Martina Reilly is the author of six successful novels: *Flipside, The Onion Girl* and *Is This Love?* published by Poolbeg in Ireland and *Something Borrowed, Wish Upon a Star* and *Wedded Blitz* published by Sphere. She has also worked as a columnist for the Irish Evening Herald. At the moment she writes a column for the *Irish Independent* while concentrating on her novels. She is a mother of two and in her 'spare' time she teaches drama at the Maynooth School of Drama, writes plays and helps out with her son's under-11 soccer team!

For more information see www.martinareilly.info

Praise for Martina Reilly

'Clever, frank and funny' – *Bella*

'Hard to put down, laugh-out-loud funny . . . perfect holiday reading' – *Woman's Way*

'Reilly is a star of the future' – *Belfast Telegraph*

'A rollicking good yarn' – *Irish Evening Herald*

'Reilly has a wonderful comic touch, both in the way she draws her characters and in her dialogue . . . a brilliant read' – *U Magazine*

All I Want Is You

MARTINA REILLY

sphere

SPHERE

First published in Great Britain in 2006 by Sphere
This paperback edition published in 2007 by Sphere

A CIP catalogue record for this book
is available from the British Library.

ISBN-13: 978-0-7515-3790-1

Typeset in Baskerville MT by
Palimpsest Book Production Limited, Grangemouth, Stirlingshire

Printed and bound in Great Britain by Clays Ltd, St Ives plc

Sphere
An imprint of
Little, Brown Book Group
Brettenham House
Lancaster Place
London WC2E 7EN

A Member of the Hachette Livre Group of Companies

www.littlebrown.co.uk

This book is dedicated to all you readers who part with your hard-earned cash so that I can keep writing. Thanks a million

This book is dedicated to those I respect who put our
post-human species right, and to the ones before
who dreamed them up.

Acknowledgements

A big thanks to Sandra O'Connell – editor of the wonderful *House* magazine – for her help with all my architectural queries.

Thanks to all in the RIAI.

Thanks to VHI and Bupa who were so generous with their time and information regarding the various health care packages available. Special thanks to Barbara Coyle of the VHI.

Thanks also to Fíona Kelly Meldon for giving her time so generously to talk to me on the assessment procedure for children with ADD and ADHD. Any mistakes are mine!!

Thanks also to all the parents of ADD children I spoke to and to HADD Family Support Group for your wonderful booklet.

Thanks also to the Irish Cancer Society.

And finally – thanks to all the staff in Annaghmackerrig artists' retreat – I couldn't have written this book without my fabulous two weeks up there. I knew at some level there had be some advantages to being a writer and I FINALLY FOUND IT!!

I'll be back!

Prologue

Embezzlement!

Shannon and Kilbane Architects, one of the most successful architectural practices in the country, is facing bankruptcy today. The firm is being prosecuted for issuing fraudulent documents pertaining to planning permissions. The matter is currently under investigation by the relevant authorities.

Shannon and Kilbane have not issued any statement in the matter.

1

I CAN STILL remember it – the day my whole life changed. And I mean just that, my WHOLE life.

At thirty-two, I was happy, only at the time I didn't realise how happy. I had a great husband and one lovely child – well, lovely except for the fact that he was completely mad, though even that was lovely.

It was nine-oh-five at night. *Fanny the Fab Nanny* was just starting up on the TV and to my delight she had her hands full that night. She had to discipline three kids who were totally wrecking their parents' house. One of them had just flung his toy train through the kitchen window and it had hit Fanny the Nanny on her face. Of course, she had to pretend that she wasn't bothered, but you could see that she was shook up. I love parenting programmes like that. Anyway, there I was watching it, and at the same time flicking through the latest issue of *Hello*. Pete was upstairs putting Billy – that's our son – to bed and Billy was shouting out that he didn't want to go to bed. In the end, I heard Pete slam Billy's door and stomp down the stairs. It struck me as odd that Pete would do that; it wasn't a Pete thing to do. He usually tried to be patient with Billy as we'd found that that was the best way to handle him, but Pete's impatience went straight out of my head because the child on the TV had

3

just told Fanny the Nanny that he'd put a laxative in her coffee. That was a laugh.

Pete came into the room and stood in the doorway, watching me. 'Hey Pete,' I giggled, 'you'll never guess what this kid has just done.' I turned to him and saw that he wasn't smiling back. Instead, he moved in beside me on the sofa, flicked off the TV and gently took *Hello* out of my hands. Pete did everything gently. He was a quiet guy, really softly spoken and he didn't flare up unless he was really mad. He had a funny look on his face – sort of sombre, which is a word I don't use very often as I haven't had to deal with many sombre people.

'Poppy,' Pete said in his sombre voice, 'I don't know how to tell you this.'

'Aw, don't say you've gone and got Billy all upset,' I glanced up at the ceiling but amazingly my son wasn't doing his usual screaming bedtime routine.

He sort of laughed a little and rolled his eyes and muttered something that sounded like 'I wish'. 'Nope, it's not that, it's a little worse than that.'

Now, I thought to myself, what could be worse that *that*? If Billy got upset it took about three hours to settle him at night. 'And it is . . . ?' I prompted.

He didn't reply immediately, instead he took my hand in his and turned it this way and that, and eventually when he did look at me, he said, 'The company has gone bust.'

I didn't understand. Or maybe I didn't want to. 'Company? What company?'

He swallowed hard. 'Mine and Adrian's company. It's gone bust.'

All I could do was stare at him.

'D'you remember Adrian's apartment complex? The one I told you about?'

4

'Nope.'

'Neither do I.' He gave a disbelieving laugh. 'Anyway, it seems Adrian was working on a big project. A huge apartment complex.'

'And?'

'It appears,' Pete swallowed hard and closed his eyes. 'It appears, Poppy, that he never had planning permission for it. He forged a planning cert., got paid money for securing the permission and started work.'

'What?'

'Oh, Christ,' he half laughed, only it wasn't a laugh laugh. 'I dunno . . .'

'Jesus.' My voice was a whisper. 'What happens now? It's not your fault.'

'It's my company as well as his.'

Adrian was Pete's partner and friend. They'd met in college, been on the same wavelength design-wise and decided ten years ago to set up in business together. It had been a bit of a struggle for them until they received an award for an extension they'd done. After that their profile had risen and the biggest moment for them had come when they'd won a major shopping centre contract. Five years later their design for the shopping centre was still brilliant.

'Yeah but—'

Pete held up his hand. 'You haven't heard the best bit,' he muttered. 'Apparently the development is illegal, the developer is losing money and he's suing us.'

'What does Adrian say?' My mind was spinning. It was like some awful dream.

'I dunno.' Another bitter laugh. 'Adrian's gone.'

'Gone? What do you mean, gone?'

'He's done a bunk. His wife doesn't know where he is.'

The SHOCK. And I write that in capitals because it was a *major* shock. Funny, charming Adrian had absconded, leaving my husband, *his* friend, to pick up the pieces. Adrian, who had been to our house for so many dinners, who had been at Billy's first birthday party, who had given me the recipe for spaghetti bolognaise – OK, I still hadn't managed to cook it, but it was a lovely recipe which he'd made up himself. That Adrian, Pete's friend, had done this, I couldn't believe.

'Are you sure he's gone?' I asked. 'Maybe . . .'

Another hard swallow. 'I found out he was gone last week.'

'Last week?'

Pete shrugged. 'Yeah. I probably should have told you before but . . .' His voice trailed off. He didn't have to say any more anyway, Pete and I understood each other. He never told me bad stuff. I think it was to protect me or something. I suppose at that moment I should have known that this was really bad because he was actually talking about it.

He continued haltingly. 'It's been in the papers today.' He handed me the copy that had been lying across a chair. I never read the newspapers – I've no concentration for anything like that. 'Embezzlement' was the headline. 'I've been with the cops most of the week, Poppy, and I kept hoping it'd just sort itself out or that there'd been a mistake.' He squeezed my hand. 'I'm sorry, Poppy, I'm awful sorry.'

I squeezed his hand back. He moved in closer to me and wrapped his arm about my shoulder. 'Adrian, our friend?'

He nodded. 'With friends like those, ey?'

I gasped out a hysterical laugh. 'So, what happens now?'

His grin faded. 'The company is in shit, Poppy. I mean, we're done for. According to our solicitors this developer is going to settle out of court for a massive amount. The insurance won't pay for that – oh, yeah, not that we have insurance.'

'What?'

'Adrian never paid the premiums, apparently.'

'*What?*'

'Three of our clients pulled out on us today. We've no more work lined up. They were major clients. And Poppy,' he sucked in his breath, 'we don't have any savings.'

'Do we not?' Of course we didn't. I knew that. Pete and I were not savers. Never had been. I'd had money all my life, I didn't know how to save, and Pete had never had money so he just loved to spend it as though it didn't mean anything to him.

'Do you see what I'm saying to you? Do you see what this means?'

Call me stupid, but I didn't. Apparently, we'd had a great eight years together and now, according to Pete, that life was over. He owed money. The firm owed money. We had to sell up, relocate, downsize.

Yeah, for thirty-two years, nothing in my world had really changed. I'd gone from one nice comfortable home to another nice comfortable home. That night, in the space of two hours, my safe, cosy world had been rocked by what was only a forewarning of the earthquakes to come.

2

I SUPPOSE, IT'S only polite, if I'm going to tell you the story of what happened after that, that I introduce myself. I'm terrible at introductions, terrible at talking to people really – though I'm much better than I used to be. I'm shy. Horribly shy. So shy that unless I'm looking great – my mousey brown hair would have to be smoothed and gleaming and smelling of expensive shampoo, my brown eyes would have to be mascaraed and painted and my face would have to be in place – I wouldn't even be able to look anyone in the eye. If you'd met me a year ago in my dressing gown and slippers, well, I'd probably have put my head down and muttered something stupid. But like I said, I'm working on the shyness bit.

So here goes . . .

I'm Poppy, Poppy Furlong, and my parents are *the* Furlongs of all the Furlong enterprises and Furlong computer parts and Furlong grocery stores and any other business that has Furlong in the title. My dad, George Furlong, set up a small computer firm in the seventies. In the eighties he cultivated it and in the nineties he sold it for a lot of money. Then he bought stocks and shares and all sorts of things like that and made even more money, and then he started taking over failing businesses and turning them around and selling them on. He was like Midas – whatever he touched made money.

I grew up in a huge six-bedroomed mansion in Dalkey and went to private schools and got piano lessons and drama lessons and ballet and Irish-dancing lessons and tap-dancing lessons and swimming lessons. It was all pretty exhausting to be honest. And what made it worse was that I wasn't an actress, I wasn't graceful and I couldn't hold a tune. The only thing I was good at was wearing clothes. I'm tall, see, and have always had a nice figure. But I think even if I didn't, I'd still have been dressed in the coolest clothes. I guess that's why I like clothes so much – I'm good at wearing them. Being good at something was important in our house, but being good at looking good was never going to make me a business woman. I really wasn't my dad's daughter. The only thing I inherited from him was my looks: brown hair, brown eyes, pale skin. I hadn't his adventurous streak, I wasn't a risk taker, and being the daughter of an entrepreneur, this was a bit of a drawback.

After I left school, Dad suddenly took an interest in me. He'd never been around much when I was growing up – always working on some new business or other – but now, now that I was ready for the work place, he kept pointing out what he thought were interesting ventures for me to get involved in. I tried hard, but like I said, I wasn't an actress. I couldn't quite be convincing enough to see the excitement in rusty old shacks and run-down businesses. And the one time he invested in a thriving business for me to run, I had major problems. He bought me a florist's. I was twenty, with no idea of what I should be doing, having spent a year travelling and failing to find enlightenment. So my dad took a decision for me and bought a little flower shop and ensconced me behind the counter. It was even worse than school. I couldn't seem to get the hang of it at all. And the allergies! The thorns! The way orders got mixed up! I couldn't estimate how much to charge clients and eventually he had to sell it on. His one business failure. It knocked my confidence a lot, to be honest.

After that he got me a job working in one of his businesses. I had to answer the phone and deal with calls. That wasn't too bad, though it was boring. All the calls were about incomprehensible things like mergers and stocks. But I stuck it out.

Then I met Pete. Lovely, cute Pete. Lovely, cute Pete who had nothing to his name but a bit of ambition. And when he set up his own business – with money he borrowed from the bank – we got married and lived, until recently, in a gorgeous five-bedroomed house.

It was about a year ago, when Pete broke the bad news, that everything started to fall apart.

3

OUR HOUSE SOLD in record time. It wasn't surprising really as we'd done a great job on it. Well, not *technically* me, but Pete and the interior decorator I'd employed had done a great job. The decorator had cost a fortune. The things he'd made us buy had cost a fortune. But in those days we had a fortune. Designer wallpaper, original art – my Angie Grimes collection of seascapes prominently displayed in our huge drawing room – under-floor heating so that no great big ugly radiators would mar the style of the rooms, good-quality wooden floors, tiled kitchen and bathroom, gorgeous kids' bedrooms. And even though Billy, my six-year-old, had drawn with blue and red marker all over his walls, the paint was of such good quality that most of it came off. Pete said it would have come off whether it was designer or not as it was wash-proof paint, but I disputed it. And not just the interior but the house itself was designer. One of Pete's designs. Big, airy, bright and friendly looking. The envy of our secluded neighbourhood.

Anyway, we got over two million for it – a three-thousand-square-foot, five-bedroomed mansion which was only eight years old. And after paying back what we owed the bank, we were left with the princely sum of four-hundred thousand. On top of that, Pete had no income as he had lost his contract for an art gallery project that he and Adrian had won against stiff competition. So all we had was a few hundred thousand to buy a house with, which is not possible in Dublin. OK, I know there are some, but not like the one we'd just left. And we couldn't get a loan as we'd no savings or business. And because Adrian had messed up so spectacularly, the only job Pete could get at such short notice was in a hotel restaurant. As far as designing went he was unemployable, being under suspicion himself, which was so unfair as Pete was the most honest guy you could ever meet.

We spent our days, when Pete was free, looking at houses. They seemed to merge together into an incomprehensible blur.

'Poppy,' Pete said after we'd looked at about our hundredth house in a week, 'you'll have to make a choice. The guy who bought our place wants us out next month. Just pick somewhere and if you hate it, we can move again.'

'I just can't bear to move, Pete,' I sniffed. A big tear hovered in the corner of my eye and I tried to make it go away. 'How'll I cope? It's not just losing the house, I won't know anyone where we're going.'

'You don't really know any of our neighbours now,' Pete said, cuddling me.

We were standing in the middle of a street but I didn't care. I liked his arms around me. Pete was my rock. The steady one. 'I do,' I said. 'I know that old lady who always chases the kids and won't let anyone park outside her house. I know her.'

'Yeah, and you hate her.'

'Not as much as I hate moving.'

'Come on,' Pete kissed me on the forehead, then wiped

a rogue tear from my cheek with his thumb. 'It'll be OK, you know.'

I nodded. 'Yeah.'

'It will, Poppy.' He cradled my face in his hands and said earnestly, 'Honest, I promise you. I'm awful sorry about this.'

'It's not your fault – I told you that.' I felt bad that he seemed to be blaming himself when it wasn't anything he'd done.

'I trusted Adrian.'

'So did I. It's just . . .' I couldn't look him in the face. I didn't want him to feel bad about things but I knew he did. I despised myself for crying. I wanted to be a strong wife, one who could support him and help him. In fact, that's what I had to do. With some major gulping and even harder resolve, I lifted up my chin and smiled. 'I know,' I said. 'But it's not fair that you can't work and that nobody wants you.'

'You want me,' he managed to grin. 'And that's all that matters to me.'

I giggled. He could always do that – make me smile when I was upset, usually by changing the subject.

'Now come on,' he pulled at my hand. 'There's one more house to look at today. It's just outside Dublin, a little bit away but you might like it.'

We collected Billy from school at two. We were a little late as the house Pete had brought me to was in Kildare. *Kildare.* Not even Dublin! I was horrified at first but it was bigger than any house we'd seen in Dublin and Pete had liked 'the light' in it and had promised me he'd make it so bright it wouldn't even be the same place in a few months. So he'd put in an offer.

When we eventually got there Billy was running about

the yard like a lunatic as his teacher looked on. I think she was calling out to him to slow down, but that was about as useful as asking the tide not to come in. Billy never slowed down, he was constantly on the go. If he ran into a wall he'd just jump up and run at it again. Pete joked that he'd be useful in a war situation.

'Billy,' I called loudly. 'Hi.' He looked towards me and tripped up. His teacher emitted a small shriek and I smiled. 'He'll be fine,' I said. 'Sorry we're late, we were held up.'

'That's OK.' His teacher, who was younger than me, was still staring anxiously at Billy. Pete had gone to help him up. 'I wanted a word anyway.'

'Oh?'

'Yes, it's about Billy. He's very energetic, isn't he?'

'Yes, I suppose that's the way with all boys,' I replied, waving over at Billy.

'Well,' she licked her lips, 'it's not just that. He's a bit disruptive in class. He's constantly jumping out of his seat.'

'Oh. Well, can't you tell him to just sit down?'

'Well yes, but—'

'Is he OK?' I called out to Pete.

'Nothing that an ice-pop won't cure,' Pete strode towards us, Billy on his shoulders. He always put Billy on his shoulders. 'Hiya,' he said to Billy's teacher. 'Sorry we were late. Has Poppy told you we were looking at houses and misjudged the time?'

'You're moving?' Billy's teacher looked from Pete to me.

'Yep.' Pete caught Billy's hands in his to keep him steady. 'Maybe out to the sticks.'

'Come on, go, Daddy,' Billy shouted. 'Run like a horse!'

'Better go,' I smiled at the teacher as Pete started to leg it across the yard with Billy squealing.

'Yeah, OK. Bye.'

14

'Oh, sorry, what were you saying about Billy?'

The teacher shrugged. 'Maybe in another school he might calm down,' she said. 'Better wait and see.'

The auctioneer rang back that night. The house in Kildare was ours.

We could move in once we'd exchanged contracts.

4

OVING DAY ARRIVED sooner than I wanted.
Everything had been packed up, boxed, labelled and placed in the hall ready for the removal guys to lift into the lorry. I'd been up since around six walking about the empty rooms, saying a silent 'goodbye' to everything. None of the neighbours had commented on the 'For Sale' sign or had even asked when we were moving. Pete was right, I wasn't that friendly with any of them and I wouldn't actually miss anyone, but it would have been nice if they'd showed some concern. Though it would have been embarrassing to admit that we were downsizing. Maybe they knew anyway.

It would have been nice to have a friend who I could have confided in. Just to say that I was scared about going to a new place and that I was scared in case money would be really tight and that Pete would be sent to jail, stuff like that. But I had no friends. I mean, I've tried to talk to people, but I never seem to get to the stage where someone will ask me over for a coffee or a chat. I don't know if it's me or them, but I've never managed to get that comfortable with anyone. I see other women going for spur-of-the-moment lunches and I wish it was me. I wish I had someone I could say 'Hey, fancy a cappuccino?' to without agonising over it for hours. But I don't. I'm just not a mixer, I guess.

Pete, on the other hand, is a mixer. He can walk into a room and everyone will gravitate towards him. And it's not that he's loud or manic or anything, he's just relaxed and easy going. I used to get worried sick about going out anywhere with him, used to hate the fact that people immediately took to him, but over the years I've got used to it, mainly because I know that he loves me. He laughs at my stupid jokes, slags off my insecurities and makes me feel special. Even when I do really impulsive things like spending huge sums of money on stuff we don't need, he grumps for a while before rolling his eyes and calling me 'Miss Money Pit'. One time, I asked him what he saw in me. The fact that he looked surprised was the best answer of all.

When the doorbell rang at seven – just as I'd said goodbye to the wine rack in the Shaker kitchen – I thought it was Gavin, Pete's oldest friend. He'd promised to help us move, and though we didn't really need him, I think Pete wanted him there. Anyway, it wasn't Gavin, it was my mother and father.

'Shit,' I hissed when I saw their tall silhouettes framed by the glass doorway. My folks are the only people who'd call anywhere at seven in the morning and expect people to be up. They're both insomniacs. My dad generally works on a Saturday, but he'd obviously decided that his daughter moving house was a bigger event in the grand scheme of things. I was honoured. I plastered on a smile and opened the door.

'Hello,' my mother gingerly stepped into the house and peered all around her. 'Oh, isn't it so bare!'

'Well, Maureen, they are moving today,' my father strode past the both of us and marched into the kitchen. 'Have you everything packed, Poppy? All ready to go?' Even when he asks a simple question, my dad sounds as if he's running an army.

'Yes.'

'Well, I've two hours free this morning before I have a meeting so I thought I'd just pop in and make sure that you've everything in correct order. These removal men like to carry things out in a certain way. Now, the big things – are they ready to go? No difficulties there?' He took out a list from his pocket and began reading from it: 'Fridge?'

'Check,' I snorted.

Dad looked impatiently at me. 'If you don't want a shoddy job, give it the adequate preparation,' he chastised. 'Now, fridge?'

'It's ready.'

'Washing machine?'

'Same.'

'Dryer?'

'Dad,' I said, 'Pete has done all this. He knows what he's doing.'

A short silence where Mam and Dad looked at each other. I knew what they were thinking: how could he know what he was doing if he let his sleazy partner wreck his business? I squirmed for him.

'Adrian was a nice guy,' I muttered mutinously.

They looked at me.

'Well, he seemed nice,' I clarified.

Dad snorted and rolled his eyes. 'If you want money, it's there,' he said. 'You know you can borrow from us any time you want. You could keep this house if you wanted. Pete could pay off his debts if he wanted.'

'Pete isn't responsible for the debts,' I snapped.

'Well,' Dad said impatiently, 'He could set up in business again if he wanted.'

They were always offering me money like that. From the day I'd walked down the aisle until now, in fact. In the beginning I'd been tempted, and Pete and I used to row over it. My argument was that they were my parents, they were entitled to offer us money. And it would be mine one day too. 'Well, for the moment it's theirs,' Pete always said, 'so let them enjoy it.' It wasn't that Pete told me *not* to accept it, it was just that I knew it would kill him if I did. So I hadn't.

'We don't need money,' I answered my father, who was poking about at the tumble dryer. 'Sure, we have a house now and everything.'

'In Kildare,' my mother sniffed.

'Kildare is,' I gulped, 'nice,' I finished. Then added, in case I hadn't been convincing, 'Lots of horses and land and green.'

'Mmmm.' Mam smiled a little too brightly. 'Well, so long as you'll be happy.'

'So, you've got over your fear of horses have you?' Dad asked smartly. 'Last time the Grand National was on the television you had to leave the room.'

'That's because a horse got injured,' I replied. And it was the truth. The camera had done a big close-up of his wild eyes and snorting nostrils and huge long legs. Ugh, I even shivered as I remembered.

There was a noise from upstairs. Pete was up. I heard him walk across our maple floorboards and head into Billy's room.

'Tea?' I asked Mam and Dad. 'We're just about to have our breakfast now.' I hoped that they would refuse. There was always tension when Pete and they got together.

'Thanks.' Mam went to the fridge and got out the one

remaining item – the milk. Putting it on the counter she called out, 'Is my favourite grandchild up yet?'

There was a shriek from upstairs as Billy recognised her voice. Dad winced. My father and my son had never really taken to one another, largely because of Billy's great ability to make a lot of noise.

'NANA!' Billy hurtled down the stairs, tripping over the last two steps and hitting his head against the edge of the stairs. The three of us gasped and Billy looked up at us uncertainly before jumping up, rubbing his head and shrieking out again, 'NANA!'

My mother opened up her arms and Billy threw himself at her. She almost fell over. 'My, haven't you got big,' she laughed.

'Too big for all that carry on,' Dad muttered.

Mam looked at me and I looked at her and we both ignored him. The best place for my father, my mother always said, was behind a desk in an office. He had no understanding of family life at all.

'So,' Mam crouched down beside Billy. 'Are you looking forward to your new house?'

We'd tried to explain the concept of moving to Billy, but I wasn't sure he'd grasped it.

Billy shrugged. 'Suppose. Mammy said she'd buy me a wrestling ring for my room.'

'Oh, great. And your granddad and I will buy you something too – what would you like?'

Billy cocked his head to one side. 'A mobile phone?'

'Oh,' Mam clapped her hands, 'you're far too young for a phone. Who'll you call?'

'You and Granddad and my other nana.' He looked at me. 'Haven't I another nana?'

'You do.'

'For all you see of her,' my mother sniffed. 'Is Pete still asking how high when she says jump?'

Pete's mother had taken to ringing and asking him to ferry her to all different places in the last couple of months. 'She's his mother,' I said. 'He wants to do it.'

'And what did she ever do for him?'

I glared at her. Billy did not need to hear comments like that and neither did Pete. 'A phone is no good to you, Billy,' I changed the subject back. 'How about some wrestlers for the ring?'

'*Loads* of wrestlers for the ring?'

'Yeah.'

'Cool. Loads of wrestlers please, Nana.'

Dad snorted. 'Wrestling – a load of rubbish if you ask me.'

Mam smiled stiffly. 'No one did ask you though, did they?' She turned to Billy. 'OK, loads of wrestlers it is.'

'Great.' Billy smiled briefly and his eyes scanned the kitchen. 'Is there any toast, Mammy?'

I'd packed the toaster away. 'Just bread.'

Billy's bottom lip quivered and he sniffed hard. 'Are we really poor now, so?'

Dad snorted derisively, Mam rushed to reassure Billy and I frantically began to look for the toaster.

'How's it going?' Pete strode into the kitchen with a nod at my mother and father. 'Hey, what's up, Bill?'

Billy blubbered about us being poor and having no toaster, generally managing to make me feel guilty. Pete laughed and scooped him up in his arms.

'The toaster is packed away, you fool. We're going out to breakfast this morning. I've booked breakfast at the hotel I work in,' he looked at me, 'as a surprise.'

'Aw, that's great.'

'Cool!' Billy agreed.

'You work in a hotel?' Mam said incredulously. She looked Pete up and down. 'Since when?'

I winced. I hadn't told them that bit of information.

'Since I lost the company,' Pete replied evenly.

'And what do you do in this hotel?'

'Wait on tables. Serve breakfast,' Pete answered.

I was mortified for him. It didn't, however, bother Pete.

'It's a good job,' I said, clasping Pete's hand in mine.

'Huh, I could give you a better job than that,' my father said, shooting a disbelieving look at me. 'You could work in one of my companies. In fact, if you proved yourself, I could give you the money to start again.'

'Thanks,' Pete said easily, 'but I intend to do it myself. So, who wants to come for breakfast?'

'Me!' Billy, oblivious to any tension, hopped from foot to foot.

'Well, go up and get dressed, so!'

'Huh, you could have come to us for your breakfast,' Mam sniffed. 'Wasting money in a hotel.'

Pete stiffened but ignored her. Instead he turned to me. 'You gonna get ready, Poppy? We've to be back here by eleven for the removal guys.'

'Well,' Mam glanced at Dad. 'We might as well go, George. Poppy and Pete won't be around.'

'You're welcome to join us,' Pete offered graciously.

'No, thanks,' Dad pocketed his list. 'I've work in a while. Come on, Maureen, we'll leave them to it.'

'Bye,' I muttered weakly as they left in the same impatient manner in which they'd come. It was a relief.

*   *   *

22

The hotel that Pete worked in was a little bit out of the city, on the road to Kildare, and though he'd pointed it out to me once or twice when we'd visited our new house, I hadn't taken too much notice of it. It was an imposing building, set up high and kind of looking down on the road below it. Pete led Billy and me into the foyer where he was greeted by the guy behind the desk like an old friend. That's what I mean about Pete. He hardly knew these people and they acted like he was their best drinking buddy.

'Hey, Pete, is this the family?'

'Uh-huh.' Pete slung his arm about my shoulder. 'This is Poppy and this is Billy. Poppy, this is Lenny.'

Lenny, who looked about a hundred, but was probably about sixty or so, shuffled out from behind his counter and took my hand between the two of his and shook it vigorously. 'Aw,' he said, in a Ronnie Drew voice, 'I have to say it now, your fella has brightened up this place since he came.'

'Has he?' I smiled up at Pete.

'Well, I was an architect,' Pete smiled back down at me.

Lenny and I laughed.

'So, in for breakfast are you?' Lenny began to walk towards a big sign that said 'Restaurant'.

'Uh-huh. We're moving today.'

They began a long conversation about how stressful moving was, how lovely Kildare was and how lucky we were to be getting out of the city. Billy hopped and jumped beside them, shouting out that he didn't want to be poor.

'You're not poor,' Lenny eventually acknowledged him. 'Look at your lovely runners.'

'Trainers,' Billy corrected. 'They are my trainers and all the cool footballers wear them and I'm hungry.'

'In we go,' Pete pushed him into the restaurant. 'See you tomorrow, Lenny, on the early shift.'

'Yeah, see ya. Take care and safe travelling.'

Once in the restaurant, Pete was greeted by what felt like a hundred more people, though obviously it couldn't have been. Pretty waitresses smiled and waved at him, the waiters came and slapped him on the shoulder and I began to feel claustrophobic with all the attention our family was getting. The whole thing went to Billy's head. First, he wanted to sit in one chair, then he decided that that chair wasn't the one he wanted, that in fact Pete's chair was the ONE. And Pete refused to give it to him. I love Pete, but sometimes he thinks that he knows how to handle his son when in fact he has no idea. He's like a parrot. If I say 'sit down' Pete immediately echoes me. Anway, that day, maybe to impress his co-workers, he decided to take a firm hand with his son.

'You can't have it,' he said to Billy. 'Sit in your own seat.'

'NOOOOOO!'

'Pete, for God's sake,' I whispered furiously as Billy began to scream and our family started getting the wrong sort of attention, 'would you just let him have it.'

'No,' Pete continued calmly eating his breakfast. 'He chose the other one.'

Billy hit him. Pete turned around and told him to stop. Billy screamed even more loudly.

'Pete,' I whispered. He was unfazed, I, however, was mortified. Everyone was looking. 'Billy, sit on my knee,' I cajoled.

Pete glared at me. 'Don't mollycoddle him,' he whispered.

'I want *that* chair!' Billy was really getting going now.

Tears were pouring down his face, which had gone furiously red. He was going to throw something if he kept it up.

'Well, you can't have it,' Pete said. 'And if you don't stop, I'm going to take you out and you'll miss out on your breakfast.'

'I hate you, Daddy!' Billy shouted and picked up his fork. But before he could throw it, Pete picked him up and tossed him over his shoulder. 'Nooooooo!'

Pete strode out of the dining room, Billy pounding his small fists uselessly on Pete's back. I was left on my own at the table eating my sausages. Well, not that I could eat them. Why couldn't Pete, for the sake of a nice breakfast, just give in to Billy this once? Jesus, we were moving, we were all upset, and he wouldn't let Billy sit in a stupid chair. I rubbed my hands over my face and tried to ignore the fact that everyone seemed mighty interested in what had just happened. In the end, after eating about one bite of sausage, I went in search of them.

They were in the foyer where Pete was talking to Lenny and both of them were ignoring Billy, who was sobbing furiously in an armchair. I glared at Pete's back before crouching down in front of Billy.

'Hey baby,' I cooed. 'Don't cry, come on.'

'Have you finished already?' Pete asked, glowering at me as I scooped Billy up in my arms.

'Well, there wasn't much conversation going on,' I said back, a bit snappily. I kissed Billy on the side of his face and tasted a salty tear. I hugged him harder.

'Well, if you're finished, I might as well go and eat *my* breakfast.'

To my horror, Pete sauntered off and left me with Lenny.

25

I felt like picking up a fork and throwing it at him myself now. Lenny and I smiled awkwardly at each other.

'I'm hungry,' Billy sniffed into my hair. 'I want a sausage.'

'Yeah, well, you should have been good inside, shouldn't you?'

He pouted. 'Daddy was mean.'

I smiled apologetically at Lenny. 'Fight over a chair,' I muttered. I could feel the beginnings of a tension headache behind my eyes.

'You go and say sorry to your daddy,' Lenny advised, poking Billy on the shoulder, 'and maybe he'll let you have a sausage. I reckon he's lonely in there all by himself.'

Billy shrugged but wouldn't commit himself.

'And the sausages are lovely today,' Lenny added, winking at me. 'Just right for ten-year-old boys like you.'

Billy lifted his head from my shoulder and smiled delightedly at Lenny. 'I'm not ten. I'm only six.'

'No way!' Lenny did a credible look of disbelief. 'Only six?'

'Uh-huh, but I'm tall for my age,' Billy said seriously. He wriggled down from my arms and went around the counter to stand beside Lenny. 'See, I'm up to your elbow almost. That's tall, isn't it?'

'Sure is,' Lenny agreed cheerfully. 'Which is why you should eat your breakfast – tall boys need it more, isn't that right, Mammy?'

'Yeah.'

Billy stared from one to the other of us. 'OK, so.' He careered off towards the restaurant.

Lenny and I smiled at each other. I was the first to turn away.

'You should go and finish your breakfast too now,' Lenny

offered. 'It can't have been much fun in there on your own.'

Tears pricked the back of my eyes and I blinked them away before he noticed. 'I was fine. I'm finished.' I sounded abrupt and I hadn't meant to. 'I wasn't hungry,' I blurted out.

Lenny nodded. 'Oh. Right, so.' Then he said, 'I suppose it's nerve-racking moving house – ruin anyone's appetite.'

'You got it.'

Another smile, which I returned, then he turned away and started to press buttons on a computer keyboard.

In my head, I flirted with all the things I could say to Lenny to keep the conversation going. I could ask him about manning the front desk, about his shifts, about his experience with kids, but just as I'd formed the questions in my head, something would distract Lenny and he'd wander away. I felt like a prat standing at the desk with no conversation so, in the end, I moved away and sat in a foyer chair, feigning interest in the décor while I waited for my husband and son to re-emerge from the dining room.

Though it had been lovely of Pete to arrange breakfast, with all the hassle, breakfast at my parents would have been better, I reckoned.

5

WE GOT BACK to the house at about ten-thirty and Gavin was waiting for us outside. Gavin, as I said before, is Pete's best mate. According to both of them, they've been through everything together – from primary school right through. Gavin's family were Pete's 'adopted' kin. Gavin's parents are dead now, but when Pete was growing up, apparently he spent way more time in Gavin's house than he spent in his own. To be honest, that's not hard to believe. Pete's family are a bit weird – I wouldn't spend time in their house unless I had to either. Pete's dad died when he was five and I know it must have been hard on his mother having to raise three kids on her own (Pete and his two brothers), but apparently it was equally hard for everyone else listening to her moan about it. His brothers emigrated as soon as they could – they live in England now – and Pete is the only one who visits his mother regularly. I do feel sorry for her – I'd hate it if Billy never came to see me – and I offer to go with Pete to see her all the time, but he hates me going so I only go when he asks me now, which is a bit of a relief if I'm honest.

As we pulled up, Gavin hopped out of his car to greet us. Gavin is an artist and a starving one at that. He went to art college, and now he spends his days working with underprivileged kids doing art workshops. He hasn't had a steady job in years and he travels about doing his drawings and basically living from hand to mouth. It doesn't bother Gavin that he just scrapes by, so it doesn't bother us either. And he's so likeable. Though when he and Pete get together they go on like a couple of kids. Gavin looked like a kid as he got out of his car, his dirty-blond over-long hair pushed behind his ears and his green combat jacket half-on, half-off his shoulders.

'Hey, all set?' he greeted us. He slammed the door of his ancient Ford and it shuddered. 'All packed up?'

'Uh-huh,' Pete nodded. He was still in a mood since the breakfast incident with Billy, but seeing Gavin made him grin, as it always did. It was good to have Gav there.

Gavin grinned back then called over to Billy. 'Hey, you, squirt. Look what I have!'

'I'm not a squirt,' Billy said indignantly.

Gavin pulled a cardboard tube from behind his back and waved it about. 'Wanna see?'

Billy bounded over to him and watched wide eyed as Gavin opened it and pulled out a rolled up tube of paper. Unrolling it, he held it out for Billy to look at.

There was a second's awed silence from Billy before 'Wow!' He turned excitedly to me. 'Mammy, look. Look what Gav's got for me!'

I crossed towards them and saw the most fantastically colourful drawing of Billy, dressed in Wrestlers gear, with a banner announcing the WWF Champion as being 'Billy Shannon – Country Bumpkin'.

'Woulda framed it, only I ran out of money,' Gavin said apologetically as he fed the picture carefully back into its tube. He handed it to Billy. 'For your new bedroom, champ.'

29

'Thanks. Thanks.' Billy, in a rare display of affection, flung his arms about Gavin and hugged his legs. 'It's great!'

'Yeah, it is,' I said, delighted to see Billy smiling. 'Thanks Gav.'

'No probs.' He flashed me a quick smile before turning back to Pete. 'So, any chance of being invited into your enormous gaff for a last look around?'

Pete jangled his keys and the two of them went up to the door, me and Billy following.

Once the door was opened, Billy pushed past everyone and raced upstairs.

'Always thought this place was too big for yez,' Gavin announced as he stood in the hallway. 'What does one family need with three houses, I use ta think.'

Pete laughed. He always laughed at Gavin's jokes, though I don't think Gavin was joking. I didn't smile. Gavin was always remarking on how big our house was and though he probably didn't mean it, I kept getting the impression that he thought Pete and I should donate all our money to charity and live in a cardboard box.

'In fact,' Gavin went on, strolling into the bare kitchen, 'your house is so big, that travelling from one end to the other you'd need a flask of coffee to keep you going.'

'Fuck off!' Pete shoved him.

'Kelly Holmes would take two days to sprint around it.'

Pete laughed loudly and his laugh made me smile.

'So, what's happening now?' Gavin leaned up against the worktop in the kitchen, his hands shoved into the pockets of his combats.

'The truck is coming at eleven,' Pete said.

'Any luck getting an architect's position yet?'

'Nope,' Pete shook his head. 'I haven't a hope until this

30

mess with Adrian is sorted out. Guilty by association – that's me.'

'Bastard Adrian,' Gavin commented. Pete shrugged. Gavin turned to me, 'Any luck yourself?' he asked.

I laughed. 'Me?'

'Yeah,' Gavin looked puzzled. 'Pete said you might have to work too.'

'Only if we're desperate,' Pete said.

'Yeah, you'd want to be desperate to send her into the workforce all right,' Gavin chortled, showing off his beautiful white teeth.

I belted him.

'You leave my wife alone,' Pete kissed me on the forehead and wrapped his arm about my shoulder. He smiled down at me, our spat in the hotel forgotten. 'She's the best dresser in the business. The best holiday booker. The best spender of money I have ever met and I love her.'

'Exactly,' I said.

Gavin smiled slightly at us. He looked, I don't know, different all of a sudden.

There was a thump from upstairs and realising that Billy wasn't in sight, I ran out of the kitchen to see what he'd done.

By five o'clock that evening we were sitting in our new house with box upon box piled up everywhere. We had run late because Billy had flooded the bathroom in the old place and we all had to mop it up before leaving. He was in big trouble and had been sent upstairs as soon as we arrived. He'd screamed and shouted and I'm sure our new neighbours wondered what they were in for, but it was quiet now – he'd fallen asleep through sheer exhaustion. The house

31

looked so small with all the clutter and my heart sank. I would have cried only that Gavin was there. The three of us sat on upturned boxes, dusty and sweaty and tired.

'I'll send out for a pizza,' Pete pulled his mobile from his pocket and began to dial. Only he dialled our ex-local pizza delivery place, and while this caused Gavin and him to crack up laughing, I had a sore sort of feeling right in my heart. This was really happening, the feeling said. Your old life is gone. Welcome to this new one.

The owners had left us a local phone book in the kitchen along with a card and a bottle of wine, so while Pete looked up the nearest pizzeria, I uncorked the wine and poured myself an enormous glass.

Gavin left at around eleven, and for the first time that day Pete and I were on our own.

'Come here,' he said, and pulled me into the circle of his arms. He kissed the tip of my nose. 'How you doing?'

'Good,' I lied.

'Really?' Pete bent down and looked up into my face.

'No,' I half giggled. The wine had made me a bit drunk. My head had that nice floaty feeling. 'But another glass of that,' I nodded at the bottle, 'and I'll be fine.'

'It's a nice house,' Pete turned me to face the room and rested his chin on my head, his arms about me. 'And when I've finished with it, Poppy, you'll love it. I promise.'

'It just looks so much smaller than what we had.' I hadn't meant to say that, it just popped out, but I couldn't help the way I felt.

'It *is* so much smaller than what we had.' That struck us both as funny and we started to laugh a little drunkenly.

'And I miss our sofa,' I muttered then. We had had to sell it as it wouldn't fit.

'It misses you.'

'Stop!' I giggled. 'Take me seriously.'

'I'll take you any way at all,' Pete nibbled my ear lobe. He pulled me tighter. 'You know the good thing about moving house?'

'What?' My voice was going all shaky, the way it always did when he was this near to me.

'Well, we have to christen every room, don't we?'

'Yeah,' I turned and began to unbutton his flies ever so gently. 'Pity it doesn't have as many rooms as the last house though.'

'You'd never last the pace if it did.' His voice had gone shaky too. I loved it when he sounded like that.

'Want to try me?'

And he didn't need to be asked twice.

6

PETE LEFT FOR work at some unholy hour the next morning. I heard him moving about downstairs before he slammed the front door and drove away. I lay in bed for a while – a new bed as our old one wouldn't fit up the stairs of the new house – and listened to the noises of our new estate. In the old house it was quiet in the mornings, though the noise of traffic could be heard faintly from the main road. Here there was the sound of traffic all right, but unbelievably I could hear birds too. All sorts of birds. It was kind of nice. They seemed to be twittering and fluttering right outside the window. I lay in bed for a while, my arms stretched over my head, trying not to think too much about where I was and the fact that I was likely to be in this house for the foreseeable future.

I concentrated on the birds and tried to focus on the nice things about living in the house, but the birds were as good as it got. And their happy chirruping couldn't stop the sort of dull ache spreading through my head. It's the only way I can describe it. I missed our house so much. I think the ache was reality knocking on the door of my brain, drip feeding me pain until I couldn't stand it any more and had to get up. Maybe if I was busy, I decided, then I wouldn't think so much. Of course, I knew that eventually I'd have to sit down and face the sadness head on, but maybe by then I'd have got used to this new place. So I got up, determined to work hard and unpack as much as I could before Pete got in. I pulled on my dressing gown and went to wake Billy.

I love looking at my son when he's sleeping. It's about the only time he's actually still enough to enjoy. He was sprawled out in bed, his arms flung at weird angles. There was a small smile just curling the tips of his lips. Above him was the picture Gavin had drawn. The likeness to Billy was uncanny. He'd captured in the face, and in the eyes especially, Billy's whole restless character. It made me smile to look at it.

Billy stirred. His eyes fluttered open. 'Mammy!'

'Hiya, baby, are you going to get up?'

He pushed himself up in bed and looked about. 'I like this room,' he said. 'Not so big and scary as my last room.'

'Good.' That was positive at least.

We smiled at each other and he hopped out of bed and legged it past me. 'I wonder if there are any boys to play with here?' he shouted over his shoulder. 'Maybe they'll let me play with them?'

Two hours later, Billy had happily found a friend. A red-headed, loud, skinny boy with gappy teeth. He was seven. I watched them out on the road kicking a football and wished I was a kid again. But then again, I'd never been good at making friends even when I was young. Whereas other kids blended in, I hung about on the fringes, too shy to ask to play, too embarrassed to be seen to be on my own. The only time I really got on with others was when my parents got me a new toy, then suddenly everyone wanted

35

to be with me. I was the first to have Tiny Tears and Talking Trisha. I had more Cindy clothes than anyone else. I revelled in those moments.

I turned away from the window and began to unpack the box of Delph we'd brought. I examined every little thing, remembering how and why we'd bought it. It made me sad and happy all at the same time. I was carefully placing a pile of Denby cups on to a shelf when the doorbell rang. The sound was so unexpected that I dropped one of my favourite cups on to the kitchen tiles where it smashed into about a million pieces. I had to pause and stay very still to compose myself. I know it was only a cup, I know it could be replaced, but at that moment, it was like every single lovely thing in my life had been taken away from me. The doorbell rang again and I felt like yelling a great big tearful 'fuck off' at the caller. Only I didn't. I plastered a smile on my face and went to open it.

A tiny woman stood there. Tiny shoulders, tiny frame, tiny little mouse-like face. Brown shiny hair was pulled back in a jaunty ponytail and blue eyes stared up at me. She had a nice gentle sort of smile though, and I found myself smiling back a little. Then I got embarrassed as I was in my tracksuit and had no make-up on.

'To say hello,' the woman said, holding out a pie dish. She sounded a bit breathless. 'I know it's hard moving into a new house – no food in, no way to cook – so I thought I'd bring you this over to help you out on your first day.'

'Oh!' I was touched. Unexpectedly, I wanted to hug her, but I knew she'd run screaming and yelling up the street. So I took the dish from her. It smelt of garlic. It was warm. It looked nicer than anything I could ever cook. 'Thanks. Thanks. That's very nice of you.'

'No problem.'

She held out her hand and, balancing the dish in one hand, I shook her hand with my free one.

'I'm Laura,' she said, 'I live next door.' She indicated her house. 'I'm Tommy's mother.'

'Tommy?'

She pointed to the red-headed kid.

'Oh, right. Tommy.' I laughed a little. 'Are there many boys around here?'

'Not too many. It's mainly girls.'

'Oh, right.' I ran out of things to say then. None of the people in our other estate would ever have dreamed of cooking for a new neighbour. They wouldn't ever have dreamed of cooking, full stop. I held up the dish. 'Thanks for this,' I said again.

Laura smiled and began to back away. 'You know where I am if you ever need anything – just knock.'

And it hit me. I should have invited her in for a cuppa. That's what Pete would have done. I wondered if it was too late. 'Tea?' I called out in desperation. 'Coffee?'

'Sorry?'

I flapped my free arm about uselessly. 'Would you like a cup of tea?'

'Oh. Oh. Well, yes, if you're not too busy.'

'No! I'm not.' I opened the door wider. 'Come in, please.'

She came in and stood in the hallway, then I walked towards the kitchen and she followed me. Of course, I'd forgotten about my smashed cup. Splinters of it lay everywhere. 'Dropped a cup just before I answered the door.'

Laura smiled.

'Sit down, do.' God, what was I going to talk to this woman about? How long did cups of tea actually last? I walked across the floor to the kettle and the broken cup crunched under my feet.

'Do you have a brush?' Laura asked.

'Of course I have.'

She looked taken aback. 'I meant, have you unpacked it yet, to sweep up the breakage? I can run next door and get mine if you like.'

I flushed. She couldn't have missed it. I mean, I'd actually thought that she thought that we were too poor to have a dustpan and brush. 'Oh, yeah, that'd be great.'

She hopped up like a rabbit and rushed out of the kitchen.

I wished I'd unpacked the knives so I could have cut my tongue off.

Laura was just brushing up the last of the cup from the floor when Gavin called by. He'd promised, if he had no work on, to come and help us unpack. I'd put the tea and biscuits on the table and was waiting for her to join me. It was a huge relief to see Gavin arrive as I was completely sweating at the thought of tea with this stranger. Like I said, I'm shy, and even though she appeared nice, conversation thus far had been stilted and restricted to talk about the kind of things boys did and what the local school was like. After the school conversation I had nowhere to go. I was like a train rapidly running out of track.

'How's it going?' Gavin asked, poking his unkempt head round the kitchen door. He paused at the sight of Laura sweeping up.

'A neighbour,' I said brightly. 'Laura.'

'Wow, this is great. Is this a "welcome to the neighbourhood" gift or something? A free clean with every house purchased?'

Laura laughed – a genuine laugh and a genuine smile. She looked younger suddenly. 'I'm Laura. I was just saying to your wife that I live next door.'

Gavin laughed and pulled at my hair. 'What do you think of that, wife?'

'He's not my husband,' I explained, slapping his hand away. 'He's a friend of my husband's though.'

'Gavin,' Gavin held out his hand.

It occurred to me then that I hadn't told her my name. Oh Jesus! It was too late now. Gavin had settled himself at the table and after taking a handful of biscuits was asking her all about the neighbourhood. She sat opposite him and talked away easily.

I got a cup down for Gavin and poured him a tea.

'Ta, Pop,' he grinned. His hand brushed mine. 'Hasn't Pete got her well trained – tea and biscuits for all his mates?'

Laura laughed again.

I sat in beside him, happy to let him do the talking.

It turned out that Laura had lived in the house next door since it was built. She didn't mention a husband and Gavin didn't ask. Apparently, the people who had owned our house had been really nice people and they'd had lovely kids and everyone had been sad to see them go. Her praise made me feel under pressure.

'So why did they go?' Gavin asked.

'Moved to a bigger house.'

Gavin choked on his biscuit and I had to get him a glass of water. As I handed it to him, he looked at me and there was laughter in his eyes. I don't know how he could find it funny.

*　　*　　*

When Pete got home, Billy decided that he was going to stay in Tommy's for tea. Laura had insisted that it was fine. 'You go and unpack and come and collect him when you're ready,' she said.

'She seems nice,' Pete said as he closed the door on her.

'Yeah, she does,' I agreed.

Pete gazed about at all the unpacked boxes. 'Now, come on beautiful wife of mine, let's make this place habitable.' He pulled out a box and peered into it. 'Great, I get to set up Billy's room and you,' he pulled out another box and winked at me, 'get to shove all this gear into the bathroom.'

'Fecker!' I tried to wrestle Billy's box from him. He tried to pull it back and we ended up on the floor, me with a handful of his hair in my hands as he begged for mercy.

'You can do Billy's room,' he groaned. 'I'll let you.'

'Ta.' I let his hair go and stood up. I pulled the box with me. He stood up too and we were face to face. He brushed strands of hair from my eyes and tucked them behind my ear.

There was a short silence. The grin slowly faded from his face. He said softly, 'I'll make you happy here, Poppy. I promise.'

I caught his hand in mine. 'You're all I need to be happy,' I said back. Well, aside from the old house, I wanted to add, but didn't. I didn't know if he would have laughed and I didn't want to hurt him.

'Me, Bill and our old house is all you need, you mean,' he grinned.

Oh, he knew me too well. I squeezed his hand slightly. 'But you and Bill are the best parts of it,' I said back. 'You'll both do for the moment.'

'Well, honey, the way things are, we're all you've got at the moment.'

No matter what, he could always make me laugh. Then we stopped laughing and stood in silence for a while, just drinking each other in. I loved those moments.

7

BILLY'S NEW SCHOOLYARD was bedlam when we walked through it for his first day. I suppose all schoolyards are a bit mad – his old school had been the same – and previously Pete and I, despite the money we'd had, had sent Billy to the local school. I'd wanted to because I'd been sent to private schools all my life and hated the trek there and back every day. I'd also hated that I'd had no friends in my area and spent weekends inside looking at nothing but the telly. Pete had wanted Billy to go local as it hadn't done him any harm. He thought private schools were a big scam. Pete thought anything different from the norm was a scam though, so I never took much notice of that.

Anyway, almost two-and-a-half months after Pete had lost his company, there was no point even considering private, and so that miserable Monday morning I led Billy by the hand into what was soon to be his new school. I wished Pete was there with me, but I think it might have upset him to see Billy wandering away into a crowd of strangers, so when he didn't offer to come I hadn't pushed it. It was upsetting for me too, though. The noise of shrieking and laughing and shouting kids was unbelievable, and when Billy huddled into me my heart broke a little. Normally he'd pelt about the place.

My high-heels kept snagging on the tarmac of the yard and I cursed myself for wearing them – but what else could I have worn? Flat heels wouldn't have looked as good with my wide trousers and it was important to create a good first impression. I'd applied my make-up carefully that morning and I knew I looked good. Slowly, following the signs, we made our way to the headmaster's office. He'd told us to come to him before school started so that he could meet Billy and so that Billy could meet his teacher. Big bright pictures of rainbows and suns and cars were hung along the walls. Photographs of various students beamed at us from frames. It seemed a nice place and my heart lifted slightly.

The plaque for Mr Harvey, Principal, was hung on a yellow door. I felt like a kid as I knocked tentatively on it. I patted my hair down and tried, unsuccessfully, to see what I looked like in the shiny surface of the door.

'Mam!' Billy tugged my hand. 'Someone said to come in.'

'Oh right. Right, so.' I pushed Billy in front of me and we entered the small room.

Two people were inside, a man – presumably the headmaster – and a young woman dressed in jeans and a tie-dyed top. I knew then I was getting old, as Billy's teacher was way younger than I was. She hardly looked old enough to have left school herself.

'This must be Billy,' the headmaster said in a big jolly voice.

Billy nodded mutely. He began to kick the floor with the toe of his shoe.

'Well, Billy, I'm Mr Harvey and this lady here, she's your teacher, Miss Walsh.'

Billy didn't look up.

'Billy, meet your new teacher,' I urged.

Miss Walsh crossed over to him and crouched down so that he could see her. 'Hiya, Billy.' She too spoke in a jolly voice. 'Are you going to come with me and meet all your new friends?'

Billy stopped kicking. 'What friends?'

'All the children in your new class. Will you come with me and meet them?' She held out her hand and Billy looked at me. I nodded and he took hold of her hand. 'Come on, so,' Miss Walsh said. 'Have you got your schoolbag?'

I hastily took Billy's bag off my shoulder and handed it to him. I didn't know if I should kiss him or not.

'Bye, Mammy,' he said. He sounded a little forlorn so I bent down and gave him a hug.

'Bye, honey. See you at two.'

His teacher mouthed a 'he'll be fine' at me before she closed the door. I turned to the headmaster. Oh God, I was going to cry. I blinked hard, feeling like such a failure for sending my child off into a room full of strangers. Mr Harvey indicated for me to sit down. He passed a box of tissues across the desk and I took one.

'Don't worry,' he muttered, sounding a little embarrassed. 'Lorna Walsh is great with the little ones.'

'I'm sure she is,' I muttered back, more than a little embarrassed.

'Now,' he was all to business, 'if you have any queries, don't hesitate to contact the school – we've a policy here of always listening to parents.' He passed a piece of paper over to me. 'That's the number of the school, my direct line and the school secretary. All right?'

'Thanks. Great.' I folded up the paper and put it in my coat pocket.

'Billy will be very happy here,' Mr Harvey went on. 'You'll see. How is he adjusting to moving? Some children can be very upset.'

'He's getting there,' I said. My voice went a bit shaky. 'He made a new friend yesterday, so that was good.'

'He'll make lots of new friends,' Mr Harvey soothed. 'You'll see. Now is there anything you want to know?'

I'm sure there was but my mind was a blank. All I could think of was poor Billy in a classroom full of kids who had probably already made their friends and wouldn't want him. 'No,' I said softly.

'Well, if you think of anything . . .' He stood up. I stood up. We shook hands and he opened the door for me. 'Bye now. Take care and welcome to the area.'

'Thanks.'

Once the door closed behind me, I bolted up the corridor and ran outside. The yard was quiet now – only one or two mothers standing about talking to each other. They were dressed in tracksuits and horrible jeans. I would never go out looking like that. Still, they chatted easily together and I envied them that.

I wished I knew where the senior infant room was so that I could have a peek inside and see Billy. I resisted the temptation to go gawking into every window I came across though and, as sedately as I could, made my way to my car. I still hadn't sold my lovely yellow Beetle. I felt I should sell it as Pete had traded his BMW for a Focus and I didn't want him to be the one making all the sacrifices. But, to my relief, no one had rung up in response to the ad I'd placed to sell it and Pete hadn't mentioned getting rid of it, so I was hoping that maybe we could still afford to run it. And it was so comforting, that tiny little bit of my former life.

I fired up the engine and was about to head back to the house, but then decided not to. Instead, I thought I'd go to my parents' house. At least there I'd feel a little at home.

My mother was just about to go out when I pulled up to the house. Well, pulled up wouldn't be an accurate description really. Drove up would be better. The house is in an enclave with eight other houses, each one with its own extra-long driveway. With six bedrooms and three drawing rooms it's way too big for them, but they'd never admit it.

Mam was just closing the door of the house when I stepped out of my car. 'Oh, Poppy,' she said sounding surprised when she saw me and flapping her hand at the closed front door, 'I'm just going out.'

'Oh. Oh right.'

She must have noticed the disappointment in my voice because she added hastily, 'I'm meeting Avril and the girls to discuss this year's fundraiser. And after that, I have to go into the city to buy something to wear for your father's retirement do on Saturday.'

What with the move, I'd completely forgotten about the fundraiser and the fact that Dad was retiring.

'Still,' Mam went on, looking me up and down, 'if you've nothing else to do, you can come in with me – to the FR meeting.'

I winced. My mother's friends were not the sort of people I particularly liked. All my life when she'd tried to drag me along to their meetings I'd managed to wriggle out of going. And besides, I knew that I'd be useless at organising a charity event. 'Aw, Mam, I don't think so.'

She gave a bit of a laugh. 'Too busy are you? Is that why you called over – you're too busy?'

She'd get in a huff if I didn't go, I realised. 'OK, fine. I'll come,' I said.

'Good,' she clasped my wrist in her bony fingers. 'And after that, we'll go into town and buy some gorgeous clothes.'

Now there was an offer I couldn't refuse.

The meeting was being held in Avril's house. Avril was my mother's best friend and had been since they'd both moved into their houses when they'd been first built. My mother had lost her husband to finance and Avril had no husband, only cats, so they bonded in a weird competitive sort of way. Neither of them liked each other very much, as far as I could see, but the veneer of friendship was polished daily with comments like 'Oh, where did you get that dress/hat/blouse?' and then telling one another how lovely they looked and how much everything had cost.

Avril met us at the door of her palatial home, immaculately dressed and with her collagen smile firmly in place. 'Hi girls,' she trilled.

However much I'd get away with being a girl, my mother and her compatriots, all over sixty, were stretching things a little.

'Now,' Avril minced her way across her marble hall and into her drawing room, where she removed two ginger furry cats from the white sofa and shooed them out of the room. 'Sit here, Maureen, do,' she sing-songed, noting my mother's black wool trousers. 'And Poppy, what a surprise. Come to inject some new blood into us, ey?'

I smiled weakly and sat down beside my mother, who was trying not to go near the cat hairs. Two others were also in the room – Phil, and Daisy. Each woman had tried to outdo the other with the dresses they wore. My mother, however, was belle of the ball. She just had style. No matter what she put on, it looked good on her, and I could see the other three enviously eyeing up her jade-green blouse. The fact that no one commented on it pleased my mother. She knew they liked it then.

'My daughter was going to be here,' Phil said beaming, 'but she had to fly to Germany last night – some emergency with her parent company apparently.'

'Emergency?' Mam said casually, picking some cat hair off her trousers and letting it drift to the ground. 'She can't have chosen her staff very well.'

Avril and Daisy sucked in their breaths and looked in glee at each other. Phil ignored the barb and instead turned to me.

'I see you've moved, Poppy. That's a nasty business with Peter's company, isn't it?'

My mother flushed. I gulped.

'Yes, it is, I suppose,' I muttered.

'And what's the news on his partner?'

'He's still missing.'

'Oh well, at least that makes him look guilty, ey?'

Before I could answer, my mother chirruped, 'But at least she's a lovely house still. And they've always wanted to move to the country.'

'Really? I prefer Dublin myself.' Avril sniffed a little. 'Now, who's for tea or coffee?'

Avril came back with three coffees and a tea on a fancy tray. She also had a plate of the most gorgeous-looking cakes. 'Baked by my own chef,' Avril announced with pride.

I was the only one to actually eat any cake. The others, my mother included, took a nibble, pronounced it fabulous and then left it by the side of their plates. They did this for two reasons. The first being that no one wanted to eat more than the other, and second because if they enjoyed them too much it would be far too much of a compliment to Avril. It was all very complicated but I'd been well tutored by my mother for years and I knew how these women operated. And they thrived on it.

'Now,' Avril was all business. 'Let's see. We decided at the last meeting to organise a fundraiser for the Irish Cancer Society. So, has anyone any ideas? Last year's event was a great success, I'm sure you'll all agree, so we need something extra special to top it.' She looked around.

Last year's event had been Avril's idea – a dinner, cooked by a celebrity chef, for which everyone had to pay a thousand a table. No one actually ate the dinner, but loads of money was raised. Ironically, it had been done in aid of those with eating disorders.

'Maureen?' Avril looked expectantly at my mother.

'I haven't given it a lot of thought, I'm afraid,' my mother replied. 'George is retiring next week and all my energies have been taken up by that. I'll have a think about it for next time.'

Avril made a disapproving clucking sound. 'Daisy?'

Daisy giggled a little nervously. 'Same here,' she twittered. 'All I could think of was a cake sale.'

'Phil?'

'A fashion show! I know loads of people in the fashion industry and we could get glimpses of their new ranges.'

'It's been done,' Avril said dismissively.

'Oh, I know. I know.' Daisy was hopping up and down. 'How about a sponsored celebrity bungee jump?'

'Oh, for God's sake,' Avril let her disdain show. 'The cake sale was a better idea. Where's the class in people jumping from a crane?' Now that Daisy was suitably chastised, she turned to me. 'Poppy, I don't suppose you've any ideas?'

'No.'

Avril bit on the top of her silver pen. 'Well, I want you all to think hard. This event has to take place before the end of the year and we need something exciting, something dynamic and something that will raise a lot of money. Something,' she added smugly, 'like last year.'

My mother poked me in the arm and whispered as Avril turned to clear the plates, 'Think now, Poppy, for next month. Get a good idea and upstage that smug woman.' Louder, she added, 'Avril, that was delicious. Can I help you clear up?'

Avril shoved the milk jug in her direction and the milk spilled everywhere.

I love the city on a Monday. It's not too crowded, though the shops we visit are never that crowded anyway. I don't know why – Paul Costelloe's hats are to die for and as for Lainey Keogh, her knitwear should have had them queuing up for miles around. I noticed people staring at my mother as we made our way into Brown Thomas. People always stared at her, she's quite beautiful in a mature woman way. Ash blonde hair, prominent cheekbones and eyes that were once big and wide. She's thin too, thinner than I am. I trailed behind her, enjoying the reaction she got from the other shoppers. She was like a bright exotic bird in a hen house.

'Now, what do you think of this?' She startled me out of my reverie by holding up a moss-green velvet dress. 'Isn't this nice?'

I cocked my head to one side. It was nice but there was something missing. 'Here,' I pulled out the midnight-blue version. 'Try this colour instead.' She held it up to herself, looked at her reflection in the mirror and nodded approvingly.

'Well done, Poppy. Yes, that's much better.'

I envied her slightly as she studied herself, swaying this way and that, the dress floating out in a gorgeous blue arc. That would have been me less than four months ago. 'It's great,' I agreed.

'Good, so let's go to the dressing rooms to try it on.' Mam looked questioningly at me. 'What are you going to bring, Poppy? Do try that green one on.' She pointed to a John Rocha dress that I had been silently admiring. 'Come on, hurry up. You might as well, you need to look good for your father's do. It'll be in all the papers, you know.'

The last thing I wanted was to be was in the papers. I'd had enough of reading about my husband in them. 'Aw, Mam, I'm not really in the mood.'

'When can you *not* be in the mood for shopping?' my mother laughed gaily. 'Don't be ridiculous, look at all the gorgeous things here. Just try something on – if you find something it'll save you another trip.'

'I have something at home that I might wear.'

A small frown line appeared between her eyes. 'What?'

'I was thinking of the blue dress I wore for the last wedding we were at.'

A pause before she tittered. 'That's last season! You can't wear that. And besides, this is your father's retirement do, you have to have something new.'

'Not from here,' I said.

'Not from here?' my mother hissed. Her smile was gone as she began to realise that I was serious. 'What do you mean? Here is as good as it gets.'

I didn't want to have to say it, but she was going to keep going on about it if I didn't. 'Here is as expensive as it gets too, Mam.'

'Yes. Because it's excellent quality. It's designer. It's . . .' she paused, suddenly understanding. 'Do you mean that it's *too* expensive?'

I shrugged, embarrassed.

There was a bit of a pause and I knew she was wondering what to say. We're not really comfortable with 'situations' in our house. When she spoke it was slowly and every word was enunciated, making me think that everyone could hear her. 'Are–you–saying–that you–and Pete–are too *poor*–to afford a dress like that?' She dragged out the word 'poor'. 'I mean, it's not that expensive.' She held up the price tag to me.

I gave an uncomfortable laugh. 'Mam, that dress is about a month of Pete's wages.'

'No!'

I nodded.

'Good *God*!'

'So, you see why I—'

'Do they not pay properly in that hotel? That's a disgrace!'

'I don't know what they pay, but it's the going rate, apparently.'

'Going rate? It should be well gone!' Mam was disgusted. She pulled the dress off the rack. 'I'll buy it for you. Huh, if my son-in-law can't make my daughter look beautiful then I will.'

'Mam, it's not Pete's fault.'

'I don't know. Him and his dodgy—'

'Mam!'

She bit her lip and made a contrite face. 'Well, mmm, maybe not.'

'Definitely not. He's doing his best. He's great and I don't need a dress.' I glared at her, feeling hurt for Pete. I folded my arms and said crossly, 'The blue one I have at home will be fine.'

'No, it won't. Please, Poppy, try the green one. I'm sorry about what I said, I just think you deserve the best.' She held the dress towards me.

'Pete *is* the best.'

'I was talking about the dress.'

I allowed myself a smile. 'Oh.'

'Oh indeed. Don't be so sensitive, Poppy. Now, will you try it on?'

'I can't.' I shook my head. God, it was one of the hardest things I had to do.

'Come on,' she pressed the dress into my hands. 'Call it a . . . a . . . an early birthday present.'

'A birthday present?'

'Yes! Your birthday is only *three* months away and I promise nothing for your actual birthday, OK?'

'Aw, I dunno.' The dress shimmered with a life of its own against me. I touched it. Cool silk. Liquid silk. God, it would look great on me.

'You just try it on and if you don't want me to buy it, then I won't,' my mother said.

I struggled with myself but the materialist in me won out. 'I suppose that won't hurt.'

'It won't hurt at all,' my mother beamed.

An hour later we left the shop, her with the blue velvet dress, strappy shoes and the most fantastic Gucci bag I'd ever seen, and for my birthday, she'd bought me the green dress. And despite my better judgement, I'd bought myself a pair of shoes to go with the dress: Jimmy Choo wedge shoes. They were a perfect match – the only thing I was really good at was shopping – I could always put together clothes that people said would never match – and these shoes were my birthday present from Pete. I swung the brown-and-cream shopping bags to and fro. I loved carrying them. I loved knowing that the label emblazoned across the front of them was going to be noticed. I loved that I had new clothes. It was like a warm cashmere jumper on a cold day.

Eventually we arrived at the Dome restaurant and bought ourselves a snack.

'He's going to be unbearable, you know,' Mam said before biting into her salad sandwich.

'Who is?' I hadn't my mother's will power. I'd bought a huge squishy cream cake and the filling squirted everywhere when I bit into it. My fingers were covered and I licked at them as my mother winced.

'Use a tissue, Poppy, for God's sake,' she said, passing me one. 'Honestly, you'd swear you never got fed.'

I ignored her and asked again. 'Who'll be unbearable?'

'Who do you think? Your father, of course. Honestly, how is he going to *bear* being retired?'

I hadn't thought of that. What would he do?

'And he'll be around the house all day.'

I hadn't thought of that either. The thought of my dad being at home with *me* all day sent chills up my spine.

'He'll have a roster for the house made out before his first week at home is over,' Mam went on, dabbing a napkin daintily at the sides of her mouth. 'He'll have days for shopping and days for walks and days for watching television – you mark my words, the man will drive me mad.'

I couldn't argue with her.

'The only consolation is that I'll be out of the house most of the time – what with my charity work and my work with the old folks and the residents' association. I'm going up for chairwoman this year, you know.'

My coffee went down the wrong way. It was a horrible sensation and made me cough like mad. Mam was disgusted. Another tissue was thrust in my direction. This time I used it.

'Chairwoman? You?'

'Don't sound so surprised,' Mam tut-tutted. 'And anyway, my election will get me out of the house, away from your father.'

'Do you not want to spend time with him?' I have to say, I was a bit taken aback.

'Yes, when it suits me. Has he ever spent time with me unless it suited him? No.'

I guess she had a point in a weird way. Dad had been a bit of a workaholic.

'But poor Dad,' I said, feeling a little sorry for him, 'thinking he's going to be spending his time with you and instead he'll be all on his own.'

'Well, I was on my own long enough when he was working,' Mam said smartly. 'Now, eat up, Poppy, and let's get back. If I know you, you'll be dying to show the dress off to that husband of yours.' Which went to show that she didn't know me at all.

I half-heartedly went about finishing the cake, wondering now, for the first time, what Pete would say about the money spent. He wouldn't be impressed, that was for sure. Maybe, the sneaky thought crept up on me, maybe I could wear the shoes and then bring them back?

'Hello. Poppy, isn't it?'

I jumped, startled. I could feel my face flush guiltily, almost as if the speaker had heard my thoughts. 'Yes.'

The old woman in front of me looked familiar, though I couldn't at first place her. Then it dawned on me: she was the old bat who hated Billy near her garden by our old house. In fact, one time she had accused him of scraping her car. What was her name again. Madge? Margie? What? 'Hi,' I blurted out.

She looked down at my shopping bags. 'Oh, well, things can't be too bad for you then,' she said in a sly voice. 'We all thought you'd lost everything.'

'All?' I went red.

'All the neighbours.'

'Oh.' I hated that they'd been talking about us. I dropped my eyes back to the table.

'I'm Maureen,' my mother filled the silence. 'And you are?'

'Martha, an old neighbour of your daughter's.'

They shook hands in the dainty, refined way that I hated.

'It's nice to see you again, Poppy,' Martha said. 'And to know that you're still OK. And do you know who bought your house?'

I shook my head. Nor did I want to.

'That film star chap, the Dublin one who's making all the movies now. Oh, I can't remember his name. He's very handsome anyway, and always has a smile for me.'

'He must be a good actor, so,' I said without thinking. Then, at Martha's indignant look, I amended, 'To be in films . . .'

'Yes.' She was still looking oddly at me. 'Yes, he is. David something or other, that's his name.'

'David Dunne?' I gasped. No way!

'That's it,' Martha nodded. Then with a smirk, she added, 'We're all thrilled to have him near us – gives the neighbourhood a bit of extra glamour and probably increases the prices too.'

'Well,' my mother stood up. 'We have to go now, don't we, Poppy.' She handed me all the bags for which I was most grateful. 'Come on now.' She turned to Martha. 'We've to visit a few more places – you know what daughters are like!' And without looking any more at her, we left.

'Bye now,' Martha called out gaily.

'Old bitch,' my mother hissed.

I know it was stupid, but Martha being the old bitch she always was had me feeling so homesick it hurt.

8

'WHERE DID YOU get that dress?' Pete asked the second he spied me at the top of the stairs. He was standing, in his navy suit, before the hall mirror, waiting on Billy and me. I'd bided my time coming down, hoping, I suppose, that he wouldn't ask about the dress.

'This?' I made a feeble attempt at looking surprised. 'Oh, didn't I tell you? My mother bought it for me last week, as an early birthday present.'

His gaze took in my gorgeously shod feet. 'And the shoes, are they new too?'

Pete was not the sort of guy to notice things like shoes, but you couldn't really miss these. They screamed 'class' and 'money' and unfortunately in the shop they'd screamed out 'BUY ME NOW'.

'Yeah,' I flashed my foot at him. Gave a giggle. 'I got these for myself. From you. For my birthday.' I joined him at the bottom of the stairs and studied my reflection in the mirror.

'Oh.' Pete looked taken aback. 'Well, I guess I should say "Happy Birthday" then.'

I felt irritated, the way you do when you know you're in the wrong. 'Thank you.'

'Your mother never would have bought you a dress before.'

'Before? Before what?'

I knew what he meant, of course, but I had to pretend I didn't. I didn't want him to think that I thought there *was* a before and after. Or that if there was that it made a difference. But of course it did. Before we had money, before we moved, before we went on holidays, before when we were happier . . . I quashed the thought.

In the bedroom, as I pulled the dress on and zipped up the dinky little concealed side fastener, my heart had lifted, just for one tiny moment. The first time I'd felt like myself since we'd moved. Feigning happiness was getting harder by the day. For both of us.

'Before I lost my company,' Pete said. 'She would never have bought it for you before that. She usually sends you flowers.'

I shrugged. 'She just wanted to treat me.'

His brown eyes darkened. 'I want to treat you too, you know.'

'And you have.' I turned to him and wrapped my arms about his waist. 'Didn't you buy me the shoes?'

'Yeah, that was nice of me, wasn't it?' He gave a little grin and kissed the top of my nose. 'How much did I spend on you, as a matter of interest?'

Fuck. Shit. 'That's not a polite question to ask.' I tried to sound flirty but failed.

'Give me a ball-park figure.'

'Well,' I licked my lips. 'It'd be what you normally spend.'

I ignored his sharp intake of breath. 'But I don't earn what I normally earn now,' he said in a pissed off voice.

'Oh yeah,' I nodded. 'Sorry. I forgot.'

He glared at me.

Of course, that made me defensive. 'I'll sell them once I've worn them, will I?' I muttered. 'You'd like that, wouldn't you?'

'No.' He paused and gulped hard. 'No, Poppy.'

I pretended to fiddle about with my hair.

'But it might be nice,' he went on, 'if you could be economical about some things.'

'Like?'

'Well the—'

'I was economical about my hair and look at it!'

'Your hair is lovely.'

'It's rotten.' I scowled at my reflection. I decided, due to guilt about the shoes and partly in the spirit of our economy drive, to sacrifice my regular hairdresser for the local one. Pete had been really proud of me but NEVER AGAIN. The girl, a twenty-year-old Goth, had butchered it. Chopped it into uneven lengths and attempted to shove a colour in. It was now a mess of red, brown and blonde highlights. I'd cried all the previous night and Pete had told me not to worry, that he'd pay for me to go back to Leroy once he got the cash together.

I stared at Pete in the mirror. The suit he was wearing was one he'd bought for a wedding we'd gone to last Christmas. It looked good on him, but he should have had something new too. He shoved his hands into his pockets and seemed to be glaring at my back. He was talking to me too, only I hadn't been listening.

'. . . and the electricity bill will cost a fortune at this rate. Poppy, there is a line in the garden for hanging out clothes, you don't have to keep using the tumble dryer.'

'I do try, Pete. But it keeps raining and the clothes wouldn't dry. I had to use it.'

'You could have put the clothes on the radiators.'

'Oh.' I hadn't thought of that. I winced. 'Sorry.'

He rolled his eyes, but he was smiling a little. 'Just

remember the next time,' he chided gently.

'Yes, Daddy,' I joked.

'Jesus, shoot me,' Pete groaned. 'I'm not like him.'

I made a face at Pete and called up the stairs, 'Hey, Billy, are you ready yet?'

'Don't want to go,' Billy shouted down. 'It'll be boring.'

'Well, you have to go, honey.'

'I want to go next door and play with Tommy.'

'Well you can't. Your granddad has invited you to his retirement and he'll be sad if you don't go.'

'So you cheer him up then!'

Pete snorted out a laugh.

'Cheeky brat,' I giggled.

'Like his mammy,' Pete kissed me on the side of my neck. 'And even though you're a money pit, you do look gorgeous, you know.'

His compliment made me shiver. I was not gorgeous, never had been, but for some weird reason Pete genuinely thought that I was. 'Awww, thanks,' I snuggled into him. 'And even though you're a big depressing moan, you're gorgeous too.'

There was a lovely moment of silence then when we just smiled at each other.

'I'll go up to him, will I?' Pete asked, nodding in Billy's direction.

'Please.'

He gave me another quick kiss before taking the stairs two at a time and bursting into Billy's room. 'I'm coming to kill you!' he shouted out and Billy went into peals of laughter. 'Aaagghhh!' Pete shouted then.

I smiled at the noise they made. Thumps and bumps came from upstairs and eventually Billy arrived down in the kitchen in a pair of jeans and a check shirt.

Jeans? Honestly. The man hadn't a clue.

'Pete, I had a nice pair of trousers out for him.'

'Us boys hate trousers,' Billy said in this cool macho voice that he'd learned from Tommy. He folded his arms and gazed at me cockily. I didn't think Tommy was a great influence.

'Too right,' Pete agreed.

'Boys have to wear things they hate when they go out.' I was not having Billy turn up to the retirement in a pair of jeans. Bad as things were, he still had nice clothes that fit him. Next year, he'd have nothing. 'Now, go up and put them on.'

Pete glanced at his watch. 'Aw, Poppy, we'll be late. Jaysus, it takes ages to get clothes on him and anyway, he's only a kid, all kids wear jeans.'

'Not on nights out – Billy up and put your trousers on!'

'But Daddy said—'

'I don't care what Daddy says, your daddy hasn't a clue about what to wear to these things. Now, up!'

Billy looked to Pete, but Pete was staring at me.

'Up!' I said again to Billy. He didn't move. 'NOW!'

'Daddy?'

'Go on up,' Pete spoke softly and without taking his eyes from me, adding, 'Your mother is the one with the social graces.'

'Aw, Pete—'

He talked over me. 'Go on up and change, you can wear your jeans tomorrow.'

'It's not fair,' Billy said, his lip trembling. Then shouted, 'I'll look like a nerd!'

'No you won't,' I said.

'Yes, I will.'

'No, you won't.'

'Yes, I will.'

'No, you won't.'

'Tommy says boys who wear trousers are nerds.'

'Well then, you better stop playing with Tommy!'

'No, I won't.'

'Yes, you—'

'Up!' Pete snapped.

Billy shot a look at him and stomped from the kitchen.

I was about to apologise to Pete for what I'd said – though he'd taken it up all wrong – when he turned from me and followed Billy up the stairs. *Great!*

9

D AD'S DO WAS being held in The Maxwell Hotel, which was the most salubrious place in town. His firm had hired out the ballroom and it seemed that anyone who was anyone was there. Unfortunately, it was anyone who was anyone in the business world, not the pop world or the film world. Consequently, the gathering had an element of the Irish summer about it. Really wet and missing its sunny side.

Pete and I walked in with Billy trailing behind us like a sad snail or something. I don't know which is worse, going out with Pete when we're having a row or bringing Billy somewhere when he's in bad form. With Pete, it's such a struggle to appear happy when he refuses to co-operate. I mean, I go all out to pretend that we're the happiest couple in coupledom while all the time he avoids my gaze and won't talk to me unless I talk to him. Bastard. Though in a funny way, I like that he's not into show. With Billy, it's just a worry in case he decides to throw a wobbler. He'd screamed his head off in the car all the way over even though, to pacify him, I'd let him bring his Star Wars sword. 'He'll hit someone with that,' Pete had muttered ominously, and I'd ignored him. Huh, if he wasn't going to speak up and look at me when he did so, he could feck off.

'Hiiiii!' My mother, ever the social butterfly, crossed towards us, her arms outstretched in greeting. She looked great in her blue velvet, a big silk wrap around her shoulders. Her gaze was a little vacant which was a sure sign she'd had a few glasses of wine. 'Oh, hiiii, Poppy. You look *fabulous* in that dress. You really do. Doesn't she look great, Pete?'

'Yeah,' Pete answered as if he couldn't care less. 'Anyone want a drink?'

'A wine,' I said frostily. 'A nice large one.'

'Maureen?'

'I'll have a wine too, thanks, Pete.'

'And get an orange for Billy,' I said.

'I want a Coke.'

'You're having an orange, your mother says so,' Pete snapped before stalking away.

'I want a Coke!' Billy half screeched.

Pete ignored him.

'COOOOKKKEEE!' Billy screamed.

'Get him a Coke, Pete,' I called out gaily to Pete's retreating back. He didn't respond but I'm sure he heard as half the room turned towards me.

'Oh, don't shout, Poppy,' Mam wittered. 'And you,' she bent down to Billy, 'You shouldn't shout either. It's not very nice.'

Billy scowled. 'I can if I want to. I can shout if I want to.'

'Oh, you can,' Mam said, with a pained look on her face, 'you can if you want everyone to think you're a rude boy.'

'GOOD!' Billy yelled. 'I WANT TO BE A RUDE BOY!'

'Oh, well then you'll have to go home,' Mam said back.

'Good,' Billy stuck out his tongue. 'I didn't want to come anyway. I hate Granddad.'

'Oh!' Mam looked horrified.

'Just ignore him,' I muttered. I gave Billy a little shove. 'Go on, honey, and see where your daddy is, will you?'

'I want to go home.'

'Go and see where Daddy is.' A light sweat broke out on my face. Please don't make a show of me, I silently prayed.

'Will he get me a Coke?'

'If you're there to tell him he will.'

'OK.' Billy, swinging his sword around his head, scampered off.

Ha, I thought, let Pete deal with him.

Mam gazed after Billy. 'I don't know how you manage to keep your sanity when he carries on like that, Poppy. Honestly, that was pure bold.'

'He isn't bold,' I said. 'He's just annoyed that I made him wear trousers instead of jeans.'

'Oh, for God's sake,' she rolled her eyes. 'Hasn't he little to be annoyed about.' Then she smiled, 'Still, he's got great spirit, hasn't he?'

'He has.'

We smiled fondly after him. He careered into the back of a man who was holding a pint of Guinness. I was about to go over and apologise when my mother pulled me away.

'Oh, no, don't, Poppy, he's a very grumpy man. And anyway, that's a horrible suit, isn't it?' She looped her arm through mine. 'I'm so glad you're here now, your father's friends are so boring.'

'So, how's Dad feeling?' I asked. 'Is he regretting his decision?'

'Oh no,' Mam shook her head and staggered a bit – she was well on – 'Does your father ever regret a decision he's made?' She pulled me towards a group of people. 'Come

66

on, come and talk to these people. They're hilarious, Poppy. They have to be the most boring people you'll ever meet in your life.'

Mam was right. These people were work horses. All they talked about was stocks, shares, bulls, and computer jargon – it was like listening to a constant business show. Still, it got me away from Pete, who I noticed had ensconced himself at the bar and was chatting easily to the barman and a few other people. Their conversation looked a lot more inter-esting than the one I was having. Loud bursts of laughter kept floating across the room to me and I wondered what they were talking about. So, in case Pete was looking at me, I plastered a smile on my face to show that I too was having a good time.

I was useless at making small talk with strangers unless Pete was beside me. I felt as if I were drowning in a sea of banality. Every couple I met seemed to be happy and contented. They smiled at each other, laughed at each other's jokes – which went completely above my head – and gener-ally enjoyed one another's company. I winced. Maybe I was just feeling paranoid. Just because I was a bit miserable, everyone else was appearing to be happier than they were. I was pondering this while pretending to listen to a man who was telling me about the time he'd bought up all the yo-yos in the country. He was in the middle of explaining how he'd sold them all at profit when I noticed that Billy wasn't with Pete. I scanned the room hastily and couldn't see him. I waited a couple of minutes, trying not to panic, just to see if I'd missed something. Nope, no sign of him.

Trying not to appear alarmed, I excused myself and crossed to the bar. Pete was, as usual, the centre of atten-tion as he told a story about the year we booked holidays over the Internet and instead of heading to Georgia in America we ended up in Russia. Of course, it had been my booking, and I cringed as everyone burst into laughter.

'Excuse me,' I said, my voice shaking slightly, the way it always did when I had to break into a group of people. 'I just want a word with Pete.'

'This is my wife,' Pete introduced me. 'Poppy.'

'Hello,' I smiled around as best I could.

'Oh, you're Furlong's daughter, are you?' a chesty blonde asked. Then she giggled and put her hand to her mouth. 'Oops, sorry I mean Mr Furlong's daughter.'

'Yep, he's my dad,' I answered. 'Pete, have you seen Billy?' I said, turning away from her.

'Nope, I thought he was with you,' Pete said in an offhand manner that only I would notice.

'I sent him to find you about an hour ago.'

'Yeah, and I gave him the Coke and he wandered off,' Pete shrugged. 'Relax, he's fine.'

'Relax?' I gaped. 'What do you mean relax? This is Billy we're talking about!'

'Who is Billy?' the blonde asked.

'Our son,' I answered, scanning the room again.

'Is he the little guy with a big sword?'

'Yeah.'

'Oh, I saw him up at the top of the room, where the tables are all set up for the speeches.' She giggled. 'Aw, he was so cute in a gorgeous pair of trousers and everything.'

'That's him,' I frantically looked to the top of the room. 'Where did you see him?'

'Just at the table. The first table.' She pointed and her blouse strained at the seams. Her boobs were right under Pete's mouth.

I didn't have time to notice Pete's reaction because, as if on cue, there came the biggest whack followed by a yell. Then Billy stood up on the table brandishing his sword like his Star Wars heroes.

'Ha. Ha. Betcha didn't think that would happen!'

'You little brat! What did you do that for?' The man shouting was about thirty-five with ginger hair but balding in the middle. There was a red welt down the side of his face where Billy had obviously hit him.

'Oh Jesus,' Pete groaned.

'You should have kept an eye on him,' I spat.

He glared at me.

The blonde clapped her hands gleefully. 'Ooohh, that's great. I've been wanting to do that since I came into the room!'

'What? Stand on a table and brandish a sword about?' some guy asked lasciviously behind her.

'Nooo, give David Hennel a good whack across the face. He's the sneakiest sneak,' she giggled. 'He stole my boyfriend's promotion from right under his nose.'

Pete and I stared horror-struck at the scene unfolding in front of our eyes. Billy was refusing to be caught, running across the tables like an acrobat, jabbing his sword at anyone who came near him.

'Ha! Ha!' he chortled. 'You shouldn't say stuff about my granddad, ha, ha.'

David Hennel was glaring at him. 'I said nothing!'

'Liar, liar, pants on fire,' Billy shrieked. 'Your nose will grow now. Ha. Ha.'

'Fuck.' Pete pushed past me on his way to collect our son. I decided that I'd better support him.

'Get down!' My father's voice rang out across the room. 'Get down from that table and apologise now!'

There was instant silence. My dad has that effect on people. Grown men quiver when he turns on them. I'd seen it happen when I'd worked for him.

'Get down!' My dad said again.

Billy glared at him. His sword wobbled in his hand. He lifted his chin up and said, 'No!'

A barely audible gasp ran around the room. Pete stopped walking and I bumped into him.

My dad strode up the room. 'Now Billy, one more chance.' Grandfather and grandson glared at one other.

Billy pointed his sword in the direction of a smirking David. 'He said you were a, a . . .' he struggled to remember what David had said. 'A bas-turd, Granddad. And I know what that means – it means a shit. Shit is turd in America.' He looked at David. 'Are you from America?' David glared at him. 'And he said you were a banker. And you're not. And he said he was glad you were leaving – sure that isn't nice?'

'I did not,' David protested. 'I was talking about someone else,' but his flush gave him away.

'No you weren't,' Billy sounded amazed. 'His name is George Furlong,' he pointed at my father, 'and you called him George Fuck Face!'

Now an audible gasp rang out. I don't know whether it was at the language or the fact that this David guy had said that about my dad.

'It was another George,' David said weakly.

'No it wasn't,' Billy jabbed his sword again. 'You said that—'

'Shut up!' David yelled.

'Did you just tell my Grandson to "shut up"?' my father asked in this really low voice.

David gulped. 'He hit me.'

Someone laughed.

'Did you make any of those comments about me?' my dad asked.

'No.'

'So you're calling a member of my family a liar then?'

David gulped. I almost felt sorry for him. 'Well, no, but—'

'So you did say those things?'

'He misunderstood.'

Pete left my side then. He marched up the room and grabbed Billy's arm. 'Out!' he said. Billy squealed.

Dad looked at Billy. 'Good boy, Billy. You did well. Go on now with your daddy.'

To my surprise, Billy jumped down off the table and, without having to be dragged anywhere, followed Pete from the room. I felt weak with relief. Meanwhile, my father was advancing on David.

'I only employ staff who are loyal. I don't employ bad-mouthers. You can clear your desk tomorrow.'

Holy Jesus! No one else seemed surprised at all.

David glared around. 'That's illegal. You can't fire me for an opinion. I'll sue you.'

'So you did venture your opinion of me?'

'No. On another George.'

'Well,' my father said smoothly. 'Let's ask the man you were talking to, shall we? Patrick, my right hand man, was David talking about me or not?'

Patrick paled. 'Well, I can't say for sure but—'

'I don't pay you for uncertainties of judgement, Patrick,' my father's voice sounded like the snap of a firecracker. 'I pay for gut feeling, for instinct. Was he or was he not calling me fuck face? It's a simple question, it requires a simple answer.'

'Well,' Patrick ran his tongue around his lips nervously. 'Well, I believe so, yes.'

'Good. Thank you. I hope you told him that I wasn't a fuck face?'

'Oh, I did.'

'My bollix you did,' David snarled.

'So, David, you can clear out your desk by tomorrow. Thanks.' Dad turned back to the room. 'Now, let's get on with the party.'

'You can't fire me, you've retired.'

Again there was silence. My father stood completely still for a few seconds, then very slowly he turned back to face David. He was a good three inches taller. 'I've not retired until the speeches are over. And I still own the company, until such time as I sell my shares. Now, if you've finished throwing your tantrums you can leave, everyone else here wants to have a good time. Come on, on with the party.'

It was an order. Everyone smiled awkwardly and turned to whomever they were standing beside and began to chat. David stood uselessly at the top of the room being ignored by everyone before storming out and slamming the door.

After the speeches, which were glowing and probably totally untrue, the press began to take photos. They took some of Dad on his own, Mam and Dad together and finally one photographer asked for one of the whole family.

'Oh, my husband isn't here,' I muttered, flushing.

'Then get him, Poppy. Come on.' My mother gave me a shove and giggled flirtatiously at the young snapper. 'Can you wait a minute?'

He nodded. 'Sure, missus.'

Reluctantly, I went in search of Pete and Billy. I found them sitting in the foyer, Pete with his tie loosened and his legs stretched out in front of him, half-asleep. Billy was rolling about on the floor, fighting imaginary bad guys.

'We have to get some photos taken,' I announced abruptly.

Pete didn't open his eyes.

Billy looked up at me. 'Are you cross with me, Mammy? Daddy said I was very bold to hit someone, even if the person was bad.' Without waiting for my answer he began jabbing the air again. Obviously my opinion didn't matter to him that much.

'Pete,' I shook him quite roughly. 'Come on, we have to get our photo taken.'

He slowly opened his eyes and stared at me. 'Right,' he sighed, sounding fed-up, 'whatever you want.' He stood up and brushed himself down. 'Come on, Billy, let's go and smile for the camera.' He held out his hand and Billy grasped it. The two walked away from me.

After the photographs – in which Billy delighted my father by wanting to 'stand guard' beside him – Pete left the room. 'I'll be downstairs when you want to go,' he said. I barely acknowledged him but my heart sank. He really was in a mood. I think I'd underestimated how hurt he'd been. But I hadn't meant anything by my comment – it had been a sort of a joke. The sort of thing women say to men all the time about clothes. I watched him leave the ballroom and I was tempted to run after him but, the stubborn bitch in me took over. He was wrecking my night. He was ruining what could have been an enjoyable night. We could have sat at the bar, the two of us, him talking to people and me hanging on to his arm, the way I do. I could have got drunk, he could have carried me to the car and we could have gone home and made love.

But instead he was sulking, he was leaving me on my own when he knew I hated that. So, I decided, if he wanted to sit in the foyer for hours waiting on me, well, he could.

10

'FUCK SAKE, FUCK sake,' was the first thing I heard the next morning. This was followed by loads of stamping about and even more cursing. I went to jump up and see what the problem was but the pain in my head pinned me to the bed. This was followed by the most horrific stomach lurch. Jesus, the worst thing of all – a hangover when I hadn't even felt drunk enough to enjoy myself. I closed my eyes and willed the pain to go away.

The bedroom door was flung open and Pete stormed in. Without even looking in my direction, he began stripping off his suit from the night before and raiding the wardrobe.

'Problem?' I asked weakly, hoping he'd notice the pain in my voice and bring me up a couple of Disprin.

His head snapped towards me. 'Yeah. Yeah I'd say there is. I've just fucking slept it out. I was supposed to be in work for six.'

Since we'd left the party at five and Pete hadn't mentioned anything about work to me the previous night, I'd assumed he'd gone straight to work. But then again, he wasn't talking to me at the time. I stole a glance at the alarm clock. It was eight o'clock. 'No point in going in now,' I murmured. 'Ring in sick.'

'Oh yeah, and lose the job.'

'You won't lose—'

'And how on earth would you know?' He pulled on a white shirt and began to haphazardly button it up. 'Jesus, what did you want to stay at the party so late for last night?'

'Don't blame me. You never told me to get home early, that you had work today.'

'Because you wouldn't care, would you?' His shirt was buttoned wrong, but I didn't tell him. 'Oh no, so long as the money keeps coming in, you couldn't care less.'

'And what is that supposed to mean?'

'It means exactly what it means.'

'Oh, an English scholar.' I was going to be sick. Jesus, I was going to be sick.

'Don't be so fucking sarcastic.'

'Don't you curse at me!'

'Well, I'm sorry my darling wife that I'm not as refined as you would like, that I'm not like your perfect parents, but hey, I am doing my best to keep the boat afloat. Meanwhile, you are doing your best to bloody sink it.'

'Pardon?' My head was hammering, spinning. I felt like I was going to collapse. And it wasn't just from the hangover.

'Ring in sick.' He did a woeful imitation of my voice. 'Well, I can't. I can't because I need this job. Because no one will employ me. Because I am considered a criminal in some circles. You, meanwhile, are off getting your hair done, your nails done, buying shoes and dresses—'

'I am not. My mother bought me that dress. My hair was cheap. I did my own nails!'

'You're still driving about in the Beetle. Wasting petrol driving to your mother's every bloody day.'

'Because I hate it here! I hate it here!' I couldn't believe

76

I just said that. Tears splashed on to my face. This wasn't real. This couldn't be happening.

'Well, honey, here is where it's at at the minute. I'm sorry I let you down, but the fact is that if we don't get some more money in soon we mightn't even be here.' He flung his trousers on to the bed. Walked about half-naked. Looked lovely. 'In fact,' he struggled with his uniform trousers, 'you need to sell that car of yours, and you need to get a job. There,' he glared at me and he zipped his flies, 'now you know.'

'A job?'

'Yes, Poppy, you need to earn some money. I mean, we can't continue to run up massive bills without paying them.'

'A job?'

'I thought we could manage on my wages, but we can't. Still, if I don't know what a kid can wear to a retirement party, what do I know, ey?'

'Oh, fuck off!'

'I intend to. I'll be at work. Try not to ring, you'll only cost us money.'

'Bastard! I wouldn't ring you if you begged me to.'

'We all might be begging soon enough.'

Then he was gone. Out the door and gone.

I bawled my eyes out.

I didn't get sick as it happens. When Billy woke up I got him to go downstairs and bring me up two tablets and a glass of water. He obeyed surprisingly quickly.

'Are you sick, Mammy?' he asked as he sat beside me on the bed and watched the Disprin dissolve in the water.

'Sort of,' I muttered, steeling myself to drink it down.

'Your eyes are all red. Have you an eye infection?'

'Yeah, sort of.'

'Poor you.' He rubbed my cheek with his little hand and it was lovely. He put his head beside mine on the pillow. 'Will I make you a cup of tea?'

'No,' I laughed a little. 'You'll end up scalding yourself. Tell you what, do you think you can dress yourself? I'll let you wear anything you want.'

'Even my jeans?'

'Yep.'

'I don't want to wear them. I think I'll wear my Star Wars gear. Then I can go and give Tommy a fright, can't I?'

'Good idea. I'll get up in a bit and make you some breakfast.'

I heard him pulling everything out of his wardrobe trying to find his Darth Vader outfit. Billy was weird like that. He seemed to identify with the baddies. Pete thought it was hilarious. I shook my head and banished Pete from my thoughts. I wondered if he'd really meant that I had to get a job. Surely not. Sure, paying for Billy to be minded would use up all my wages. He'd only said it because he was angry.

That was all.

I was up at around two o'clock – just. Billy had scavenged some breakfast for himself and left to go next door. He'd upturned the carton of milk in his haste to escape and it was all over the floor. I decided to eat something before I tackled it. By then I was feeling better. My head had receded to a dull ache and my stomach was rumbling for food. I looked in the bread bin to make myself some toast but it was bare. The only thing in the presses was Billy's Coco-Pops. And the milk was all over the floor.

'Damn,' I muttered and then more tears came. I don't know why, they just spilled out all over my cheeks and I sat down at the table and howled. It felt good actually. All the tightness around my chest lifted and my shoulders didn't seem as stiff. I cried for everything. For the row we'd had, for the house we'd lost, for the life I had. OK, on the grand scale of things, no one had died and I did have Pete and Billy, but so far, in my life, this was the worst thing I'd ever had to deal with and I felt I was messing up so badly. Crying was a relief. All the tension came back abruptly when the doorbell rang though. Jesus.

I furiously scrubbed my face and thought about not answering. But Billy was outside and he was bound to tell whoever it was that I was in. And if I didn't answer then he would panic.

The bell went again. Then I heard Laura's voice asking Billy if I was up.

'Yeah. She is.' I heard him reply.

Laura hadn't really called in since that first time. I couldn't blame her, I hardly knew what to say to her when we met in the street. I just nodded a 'good morning' and she did the same back and we went our separate ways. She seemed very nice – quiet and kind and motherly. Billy thought she was great. Apparently she made lovely cakes and things. Anyway, she was ringing my door and peering through the glass and I wondered what it could be that made her so determined that I answer.

So I did. Answer, I mean.

Her first reaction was shock, which she tried to cover over with a wobbly smile. 'Oh, hello, hello, Poppy,' she said, her eyes darting all over the place so that she wouldn't have to look at my swollen eyelids. 'I, eh, well, Billy said you were sick and, well,' she was peering hard at her toes, 'and, well, I'm going out to the cinema with Tommy and I thought,

79

well, if you could do with a break I'd bring Billy too.'

'Oh,' I gulped before my eyes started to water at the unexpected kindness. I'd never have thought of doing that for anyone. 'Oh, yes, that'd be lovely.' The 'lovely' was a sniffled sob.

For a second, Laura stiffened, then the mother in her came out. She put her arm on mine. 'Oh, what's wrong? Is it very bad? Are you OK?'

I nodded hastily. 'Fine, I'm fine.'

'You don't look fine. Has something happened?'

'No.' I scrubbed my face hard. 'Nothing has happened.'

'Just having a bad day, ey?'

'Something like that.'

'Well, would you like to come to the cinema too?' She paused, then continued, 'It's a funny film. Might cheer you up.'

I hiccuped out a laugh. 'No, it's fine.'

'Will I make you a cup of coffee?'

'I've no milk.' I was a hopeless housekeeper.

'I have some. Come into my place. Billy and Tommy are playing on the green for the minute so they won't bother us.'

'Oh.'

'It's OK if you don't want to. I just thought—'

'No,' I interrupted her. 'No, I'd like that.'

'Good.' She smiled at me.

I smiled back. It was the first time in my life someone had asked me for coffee. How could I have refused?

Laura's house was the same as mine. Well, the same as mine before Pete had insisted on putting in mirrors and glass and stuff to make ours look bigger and brighter. He'd even got me to paint one of the rooms yellow, which I'd made a bit of a mess of, but it was still better than what had been there before. Laura seemed to like brown a lot. The kitchen had brown floor tiles and brown presses. A cream net curtain hung in the window.

She walked over to her kettle and filled it. 'Tea? Coffee? Something stronger?'

'I had the something stronger last night.'

'Ouch.'

'Exactly.'

'Tea OK?'

'Yeah.'

There was silence as she went about getting biscuits down and putting sugar on the table. She was a lot more casual than me. Instead of a plate, she just dumped the biscuits on to the table in their packet. The same for the sugar. I liked that.

'So,' she sat opposite me as we waited for the kettle to boil. 'How are you settling in? Billy seems to be happy.'

I stared at my hands. I had told a lie that morning. I had actually paid for them to be manicured the day before – I know I shouldn't have, but it was a special offer and had only cost twelve euro after all. At least they looked good even if the rest of me was falling apart. I realised suddenly that I hadn't even brushed my hair or put on any make-up. I probably looked a sight. The thought made me shudder a little. I felt like running back inside and painting my face and then appearing again.

'Well?' Laura probed, looking at me in a concerned way.

'Yeah, Billy is OK, I think. He's like his dad, they'd adapt anywhere.'

'Not like you?' It was a gentle question.

I shrugged. 'I liked my old house, that's all.'

'So why move?' She got up to fill the teapot.

I didn't want to say it, it was humiliating. I opened my mouth and nothing came out.

'Sorry,' Laura said. 'None of my business.'

'No, it's just . . .' I gulped and steeled myself. 'We lost our money.' It was the first time I'd said it out loud. I hadn't even told my folks directly. I'd only said we were moving, they'd read the rest in the paper. Saying that we'd lost our money made it terribly real. And frightening. Not that it hadn't been up to now, but saying it made it worse.

'Lost? How?'

'Pete's business partner was on the fiddle. He forged planning certs. and got money up front and did a runner. Now poor Pete is under investigation and he did nothing wrong.'

'No!' Her mouth dropped. 'That's terrible.'

'Yeah. And Pete loved his job, you know. Now it's a nightmare.'

'That's terrible. Oh, poor you.'

It was the first time anyone had said that. 'Poor Pete,' I said, feeling a stab of guilt about this morning. 'It was worse on him. He built that company up from nothing. It was his baby, you know. The architects' association,' I couldn't remember the name of it, 'well, they might strike him out too. Anyway, sometimes, I just get down over it.'

''Course you do. Everyone gets down over things.'

The way she said it was weird, as if she knew what I meant. I stole a glance at her but she was busy pouring water into the cups.

We didn't say any more on the subject after that. She poured me my tea and urged me to eat a double-chocolate-chip cookie. I took one, had a nibble and put it on the side of my plate. 'Lovely,' I said.

'It's nice around here,' she said as she munched. 'Like, the people are nice and there's great freedom for the kids.'

She had finished her biscuit and was reaching out for another. I took up my biscuit and took another nibble. I watched her take a huge bite out of the second biscuit and decided that it might be a bit rude to leave a half-eaten something in this house. So I took a big bite as well. Gorgeous.

'You'll get used to it,' Laura pronounced through a mouthful of chocolate.

I didn't want to get used to it though. I didn't want my life to be spent getting used to something. 'I just want to be in love with it,' I said, without meaning to. 'I want to love my life.'

Laura said nothing, just patted my hand. I hoped she knew that I wasn't criticising her life.

After Laura had taken the kids to the cinema, I sat by my phone. Talking to her had been good. Nice. I vowed to invite her back in for coffee one day. And I would. And I'd buy those gorgeous biscuits she'd had. Normally I don't eat a lot of sweet things, but those biscuits had been delicious.

Anyway, talking about things to her had made me feel really bad for Pete. There he was working in a hotel when he should have been designing beautiful buildings. He was serving breakfast when he should have been on site seeing his vision become a 3-D reality. His business had been his dream come true, he'd built it from a few thousand quid that the bank had lent him and Adrian, and while I'd cried and moaned about having to move house, he'd accepted it all with the good grace that he accepted everything. Never complaining, never really talking about it. And what had I done? Kept him up all night when he should have been sleeping. No wonder he'd been mad.

And so I dialled his number.

It was like making a call to a boy that you're not quite sure fancies you. I was afraid he'd still be mad and throw my peace gesture back in my face.

'Hello, The Jefferson Hotel.'

It was the old guy. I tried to remember his name. Lenny! That was it. 'Hi, Lenny, it's Poppy.'

'Poppy?'

'Pete Shannon's wife. Can I talk to him, please.'

'Oh, hello, Poppy, how are you? You must have had a great night last night and worn that fella of yours out.'

I managed a laugh. 'Something like that. Is he there?'

'I'll put you through to the kitchens now. Hang on.'

There was a lot of buzzing and clicking before I heard, 'Hello, kitchens.'

'I'm looking for Pete Shannon.'

'Aren't we all, love. He's taken I'm afraid.' There was a loud cackle before someone yelled, 'Pete. Pete! A call for you.'

Huh, I thought, just what was Pete *doing* in that place? I had a good mind to hang up, but before I could I heard his voice. 'Pete Shannon here.'

'Poppy Shannon here,' I said in a low voice. 'Just wasting money by ringing you up.'

There was a pause. 'Hiya missus,' he said then, and I could tell he was smiling. 'Everything OK?'

'Yeah. Just wanted to ring you up.'

'Good. I was going to ring you later.'

'Were you?' I was smiling now, but my voice sounded really forlorn.

84

''Course I was,' he replied in his lovely tender way. 'Sorry about this morning, I shouldn't have shouted at you like that.'

'And I'm sorry about yesterday. I was only slagging you. I just meant that men don't know what to wear to things, that's all.'

'Yeah, and I took it as an insult to my manhood.' He was joking now and I smiled and blinked back tears all in one go. 'I fucking love you, Poppy. I do.'

'Don't curse at me.'

We both laughed.

'See you later.'

'Yeah, make it as soon as you can,' I said, then added, 'Billy is off at the cinema.'

He knew what that meant.

I lay curled up in his arms after the best sex ever. He kissed me lightly on the forehead. 'I love you.'

'How much?' It was a game we played.

'As much as my life,' he said.

'I love you more.'

'How much?'

'As much as my life.'

He laughed. 'Bitch!'

And he loved me all over again.

11

'YOUR MOTHER IS never here!'

I'd never seen my father so agitated over anything in his life before. This was a man who could fire people at will, downsize massive companies, and he was having a hissy fit because his wife wasn't dancing attendance on him.

'Oh, I'm sure she is,' I mollified. I was sitting in their enormous dining room. A huge piano to my right and some massively expensive work of art that looked like a horror movie to my left. I loved the room but hated my father's taste.

'She went out this morning,' Dad went on, running his hand through his thick grey hair. 'I asked her where she was going and she said that she was going to meet some people to lobby them for her election to the residents' association.'

'Isn't it great,' I said, 'that she cares enough to go on the residents' committee?'

'How can it take,' Dad stopped pacing and looked at his watch, 'three hours to lobby people? I mean, what is she doing? Brainwashing them? Giving them her services?'

'Dad!'

'I'm all alone here.'

I said nothing.

'Huh, I'd nearly go out in search of a partner myself. It'd be nice to have some company.'

Something in his words stirred a germ of an idea in my head. I smiled suddenly and this seemed to irritate Dad.

'Are you laughing at me?'

'No. Look, she probably went out for lunch or something.' I wished I hadn't come. I'd been driving over every day to talk to my mother and that day I'd decided to drive over despite her being out as I didn't want my dad's feelings to be hurt. Not that I really knew how to talk to him since I'd never had much opportunity before.

'She could have gone with me!' Dad plonked down on a sofa. Not the one I was on – another one, opposite me, about twenty feet away from me. 'I mean, I told her that today was our "going out" day. I'd planned for us to see some of the museums in Dublin today.'

'Go on your own.'

'No. There's no fun. I'd wanted to tell your mother all about the artefacts. She's not well up on those things, I thought she might like to learn things like that.'

I bit my lip. My mother. Learn about old things. She steered clear of anything old.

'Will you come, Poppy?'

I winced. 'Oooooh . . .'

'It'll be fun. Educational.'

'No disrespect, Dad, but fun and education generally don't go together in the same sentence.'

'Oh, they do,' he nodded vigorously. 'All you need is a good teacher.'

Why had I come? His expectant look made me feel a bit sorry for him. 'Well, I have to be back for two.'

'Fine.'

'OK, so.'

'Good. I'll get my keys. Prepare to be dazzled.'

Dazzled was not the word I would have chosen. I would have gone into a room, looked about and walked out. My father, on the other hand, inspected everything. He pointed out things to me and told me their history. The man was a genius. I'd got the worst of both worlds: I'd inherited my mother's brains and my dad's looks – or lack of them.

'Now this,' my dad pointed to a rusted piece of metal that didn't look as if it merited a case on its own. 'This was the top of a very special spear that was unearthed in . . .'

I tuned out. I wondered where Mam was. Whatever she was doing, it was bound to be more interesting than this. Grafton Street was only a few minutes away from the museum, it would be lovely to go over and have a look about.

'Poppy,' Dad said sternly, 'are you listening?'

'Huh? Oh yeah, yeah, Dad this is great. I'm learning loads.'

That seemed to satisfy him and he continued on about the little piece of rusty metal for the next thirty minutes. We didn't even get around half the museum and my blood ran cold when my father said, 'Well, we can do the rest next week, ey, Poppy?'

'Right. Sure.' I'd have to think of some urgent appointment.

'Now,' Dad took a list from his pocket. 'Tomorrow will be gardening day. If you brought up some gloves, Poppy, that would be ideal. Your mother doesn't like the garden. She told me. Anyway, if you like, I've a list of plants that we can buy from the garden centre and I'll do that when I get home. So, if you're up at the house around ten, that would be great.'

I gawped at him. Gardening? As far as I knew, he'd never gardened in his life. In fact, he had a gardener. 'Don't you have a gardener?'

'Yes, but I'm planning on doing some of the garden myself now. With you of course.'

My heart constricted. 'Me?'

'Yes, well, you've nothing to do, have you? You and I can have a great time, Poppy. And just think, when Billy is in school till later, we can stay out even longer.'

'Aw, Dad—'

'And money is no problem, I'll pay for everything. I know you're both strapped at the minute.'

'Dad, I have housework.'

'I'll pay for a housekeeper. It'll be my gift to you.'

'No!'

He blinked, a little hurt I think. I'd never talked to him like that before.

'I mean,' I stumbled to a halt and tried to say gently, 'well, I can go out sometimes, just not all the time.'

He looked relieved. 'Oh, that's fine. My rota is flexible. The day you can't come, I'll fix things around the house.'

The day? THE DAY?

Jesus.

Gavin arrived up for dinner that night. Gavin is not the sort of guy who you invite to dinner, he just appears. His days are never really that organised so if he's free around dinner time, he comes over. I think Pete, Billy and me are *his* adopted kin now.

'Wow,' he said, as he stood in the centre of the kitchen, 'you've made this place look cool.'

'Yeah, right.' I gave him a shove. 'We haven't done anything with it. Pete just reorganised things a little.'

'Yeah, looks cool.' He touched one of the glass panels that Pete had put in to reflect the light on to the surfaces to make the room appear bigger. 'Pretty nifty. That guy of yours is not a bad designer, ey?'

I shrugged.

Gavin gave me a brief squeeze about the shoulders. 'So, how you getting on?'

'Fine.' I pulled some forks from the drawer to set the table. 'No complaints.'

'Miracles will never cease,' he joked. 'And Pete?'

'He's been a bit quiet, but he's a lot on his mind.'

'Being married to you would do that to him OK.'

'Fuck off!'

'Ohhhh, you said a bad word, Mammy,' Billy bounced in, covered in muck. Tommy, equally filthy, slouched in behind him.

'Aw, Billy, what were you doing?'

'Playing football. I got put in goal and had to dive for everything. Like this.' He did a dramatic jump in the air, fell on to the floor and rolled over. 'I saved loads. Tommy said I was the best goalie on the estate. Hiya, Gav.'

'Hiya.' Gavin looked at him in amusement. 'I'll bet you're crap in goal. Real goalies don't get dirty.'

'Do so!'

'Well, go on, show me how good you are. We'll go out on the green and you can save my shots.'

I stifled a laugh. Gavin is over six foot and looks taller because he's as skinny as a chronic anorexic from all his vegetarianism and pot-noodle dinners.

Billy's neck stretched backwards really hard and he squinted upwards. 'You're bigger than me.'

'Lots bigger than him,' Tommy agreed.

'Yeah, I am,' Gavin shrugged nonchalantly. 'But if Billy's such a super goalie, which I'll bet he's not, he should be able to save my shots.'

'He's a mega goalie,' Tommy sneered. 'You should see him dive.'

'Yeah, like this.' Billy did another dive and walloped himself on the floor.

'Jesus, Billy!'

'Another curse, Mammy,' Billy said accusingly.

'Sorry. Blame Gav,' I muttered.

'So, you gonna challenge me?' Gavin pretended to swagger.

'Yeah!' Tommy nudged Billy. 'Come on, Shannon, let's show him.'

'Yeah!'

Billy wasn't as certain and I grinned. 'Go on, out!' I gestured for them to go. Gavin tended to drive Billy more mental than normal and it was better him doing it outside than in.

'Sure?' Gavin looked at me.

'Yeah, go on. I'll do the happy housewife thing and make you your dinner.'

'Make?' Gavin winced.

'Don't slag me,' I said. 'My cooking is a lot better now.'

'So, yez don't get the take-aways any more? You cook all the time?'

'Except Fridays. Pete says it's too expensive otherwise.' I felt a little wrench as I said it. Pete was saying that a lot these days. No matter how much I economised – and I had been doing my best despite the odd slip up – Pete never seemed to be satisfied.

'Here, I'll buy.' Gavin dug his hand into his tattered jeans and pulled out a twenty and a ten. 'Go on, my shout.'

'Oh, I couldn't. You're our guest.'

'Come on, Gav.' Billy, bouncing from foot to foot, pulled on his arm.

'Order some pizzas and chips,' Gavin pressed thirty into my hand. 'Go on, I can't have those gorgeous hands peeling spuds on my account.'

He left before I could thank him.

'So,' I put a plate in front of Gavin while Pete carried his and Billy's to the table, 'Dad has me all lined up to garden with him tomorrow.'

Gavin laughed. 'I'd like to see you get your fancy nails dirty digging up stuff,' he chortled. 'Jesus, you wouldn't last two minutes.'

'That's my wife you're talking about,' Pete plonked down on to a chair and grinned at me. 'And you're right.'

They both laughed and I belted Pete across the head.

'So, what are you going to do?' Gavin cut himself a huge piece of pizza.

'I'll go tomorrow but I can't go every day. I had a look at his list. It's amazing. He has a day for going out, a day for the garden, a day for polishing things, a day for community involvement – whatever that means – a day for visiting me and some other stuff that I can't remember. I think he thinks that I'm going to be his substitute wife, and like, I don't mind a few things but a whole *load* of stuff?'

'It's pretty heavy all right,' Gavin agreed. I reckon he was starving; his slice of pizza was almost gone. Billy was looking at him eat in fascination.

'Eat up, Billy,' I said.

Billy is the worst eater. He can't sit still at the table at all. He knocks things, spills things, does everything except eat, in fact.

Billy put the tiniest chip into his mouth.

'Another one,' Pete said sternly.

Billy pouted.

'Race you,' Gavin challenged.

The two of them began shovelling chips up off their plates and getting them everywhere. Billy was choking with laughter as chips fell out of his mouth.

'Jesus, one kid is enough,' I groaned.

'There is a way you can get out of it, you know,' Pete said.

'Get out of what?'

'Seeing your dad every day.'

One of Billy's half-eaten chips landed on my jeans. 'Killing myself is a bit drastic,' I joked, flicking it back at him.

Gavin laughed loudly, exposing his own mouthful of half-eaten chips.

'Gav, that's disgusting.'

Another laugh.

I turned back to Pete. 'So, go on, boy wonder, how can I escape my father's desperate clutches?'

Pete bit his lip. 'Well,' he said, in his I'm-a-little-nervous-of-your-reaction-but-I'm-pretending-not-to-be voice, you could always get a job.'

'A job?'

Gavin stopped his shovelling and looked from one of us to the other.

'Getting a job is even more drastic than killing myself,' I giggled.

'Not as drastic as losing this house,' Pete said.

And it dawned on me that he wasn't joking. 'You're not joking?'

'I'm not joking. Why would I joke?'

'Whofs noff hokhd,' Billy said, mashed chips falling all over the place. We all ignored him.

'A job?'

'It'd be good for you,' Pete said, but I don't think he really believed it. 'You know, it'd get you out of the house.'

'I do get out of the house.'

'Not this house, your parents' house,' Pete replied.

Gavin guffawed and promptly began to choke. Pete walloped him on the back and ran to pour him some water.

'There's nothing wrong with my parents' house.'

Gavin, spluttering like his ancient car, took the water from Pete.

'You're always over there,' Pete continued. 'You'd be better off getting out and meeting people.'

'She does meet people,' Billy piped up. He had lost interest in the race and was mashing his already mashed-up chips into his jeans. 'She meets Laura all the time.'

I suppose inviting Laura in for coffee was counted as meeting up – though Laura, much to my embarrassment had refused. Apparently, she worked in the mornings. I thought it was just an excuse. I was never going to ask her again, I vowed to myself.

'Poppy,' Pete said, sitting back down again, satisfied that his friend wasn't going to choke to death, 'you need to get a job if it's only to keep that yellow car of yours.'

I blinked. 'Pardon?'

'Otherwise that car will have to go. Do you know how much the road tax is on it?'

'No.'

'Well then, I suggest you look at the bill that arrived the other day.'

'I thought you paid it.'

'I did, but it's put a huge dent in our income for the month.'

I looked at Gavin and jabbed my fork in Pete's direction. 'This fella is always on about money these days. Didn't I tell you that, didn't I?'

'Because we don't have any, dear one.' Though Pete spoke in a jocular voice, there was an unmistakable edge behind his words.

The tone of the conversation had changed suddenly. Things like that were happening a lot these days, the two of us seemed to have petty little disputes over things that wouldn't have bothered us before. Gavin must have sensed it because he stood up, saying, 'Well guys, I'll take that as my cue to go. Thanks for dinner, Poppy.'

'Thank *you*,' I said sharply.

'Talk soon,' he said to Pete.

'Sure, yeah.'

Neither of us looked at him.

'Now see what you did,' I glared at Pete. 'You frightened Gav off.'

'Nope, he didn't,' Gavin shouted from the hallway. 'I have to go anyway.' There came the slam of the front door as he left.

Huh, I thought, he always stuck up for Pete.

There was a bit of a silence after that. I don't know what Pete was thinking, but my mind was reeling. A job? Me? Jesus, what would I do?

'Maybe I shouldn't have brought it up in front of Gavin,' Pete conceded.

'No, you shouldn't,' I said back crossly.

He looked apologetically at me as I glowered.

'Can I go now?' Billy asked, uneasily.

'No!' I pointed at his plate. 'You have to eat everything!'

'I'm not hungry.'

'Right, well there's no dessert for you then.'

'Good.' Billy folded his arms and swung his legs. 'Can I go then?'

'And no sweets tomorrow.'

'That's not fair! This is today.'

I shrugged.

Billy bad-temperedly picked up a slice of pizza and shoved it wholesale into his mouth.

'Eat properly!' I yelled.

Billy shoved his pizza in harder.

'Stop that,' I shouted, making to grab the pizza back.

Billy jumped up from the table and danced in front of me, his pizza dangling from his mouth.

'Billy!' I snapped.

'Here,' Pete picked up a chip and held it out for him. 'Eat this up and I'll give you an ice-pop.'

His half-eaten pizza dropped on to the floor as he looked at the chip. 'Just this one?'

'Well, this and one more and a bite of pizza.'

'You're undoing what I said,' I muttered loudly.

Pete didn't reply. He fed Billy his tiny dinner and dug out an ice-pop for him from the freezer.

'I need one for Tommy.'

Pete handed him another one.

Billy legged it out the back door without closing it.

'You undid what I said,' I repeated, standing up to close the door.

'You were taking your bad mood out on him and it wasn't fair,' Pete replied in a maddeningly reasonable tone.

'Well, I wouldn't have been in a bad mood if you hadn't ordered me out to work.'

'Don't be ridiculous, I didn't order you to do anything.'

'So what's this about a job?'

'I told you before that you need to get some work, Poppy, you just didn't listen to me.'

'You said that during a row. I thought you didn't mean it. And anyway, I've been good, using the line and everything.'

'I know you have.' He sounded upset. He ran his hand through his hair. 'But, well, things are getting worse, Poppy. Money is really tight.'

'Is it? Really tight? But we hardly ever spend anything.' We hadn't gone out in ages or done anything interesting. I sat down at the table again and stared at my dinner. I didn't feel hungry any more.

'We're only just keeping afloat, Poppy.'

'I can't get a job, Pete.'

'Why?'

I swallowed and shrugged and muttered in humiliation, 'What will I do? I can't *do* anything.'

'Of course you can,' he moved to the seat beside me and took my hand in his. He gave it a gentle squeeze. 'Like, you could work in a supermarket, they'd train you in.'

Oh God, I couldn't wear a horrible polyester uniform. And besides, I'd be useless. 'I'd be useless.'

'No you wouldn't.' He sighed despondently. 'We need some extra money, Poppy.'

'But what about Billy?'

'He's in school until two. You could work from nine till one.'

I bit my lip. I felt a little sick. Me? Working? Where? I knew I'd mess up if I went back to the workforce. 'Do we really need the money?'

'Yeah, we really need the money.'

'But you had it all worked out, you said—'

'Do you really need your car? And those shoes you bought?' he interrupted.

I nodded mutely. I couldn't part with those things. Especially the car. Everyone admired that car.

'Then, dearest, we need the money.'

We didn't talk much after that. My mind was reeling – I was terrified of getting a job. Me and the work force were just not compatible. All my job failures danced in front of my eyes. My dad's disappointment in me would be mirrored by Pete's now.

I don't know what Pete was thinking as he helped me clean the kitchen. He kept glancing at me as if he wanted to say something and then turning away when I caught his eye.

After the kitchen was cleaned I went into the television room to watch another of those childcare programmes. I was hoping they'd do a feature on bedtime as I couldn't ever get Billy to go to bed. Instead he always jumped and shouted and sung. It was all a bit of a nightmare to be honest. Pete took his mail and went upstairs to read it. He usually did that. He'd sprawl out on the bed, read the paper, groan over the bills and then join me downstairs for a chat.

I was dreading our chat that night. Only Pete didn't come down, so at seven-thirty I went in search of him. Well, search is the wrong word really with our little house, but anyway, I went to look for him. I desperately didn't want another fight so soon after our last one. If he wanted me to get a job, well, I'd try, I vowed. Anything to stop the bickering.

He was sitting on the bed, but instead of reading the paper, he was flicking through an old scrap book we had. There were pictures in it of our happy moments. Bits of newspaper cuttings, notices of our wedding in the social columns, stuff like that. I didn't know which one Pete was gazing at but there was such a look of dejection on his face that I gasped.

'Hey,' he greeted me, attempting to close the book.

'What were you looking at?' I crossed towards him.

He smiled ruefully and pointed to the newspaper headline, 'Fledgling Firm Wins Shopping Centre Contract'. A black-and-white of him and Adrian with their hard hats on beamed out at me from the page. Adrian with his long, lanky frame and endearing smile. The bastard.

'Aw, Pete,' I sat beside him on the bed and ruffled his hair.

'Happy times, ey?'

'Yeah. But they'll come again.' His silence frightened me. 'They will,' I said more firmly.

Slowly, he handed me a letter. I recognised the envelope as one that had arrived earlier the previous week. 'I was going to tell you at some stage,' he muttered.

I turned the envelope over and over in my hands, reluctant to open it. 'What does it say?' A feeling of nausea washed over me.

'Adrian emptied the company's account, that's why he's gone. There isn't even money to finish jobs.'

There was nothing I could say.

'He was on the fiddle long before the planning permission fraud.'

'Oh, Pete.'

'And we're being sued left, right and centre.'

I wrapped my arms about him. 'You should have told me, Pete.'

He nodded briefly and sighed. 'I hate it that you have to work, Poppy, I do. I didn't want to tell you. I guess that's why I yelled it at you when we rowed, it seemed the easiest thing to do. And today, when Gav was here, well, I dunno, I thought it might sound less drastic or something.' He paused and averted his eyes from mine.

'You should have told me about this letter, Pete.'

'You see why you need a job, Poppy. If things go bad . . .' He didn't continue, just rested his head against mine.

I swore that if Adrian ever showed up I would kill him for doing this to Pete. 'Is there any chance we could find Adrian ourselves?' I asked suddenly. He looked at me quizzically. 'You know, get a . . . a private investigator or something?'

He laughed a little. 'Poppy, we've no money. How'd we pay him?'

'My dad might.'

'No!' He shook his head. 'No way. He'd never let us forget it.'

'Pete, you're being sued here for something you didn't do. Come on!'

He looked at me before cupping my face in his hands. 'It's my mess, Poppy, and I'll sort it out. Adrian was a decent guy, he's probably *still* a decent guy, I dunno what happened to him, but for now we just have to wait.'

'For what? For you to go to jail? For us to lose our house?'

'No.' He shook his head and turned back to the scrap book. 'Jesus, Poppy, if I thought for one second that your dad could find him and that if he was found he'd tell the truth then yeah, I'd swallow my pride and go for it. But I don't know the guy who did this to me, to his wife. What's he gonna say, ey?'

He had a point, I suppose. 'But still . . .'

'If he's gonna tell the truth, he'll show up. That's what I think.'

'Yeah.' I didn't want him swallowing his pride for no result. He'd had enough of it battered out of him already. 'OK.'

He kissed me softly.

12

THE NEXT 'FUNDRAISER girls' meeting was held at Daisy's house. Daisy's real name was Dayshia, but everyone called her Daisy. In my opinion, Daisy suited her a lot better as it had a childish frivolous sound to it. Daisy's house was all puffed pink cushions and floral curtains and flouncy lampshades. Her carpets were full of fussy designs and her wallpaper was flocked and madly expensive. Statues of naked men adorned the hallway while a huge oil of Daisy exposing her breasts dominated the sitting room. She'd had it done by an up-and-coming artist and my mother had predicted a glum future for the young man. 'Sure, if he thought Daisy was that well endowed,' she'd said, 'his eyesight can't be up to much.' I'd laughed.

Daisy sat on her patterned sofa as her cleaning woman came in with a tray. On it was coffee, tea and even fancier cakes than we'd had at Avril's. These cakes were sculptures of Daisy done in pastry, cream and jam.

'Gustav made them for me especially,' Daisy giggled. Gustav was her protégé chef.

The usual oohing and aaahing abounded and then we all bit a piece out of Daisy's miniature anatomies. I went for her leg while the others bit off her head.

'Now,' Daisy arranged her elaborate gypsy-style skirt about

her plump legs. 'Last month we decided that the Cancer Society was going to be a worthy beneficiary of our fundraising efforts this year. The thing that stumped us last time was what exactly we are going to do. I hope you all had a think.' She looked around expectantly. 'Avril?'

Avril licked her lips and coughed slightly. She moved about, pretending, I think, that she wasn't exactly comfortable on Daisy's expensive sofa. 'I think that we should do what we did last year, after all—'

'No,' Daisy interrupted, tossing her ringlets. 'That shows no imagination. The media won't cover another event like that again. No, something else please?'

Avril did a very unladylike snort and folded her arms. I reckon she wasn't going to partake in any more conversation.

'Phil?'

'A sponsored parachute jump?'

My mother laughed. 'Phil, can you see us parachuting out of a plane?'

'A sponsored *celebrity* parachute jump?'

'And what happens if someone gets hurt? Or dies? Or has a heart attack on the way down?'

Phil shrugged.

'And we're celebrities of sorts,' my mother went on. 'What if we are expected to do it? I'm not jumping out of a plane for anyone. Huh, the experience will probably end up with me in hospital needing a fundraiser for myself.'

Now Phil snorted and folded her arms.

'Well,' Daisy tittered. 'This is going great. Maureen, have you a suggestion?'

My mother shivered in delight. I'd passed my idea on to her and she thought it was great. 'Well, Poppy and I did have a bit of a brainstorm and she came up with an idea that we think could work.'

'Oh?' they all said together.

I squirmed in my seat. If they hated it, I'd feel ridiculous.

'A celebrity auction.'

'What?' Avril wrinkled her nose in distain. 'Celebrities auctioning their junk?'

'No,' my mother beamed. 'Celebrities auctioning *themselves*. For a dinner date, a concert date, whatever. The thing is, the bidder has to provide the entertainment. It can be as simple as a meal in McDonald's and they can place a bid on the celebrity to go out with them.'

The idea was met with a stunned silence.

'Good, ey?' my mother said in her smug voice. 'And say, for instance, someone just wants to chat to the celebrity about getting started in whatever trade the celebrity is involved in, or wants the celebrity to speak to a group of people about acting or business or whatever, they can bid on that too. The point is, the celebrity has to do what the winning bidder wants him or her to do.'

'Oh,' Daisy gave a giggle and wrapped her fat little arms about herself. 'Pity we couldn't get Johnny Depp interested. I'd have lots of ideas for him.'

'Within reason,' my mother sniffed.

More silence.

'Well?' I asked nervously. 'Will it work?'

Phil was the first to give it her full approval. 'I know a few actors,' she said. 'And I'm sure they'll know others – actors are good for this sort of thing, they'll love the publicity.'

'And writers. They'd do anything for publicity. Sure, only

last week I saw one of them in the paper telling everyone what she feeds her children for dinner.'

'And I can talk to Zed,' Daisy pointed at her portrait. 'He's single, he'd put himself up for auction.'

'Yes, handsome, single celebs would be best,' Avril nodded. 'There's plenty of desperate women out there who could do with one.'

'And desperate men,' I smiled, relieved that they'd liked the idea. 'Daisy, would you not put yourself up? You're single.'

Daisy's eyes gleamed. 'Ohhhhh.'

'I hope you're not saying, Poppy,' my mother had her stir-the-shit voice on, 'that a man would have to be desperate to bid for Daisy?'

'Oooh,' Daisy said, her mouth wobbling. 'That's horrible!'

'I didn't mean that,' I punched my mother playfully and smiled at Daisy's aghast face. '*Honestly*, Daisy.'

'No, of course she didn't,' my mother said. 'It was just a joke, Daisy.'

'Oh,' Daisy said again.

'But really,' my mother said, 'an auction would be quite fun, don't you think?'

'Yes.'

'Yes, I think so.'

'Yes.'

'Lots of fun – if Johnny Depp were there.'

They all giggled like schoolgirls.

And at that moment, in those few minutes before they checked themselves, I saw glimpses of what these women might be if they weren't so wary of each other.

13

'So, what qualities do you think you can bring to this position?'

Despite being made chief organiser for the celebrity auction – which frankly terrified me as I'd never done anything like that before – I still had to find a job. I'd applied for loads . . . and I'd been turned down for loads before I even reached the interview stage. This one, however, I'd been hopeful of. Assistant Manager in a posh clothes shop; my dream job.

'Well,' the woman asked again, 'what qualities have you to bring to your position of Assistant Manager?'

This question, I hadn't been prepared for. I bit my lip and winced. WHAT QUALITIES DID I HAVE??? I stared at the twenty-something woman who was asking me and I just wanted to get down on my knees and beg for the job. No more questions please, I wanted to howl.

'Well,' I licked my lips and shifted about on the hard chair, 'very, very, very *unique* qualities actually.'

'Such as?'

'Well . . . for instance . . . I have a lovely wardrobe of clothes that I can wear in every day and so therefore I can make your shop look even more upmarket.'

A silence. I think it was a disbelieving silence.

When she eventually decided to speak, it was in a very low voice. 'My shop is upmarket. It's an upmarket clothes shop. That's why it's called Upmarket.'

Shit! Shit! Shit! 'Yes,' I struggled to justify myself, 'but you don't sell Prada or Gucci, do you? I could introduce your customers to those brands.'

'And make them shop somewhere else?'

'Well, no. I just thought . . .'

She said that she'd let me know.

'And what qualities do you think you can bring to the job?'

Brilliant. Pete had tutored me on this one. I pretended to think deeply. 'Well, I suppose I'm very hardworking, *very* honest and I'll always be on time for work.'

'Yes, I'm sure you will, but what *personal* qualities do you have that would make me choose you over another hard-working, honest, punctual person?'

'Sorry?'

She clicked her pen. She had been doing that all through the interview and it was getting on my nerves. 'You know. You. As a person.'

'Me? As a person?'

'Yes.'

I was like a rabbit caught in headlights. I fell back on the one thing I knew I did well.

'I . . . Well . . . I'll wear nice clothes into work. All my designer labels. Make your shop look more upmarket.'

Her eyes narrowed. 'Our customers shop here because they can't afford upmarket prices.'

'Oh.'

'And if you work here, you'll be wearing the stock.'

'Oh.'

She said she'd let me know too.

'So what personal qualities can you bring to this position?'

Yes! I wanted to shout with joy. Obviously every inter-
viewer had read the same books on interview techniques.
Once more I feigned deep thought.

'Well, I'm friendly. I'll get on with the customers. People
tend to like me.' If only it were true, my mind screamed at
me. But hey, this was an interview, I was supposed to lie.

'And what if you were faced with a grumpy customer
who didn't like you?'

'Sorry?'

'If a customer was stealing something, what would you
do? Or if he said that you were too slow or that you'd overcharged him?'

I gawped at her.

'Well? Any ideas?'

Not one. I felt like standing up and leaving. This could
go on for ever. I wondered whether I should just ask my
father for a job, though I reckoned all the staff would hate
me. How had Pete got the hotel job? How did people get
jobs? 'I've never really dealt with the public before,' I
admitted. I left out the word 'successfully'. I'd never actually *successfully* dealt with the public before. 'I suppose I'd
just have to see what the problem was and deal with it.'

'So you'd try to calm the customer down, would you?'

I stared at her some more. It was almost as if she was
giving me the answer. 'Well, yes,' I nodded. 'That would be
good.'

'And the person stealing?'

I gulped. 'Does it happen a lot then?' I'm not quite sure, but it looked as if she was about to laugh.

'Well, it can,' she acknowledged.

'Well, if someone were stealing, you'd have to have proof, and then maybe, I dunno, ring the police?'

'Ring the police,' she nodded, obviously impressed. 'Good,' She looked at her watch. 'Thanks, Poppy. I'll let you know.' Then she held out her hand. 'I'm Isobel, by the way.'

The way she shook my hand, all sort of firm, gave me great hope.

Two hours later, I got offered the job. I'd get one day of training – which made me think it'd be a cake-walk – and then I'd be behind a till in O'Leary's 'everything's almost a euro' shop. The hours were from nine-thirty to one o'clock.

Pete was very proud of me. He said that this job was just a start, that I could maybe get another job once I had some experience. My father was horrified. He wondered what was happening to the women in the Furlong family. His wife out all day, doing God's work, and his daughter out all morning doing work. God! He could have got me a job, he said. He could have paid me more. When I told Pete this, he said that if I wanted to work for my dad I could. But in getting my own job, it was the first time in my life I'd actually managed to get something by myself, and didn't that make me feel good?

I have to say, I hadn't thought about it like that, but when I did, I told Pete that it was the second thing I'd got on my own. I told him that *he* was the first.

'Yeah, and you'll love working as much as you love me,' he said.

I could only hope so.

14

WAITING IN THE school line with Billy was hell. I generally tried to avoid it as much as possible by arriving down at the schoolyard just as his class was about to go in. All the other mothers seemed to know each other and, despite my best attempts at smiling and appearing friendly, they didn't show any interest in talking to me. Still, I suppose if I saw a person smiling into middle distance, I'd keep my own distance too. But it was awful being the only one with no one to talk to.

The first day of my job, however, I had brought Billy down early because I had to be in for half-nine, which meant that I couldn't wait with him. I walked him to his line, smiled at the other mothers there without actually saying hello and placed his bag on the ground.

'Now, honey, I'll be back at two to pick you up, but you have to be a good boy and let me go now.'

'No! I want you to stay.'

'I can't. I've a job to go to.' God, it felt weird saying that.

'Only in the euro shop!'

I cringed. I figured everyone heard. 'It's still a job and I have to go.'

'Nooo. Mammy, please.' He grasped my hand tightly. 'I don't want to be on my own. No one will let me play.'

'Of course they will.'

'No,' he shook his head vigorously. 'They don't like me.'

'Of course they do. Now, come on.' I tried to prise my hand away from his but he started to scream. Everyone looked. For the first time ever, I was noticed in the yard.

'He's a bit upset,' I explained unnecessarily to no one in particular.

Sympathetic nods were given. A couple of wry smiles.

Billy continued to draw attention to himself by yelling 'Don't go' at the top of his voice.

'Billy,' I bent down to his level and whispered so he'd have to stop yelling to listen to me. 'Please let me go. I can't be late on my first day.'

'They don't like meeeeee!' He did a sort of dance too, which was a sure sign he was going to make this difficult for me. 'Mammy please, just until we go in.'

God, if I left him now, they'd all think I was a right cow. If I didn't leave him now, I'd lose my job before I got it.

'Billy,' I strove to sound calm; if he detected any urgency in me to be away, I'd be stuck there. 'Look, if I lose my job, I won't be able to get you an Undertaker. Now do you want him or not?'

His screaming abated. He cocked his dark head to one side and regarded me with his dad's green eyes. 'An Undertaker?'

'Yes, he was meant to be a surprise for you. Do you want him?'

'Yeah!'

'So let me go.'

He let my arm go and raced off. I watched him run up to a group of boys. They must have been kids from his class. Pushing himself among them, he yelled, 'I'm getting an Undertaker. Ha, ha, ha, ha.'

I was just giving myself a mental pat on the back when I heard one of the boys say, 'So what? We still won't like you.' Billy pushed him but I pretended not to see. Instead, I quickly walked away. The little brat deserved it.

Tears blurring my eyes, I left the yard without looking back.

I was still upset when I arrived at the euro shop. I'd been told to go around the back and let myself into the coffee-cum-storeroom with the key I'd been given.

There was an obese woman there when I entered. She was hunched over a cup of coffee, a fag dangling from her mouth. Her hair was dyed jet black and had been for years, I'd say, because it was coarse and fuzzy. She really could have done with a good hairdresser. Her face was red with all sorts of spidery veins snaking about her cheeks like tramlines. Hard, would describe her best. I reckoned her to be about forty. It was a relief, because though I'd never actually been in a bargain shop before, I knew that most of the staff were teenagers and I really didn't want to be with a load of teens. Anyway, this woman eyed me up as I entered. Then she turned back to her coffee without saying anything.

'Hello,' I ventured. 'I'm Poppy.'

'Fair play to you.' Her fag jumped up and down as she talked. It must have been glued to her lip.

I wanted to tell her that she shouldn't be smoking in the workplace, but I reckoned that that would really set her against me. 'What's your name?' I tried.

'Look,' she took the fag from her mouth and flicked the ash all over the place. 'We're only working together, we're not going to be best mates, OK?'

I blanched. Well, there was another female friendship destroyed before it had even begun. What was it about me?

'You're dressed pretty fancy for a dive like this,' she spat out then.

'I just wore what I thought appropriate.'

She snorted derisively, rolled her eyes and then said, 'Charlotte was not a thief, do you get me?'

I was confused by the abrupt change of subject – presuming we had actually been on a subject. 'Eh, I don't know Charlotte.'

'Yeah, well, I'm just telling you.'

'Well, thanks for the information. I'll bear it in mind.'

'Yeah, you do that. You bear that in mind.'

'Fine.'

'Charlotte worked here until a few weeks ago. You stole her job, d'ya get me? If anyone's a thief, it's you.' She took her fag out and jabbed it in my direction.

'Right.' I looked about for a chair to sit down on. Really, this woman was intimidating. I reckoned that at least if I sat down, I'd have a reason for feeling smaller than her.

'You can't sit there, that's Charlotte's chair.'

I hesitated, half-up and half-down. In the end, because of her glare, I decided to stay standing.

The woman stood up and flesh wobbled. Honestly, if I were her size, I would have worn some nice loose trousers and a smock top. She wore pedal pushers and a tight, short T-shirt. Loose flesh dripped over her waistband. A big tattoo of a butterfly wobbled on her side. She went around the small room making herself some more coffee. She had major difficulty navigating her way between the table and chairs. I longed to make myself a cuppa, but I'd probably be using Charlotte's cup or something. I stood like a spare as she pottered about. For the first time in my life, I longed for work to start so that I could be away from her.

Work started at nine-forty-five. The woman who had interviewed me for the job , Isobel, arrived and, with a big cheery smile, reintroduced me to the other woman.

'Maxi,' she said, 'I see you've met Poppy.'

'I've got to get me till, Isobel,' Maxi said by way of response.

Her tone was lighter though. It was obvious who the boss was.

'Well,' Isobel smiled brightly, 'I'm going to show Poppy the ropes today and then if she has any problems, won't you help her?'

Maxi shot me a glare that would have rivalled Chernobyl for potency and shrugged.

'She's a little difficult but you'll get to like her,' Isobel whispered to me. I don't think she actually believed it because she laughed a little at the end of her sentence. 'She's a teeny bit annoyed at the moment as we had a little trouble in the shop a few weeks ago.'

I said nothing, just watched as Isobel placed cash into the till drawer.

'Fifties here, then twenties and so on,' she said, changing the subject. Then she started to put the coins in. 'You have a two-hundred euro float,' she explained, 'so when you do your balancing at the end of the day, you'll be two hundred over, OK?'

It wasn't. I hadn't a clue what she was talking about. I reckoned I'd learn on the job.

'If you're less than two hundred over you know you've made a mistake. If you're more than two hundred over,' she grinned broadly, 'that's not too bad.'

I laughed because I think I was expected to.

'Now, come along and I'll show you the shop.'

I followed her around what was a sizeable shop. Nothing was over two euro. I was amazed by the little lamps that were only one euro fifty and actually worked. 'No way!'

Isobel laughed. 'I wish all our customers were like that,' she grinned. 'Some of them expect it for nothing.' There were cheap sweets and cheap toilet rolls and cheap deodorants. Lots of stuff. God, if I bought things here, I reckoned I could save a fortune on our household bills. How come no one had ever told me about places like this before?

Back at the tills, Maxi was across from me, sitting behind hers like a Buddha, her arms crossed, her numerous chins resting on her enormous chest.

I took my place behind my till. I sat up very straight because I'd read somewhere that a poor posture could damage my back.

Isobel went to the door and opened it. 'It's usually busy in the mornings,' she explained. 'That's why I need you then.'

'I could manage on me own,' Maxi said.

'Well, I'm sure you could,' Isobel said, and there was a touch of ice in her voice, 'but two is better than one, ey?'

'Two, as in me and Charlotte,' Maxi growled. 'Not as in Miss Poppy Perfect over there.'

Isobel came to stand behind me. 'She's nice when you get to know her,' she whispered in a sort of panicked manner.

Trouble was, I had no desire to know her.

The shop did great business. Or maybe it only looked great because I was so slow on the till that massive queues kept building up. In fact, it was almost as if everyone queued up at my till because Maxi didn't seem to be doing anything. I noticed her waving people in my direction now and again. It was awful. I could hear mutterings of discontent come floating up the line at me. Things like, 'What's taking so long?' or 'I think she's new'. Someone even said, 'What's her majesty doing working in a joint like this?' People laughed a lot at that. Still, it was better than them complaining.

Maxi, on the other hand, when she did a bit of work, was like Sharon Shannon with the speed she could press the till buttons. She only did this when Isobel appeared, which wasn't often. Still, she didn't smile at anyone or tell them to enjoy their purchases. I think that was bad. I made a point of saying 'good morning' and 'thank you' and 'I hope you like the lamps' or the deodorant or whatever. I drew the line when someone bought toilet rolls though, because there is not a lot you can say about purchases like that, is there? Loads of people bought them, which isn't surprising, I suppose, as you always need toilet paper. But these people didn't buy one or two rolls they bought *loads*. I think I would have been embarrassed carrying twenty toilet rolls down the street.

It was mainly young mothers who came in and Isobel told me that though the shop did well, a lot of the custom was from the same people. She seemed nice, though horribly efficient and businesslike. Efficient people scare me a little. They remind me of my old teachers and most especially of my dad, and I keep thinking that they expect more of me than I can actually deliver. I wondered if she owned the shop or whether she just ran it for someone. Imagine if she owned it. Imagine being that dynamic to actually own your own shop at her age. Still, Pete had owned his own business until it went bust. And my dad started off young too.

I was, it seemed, surrounded by successful people. And none of it would ever rub off on me.

15

BY ONE O'CLOCK I was exhausted. My eyes were sore, my fingers were stiff and my blouse was sticking to me with perspiration. Still, it was dry-clean only, so the smell would come out. It wasn't as if it was hot in the shop, it was just that I broke out in a sweat every time it looked like something was going to go wrong. Anyway, Isobel showed me how to do a balance on the till which involved my having to estimate how much was in each drawer. I was useless at that.

'You'll get the hang of it,' she told me. Then she pressed a button and the total that I'd taken in came up on the screen.

'Wow!'

Isobel laughed. 'Now count your money and make sure that that's what you have. Write it on to one of these sheets,' she handed me a sheet, 'and lodge it in the safe.'

'Right.' The responsibility almost overwhelmed me. With a shaking hand I began to count out the money. It took me ages. I just wanted to be sure I was doing it right.

'Oh God, I must have overcharged someone,' I groaned after I'd done it about ten times.

Isobel turned from her paper. 'Why?'

'It's two hundred over what the till says.'

'Your float?'

'What?'

'Your money at the start of the day – you have to take that out?'

'Oh. Yeah.' The relief. I subtracted it and realised that I'd balanced to the penny. It made me feel quite proud of myself. In business studies class in school I could never even balance pretend accounts. My business studies teacher had made a remark once about how she hoped my father wouldn't leave his companies to me. I hoped that too.

I jabbed at my piece of paper. 'I write it all down here, is that it.'

Isobel nodded and very nicely helped me fill it out.

My first day at work was over. I was so happy that I called out a 'goodbye' to Maxi. She didn't reply.

Of course, I only realised once I was on the street that I was late for Billy. I'd spent so long trying to balance my till that I hadn't been aware that it was almost two. Hopping into my car, I drove like a maniac over to the school. It was after ten past when I arrived and, full of apologies, I ran into Billy's classroom. He was sitting at his desk, a pile of cubes and things scattered all around him and his teacher was sitting at the front of the room.

'Oh my God,' I was completely breathless. 'I am so sorry. I just started work today and honestly, I didn't realise the time. I do apologise.'

'Mammy!' Billy jumped up from the table and, without seeming to notice, upended everything. Crayons and roundy things and bricks smashed to the floor. He hurled himself at me. 'I was crying. I was crying.'

'He's OK now, aren't you?' Miss Walsh rubbed his head.

'No!' Billy glared at her. 'No, I'm not!'

'Billy!' I said, mortified. 'You don't talk to your teacher

like that. Now, be a good boy and pick up all the things that fell on the floor.'

'I want to go home.'

'So do I, honey, I've had a hard morning earning money for an Undertaker, but really, you have to pick up the things you dropped.'

'Does he scatter a lot of things at home?' Miss Walsh asked as she stooped to retrieve some crayons at her feet.

'All the time. He never stops knocking into things and banging things over. But sure, that's boys for you.' I got down to pick some things up too. It was hard in my tight-fitting Chanel skirt.

'Billy, can you go into the yard and play for a bit,' Miss Walsh said. She threw him a small football. 'Go and practise your kicks and in P.E. tomorrow, I'll put you in the striker's position.'

'Cool.' Billy caught the ball and raced out of the room. We both watched him disappear out of the door and re-appear a few seconds later in the yard.

It suddenly dawned on me that she'd done it for a reason, the reason being that she wanted a chat with me. My blood ran cold. She was either going to tell me he was advanced, which I seriously doubted as he wouldn't sit still long enough for me to do his letters with him, or that he was in trouble – which seemed likely.

'He's very lively,' she began.

I held my hand up. 'Is he in trouble?'

She paused before answering, 'No, I wouldn't say he's in trouble.'

'So,' I was almost afraid to go on, 'what *would* you say?'

'I would say that Billy is almost too lively, that's what I'd say. He's been here a few weeks now, Mrs Shannon—'

'Poppy.'

'Poppy, he's been here a few weeks and to be honest, he hasn't made any friends. He's constantly pulling and fighting and jostling for position with everyone. He jumps up out of his seat and shouts in the middle of class. He fights in the yard with the other boys.'

My heart had stopped, at least that's what it felt like. I don't think there is anything worse than being told that your child just doesn't meet standard requirements. 'Well, maybe it's their fault too,' I stammered out. I didn't want to sound confrontational, but I felt that I had to stick up for Billy in some small way.

'Poppy,' she said, and I winced at the sympathy in her voice, 'there were never any fights before this. And to be frank, fighting in the yard is not acceptable behaviour in this school.'

'Yes, I know.' I stared at my hands. Willed myself not to cry. 'I'll have a word with him. Try and find out what's going on.'

'Look.' She pointed out the window. Billy had abandoned the football and was trying to haul himself up on the wall surrounding the yard. The wall was ten foot high at least. 'His behaviour is very impulsive too,' Miss Walsh said gently, 'and he's constantly seeking attention.' She knocked hard on the window and Billy, after glancing at her stern face, hopped down.

'Aren't all boys like that?' I asked. My voice had become quite faint.

'Sit down, do.' Miss Walsh pointed to a chair. I sat, squashed in a junior-infant seat. She sat opposite me. 'It's just a feeling I have. I know I haven't been teaching that long, but one of the other teachers commented on it too. I

121

think,' she paused diplomatically, 'I think it might be a good idea to have him assessed for ADD.'

'ADD?'

'Attention Deficit Disorder. Sometimes it goes hand in hand with hyperactivity.'

I blinked. Once. Twice. I'd never heard of ADD, but I didn't want to say it.

'Did he have these problems at his old school?'

Something half-remembered came to me. Hadn't his other teacher said that he was a little energetic or something? But he'd been fine the year before, as far as I could recall. Or maybe no one had said anything. So I shook my head, 'No, not that I'm aware of.'

'Does he find it hard to sleep, say, when the clocks go back or forward?'

'No,' I gave a wobbly smile, 'he finds it hard to sleep all the time.'

She smiled back, though it didn't seem a real smile. More sympathetic than anything. 'OK,' she nodded. 'Poppy, if he does have ADD we can get him assessed through the school or you could bring him to a GP and get it done privately. But I think maybe you should start by having a word with him about his behaviour and if it doesn't improve, just get him checked out, OK?'

'Check it out how?'

'Well, the school has a funding allocation that is used for this kind of assessment, though it might take a while. Here,' she stood up and rooted about in the desk drawer and pulled out a pamphlet, 'this will give you some idea just what ADD is. You can have a read of it and maybe see if any of it applies to Billy.'

As if in a dream, I took it from her. 'He says the other

children don't like him.' I thought I was going to cry. I bit down hard on my lip.

Miss Walsh looked apologetic. 'He is finding it hard to fit in,' she admitted. 'Did he have friends at his old school?'

I thought back. I shrugged. 'I don't know. But he plays with Tommy on our street. He's in first class here.'

'Tommy Mahon?'

I flushed as I realised that I didn't know Tommy's second name. 'Yeah, I think so.'

'Well, look, have a talk with him and see what happens. Meanwhile, I'll keep an eye on him here and make sure the children involve him in things. How about that?'

What could I say? I had to nod and agree.

I walked out of the room in a bit of a daze to find Billy balancing on top of the wall, shouting that he was going to become a high-wire walker in a circus when he grew up. I ordered him down and down he came. I hugged him hard. Harder than I've ever hugged him before.

'Mam, get off!' He pushed me away and laughed.

He was beautiful.

16

I READ THE ADD pamphlet over a coffee. I usually hate reading, but I made an effort because I had to see if any of the stuff in it applied to Billy. I was in the middle of a page that described the type of difficulties ADD children have when Pete arrived home.

'Well, how'd it go?' He crossed to me and pulled gently on my hair. 'Well?' he asked again.

He seemed happier today, happy enough that I envied him. Adaptable, sociable Pete who could be happy anywhere. I'd thought that he'd miss his job – designing buildings, recommending materials, being on site to oversee his projects – but no, Pete, it appeared, was quite content to serve breakfasts to complete strangers. He kept telling me that he was getting all the creative thrills he needed by redesigning our house. And to be fair, he had done quite a job. It no longer looked the same place. He had used all the natural light and channelled it into making the rooms look bigger and airier than they had. The kitchen, where I was sitting at the table with a sodden tissue screwed up in my fist, was at that moment flooded with sunshine. It hit the shiny tiles and the bright windows and bounced off the glass.

'Hey,' Pete sat in beside me, all concern as he noticed the tissue and my red eyes.

'What happened? Was it really bad? You know if—'

I shook my head. 'Bad, but not that bad.'

'Hey,' he said again. He tenderly pulled my hand down from my face and grasped it.

'What's wrong, so?'

'Billy.'

His face paled.

'No,' I rushed to reassure him. 'He's fine. It's just, it's just . . .' my voice broke.

'Just what?'

And I told him, in big halting sentences, what the teacher had said. Then I pushed the pamphlet towards him. 'Some of the stuff in this describes what Billy does.'

For a second, he was quiet, then he gave me a sort of incredulous look. 'Billy?' He nodded towards the page. 'That?'

'Yep.'

'And you believe her?' His tone of voice implied that he certainly didn't.

'Well, I don't know. This book says that ADD children are impulsive, and Billy is, isn't he? And it says that—'

'There is nothing wrong with Billy,' Pete said with such conviction that my heart lifted. 'Yeah, OK, he's always running around, but she's the teacher, she should be able to control him.'

'I think she's tried—'

'Well, not hard enough, obviously,' Pete snorted. He stood up. 'Don't be worrying, Poppy. It's nothing. We'll have a talk with him, OK?'

I pushed my hair from my face. 'Really?'

'Really.' His back was to me and he was filling the kettle. 'D'you want another coffee?'

125

'Yeah, go on.' Maybe he was right. Billy was just an exuberant boy. Full of life. There was nothing wrong with that.

My mother rang that night to see how I'd fared. I gave her a sanitised version of events. Very sanitised. I hadn't even told her it was a euro shop I was working in. I'd just said it was a small shop. It wasn't my fault that my mother assumed it was an exclusive boutique.

'And is it good value?' she asked. 'I know some of these smaller places can be a bit of a rip off.'

'Very good value,' I told her.

'Oh, I must shop there one day, so,' she said. 'What labels do you stock?'

I made up a few posh-sounding labels. 'Isobella, Maxi and Euro.'

'Oh!' I could picture her at the other end, her nose wrinkled up trying to recall anything she'd seen by Isobella, Maxi or Euro. 'Interesting,' was all she said.

'And how's the residents' association lobbying progressing?' I asked, trying to divert her attention. 'Any news there?'

'Well, we're expecting a good turn-out as I've told everyone that it's on. And I'm popular and well known due to my charity work, so I think I'm a shoe-in. It's on in a few weeks' time.'

'Oh? Really? Good.'

'Yes, isn't it? And your father is nominating me. Isn't that nice of him?'

Oh, well, at least they were agreed on something. Sometimes I worried about my parents. 'Really nice of him,' I said fervently.

'Of course it's nice. Oh *stop*!' she said impatiently. 'As you

126

can probably hear, your father wants a word. He's poking me in the back, so I'll go. I'll pass you on to him. Bye-bye, love.'

'Poppy,' he barked.

'Hi Dad.'

'So, the job went well then?'

'Yes, great.'

'Well, tomorrow is my day for visiting you, so will I come over in the afternoon?'

'Eh—'

'Around two-thirty?'

'Actually, Dad, maybe you could do me a favour. Could you collect Billy from school for me, just in case I'm late. I was late today as I'm only just getting used to counting up all the money and things.'

'Oh yes, that's no problem.' He sounded pleased to have something to do. 'I'll drive down and get him. I'll meet you back at your house, how about that?'

'OK.'

Without even saying good-bye, he hung up.

Laura called by later that evening. I hadn't talked to her much since she'd refused my offer of coffee. I'd begun to think I'd messed up. I mean, what was the etiquette in relation to cups of coffee in neighbours' houses. Did they just happen? Were they arranged in advance? I suppose in my previous big detached house, with our neighbours a whole big massive garden away, I'd never had to worry about things like that. I hardly ever saw my neighbours, and when I did, no one discussed coffee or kids. They talked about functions and clothes and shops, things I was comfortable with. But now, now it was ordinary personal stuff, and I found that hard.

'Hi, Poppy,' Laura said in her nervous manner. 'I was just

wondering—' Then she stopped and her eyes widened as she said, 'Wow!'

'What?'

'Your house! Wow!'

I was completely confused.

'You've changed it. It looks great!'

I laughed a little. 'Thanks. That's Pete's doing. He was an architect in a previous life.'

She was still gawking about. I found her lack of reserve very amusing; I'd never have been so open in my admiration of anything. 'D'you want to see what he did with the rest of the place? He's done the bathroom too, and the kitchen. He's going to try the bedrooms next.'

She flushed and took a step back. 'Oh no, that's not what I came about. Oh, I couldn't . . .'

'Well, you could. Come on. It's probably a mess as I haven't cleaned it today.' Now it was my turn to flush. 'I started a job today. Not a very nice job but the best I could get.'

'Oh. Where?'

I flirted with lying, but then decided in favour of the embarrassing truth. Our little Kildare town was a small place after all. 'In the euro shop.'

Her eyes almost popped out of her head. 'Isobel's shop? The one that was in the local papers a few weeks back?'

'There is an Isobel, yes.'

'Oh. My. God.' She put a hand to her mouth.

'What?'

'Oh, nothing.' Hand down, she smiled brightly. 'Nothing. Probably not the same place.'

'The same place as what?'

'As was in the paper.'

'*What* was in the paper?'

She clamped her lips tight shut. She reminded me of Billy.

'Go on, tell me, Laura. Was it bad?' I gave a little laugh. I mean, how bad could it be?

'Well,' she began a bit hesitantly. She flapped her arms about as she spoke. 'There was a story all about one of the staff robbing this shop – probably not yours – and the boss, Isobel, fired one of the girls.'

'Sounds like the same place,' I said casually as her face dropped. 'Laura, *what*?'

'Ooooh,' Laura was like a schoolgirl as she hopped from foot to foot. 'Well, it's just, well, the girl she fired, well, you see, her sister worked in the shop with her.'

I suddenly felt queasy.

'And this girl, well, apparently she's been fired from lots of jobs. And apparently, because her sister is well known in the area, no one will take the job – out of respect for her.' She gave a bit of a laugh. 'Well, except you, apparently.'

'What?!'

Laura gulped. 'Well, I think it's great. Good for you.'

Jesus. Jesus. JESUS! No wonder I'd got the job. I'd probably been the only one to apply for it.

Laura shrugged, a little ruefully. 'Maybe I shouldn't have said anything. Maybe it's a different shop.'

'Yeah.' I barely heard her. Maybe I should quit, I thought. In fact, I figured that's *exactly* what I should do. But my car. And Billy's wrestling figure. And all the people who were queuing up to sue Pete. And maybe it would be better to quit when I found another job. And that mightn't take too long. I'd get experience and move on. ASAP.

'Sorry,' Laura said meekly.

'No, no, it's fine.' I smiled and laughed and sounded false even to myself. 'Fine.'

'Anyway, is Tommy here?' Laura broke into my thoughts.

'Yep,' I gave a forced smile and thumbed up the stairs. 'Can you not hear them?' Thumps and banging came from Billy's bedroom.

Two months, tops. I'd be outa there. 'They're playing something upstairs. Sure, come on up and see the place.'

She didn't protest this time. I think she was dying to see it. I suppose I was used to Pete doing things so it didn't impress me as much as it should have, but Laura was agog.

'Your bathroom looks huge!' she exclaimed.

'All mirrors.'

'Yeah, but still. Wow!'

She was even more agog when she saw what her son and my son had been up to in the bedroom. I was mortified. I looked like a completely negligent parent. They'd been jumping down off the windowsill on to Billy's beanbag. That mightn't have been so bad if the window had been closed, but it wasn't. The idea, apparently, had been to stand in the open window and let the breeze blow their hair about before they launched themselves downwards.

'JESUS!' Laura grabbed Tommy, who was about to climb on to the ledge. 'What are you doing?'

It was a shock to hear her yelling. I hadn't thought she was capable of it.

'Playing,' Tommy said sulkily. 'Billy's best game so far, this is.'

'I'm sorry,' I muttered feebly as she dragged a howling Tommy from the bedroom.

'That's dangerous,' she berated him loudly as she yanked him down the stairs and out the door. 'I'm not letting you and Billy play together again if this is what you do!'

I stood, stock still, in the centre of the bedroom glaring at my son. He was oblivious to what was wrong with his game. 'You could have hurt yourself badly if you'd fallen out,' was all I could manage to say.

'We wouldn't have fallen out, Mammy,' Billy explained. 'See, we held on to the frame, right here.' He attempted to climb up again so that he could show me exactly what he meant, but I pulled him back.

'If you ever, ever attempt anything like that again, you'll be grounded for a month! Now,' I pointed to his bed, 'put on your pyjamas.'

'But it's early.'

'No it's not, now go on!' I slammed the window closed. I turned and left him shouting after me.

Two hours later, after he'd calmed down and was tucked up in bed, I sat beside him and stroked his hair. He let me do little things like that when no one else was around. He looked lovely, with his big green eyes and sallow skin.

'Billy,' I said, 'I was talking to your teacher today.' He squirmed a little and turned from me. 'She said you fight a lot in the yard. Do you hit people?'

He shrugged and muttered something.

'Billy?'

'They don't like me,' he snapped. 'They laugh at me.'

'Why?'

'I dunno. They call me show-off and don't let me play games. I don't like those boys.'

'Well, even if you don't like them, you can't hit them. That's wrong.'

'So?'

'Billy, you'll get into trouble.'

'So will they.'

'I don't care about them, I care about you. I don't want you getting into trouble at school.'

He said nothing, just stared at me mutinously.

I searched for something to make him be good. 'Look, I'll buy you two wrestlers if you behave, OK?'

He thought about it for a second. 'OK. Two of the big ones. No one else will have those.'

'Right. Fine.' I kissed the top of his head. 'Night now.'

'Night, night, Mammy.'

17

'**Y**OU CAN'T LEAVE,' Isobel pointed out, pulling some paper from the drawer. 'You have to give me a month's notice. See, you signed it when you took the job.'

And there it was, in black and white – well blue actually – my signature in my very best writing.

'But you never told me the history of the job,' I protested. Pete had told me to quit if I wanted. I wanted. So I'd tried to quit. But like everything else I'd ever tried to do, I was failing miserably.

'You never asked. It's not compulsory. Anyway, it was all over the papers, I just assumed you knew.' Her blue eyes, which up until then had been all kindness, were hard and flinty. She gave an indifferent shrug. 'You can work for a month and then you can go, if you like.'

There was nothing I could do about it. I reckon she'd sue me otherwise, and I didn't need a job to actually *cost* me money. 'OK,' I said, 'as of today I give you a month's notice.'

'Fine.' Isobel pursed her lips. 'But Maxi will come around.'

Yeah. Right. I pursed my lips too. And folded my arms.

'Just say things improve within the month,' Isobel put to me, her voice a little softer, 'would you consider staying on then?'

A month. If I could stick Maxi for a month would that mean I'd manage from then onwards? It'd be a strain. 'I dunno,' I said. 'It's not easy working with Maxi.'

'I took Charlotte on as a favour to Maxi. No one else would touch her. She let us both down, and the sooner Maxi realises that, the better,' Isobel said impatiently. 'The girl was caught on camera stealing the fuzzy dusters. Maxi has seen the footage but she won't believe it.'

'That doesn't matter. I feel—'

'I mean, if I'd known that Charlotte was going to steal from my shop systematically, from right under my nose, I wouldn't have touched her with a . . .' her eyes scanned the room, 'with a pair of extra-strong insulated rubber gloves.' She held up the gloves before shoving them in my face. 'They're a bargain. Sixty cents.'

'Yes, but you did employ her and you should have told me the situation I was getting myself into.' That's what Pete had told me to say and it sounded good.

'Well, work your month's notice then get out,' Isobel looked at me disdainfully. 'But for now, get your float and go out on to the shop floor. We open in five minutes.'

'But Maxi—?'

'Is sick,' Isobel said. 'So you won't have to worry about working with her today, will you?'

Jesus, I was all on my own in the shop.

Isobel smirked a little. I think she thought it served me right. 'If you need help, I'll be around. I'll be in here doing the accounts. But, eh, don't leave your till unattended or some kid will rob it. OK?'

'OK.' How could I get her help if I couldn't leave the till?

*   *   *

The answer, of course, was that I couldn't. That morning, I have to say, was the worst of my life. It was even worse than downsizing our house. From nine until one I worked my bum off. Well, if I could have worked my bum off, I'd probably have stayed in the job. But anyway, suffice to say I was KNACKERED. It was hell. Queues at one stage were out the door. In fact, I'm sure a lot of the stock went out the door without being paid for. I saw one girl legging it off down the street with a bunch of candles that I didn't remember taking for.

'Have you paid for those candles?' I shouted as she went to sneak out the door.

'Aw, sure if she hasn't, love,' some auld wan cackled, 'I'm sure she'll get her fingers burned.'

The shop exploded into laughter.

'Come back here,' I called out. 'Come back and pay for those candles!'

'Can't hear ya,' the same auld wan said. 'She must have wax in her ears.'

There was more laughter.

I glared at the old woman. 'Stealing things is not funny,' I said. My comment was met by an eerie silence. Foolishly I thought I'd hit on a nerve. 'Not funny at all,' I said again, really loudly, taking the woman's purchases from her and cashing them up.

'I wouldn't say that too loud, love,' the woman advised. 'Maxi mightn't like it.'

'Five euro please,' I held out my hand. It only shook a little. I managed a smile at the old woman as I took her money. 'Enjoy the perfume,' I said.

'Perfume, my arse,' the woman said. 'It's great stuff for keeping the cats away from my garden, now. I spray it on my trees and flowers. My fella reckons it smells like lion's piss.'

'Great.' I flashed her a weak smile. 'Next!'

The next customer was a young girl. She was buying fancy soap for fifty cents. How fancy could a bar of soap for fifty cents actually be, I wondered. 'Fifty cents,' I said, holding out my hand.

'I like your blouse,' she said, looking at me in admiration. 'Where did you get it?'

It was the first nice thing anyone had said to me in the shop so far. I blushed, grateful for the comment. 'Thanks. I got it in House of Fraser.'

'Oh.' She handed me over the money. 'That's an expensive place.'

'Yes. Enjoy the soap.'

'Does working here pay well then?'

'It pays all right.'

'Did it cost you a week's wages to get that top?'

I thought about how much the top was. I thought about how much I was getting. I was never very good at maths, but it had cost about three weeks' wages. 'About three weeks',' I answered.

'Wow!' Her jaw dropped. 'Hey,' she yelled out. 'Her top cost her three weeks' wages!'

Heads craned to see the top. I flushed. I didn't think people behind tills were supposed to be the centre of attention. Anytime I'd gone into a shop, I'd never even noticed the people serving me. They were anonymous, faceless beings that took your money. I reckon I was doing this job all wrong.

But wrong or not, there was still a queue at one o'clock. And at half-one. By one-forty-five, I was in a sweat. I had to go. I took my till out amid much protest and marched into Isobel.

'Isobel, I have to go now.'

She looked up from her romantic novel. Accounts, my arse.

'You can't,' she said, eyes wide. 'When there is only one member of staff, you have to work the full day.'

'No. I told you I could only work until one. That was the deal.'

She shook her head and stood up, went to the filing cabinet and, yep, pulled out my contract. 'It says here that you will work when other members of staff are ill.' She pointed to a clause, which I read.

'But my little boy . . .'

'Sorry.'

I looked at my till, then I looked at her. 'I have to make a phone call,' I said resignedly. Isobel tossed her head. 'Well, be brief. I'll cover for you until two-thirty. You can have your lunch now, collect your boy or whatever, but you have to be back for two-thirty, OK?' She took Maxi's till from the safe and waltzed from the office.

Huh, to think I'd thought she was nice. I was tempted to steal from her myself.

I phoned Dad who said that yes, he would mind Billy for the day. I think he was a little chuffed. He seemed to have grown quite fond of his grandson ever since Billy had hit that guy on the head with the sword. 'You work away,' he told me. 'They obviously need you badly.' I agreed that they did. Then, putting down the phone, I glanced around the dingy storeroom and I felt sick. Where had my life gone?

*　　*　　*

Lunch on my own was a strange affair. I'd never been into any of the cafés in the town before, preferring instead to eat at my mother's or at home. I chose the nicest one and sat down at a table. It was quite empty, as I guess the lunch rush hour must have been over. A few people sat drinking coffee and eating scones and they glanced at me as I sat in my seat. Eventually, after about ten minutes, a man approached me.

'Excuse me, madam, tables are for customers only.'

'Yes, I know.'

He gestured with his arms. 'Customers are people who buy things.'

I think he was being sarcastic. 'Pardon?'

'Well, are you a customer or not?'

'I'd like to be,' I said. 'Only no one has taken my order yet.' Ha, I thought, that'd show you and your very bad service.

'It's self-service.' He gestured to the counter. 'You say what you want, you take it, we charge for it and then you sit down.'

I think someone sniggered behind me.

'Oh.' I stood up, my bag falling to the ground. 'Oh, I am sorry. I just thought . . .'

'And we just thought you were a lunatic,' the man laughed.

I smiled a little and flushed a lot. I ordered a salad roll and a coffee. He made up the roll for me and gave me a coffee.

'Free coffee for first-time customers,' he said as he placed it with a flourish on my tray. 'Come in again.'

'I didn't get free coffee my first time,' a woman grumbled.

'That's 'cause you're still a virgin,' the woman with her laughed.

138

'Ha bloody ha.'

The man came down with two coffees for them.

It was a nice café. And cheap – which I'm sure would have pleased Pete.

At five o'clock I was ready to lie down and die. My legs were stiff and my fingers ached. My head seemed stuffed with so many thoughts that they all seemed to get jammed as they fought for space.

'I'm going now,' I said to Isobel as I handed her my cash.

'Thanks,' Isobel glanced down at my receipt roll. 'My, you have taken a lot in today.' She smirked a bit. 'You must have worked hard.'

I felt like a schoolchild. 'I did. It was very busy.'

'Well, Maxi has said that she will be sick again tomorrow, so maybe you should make arrangements for your little boy to be minded again.'

'But you said yesterday that two was better than one.'

'Which it is,' Isobel nodded. 'But Maxi is sick. What can I do?'

You could work, I felt like saying. Only I didn't. 'What indeed,' I muttered. I walked out, feeling my heart sink as low as my life.

When I got back home my father was out in the garden. Billy was racing like a lunatic around in circles.

'See, if I go a bit faster, Granddad, I can make myself feel sick.'

'Excellent,' my father said dryly. 'I'm sure that must give you a real sense of pride.'

'Whoa!' Billy ran into the wall and collapsed on to the ground. 'I'm spinning around the world,' he shrieked. 'Whoa!'

'Hi, Dad,' I called, startling him. 'Thanks for today.'

'No problem.' He was looking in bewilderment at my son who was staggering to his feet.

'Granddad took me to the museum,' Billy stood up and wobbled dangerously. 'And he showed me all the old weapons and stuff.'

'And he nearly knocked down a dinosaur,' Dad continued. 'So we got thrown out.'

'So instead, we went to Stephen's Green,' Billy began to wobble towards me. 'And I went on the swings.'

'Great.' I made my way into the house, my dad following me. 'Would you like some tea, Dad? Pete is due home any second – I'll make some toasted sandwiches or something.'

Dad looked at his watch. 'Oh, I don't think so. Your mother gets in in twenty minutes. If I hurry, I'll make it to the Chinese and have it on the table when she gets back. She likes to eat when she comes in.'

Just then, his mobile rang. I left him talking into it as I trod wearily into the kitchen. Making a sandwich suddenly seemed as difficult as solving an algebra problem. I had just buttered the bread and switched on the toasted-sandwich maker when Dad came in.

'Your mother,' he said, pocketing his phone. 'She's heading out for dinner with some friends from the old folks thingy she does, so I think I'll stay and keep you company, if that's OK.' He took a piece of typed paper from his pocket. 'The garden is going to have to wait until tomorrow.'

'Oh, Dad,' I winced as I asked him, 'is there any chance you could mind Billy tomorrow? That girl I work with is sick and I have to work until five again. Apparently it's in my contract.'

'It doesn't sound much of a shop with only two staff,' Dad muttered.

I shrugged.

He consulted his paper. 'Well, I suppose I can take him from two. Maybe I'll do some gardening in the morning and he can help me plant things in the afternoon – would he like that do you think?'

'He'd love it,' I said in a big false cheery voice. I took some more bread out. 'So, what would you like? Cheese? Ham?'

He glanced at my bargain-basement cheese and my rubbery ham. 'I think a tomato or two and some mayonnaise will suit me, thank you.' Then he dusted his suit down and sat at the table. 'Vine tomatoes,' he specified.

I took out my non-vine tomatoes and cut them up before he could notice. 'I've only got these – semi-vine ones,' I lied. 'They're the next big thing, apparently.'

'Oh.' He looked sceptical. 'Right. Well, I'll try those, so.'

'Great.' Chop. Chop. Chop. 'They're an acquired taste. A bit like fine wine.'

'Oh.' He was impressed now.

A bit like this new life, I thought. Only it wasn't so much the 'fine' as an acquired taste.

I made Dad his sandwich, which he declared horrible, and sat down opposite him and ate mine.

'I don't know how you can eat that,' he muttered as bits of cheese dribbled down my chin. 'Honestly, Poppy, whoever told you those tomatoes were the next big thing should be shot.'

'I like them.'

'Oh. OK. Whatever.' He studied his hands, then he stood up and walked to the window, made a remark about Billy going very high on the swing before sitting back down again at the table.

I suddenly realised that we'd never actually had a proper conversation before, not a real, adult, grown-up one. He'd flitted in and out of my life, dispensing presents and stern advice. I sought for something to say to him. It was worse than talking to other women. 'So, eh, how's retirement going?' I eventually asked.

'Ooooh, great,' he answered, nodding vigorously. I don't think he knew what to say to me either. There was a bit of a silence before he added, 'Lots of free time to do what I want.'

'Good.'

'For instance, the other day I spent approximately two hours twenty minutes in the gallery. Then I did some of the museums and then I spent the rest of the afternoon strolling about the city. I even went on a tour. Did you know the Bank of Ireland on Dame Street has no windows?'

'Yes.'

He looked surprised.

'Pete told me that.'

'Oh.' His thunder stolen, he settled into silence again.

'Well, it all sounds good.'

'It is.' He jabbed his half-eaten sandwich. 'It would be even better if your mother were around sometimes.'

I didn't reply. There was no way my mother would be giving up her life.

'What does she need all those organisations for? I asked her that only this morning. She got in a huff and said something cryptic about them being there for her when others suited themselves. Weird. Anyway, now she's not even bothering to come home on time.'

'You said she'd gone for a drink with her friends.'

'To get at me,' Dad poked himself in the chest. 'Huh, why does she need to go out for a drink with women she

142

hardly knows? She could go anywhere in the world and get the best drink and instead she's going to a city-centre pub with a load of strangers. All to get at me.'

'Oh, Dad, I hardly think so.'

'Anyway,' he said a little sulkily, 'retirement is fine.'

The subject was closed.

I picked up our plates and carried them to the sink. I opened the back door and threw my dad's half-eaten sambo out for the birds.

'You shouldn't do that,' he remarked. 'You'll attract rats.'

'We've had none so far.'

'Oh, you will. Mark my words. *Jesus*, what is that child doing?'

Billy was on his swing. There were piles of toys arranged in a line underneath the swing. Billy was going higher and higher. Just as I was about to knock on the window, he let go of the swing and went sailing through the air, over the toys and on to the ground. I let out a small shriek as my father cursed slightly.

'Ten toys today.' Billy jumped up and began dancing about the garden. He yelled out, over the wall, 'Hey, Tommy, ten toys today! I broke your record!'

'Billy!' I hammered hard on the window. 'You don't do that – you'll get hurt!'

'I'm fine!' He continued his dance about the garden.

'Listen to your mother!' My father yelled loudly. 'That was dangerous!'

Billy paused and looked wide-eyed at my dad. 'But Granddad,' he said, in a tone of complete confusion, '*ten* toys. Come on!'

'He'll kill himself,' my father predicted ominously. 'One day, he'll kill himself.'

'No he won't,' I opened the dishwasher bad-temperedly. 'He's fine.' I began to stow the dishes in it.

After a bit, Dad asked, 'Why are you stacking the small plates that way?'

'Because I always do,' I replied through gritted teeth.

'Would they not be better on the lower levels,' Dad asked. 'You'd use up a lot less space.' He peered into the dishwasher. 'Yes, it's the same one as your mother and I have. I made out a chart to show her the best way to arrange things. All the permutations are there. Now, let me see. Give me the plates.'

Resignedly, I handed him the dishes. My mother was right to get out, I thought.

Very carefully, he placed the two plates in the washer. 'Now, this is where you put the saucepans,' he continued, taking out a pen and paper from his jacket pocket and drawing a rough sketch of the dishwasher, 'but if you have baking trays, don't put the saucepans here, put them there.'

'Great.' I smiled quickly. 'Look, Dad, I have to go next door, you draw that out for me and I'll put it on the fridge, OK?'

'Yes, yes. No problem. Off you go.'

I left him, bent over his drawings as I exited the kitchen.

I hadn't planned on calling on Laura so early, but anything was better than listening to my father drone on about dishwashers. My heart pounded slightly as I rang her doorbell. This was a whole new territory for me, as maybe it would be for any mother whose child had just started making friends. She answered the door and her face broke into a smile when she saw me. It was kind of nice.

'Laura, hi,' I said. 'I, eh, just called in about last night. I'm sorry, I should have been keeping an eye on them.'

'No, no, no.' Laura pulled her door open wider. 'No. Come in. I was going to call on you later after dinner.'

'Oh, I'm disturbing your dinner – I'll go.'

'Don't be silly. Where's Billy?'

'In our back garden trying to kill himself, yet again. But I have my dad keeping an eye on him.'

She beckoned me in. 'We're just having chips, d'you want some?'

'No. No thanks.'

She crossed to Tommy. 'Have you finished?'

Tommy looked up. He grinned when he saw me. 'Yeah. Can I go into Billy now?'

'You can. But remember, you're seven – you're in charge. No dangerous stuff.'

Tommy raced off without answering. Laura laughed gently after him before turning to put the kettle on. 'I get a bit overprotective at times,' she said from over her shoulder.

'Your son was standing at an upstairs open window – I'd be overprotective too.'

My answer made us both giggle at the same time. She looked years younger when she laughed. Then, for some reason, I felt uncomfortable laughing with her and stopped. And I felt myself going all red. She must have noticed because she stopped too.

'I'm worse than I should be,' she admitted. 'His dad died four years ago, in an accident.'

'Oh.' I wasn't expecting that. 'God, I'm sorry.'

'Thanks.' She smiled a little sadly.

I didn't know what else to say. So I looked down at my hands and fiddled with my wedding ring. Then I stopped fiddling with it, because her husband was dead.

'It was so sudden, you know,' Laura began talking again.

'Like, that morning he was there, Tommy was chattering away and I was trying to coax him to eat his breakfast, and then Dan stood up and kissed me.' She put her fingers to her lips. 'Right here. Then he kissed Tommy, then he said "goodbye" and I hardly even looked up. I didn't even walk out to the door with him or anything.'

I think she was about to cry. I didn't know what I should do. Her telling me something so private transfixed me.

'Like, if I had only known that it would be the last time I'd see him, Poppy, I—' she stopped and swallowed hard. 'Anyway, he left to go to work and then two hours later he fell from a scaffold.'

'Oh God.'

'He was dead when he hit the ground, they said. And I know it might sound awful, but the shock of his death was nearly worse than him being dead.'

'Really?'

'Yeah, it changed me a lot. For the first time ever, I realised that life can change, just like that.' She clicked her fingers.

My life had changed that suddenly too, I thought. Then I quashed it. Jesus, how can you make that comparison, I scolded myself.

'I never used to worry,' Laura went on. 'But now,' she gave a rueful smile, 'I worry all the time. About stupid things mostly, but mainly about Tommy, though I try not to show it. Then, yesterday, when I saw him standing in your upstairs window, it hit me all over again, how easily things can happen.'

'You must think I'm a right selfish bitch moaning about moving house.'

'Nope,' she reassured me. 'When you have a perfect life and then it goes, that's awful for anyone.'

'It's still not as awful as what happened you.'

'Yeah, my life is worse than yours all right.'

To my surprise, she giggled, and I found myself giggling too.

'So, I'm sorry for storming out.'

'Jesus, don't be. Next time, though, could you yell out that our windows are a danger? Wooden frames are crap for kids to hold on to, that's what you say.' At her puzzled look I said, 'I want weather glaze and Pete says we can't afford it yet.' What had I told her that for? I reddened again.

Laura smiled. 'You and Pete are a great couple. He'd do anything for you, I reckon.'

The kettle clicked off. 'Coffee?' she asked.

'Great.'

When I got back, the map of the internal layout of our dishwasher was secured to the fridge. Billy's drawings had been taken down to accommodate it. Pete was at the table drinking coffee and eating his sandwich. My father was across from him, reading the paper. There was silence between them. I reckon there'd been some sort of a row. But as was usual, it was better to ignore it – though Pete was bound to be in bad form now. 'Where are the boys?' I asked.

'Watching TV,' Pete answered shortly.

'Rubbish TV,' my dad interjected. 'Cartoon network – it would suit them better to watch the geography channel or something.'

Pete looked ready to say something so I jumped in with, 'Hey, thanks for the plan, Dad.' I thumbed to the fridge.

Dad nodded and put down his paper. 'You'll find it invaluable. I've also taken the liberty of giving Pete a list of the cheapest places to buy various foodstuffs.' Pete, as if on cue, held it up, smiling stiffly. 'In the last few weeks, I've begun visiting various food shops and comparing prices. Just because I've money it doesn't mean I squander it. Your mother and I went to eight different places last week to do our shopping.' Pete began to laugh and then to pretend that he was coughing. Dad looked sharply at him before standing up. 'Now, I'll take my leave. Thanks for tea and I'll return the compliment tomorrow. You can pick Billy up from my house. Perhaps you could all visit us on Sunday – it might mean your mother will actually stay home.'

'I'm heading off to visit my mother,' Pete said, a bit rudely I thought.

Dad looked at me. I shrugged. 'I'll get back to you, Dad,' I said.

Dad sighed. 'OK, see you tomorrow anyway.' He pulled his jacket on and made his way to the door. 'Bye, Poppy.'

'Bye, Dad, and thanks for today,' I said, following him to see him out.

'You get a copy of your work contract and let me see it,' he advised. 'I'll go over it for you – it all seems a little odd.'

'Yeah. Thanks. Bye,' I called out, closing the door. 'So you're visiting your mother, ey?' I challenged the minute I got back to the kitchen.

'Yep.' Pete drained his cup and stood up. He crossed to the fridge and stared at my father's plan. 'She rang me to come down. She wants to tell me something, she said. Now, where does this go in the dishwasher?'

'There is no need to be sarcastic, my dad was only trying to help. I'd have been lost without him today.'

'You were meant to leave your job today.'

'Yeah, well, I can't – I've to work a month first. Anyway,

let's not get off the subject – why won't you come to my folks on Sunday?'

Pete strode towards the dishwasher and fired his cup in. 'Because I do have to visit my mother. And anyway, it's not me they want to see – it's you and Bill.'

'I don't care, you're my husband. I want you there.'

'Well, I can't go.'

'Don't want to go, more like.'

He shrugged and didn't reply.

It annoyed me. 'You'd rather visit your mother who never ever invites us down than visit my folks who at least have the decency to invite you over.'

'Oh, that's right, make your folks out to be better than mine.'

'They are.'

'Sure,' Pete glared at me. 'Sure they are.'

'Well, they care enough to babysit.'

'He only did it because he's bored. The man is bored out of his tree. Face it, you never saw him as much in your life before.'

'Don't you criticise my dad!'

'Well, don't criticise my mother.'

'OK, I won't, so. Let's all go and visit her on Sunday. In fact, let's go Saturday after your shift and stay there over the weekend. I'm sure she'd *love* that.'

His face dropped.

'I'll tell Billy he's going to see his other grandmother at last.' With that I waltzed out of the kitchen.

18

O N SATURDAY, I packed our bags ready for the off.
Billy was jumping about the place with excitement.
He'd only ever seen his Granny Shannon twice in his life.
The first time was at his christening, which he obviously
didn't remember, and the second time was when we visited
her one Easter. He'd been two then and he'd succeeded in
breaking her favourite bowl. I'd bought her another one,
just the same, but according to her, it wasn't the same. Not
the same at all. Not at all. At all. She and Pete had a row
about it and we'd left early. He hadn't let me visit her since,
even though I'd tried. Family being around is important, I
think. And Billy had a right to get to know his other granny.

'I see you're still coming,' Pete remarked sourly as he
surveyed our bags.

'I see you're still delighted about it,' I said back as lightly
as I could. Pete was nervous about the trip and I was doing
my best to make allowances for him. He hadn't really talked
to me in the last couple of days except to say that I was
being ridiculous about it and that I should visit my own
parents. I remained stubborn.

Pete hefted our bags up on to his shoulder and stomped
downstairs with them. I watched from the window as he
threw them into the boot of the car. Torpedoed them in

would be more like it. Then he slammed down the boot and stood for a second just staring at the blue paintwork of the car. As I watched from the window, there was something in his bowed head that got me. Something about the way his shoulders slumped that sent me hurtling down the stairs and out into the front garden. I wrapped my arms about him and rested my head against him. 'It'll be fine,' I said. 'You'll see.'

He said nothing, though he wrapped his arm about me and pulled me in tighter.

It was around three when we pulled up to Pete's mother's house. I keep calling her Pete's mother in my head because her name doesn't suit her. She's a big stocky country woman with a red, deeply lined face. The deepest line is the vertical slash between her eyebrows which gives her a cross look. She has huge forearms and her hair is a sort of bristly blondey brown. In her day, I'd imagine that she was quite pretty as she has Pete's big green eyes. Her name is Thelma.

She didn't come out to meet us as we got out of the car, Pete dragging all our bags. Billy was hopping about from foot to foot, running up and down the small little driveway, pointing out flowers and picking up pebbles. I stood beside Pete as he unlocked the front door and went inside to a dark little hallway.

'Mammy,' he called, 'it's me.'

I could never get used to Pete saying 'Mammy'. It was a childish way of speaking, I thought. Maybe it was a country thing, I don't know.

'I wasn't expecting you until later,' she shouted out from the kitchen. 'I haven't a thing in the house for ye.'

Pete rolled his eyes at me and I squeezed his hand.

151

'I'll bring you down to the shops later,' he said, entering the kitchen. 'Poppy and Billy are here too.'

I have to say, I got a bit of a shock when I saw her. She'd lost a little weight and didn't look as imposing as she used to. Or maybe I just wasn't in awe of her as much as before.

'Oh,' she said and her head shot up. The slash between her eyebrows deepened a little more. 'Oh. What's the occasion?'

'Poppy wanted to come,' Pete said abruptly, leaving my side. 'And Billy was dying to come too.'

'Well, that means I've to get in even more food. Don't sit down there,' she barked at me, 'I've only just ironed the clothes on the back of that chair.'

'Sorry, Thelma,' I answered. Nope, my awe was still there.

'And where's the young fella? I hope he's not out there destroying the garden.'

'Hiya Nana!' Billy burst into the kitchen. Then stopped abruptly. He looked her up and down before coming to cower at my side. 'She looks cross,' he said loudly.

No one could deny this so it was ignored.

'I suppose you want a cup of tea?'

'Well, it was a long journey,' Pete took this as an invitation to fill the kettle. Water splashed into it and he plugged it in.

The kitchen hadn't changed much since I'd first been here – as Pete's girlfriend. It was a real country kitchen, all walls and a range. Thelma had done nothing to brighten it up, however, and it was gloomy and messy.

'Tea is in the press,' Thelma barked. 'And before you ask, I've no coffee. I wasn't expecting you this early.'

'Fine.' He turned to Billy. 'D'you want some water, Bill?'

'Is there no juice?'

Thelma cackled. 'How could there be juice? I didn't even know you were coming, child.'

'Well, for the next time, could I have some juice?'

'I might be able to get it in by the time you're eleven all right. That'll probably be the next time.'

Neither Pete nor I rose to the bait. Pete because he figured it wasn't worth it and me because I was now terrified. Every time I met her, I wondered how she could have given birth to Pete.

Thelma looked from one to the other of us before going back to folding her ironed clothes. When she'd taken the ones from the chair, I gingerly sat down. Billy seemed to sense the atmosphere because he sat quietly too. Well, quietly for him, his legs kept jiggling up and down.

'So, have they caught him yet?' Thelma barked out just as the kettle clicked off.

'Who?' Pete asked as he poured three cups of tea.

'That shyster that ran off with all your money!'

'Nope.'

'And would you not look for him yourself?'

'I've a job to keep down. I don't have the cash and I wouldn't have a clue where to start. And anyway, even if they do catch him, I won't be getting my money back.'

'Well, if it were me, I'd go after him. Huh, I don't know why I wasted all that money on college for you, and now look – you're waiting on tables.'

'You didn't want me to go into business anyway, Mammy.'

'Yes, but you did. And now look. Now you've lost that and you wait on tables.'

'I haven't lost it, not yet,' Pete sounded a little cross. 'And the RIAI said that until Adrian is caught they won't expel me. I'm only suspended.'

So they'd suspended him. He hadn't told me that. But before I could say anything, Billy piped up, 'He works in a nice place – it's a hotel.'

'Waiting on tables, pah!' She took a sup of her tea. 'Have you forgotten that I like sugar?'

'I'll get it,' I stood up. There was no way, while I was there, that she was going to order Pete about. He did enough for her.

'Sure, you're never here, you don't know where it is.'

'I'm sure it'll be where it was the last time,' I said over my shoulder as I reached into a press, hoping to hell this was where it was the last time. 'Nothing else seems to have changed.'

'So I see,' she remarked back, eyeing me up and down. 'How's your own job going? Pete told me you were working too now.'

'It's going fine.' My fumbling hands found the sugar and I pulled it down and put it on the table in front of her.

'Must be a change for you,' she said sourly. Then, she opened the sugar and, without using a spoon, she poured it directly from the packet into her cup.

'Wow,' Billy said as tonnes of sugar made the tea rise up in the cup. 'You sure do take a lot of sugar.'

'And what's wrong with that?'

'Sugar gives you worms – you must have loads of worms.'

I spluttered on my cup of tea as beside me Pete winced.

'I don't have any worms, thank you very much! Only dirty people who don't wash their hands get worms.'

'Come on, Billy, I'll show you around outside. Let's have a look at your Nana's farm.' I held out my hand for him and he jumped up, knocking against the table and making my tea slop out.

154

'I'll wipe it,' Pete said. 'Go on out.'

Thelma had about five acres of land on which she had sheep and cows. Billy, who had never really been to the countryside before, was fascinated. He hopped over a gate and ran towards the sheep and they scattered. I let him run around after them as I leaned back against the little stone wall and watched him. The sky was a brilliant blue with not a cloud in sight. And everywhere was so silent, except for Billy's whoops and cheers, and as I watched him cavort about like a mad thing, I suddenly felt strange. Peaceful or something.

It didn't last, however. Thelma arrived out, wrapped up in a big shawl, and yelled at Billy to stop making so much noise.

'You'll frighten the animals,' she scolded.

Billy glanced at her and obviously decided that she wasn't a woman to be messed with. He stopped, like something out of a cartoon, in mid-step.

'That's better,' Thelma nodded. Then she turned to Pete who had come out with her.

'Right, drive me to the town, will you. I've to go to the doctor and then stock up on some food.' She looked accusingly at us.

'You were only at the doctor the last time I came,' Pete said.

'And when was that?' Thelma arched her thick eyebrows. 'Before you moved.'

'Yeah and no one needs to visit their doctor every month.'

'And you'd know, would you? You being a bankrupt architect.'

'Mammy, I'm only saying—'

'Well,' Thelma pulled her shawl about her, 'there is no need.'

155

'Can I come to town?' Billy asked.

'No,' she snapped. 'You make too much noise.'

'You and Mammy stay here and have a look about,' Pete suggested in a don't-ask-any-questions type of voice.

'But I want to go to town,' Billy whined.

'And I want to go to America and live in a big house, but I can't,' said Thelma, 'so just accept it.' Then she turned and marched off towards the car.

Pete ran after her like a lackey.

Later that night, when Pete and I were in bed and Billy was snoozing on the floor – Thelma hadn't expected us and she had nothing for Billy to sleep on – I asked Pete about the suspension.

'It's nothing,' he muttered. 'They haven't expelled me yet and they won't until they have proof, and I did nothing wrong so don't worry, ey?' He pulled me to him in the dim light and kissed my forehead. 'In fact, it's a vote of confidence from them.'

'You should have told me.'

'I didn't want to worry you.'

'Pete, you not telling me things worries me.'

He kissed me again and said, 'She usually hates doctors.'

The change of subject wrong-footed me. 'Huh?' The bed was like nails.

'She never goes to doctors – she thinks they're all chancers. And she was awful quiet when she came out of the surgery.'

I detected a note of anxiety in his voice, so I raised myself up on an elbow and looked down at him. 'Was she?'

'Yeah.'

'And did you ask her if there was something wrong?'

He shrugged. 'Nope. I asked her the last time she went

156

and I was told that having abandoned her, I had no right to know.'

I almost laughed. Almost. 'Pete,' I said, 'can you see your mother not complaining if something is wrong? The woman would be in her element.'

He smiled a little. 'Yeah. Yeah I guess.'

Then I switched off the side lamp and went to sleep.

19

THERE WAS CERTAINLY nothing wrong with the woman the next day. She woke us up by pounding on the bedroom door. I sat bolt upright, my heart hammering, not having a clue where I was.

'Mass is on in an hour. Get up now.'

'Shit,' Pete groaned, hauling himself up beside me. 'Mammy, can you not do that!'

'I don't know what sort of a life you live in Dublin, but you'll go to mass while you're here. Say a few prayers – it might just save your souls.'

'We live in Kildare now,' Billy said loudly. 'Not Dublin.'

'Don't be cheeky!' She stomped off down the stairs.

'Well,' I rolled over in the bed. 'I'm not getting up.'

'I did that once,' Pete said, crawling out from under the covers, 'it's not worth it, believe me.'

And of course if he wasn't doing it, I didn't have the nerve to do it on my own.

Mass wasn't too bad. The priest had us in and out in less than forty minutes. And it was nice to sit in the church and let the prayers roll over me and just think. Though, not having gone in ages, I hadn't a clue when to stand or sit or kneel or anything. And Billy was like a jack-in-the-box, mooching and wriggling and rolling about on the ground. Thelma was not impressed at all.

'There'll be no more juice for you with that carry on,' she told him as we left the church.

'I don't care, I like my other nana better than you anyway.'

'And I like my other grandchild better than you,' Thelma retorted.

Hurt flashed across Pete's face but unbelievably he said nothing.

'Oh,' I said, annoyance overcoming my fear, 'so you've seen him have you? When did he visit?'

Thelma flushed. 'I've seen photographs of him,' she said defensively, straightening herself up. 'A very handsome child with blond hair and nice blue eyes.'

'Yes, he is handsome,' Pete agreed.

'But he hasn't visited?' I asked as if I was surprised. I ignored Pete's poking me to shut up. 'And what age is he now, four? Five?'

'Five. And he's advanced. And he—'

'And in five years you haven't once seen him. My God!'

Thelma puffed herself up, like a bird about to go on the attack. 'Well, I haven't exactly—'

'Now, who's for coffee?' Pete interrupted. 'There's a nice coffee shop just a walk away.'

'I could certainly do with one,' Thelma shot me a malevolent look. 'A good strong one.'

I felt like thumping Pete. How could he just let her get away with saying the things she was saying?

Things got worse as the day progressed. I began to think that Pete must have been right when he'd suggested that I should have gone to visit my own parents. Thelma hated me. She always had done, from the very first time we'd met. Only, because she was Pete's mother, I'd valiantly tried to ignore it. To be honest, she acted like she hated Pete too, the way she ordered him about. But she was his mother so she couldn't have.

She insisted on making the dinner. My offers of help were ignored. When she finally dished up, I got the tiniest piece of ham, one potato and a spoonful of cabbage. In fact my dinner was so small Billy thought it was his.

'That's your mammy's,' Thelma said slapping his hand away. 'I know she has to watch her weight.'

'Thanks.' I bit my lip, determined to stay calm.

'Well, I don't have to watch my weight, and I'm hungry,' Billy said. 'And I like ham.'

'We all like ham,' Thelma announced. 'But I only bought enough for Peter and me. I didn't know you and your mother were coming so you'll just have to make do.'

Bitch. Bitch. Bitch. 'Here,' I gave Billy my miserable little mouthful. 'You take it – it tastes funny.'

Pete kicked me under the table, I kicked him back.

'Oh, not up to your usual take-away meals, is it not?' Thelma said cheerfully. The first cheerful thing she'd said since we arrived. 'Peter loves his Sunday ham here, don't you, Peter?'

I looked at him. He looked at me. Then he looked at his mother. Then she looked at me. Then we both looked at Pete again. He caught my hand under the table. 'Poppy cooks nice ham, too,' he said. He was a terrible liar.

His mother served him an even smaller piece than she'd given me. For herself, she reserved a big plateful and then only nibbled at it.

Bitch, I thought. Bitch. Bitch. Bitch.

160

Needless to say, we left early. Pete had our bags in the car by three. Billy was sitting in the car without having to be coaxed or bribed. I sat in too, without saying goodbye to our hostess. In fact, I was nearly about to tell Pete just to drive off without talking to her, when he said, 'I'll just go and thank her.'

It took all my will power to ask 'for what?' but I let him go. I felt sorry for him. I wondered why he bothered going to see her if that was the way he was treated. I wondered why she treated him like that. I wondered why, for the last few months, he had been at her beck and call, driving her to the shops and collecting her afterwards. I'd have told her where to go.

He was in with her for a while and I was sorely tempted to start beeping the horn for him to hurry up. When he did come out, he was stony faced and without saying a word, he started the car.

'Well,' Billy said. 'I am never going back to see her again.'

I laughed.

Pete said nothing, all the way back to Kildare.

I didn't know if there was going to be a row when we got back or not. And if there was going to be a row, I didn't quite know what it would be about. All I knew was that as I unpacked the clothes, Pete paced up and down behind me like some kind of caged animal. I don't even know if he was aware he was doing it. Billy was in his room, jumping about on his bed as both of us tried to ignore him. He was meant to be going asleep. I took my good skirt from the case and shook it slightly to get the creases out. Behind me, Pete cleared his throat. I stiffened but continued what I was doing.

'She's sick,' Pete blurted out. At my puzzled look, he added, 'My mother, she's, eh, she's not well.'

161

'What?' I froze, with the skirt in mid-air. 'How?' Then, 'When? Well?'

Pete shrugged. He continued to stare at me. He was pale, I noticed, with a bit of a heart wrench. I'd been so angry towards that woman that I hadn't noticed how pale he was.

'When did you find out?' I asked, dropping the skirt on to the bed. 'Today?'

He nodded. 'Yeah.' A semi-smile flickered for an instant. 'When I went in to say goodbye to her, she gave me an earful about bringing you down when she had specifically requested me on my own.'

I flushed. Me and my stubbornness.

'And I said that you had insisted on coming, that you were dying to see her.'

'You didn't!'

He smiled a little again. 'Yeah, I did. And she said that you weren't the only one that was dying.'

'What?'

'That's what *I* said.'

I know it wasn't right or appropriate, but the way Pete was telling this story, was making me grin, and I desperately didn't want to.

'And she stood up and said, really loudly, I don't suppose either of you care that I have cancer.'

'No!'

'And I said, "How could I care when I hadn't known," and then I said, "You have cancer?" and she said, "That's what I said."'

'Jesus.'

'Who has cancer?' Billy called out from his room.

'Go to sleep!' I called back. 'I swear, Billy, if you don't go to sleep, there'll be no sweets tomorrow.'

'So?' Billy jumped harder on his bed. 'I don't care! I don't care!'

'She has to have a breast removed,' Pete went on, ignoring the commotion Billy was making. 'And maybe some more treatment, depending on what they find.'

My stomach heaved. Operations and blood and stuff always made me queasy. I'd almost passed out when I'd been handed Billy when he was born.

'And,' Pete shuffled uneasily and dropped his gaze, 'she can only get the treatment in Dublin, it's the nearest place for her.'

I felt as trapped as one of those ladies in the silent movies tied to train tracks. Before Pete spoke I could see the train coming.

'And, well, Poppy, I was wondering if she could stay here. It'd be too much travelling for her going up and down and if she's not well . . .' his voice trailed off and he looked up at me from under his dark eyelashes.

What could I say? It's not that I wouldn't help her – she was welcome to stay – I just wasn't sure that we would be able to withstand it. 'She can stay, but I'm telling you, Pete, she can't come between us,' were the first words out of my mouth.

'She won't.'

I needed to clarify this. I had to before he moved her in. 'Pete,' I said, trying not to sound confrontational, 'you wouldn't even stick up for your son today when she said she preferred a photograph to him.'

'That was just nonsense.'

'Not to me, it wasn't. She was slagging off our son.'

'She just says things.'

'Not about our child, she doesn't. You should have backed me up, Pete.'

'There was no need to defend him. The whole thing was ridiculous.'

'Pete, if she stays, she treats you and me with a bit of respect, that's all I'm asking.'

'She'll be sick, Poppy. For God's sake!' He glared at me.

'Pete, all I'm saying is that if she says things I'll want to defend myself without you getting annoyed.' His lips thinned out and I tried again. 'I feel for her, I do, honestly, and I'll be good to her. But she can't be let walk all over us like she did this weekend. I can't live like that.'

'Well, your family walks all over me.'

Jesus, this was developing into a row and I hadn't meant it to. 'Look, she can stay, OK. Let's just forget it.'

'I'm expected to take it from your folks, aren't I? When your dad makes remarks about people being successful, I just have to sit there knowing he never wanted me to marry you in the first place. When your mother buys you expensive dresses, I'm supposed to like them, knowing she knows I can't afford that kind of thing.'

'Pete, let's stop this.' God. God. God.

'When your dad criticises the programmes that I let Billy watch, I know he's doing that because he reckons I'm not intelligent enough.'

'Oh Jesus!' I raised my eyes and my voice.

'Don't fight!' Billy called in from his bedroom. 'Don't fight!'

'We're not,' I lied, trying to sound happy. 'We're just discussing things.'

'D'you know what he said to me the other day he was here, do you?' Pete hissed.

'Are you asking if I'm psychic?'

'Yous *are* fighting!' Billy shouted.

'He said that I had no control over Billy. That the kid was wild and that it was my fault. Mine.'

'That's my dad, he just says things.'

'Yeah, and so does my mother.'

'Your mother is worse.'

'Ha, at least I saw my mother when I was growing up. More than you can say for your dad!'

'He was busy working. And you shut up,' I marched towards him and hissed, poking my finger in his direction. 'You shut up.'

'No, I won't. That's why your dad is here so much now – he has nothing to do.'

'My dad can come here whenever he likes, and you hating him won't stop it!'

'And so can my mother. She's coming up, and I don't care how you feel about it.' And he yanked open the door and walked out of the room, leaving me completely speechless.

20

WHAT PETE SAID was true. My parents had never wanted me to marry him. I think they expected me to end up on the arm of some incredibly rich, successful businessman who would show me the world. They wanted me to marry a guy who would buy me my every whim, including a massive house in one of the most ridiculously expensive parts of Dublin. I'd wanted that too. At the time, I wanted exactly what my parents had. And then I'd met Pete. At a funeral. Harry Hopper's funeral to be precise.

Harry had been a work colleague of my dad's. And because he worked with my dad – or rather *for* my dad – I'd joked, quite irreverently, that he'd obviously died of over-work. My dad had been disgusted. He'd told me to have some respect. Harry was a good man, he said. Everybody liked Harry. I'd made a face and got a disapproving face from my mother in return. Anyhow, because Dad knew him, he dragged me and my mother to the funeral. Dad had marched boldly up the church as Mam and I followed in his wake. Once at the front, he had shaken hands with the mourners. 'Saves some time at the end,' he'd whispered to Mam when he slid into the seat beside us a few moments later.

Anyway, as we were sitting there listening to the sniffs and whispers and shuffling that goes on in a church before the show begins, Pete arrived. He squeezed in beside us just as the mass began. Well, beside me, actually. His shoulder brushed off mine, his leg touched mine. He kept trying to move away but it was impossible. Harry must have been a popular guy indeed because the place was packed. Five minutes into the service Pete had started shifting about in his seat. I could see my father growing annoyed with him. It didn't bother Pete, he turned right around in his seat and gawked at the people behind. Then he gawked at me. Eventually he whispered, 'Whose funeral is this?'

His eyes, so large and green and innocent-looking, made me catch my breath. I blushed a bit before answering, 'Harry Hopper's.'

'Shit,' he winced. 'Jesus, I'm at the wrong funeral.'

Despite my shyness with new people, I exploded in giggles. Mam nudged me. We were right at the front.

'I'm meant to be at Andy Grace's. Do you know where that is?'

'Sorry, I haven't got my funeral guidebook with me.'

Now it was his turn to laugh, and Pete does not do quiet laughter. He gave a guffaw that he tried to turn into a cough. Dad glared at him. Mam stiffened. I bit my lip and tears came out of my eyes.

Pete gulped. 'I thought Harry was a sort of nickname for Andy,' he muttered to me.

'Mmm.' I decided not to answer. I'd only laugh.

'He was my teacher in college. Nice guy.'

'Mmm.'

'Aw, well, I suppose old Harry Hopper was a nice man too.'

'Mmm.'

'I hate funerals. The only one I'll like will be my own – all that attention will be nice.'

I giggled again.

'Stop!' Mam hissed to me. She glared at Pete. He tipped his forehead and smiled cheerily at her.

Harry Hopper's funeral went to Mount Argus. Pete decided to follow the coffin because his teacher's funeral was going there too. I saw him jump into a battered car and I remember the way he waved at me. I'd waved back and felt a sort of thrill just looking at him. I think I knew then that I was going to marry him.

As luck had it, his funeral arrived at the graveyard the same time as ours. As I watched him walk over to join it, I remember feeling sort of empty. He'd asked me out as we were leaving. I'd liked the way he'd braved the disapproving looks of my mother and father as he said, 'If you're going to any more funerals in the future, can I come with you?' I'd told him I'd prefer a trip to the cinema. He'd agreed and we'd met the next night.

Pete turned up at the wrong funeral and had charmed his way into my life. He had no money, no house and a car that only started when it felt like it. But he had childlike green eyes and an open grin. He had good friends and he made me laugh and I fell hugely in love with him. He knew how my parents felt about him, though they never actually said it, and he told me that he wouldn't marry me until he had his business up and running. I think he thought it would win their approval. It hadn't, and nothing he had done since had made them like him any better. They had just never got over their dreams for me.

However, it worked in reverse too. Pete's mother hadn't wanted Pete to marry me. I think she thought that Pete would wind up working and living from home and that he would mind her until the end of her days. At the time I met Pete, he was in college finishing his degree and he'd trot home to her every weekend. Gavin and I used to slag him about it, but in a funny kind of a way it appealed to me. I used to think that if he looked after his mother like that, why then, he would take the same care of me. He'd never leave me alone and he'd always be there. And I'd been right. Only he couldn't be with me and with his mother at the same time, so he curbed his visits to her to once a fortnight. And because of this, I reckon, she began to dislike me even before she met me.

The first time I ever visited, I'd made a huge effort to impress. I'd bought new clothes, purchased some really extravagant chocolates as a gift for her and even got my hair done.

'Now, our house isn't like yours,' Pete warned me about a million times. 'It's small and, well, my mother isn't into doing it up or anything.'

'Pete,' I said, 'if you were the son of Satan and you lived in hell, I wouldn't mind.'

It turned out that he was the son of Satan.

Satan had met us at the front door as we pulled up in front of the house. Her first comment as I stepped out of the car was, 'Oh, mixing with very fancy people now, aren't you Peter?' Then she'd turned on her heel and walked in.

The woman's tongue was as sharp as a bee sting. And when she wasn't being sharp she was ignoring the conversation I was trying to make and engaging Pete in another type of conversation. I'd spent two days of hell under her roof, and it was a long time before I went back. I was married by then and there was nothing she could do. Then

Pete and I had rowed about it as he didn't want me to visit her, but I'd insisted, convinced that the fact I was expecting her grandchild would be a cause for celebration.

'Kids,' she'd said. 'I raised three of them on my own and what thanks do they give you?' she paused dramatically, 'Nothing.' She nodded ominously at my belly. 'That's what'll happen to you.'

It was the only time I can remember that Pete stood up to her. He took my hand and pulled me from the house. Then, without saying a word to her, he drove us both home.

A small gift when Billy was born had restored communications between them, but her dislike of me had grown. And now, now she was coming to our house. The thought petrified me. Pete and I were having a hard enough time of things as it was without her driving her oar in. And despite what Pete promised, I knew he found it hard to stand up to her. He was soft. That's why he'd ended up taking care of her when his two brothers had bunked off. And I'd loved that about him.

I heard him downstairs marching about the place – I think he was getting beer out of the fridge or something. I think he was expecting me to go down after him, and maybe I should have. After all, he'd just discovered that his mother was sick and it had to have been a huge shock. I'd hate it if anything happened to my parents. But he'd said my parents were awful. That hurt. At least they cared enough to offer us money when we were stuck. His mother wouldn't give us so much as a bloody smile, for Christ's sake.

I shoved a pile of my clothes into the wardrobe, mentally cursing it for not being a walk-in wardrobe like at our last house. But still, the thought nagged at me that I should go and see if he was all right.

'Poppy?'

Pete's voice startled me. I jumped, clothes tumbling to the floor. 'Yeah?' I said cautiously.

'Sorry.'

I gulped. I considered hugging him, but for the first time in our marriage I didn't know how he'd react. Or even quite what he was sorry for.

'I'm sorry for not sticking up for Billy. I should have.'

'Good.' Like a thick, I had tears in my eyes. 'That hurt.'

'Yeah, I know.' He crossed over to me and wrapped his arms around me. 'Jesus, Poppy, I dunno what's happening to us.'

I pulled him in tight. 'Me neither.'

'I'm doing me best, honestly.'

'Yeah. I know that.'

He kissed the top of my head. 'And I'm so proud of you with the job and all. I know it's not easy.'

'It's fine.'

We stood for a while, just holding each other. Then he said cautiously, 'And my mother is only coming if you say so – that's what I told her.'

'She is welcome to come, Pete. She's your mother. I have no problem with that.'

'It's a lot to ask, I know that.'

'A lot? A lot? This will earn me permanent sainthood!'

He smiled. Then his smile faded. 'She'll be a nightmare, I know that, Poppy.'

'Pete, I've lost my house, I'm working in a euro shop, my kid fights with his classmates, my dad is using me as his surrogate wife – how much worse can it get?'

And surprisingly, we both started to laugh. Then I noticed that Pete had tears in his eyes and he was trying not to let me notice, and I thought to myself, he loves that horrible woman. She brought him up, she made him the wonderful person he is, so there had to be some good in her, and bloody hell, I was going to try and find it. Or kill her, or myself, in the process.

21

I WAS PUTTING Billy's lunch into his bag over a week later
when I found the note. At first I thought it was about
days off or sports days or something, but when I opened it
up I saw that it was handwritten. My heart stopped. Oh
Jesus, I thought, what had he done now?

Dear Poppy, the note read, *could you please make an arrange-*
ment for you and your husband to see me next week regarding our last
conversation about Billy's behaviour. Thank you. It was signed by
Billy's teacher and the principal too.

I reread the note and then I read it a third time. What
did it mean? Billy came slouching into the kitchen, his
uniform askew and, as I was straightening his tie, I asked
casually, 'Billy, have you been in trouble in school lately?'

His eyes darkened. 'I hate school,' he said.

'Yes, so you've said about a million times, but have you
actually been in trouble with your teacher?'

'What did you put in my lunch box?'

'Billy, answer my question!'

He jumped at my sharp voice – normally I don't shout
at him. Apparently shouting is bad for kids. I saw it on one
of the parenting programmes on the telly. 'Well?' I
demanded, still shouting since it was having a good effect
on him.

'Everybody hates me,' he said. He didn't sound sad about it, just kind of angry.

'No they don't,' I scoffed.

'They *do*.'

'Why? Why do they hate you?'

He shrugged and stared mutinously at his trainers. 'I dunno. They call me a liar and a show-off and everything.'

'Why?' I knelt down so that I was at his height. The parenting programme had advised mothers to do that. 'How do you show off?'

'I dunno. And then when they say it to me, I hit them.' He did a sort of half-jump and punched the air with his fist. 'Like this – POW!'

I recoiled. 'Billy, you shouldn't hit anyone. Who have you hit?'

Another shrug.

'Billy?'

'Dunno. Just boys in my class. They just cry then.'

I didn't know what else to say. A cold hard band had clenched around my chest and I wished that I didn't have to take him to school. I wanted to hide him away from the horrible boys who teased him. I wanted to hide myself away from this life that was getting more fraught with every passing week. 'Don't hit anyone today, OK?' I held out the note. 'Your teacher wants to see me and Daddy. That's not a good thing.'

'What did you put in my lunch box?' He danced away from me and pulled it out of his bag. When he saw it was sandwiches, he made a face. 'I hate them.'

I ignored his moans and went in search of his coat.

* * *

Maxi was at her till when I arrived into work. Isobel looked pointedly at her watch as I sidled by her with my own cash drawer. I didn't bother saying anything – I was fed up trying to be pleasant to unpleasant people. Instead, I ignored both her and Maxi, and concentrated on shoving my cash drawer into the register. Isobel, obviously sensing my mood, said nothing as she opened up the shop.

'I'm heading off to the wholesalers this morning,' she said brightly a few minutes later, poking her head out of the back room. 'See you both later.'

'Yeah,' Maxi nodded.

I gave a brief nod too.

Thirty minutes went by and no one came in. I grew bored sitting at the register so I thought I'd try to compose the letter for the charity auction that would be sent out to the various celebrities and their agents. I had been putting it off as I hated writing letters, but with a meeting coming up I had to have something to show the rest of the women. I took my notebook and pen from my bag and tried various openings.

Dear (whoever), I would be obliged if you would consider

– too boring.

Dear (whoever), Would you like to help raise money for

– too common.

Dear (whoever), The most exciting charity event will take place in November and we want YOU on board

That sounded good. Maybe a picture of Uncle Sam or something could be included with the letter. Some flattery wouldn't go astray either.

As a well-known celebrity, you would be ideally placed to help the . . .

'What are you doing?' Maxi asked.

I glanced across the shop at her. The nosy cow – she hadn't bothered talking to me all morning. 'Nothing,' I said.

'You are, you're writing something down.' Her tone was accusing. 'I hope you're not writing a report on me. I can't help it if there's no customers in.'

I shot her what I hoped was a disdainful look. 'No, Maxi, I'm not writing a report on you.'

'Good.' She folded her enormous arms and glared at me. 'Is it for another job?' She couldn't disguise the hopeful note in her voice.

'No.' Despite being uncomfortable in her presence, I relished her crestfallen expression before turning back to my letter and rereading the little I'd written. Damn, the stupid woman had ruined my train of thought.

'So, what are you writing?'

I didn't reply.

'Well? Is it to do with the job, 'cause unless it is, Isobel won't like it.'

'I don't care,' I said. 'I don't care if I get the sack. In fact, I'd be happy to leave now, so you run along and tell Isobel that I was writing in work if you want to.' I marvelled at my braveness. Standing up to the mother-in-law from hell had its advantages, Maxi seemed like a pussycat now.

Her mouth hardened. 'I'm not a rat.'

That was debatable, I felt like saying, only I didn't.

'Is it a birthday card?' Maxi asked.

'Nope.'

'Is it for a school application or something?'

'Nope.'

'Do you just like writing?'

'No.' Jesus, if I didn't tell her, she'd keep going. 'I'm writing a letter to try to get famous people to do something for me.'

Maxi's mouth fell open. I saw her enormous teeth and her big tongue. 'Wha'? Famous people do stuff for you if you write to them? I never knew that.'

'They don't do stuff just because you write to them,' I explained. 'They have to consider it. I'm writing to see if these people will consider getting involved in a charity auction I'm running.'

'A wha'?'

'A charity auction.' Of course then I had to explain to her what a charity auction was and what our cause was. To my surprise, she seemed a little impressed.

'My husband, now he died of cancer.' She nodded vigorously. 'Terrible it was. One day he was fine, the next, BAM!' she hit her fist off the counter, making her till jump.

'Oh.' I put down my pen. 'Sorry to hear that.'

'Why? Did you know him?'

'No, but it must have been hard on you.'

She shrugged and her face softened a little. 'Yeah. Yeah, it was hard. But I manage. Got this job, haven't I?'

'Yeah.'

She nodded in the direction of my pen. 'You write away, so. Put up your closed sign and concentrate on the letter.'

'Oh.' I put up my closed sign, wondering if there was going to be a catch. 'Oh, right, OK. Thanks, Maxi.'

'And if you have to do anything else about the auction, you just do it. It's nice to know people do stuff like that. Do you get paid?'

'No.'

'Fair dues.' She nodded again. Her fuzzy black hair sprung up and down. 'The auction sounds great. Can anyone go?'

'Eh, yeah, by invite.'

'Good. Send me an invite. I might get a few of me bingo mates and we can all club together and make a bid on someone. Charlotte might even come.'

Jesus!

22

M Y MOTHER WAS in bad humour. I didn't bother to ask why – it was safer that way. She snapped at me continually as she drove me over to Phil's house. The only thing that took her out of herself was when I told her about Pete's mother. She was horrified. In fact she was so horrified that she put her foot on the brake instead of the accelerator, throwing us both forward.

'Sorry, sorry, sorry,' she apologised to me as she restarted the car and ignored the horn blasting from the man behind us. 'So,' she said as the car began to move again, 'that woman has cancer?' She always called Pete's mother 'that woman'.

'Yes.'

'That's awful. I know she's awful and everything but that *is* awful.'

'So, she's coming to live with us while she's being treated.'

'No!' Mam's head swivelled to look at me. She almost rear-ended a fancy-looking car in front. 'No!' The guy behind us was now giving my mother the two fingers.

'Mam, will you mind the road!'

'That woman is coming to live with you?' Her brow wrinkled. She was totally oblivious to the stress she was causing to other motorists. 'Is there nowhere else she can go?'

'No.' I gave a little laugh. 'She barely has friends at home, she'd hardly have them up here.'

'True. Oh God,' Mam made an anguished face. 'How long will she be around for?'

'A few months at least. Pete doesn't see any point in her travelling home after her treatment – he says she might as well stay with us until it's all over.'

'Easy for him to say, he's out all day.'

'Well, I'll be out in the mornings, so I'll just have to put up with her in the afternoons.'

Mam laid her hand on mine. 'You can come to me any time, you know that.'

'Thanks.' I patted her hand back. 'But I'll be fine. Honestly.'

I wondered if she knew I was lying.

Phil's house was smaller than everyone else's. Well, everyone's except mine. Two-thousand-foot small. As if to compensate for it, she drove an enormous jeep. The vehicle took up most of her driveway and hence parking there was impossible. Mam grumbled as she was forced to drive around Phil's estate looking for somewhere to park.

'What does she need a big car like that for?' she moaned as she manoeuvred her car into a space. 'Honestly, there's only herself to drive about. You'd swear she had an army of children.'

I said nothing. The four of them continually griped and complained about one another. How they remained friends was a mystery to me.

'Now,' Mam pulled her handbag from the back seat, 'let's go and see what brilliant ideas they've conjured up.'

The others were waiting on us. They sat, dressed in their finery, on Phil's over-large sofa. If Phil had been a man the

Freudian experts would have had a field day. Everything in the room was large except for the room itself. And I wouldn't mind, but it was a lovely proportioned room. It could have been so cosy if she'd only accepted it for what it was. Instead, she was determined to make it into something it most definitely wasn't.

'Well,' Phil eyed us up as we came in, 'here we all are at last. Now, have we all been working hard this month? I'll go first, shall I? Seeing as I'm the coordinator for today.'

The others nodded indifferently.

'Now, let me see,' Phil tapped her pen against her teeth and studied a little notebook she was holding. 'I was to book a room for our purposes and I spent the month going from place to place. Eventually, The Glenstone Hotel offered me a room for free. So I went to see that and it's a nice size, and they'll provide a bar and sandwiches and everything.' She sat back and smiled around at us all. 'Of course, I only provisionally booked it so one of you girls can come and see if it's suitable.'

'I'll go,' Daisy offered.

Phil arranged to meet her the next day. 'Now, what else – oh yes, publicity. Poppy, did you do up something for us?'

'Well,' I licked my lips, 'I thought a letter to all the celebrities and their agents would work along with an Uncle Sam-type poster.' I unrolled a poster that I'd got Gavin to sketch up for me. It was a caricature of the four women (stolen from photos my mother had) with the slogan *We Want You!* I'd been a bit apprehensive about showing it to them as I was afraid they might take offence, but unbelievably they loved it. I'd thought all was well until Daisy asked, 'But why did the artist draw those women? Surely our faces would have been better.'

Avril laughed. 'Darling,' she said patronisingly, 'we might look good for our age but even *I*'m not deluded enough to think that I'd entice a young hunky man to do what I want him to do. No, those funny faces are better.'

'Right,' Daisy said doubtfully. 'OK.'

Hastily I folded up the poster before anyone else said anything. There was no way this poster was being dumped – it was genius, I thought. It had been Gavin's idea to do their faces. 'And now for my letter,' I said, unfolding it. 'I plan to email most of the agencies with it. Then I'll send out the poster.'

They clucked approvingly at this. Computers were not their forte – nor mine – but Pete said he'd take care of it for me.

'OK,' I took a deep breath and my voice shook a little as I read out what I'd written. It was like being in school again and being asked to read out a story you'd done. By the time I reached the end, my voice was squeaking. 'So, go on, give that body and wonderful personality away to someone who probably doesn't deserve it for a cause that most definitely does.' I stopped and looked around nervously. 'That's it.'

There was a silence that to my ears seemed to last for ages, but then my mother clapped her hands. 'Oh, that's wonderful, Poppy. If I were a celebrity I'd definitely auction myself.'

'It's one thing auctioning yourself, quite another getting someone to buy you,' Avril sniggered.

Mam looked offended. 'And what's that supposed to mean?' she demanded imperiously.

'Nothing,' Avril replied innocently, batting her cosmetically enhanced eyes. 'It's just that some people would fetch more than others.'

'Now, now, girls,' Phil said gaily, 'let's move on. Daisy what have you—'

'I'd get more than you any day,' my mother hissed. Her bad mood re-emerged. She tossed her blonde hair over her shoulders.

'Of course you would,' Avril said mockingly. 'More rejections.'

'Girls,' Phil clapped her hands like a schoolteacher.

'I took the liberty of phoning RTE,' Daisy began, trying to talk over my mother and Avril who were getting quite nasty. 'But unfortunately they said that unless—'

'Let's put ourselves up for auction and see who gets the most then,' Avril sneered.

'I will not subject myself to that humiliation,' my mother gasped.

'Oh, well, I see,' Avril smugly began to study her nail varnish which was a bright pink. 'It'd be humiliating for you all right. I mean, you must be what, ten years older than I am? But still and all, I'd have thought you'd be used to rejection.'

'I—am—not!' My mother was outraged. Though whether it was at the ten-year slur or the rejection one, I'm not sure.

'Like I said, I phoned RTE and they're very interested providing we—'

'Well then,' Avril quirked her eyebrows. 'Show me the money.'

'Ridiculous,' my mother hissed.

Avril said nothing.

'RTE are very interested in publicising the auction provided that we—'

'OK then, you're on,' my mother snapped.

'Mam!' I couldn't believe it. 'You can't!'

183

'She just did,' Avril smirked.

'This is childish,' I glared at the two of them. 'It's celebrities we're trying to attract.'

'And we are celebrities around here,' Avril said. 'Everyone knows us and our good works.'

I suppose she had a point. They weren't exactly the humble charity givers that were mentioned in the bible. No, my mother and her friends were the guys that went to the top of the church and announced to everyone just how generous and upright they were. So, yes, I suppose people did know them.

'Well,' Daisy licked her lips. 'Can I continue now?'

Mam smiled uneasily at me and I refused to smile back. My mother, up for auction. What would Dad say?

'Well, the person who gets her will probably see more of her than I do,' Dad muttered as I let myself into my house. He'd agreed to mind Billy again for me as I'd gone to the meeting straight after work. 'Now, Poppy, Billy has done his homework – though I must say, his reading isn't very good. He got a book home to read and he couldn't make head nor tail out of it.'

'He's not supposed to be able to understand it, Dad. I have to read it for him and he points out the words as I go.'

'Well, he never said.'

I put some water into the kettle to make myself a cuppa.

'And that woman from next door called in,' Dad followed me down the kitchen. 'Apparently her TV wasn't working and she wanted to know if yours was.'

'Oh, and was it?'

'Well, yes it was, so I offered to have a look at hers. Her

184

aeriel had come out and she'd put it in the wrong socket. She's a nervous kind of woman, isn't she?'

'Yes, I suppose.'

Dad looked around the kitchen and said wonderingly, 'I couldn't believe it, but her house is even smaller than yours.'

I clamped down my irritation. 'It's not, it's just that Pete has made the most of the space in here. See, he's put in shiny tiles so that they reflect the light – it makes the room look bigger,' I explained once again.

Dad had a good look at the tiles. 'Oh, right, I see. Very good. It's a wonder he's still messing about being a waiter, isn't it?'

I ignored the comment. 'Tea?' I asked instead.

He nodded. 'Yes, I'll stay for a while, if you don't mind. Your mother isn't talking to me and I'd rather not meet her until later.' He sat down at the table and looked at me. 'Just a little milk now, Poppy. You always use too much, and for someone who hasn't much money it's a bit wasteful.'

'Dad, saving on a bit of extra milk is hardly going to pay the mortgage for a month,' I scoffed, pouring only a small amount of milk into his cup all the same. When we were sitting opposite each other, I asked apprehensively, 'So, what's the story with you and Mam? She was in a pretty bad mood today all right.'

Dad rolled his eyes and took a sip from his mug. 'It's not as if I did it on purpose,' he muttered. 'But you know your mother, she takes offence easily.'

I said nothing. There was no best way to reply to this.

'The residents' association election was on last night,' Dad continued eventually. 'And as you know, your mother had her heart set on being chairwoman. Why, I don't know.

185

I think she wants to plant flowers or something at the front of the estate. Anyway, I nominated her.'

'Good.'

Dad licked his lips. 'Only, well, one of the neighbours nominated me. It's not as if I asked him to. So your mother said that I wasn't interested in the election and that she was up for it and that the two of us couldn't go up against each other. And then it struck me: why shouldn't I go up? Your mother is never around and it'd be interesting. So I said that I would like to go up. Then Avril – that woman who your mother likes – she said, very nicely, that she seconded my chairmanship. And your mother went ballistic. And Avril said that I'd be good for the job as I'd been a busi- nessman and that I'd be good at negotiating things, like the price for the upkeep of the estate and things like that.'

So that's why Mam and Avril had been at loggerheads this morning, I thought.

'And your mother took offence at this. She took it person- ally. She told Avril that she didn't know the first thing about me, and Avril said that she knew your mother and that all your mother would be interested in would be the grass verge outside her own house.'

'No!'

'And I said that that wasn't fair and that Avril should take it back,' Dad said self-righteously. 'And Avril said she would, but only if I went up for election. And your mother said that she didn't care if Avril never took it back. Anyway, the upshot of it is that I'm in charge of the residents' associa- tion and your mother isn't.'

'Oh.'

Dad sighed deeply. 'Well, your mother lost all credibility when she started shouting. You can't be emotional and be on a committee, I told her. But she wouldn't listen. She stormed out and I have to say, I was a bit hurt at her lack of support for me.' He took a gulp of his tea. 'But do you know what, Poppy, I'm looking forward to the challenge of it. It'll give me something to do. Of course, I had to reschedule my timetable to fit it in, but it slots in nicely. A meeting once a month but more if something urgent comes up.'

I was about to ask what urgent things can come up in a residents' association when Billy charged in through the back door, slamming it open and making the glass panes rattle. 'Billy!' I jumped a little.

'Go outside,' my father ordered, 'and come in again properly!'

I was about to tell my dad not to talk to Billy like that, when to my surprise, Billy bowed his head and meekly exited. Then, a second later, he pushed open the door gently and closed it just as gently.

'Good,' my father said, without a hint of a smile. 'That's two karate chops now. Three more and I'll buy you something.'

Billy beamed and bounced out into the hall.

'Karate chops?' I asked, stunned at this quiet version of my son, not quite sure whether I liked it. Or the fact that there seemed to be some sort of bribery going on. 'What's all that about?'

'It's about behaving himself. Honestly, Poppy, you and that husband of yours seem content to let him run wild. Well, while I'm in charge, he'll do things my way.'

I glared at him. 'He doesn't run wild.'

'I merely use a reward system, it's no different to what my employees were used to when I was in charge.

187

Performance-based rewards. If Billy shuts the door quietly, he gets a karate chop. If he doesn't shout, he gets tanks, and so on. He seems to like it.'

'Sort of like a star chart?'

'Star chart?'

'Getting stars if you're good.'

Dad nodded. 'Yes, I suppose.'

Billy had hated star charts when I'd tried it with him. I'd even got Pete to do it out on the computer so that it looked really cool, but he'd turned his nose up at it. 'Who wants stupid stars anyway,' he'd scoffed. 'They're for girls.' I'd never thought of tanks or guns or stuff like that.

'Do you watch parenting programmes, Dad?'

He began to choke on his tea. After he'd spluttered and coughed he looked at me as if I was a loon. 'Parenting programmes? What on earth would I watch those for?'

And I kicked myself for the question. I mean, what would he know about parenting – he hadn't even been there when I was growing up.

188

23

PETE LOOKED LOVELY in a suit. He hadn't worn a suit since that horrible night of my father's retirement do, which seemed so long ago. It was his navy blue suit, and to me, having not seen it in ages, it didn't look as dated any more. He looked scrummy, his dark hair just the right side of messed up and his green eyes, as ever, huge and innocent. He looked ripe for corruption. The tight line of his jaw betrayed his anxiety though.

'What do you suppose she wants?' he asked me.

'I dunno.' I was trying to squeeze myself into a skirt. It wasn't working. Frustrated, I gazed at it. 'I couldn't have put on that much weight,' I said. 'It was never that tight before.' But before, I'd spent three mornings a week at the gym, not sitting behind a till. I yanked the skirt up viciously and I heard an on ominous tearing sound. 'Oh shit!' Tears, never far away sprung to my eyes. 'This is just typical. My favourite skirt and now it's ripped – just like everything else in my life.' I threw it across the room and sat down on the bed, putting my face in my hands as the stupid, stupid tears leaked out of my eyes.

Pete sat down awkwardly beside me. 'I dunno, I think it might look nice with a big hole in the backside of it. I'd enjoy looking at it anyway.'

I couldn't laugh. 'It's not funny, Pete,' I sobbed. 'How can you make a joke out of it!'

He said nothing for a second and the only sound was from me crying and trying not to. Then he rubbed me on the back and said, 'Isn't it better to laugh than cry, ey?' His fingers wound their way through my hair. 'The worse things are, the more you should laugh, Poppy. Breaks it all up.'

'Well, if that's the case, we should be in hysterics,' I hiccuped, half-snappily.

So he started to tickle me.

We were late for our appointment. So much for responsible parenting. But I had to redo my eyes because all my mascara had run. There was also some stubble rash on my face that had to be concealed as Pete had taken advantage of me crying and tried to have sex with me. And how could I disappoint him? I mean, his mother was arriving in two days and that would be the end of any sort of a sex life as far as I was concerned.

Pete was on a half-day from work and I'd asked my dad to pick Billy up from school as we had a two-thirty appointment with Billy's principal. And though neither of us would admit it to each other, we were bricking it.

Anyhow, we arrived ten minutes late full of apologies. The principal and Miss Walsh were very nice about it and asked us to sit down. Pete grasped my hand under the table. I liked that, it meant we were in it together.

'Now,' Mr Harvey said, clasping his hands together in front of him, 'Miss Walsh and I would like to have a word with you about Billy.'

I swallowed. Pete tensed beside me.

'We both feel that Billy is just not settling into school here.'

'How?' Pete asked, and there was an edge to his voice.

Mr Harvey sensed it too and he flushed a little. 'I know this is hard for you both, but please bear with me – we're only doing this with Billy's best interests in mind.'

'I know you are,' I said firmly, giving Pete's hand a squeeze to make him shut up. 'Please, has he been in trouble again?'

Mr Harvey turned to Miss Walsh who paused. She looked like she was choosing her words carefully and I didn't like that, it always meant bad news. 'Well, I've been observing him for the past while and despite my best efforts he seems unable to get on with his own peer group. There is always some scrap in the yard and Billy is usually in the middle of it.'

'He says they tease him,' I defended my son, beginning to sound like Pete now. 'He says they call him a show-off.'

Miss Walsh bowed her head. Then lifted it up again. Here it comes, I thought, in a sort of semi-suicidal way, the words that will shatter us.

'He breaks up their games, insisting that his games are better. He's always interrupting the other children when they're talking. He encourages them to climb the school walls which, quite frankly, is dangerous.' She paused again. 'And I asked the special needs teacher we have here to see him and we both agree that his work in school is not up to the standard of his age group. He's finding it a terrible struggle, Poppy.'

From the corner of my eye I saw Pete gulp hard. He went a little pale too.

'Oh,' was all I could manage. It was as if I'd been hit, very hard, in the stomach.

'He's very good at things that interest him,' Miss Walsh went on, trying, I think, to be kind. 'But, I do think that

Billy needs to be assessed. That he needs to see someone in relation to his behaviour.'

'See someone?' Pete let go of my hand and stood up. 'What exactly are you saying?'

'Mr Shannon, please sit down,' Mr Harvey urged.

'No,' Pete barked. 'What are you saying? That there is something wrong with our son? That he's disturbed or something?'

'Mr Shannon, if you'd please sit down!' His tone was more exasperated now.

'No! What are you saying?'

'Pete,' I stood up and touched his arm. 'Please, sit down. Come on.'

He turned to me, his lovely green eyes blazing. 'I am not going to sit here and be told that my son is ill. There's nothing wrong with him.' He jabbed his finger in the direction of Miss Walsh. 'It's not our fault you can't control him.'

'Pete!'

Miss Walsh seemed unperturbed. 'I'm sorry you feel that way—'

'I'm going.' Pete looked at me. 'Poppy?'

I shook my head and sat back down. Somehow, I'd known. Billy had always been a little wild, a little hyper, but it seemed to be getting worse. The only person who had any control over him was my dad, which was completely tragic as the man had had no parenting skills whatsoever. 'Sit down, Pete.'

His reply was a slam of the classroom door.

There was silence after he left. I was acutely embarrassed. 'Sorry about that,' I muttered, unable to look them in the face. 'He's been under a lot of stress recently and I think this is just, well, it's too much for him.'

They said nothing.

'He's not normally like that,' I said then, beginning to babble. 'Usually it's me storming out and slamming doors.' I attempted a smile, which wobbled like jelly.

It seemed to ease things. Miss Walsh smiled back a little. 'Well, maybe you can talk to your husband yourself,' she said as she drew out a sheet of paper. 'Now, as you know we've school summer holidays soon and unfortunately we've used up our assessment funding for this year. If Billy is to be assessed, through the school, we can arrange for it to be done next academic year. But both you and your husband would need to sign a consent form.' She handed me a form which I numbly took from her.

'You can, if you like,' Mr Harvey said, and his voice was gentle, 'arrange for a private assessment yourself. Bring Billy to a GP who will refer him on to a psychologist. It's expensive but you can claim the money on your tax return.'

I stared at him blankly.

'If it were me,' Mr Harvey continued, 'I would get him sorted out during the school holidays. That way, if any special requirements are needed in school, they can be arranged before Billy comes back. Or if Billy needs medication, he'd have time to get used to it. And then, when school starts, we can meet with you about any recommendations made for his education.' He paused, gauging my reaction before continuing. 'It's entirely up to you, but if you do get him assessed during the holidays, you'll have to fill out some assessment forms, and so will Miss Walsh.'

'Here's my home address,' Miss Walsh said, passing me another piece of paper.

I stared dumbly at the page. Psychologists? Billy needed a psychologist? In that moment, I knew what failure was. I had failed at the only thing I'd ever thought I might stand a chance at. The words on the page danced in front of my eyes, in and out, in and out.

'Would you like a drink of water?' Miss Walsh asked.

I shook my head, stood up and pocketed the page in my coat. 'No, no, I'll go now. Thank you. Thank you.'

I don't know what she said after that, I couldn't even hear her.

Pete was lounging against the car when I stumbled from the building. He looked shamefaced at me. 'Sorry for leaving you,' he muttered.

'Billy needs to go to the doctor.'

He glared at me. 'He does not. There is nothing wrong with our son.'

'You didn't stay to hear it all, did you?' I taunted, wrenching open the car door. 'So don't talk about what you don't know.'

Wisely, he didn't reply.

24

I SPENT THE next few days in a bit of a daze trying, I suppose, to get my head around the fact that Billy wasn't normal. Whatever normal was. I suppose, in a subliminal way, I had always suspected it but was afraid to confront it. Instead, I'd watch parenting programmes featuring the most bizarrely behaved kids and think to myself, well, at least Billy isn't *that* bad. And in every case, in these programmes, it was the parents' fault, so I'd figured all I had to do was copy the woman on the telly, or be more patient, or whatever. Only it hadn't worked.

I spent those days studying Billy every second I could, wondering just what it was about him that was different. But I knew. It was as if there was an energy force trapped inside him that was bouncing off his bones and skin trying to get out. And the force of it trying to escape meant that Billy bounced from one thing to another. And it wasn't just that, I observed, it was his aggressiveness too. The way at six years of age he could shout and demand things from Tommy, and Tommy, being the good-natured child he was, always gave in, to prevent fights. I studied my child and realised, with slight horror, that I was looking for his flaws and ignoring his good points: the way he'd cuddle me hard, his sense of humour, and yes, his boundless energy. I liked his energy. His verve. It was him.

I tried to talk to Pete about it. I showed him the consent form we had to sign. He took it from me and I said, 'Do you think we should get him assessed?' And his reply was, 'Well, if you think so,' and 'if it bothers you so much.' There was no 'we'. It implied that I was dissatisfied with my son and that he thought that Billy was fine. It also implied that if things went wrong, I'd be blamed. There was no way I was making a decision on my own like that. When I pressed him, it'd make no difference. I felt as if I was banging my head against a wall. In fairness, he did eventually sign the form, but I couldn't bring myself to drop it into the school. Instead, I went about asking everyone what they thought.

My mother was against it. In fact she was appalled by the very notion. 'You only go to one of these people when you're old and have no one to talk to,' she snapped. 'Or if you're old and have made a gigantic mess of your life. Now, honestly, Poppy, what would a six-year-old have to tell a psychiatrist?'

'Psychologist, Mam,' I corrected her.

'All the same,' she snorted. Then she said, 'I need one of those though. I mean, who have I got to talk to, ey? Your father is spending more and more time reading up on by-laws and council grants and things like that. That should be me. Me!' And there followed a long rant about my father. Then she decided to buy a dress to cheer herself up.

Dad, surprisingly, wasn't as shocked as my mother. Though he thought a bit of discipline was all Billy needed. 'You and Pete have the child ruined. Pete lets him get away with murder. Yesterday, before you came home, Pete arrived back and because he wasn't paying enough attention to Billy, Billy hit him. A big wallop, right on the leg.'

'Pete wouldn't let Billy get away with that.' If anything,

I was the soft one. I thought of all the times Pete had tried to impose some kind of discipline and I'd intervened. The thought made me squirm.

'Well, he did. And I said, "Are you going to discipline that child?" and he glared at me.'

'Well, Dad, maybe you shouldn't have said anything. Pete's a bit upset about—'

'Being upset about things doesn't mean that you let your child get away with murder.'

I laughed a little. 'Dad, it was hardly murder.'

'A bit of discipline,' Dad said sagely.

It was more than discipline though. I'm sure his teacher disciplined him in school and it still hadn't done any good. For days I tortured myself over what I should do. And then, the arrival of Pete's mother pushed it to the back of my mind. I never thought I'd welcome that woman but it was easier to accept her arrival than it was to ponder over Billy.

Saturday morning. Pete, after giving me a brief kiss, left the house to go down to his childhood home to pick his mother up. Both of us had been up early since neither of us could sleep. I'd spent the previous evening cleaning out the bigger box-room in preparation for her arrival. I'd washed it down and tidied it up. Freshly laundered curtains hung in the windows and I'd even bought her a new duvet cover and sheets. Pete had hung a full-length mirror on one wall and the way it made the room bigger was quite amazing. The two of us had stared around when we'd finished, pleased with our work. 'She'll like it,' I remarked. He'd looked at me gratefully, but the issue of Billy still danced between us and neither of us could quite bring ourselves to embrace the other. Instead, I'd asked him if he wanted some supper.

Gavin called over about an hour after Pete left. I hadn't been expecting him but it was such a relief to see him. As I watched him saunter up our drive, I suddenly envied him his relatively carefree life. He had a look of someone completely content with his world. His long hair, which I'd bet hadn't seen a hairdresser in years, suited his arty look of tattered jeans and a combat jacket.

'Hi!' I opened the door before he could knock and couldn't help the smile breaking out on my face.

'Hi yourself,' he came in and looked about. 'Godzilla not here yet?'

'Stop!' I flapped my arm at him and led the way to the kitchen. 'The poor woman is sick.'

'Yeah, guess so.' He sat down at the table and pulled a load of sweets from his pocket. 'For Bill. Where is he?'

'At Tommy's.' I bit my lip. 'Gav, would you mind if I asked you to take them back? I'm trying to ban sweets from the house for the moment.'

'Ban sweets?' Gavin quirked an eyebrow. 'Have you gone mad, woman? Has the stress of having the mother-in-law from hell in your house completely wrecked your brain?'

'Stop!' I said again. 'She's sick!'

He gave an unrepentant grin. 'So, what's the story?' He looked me up and down and, to my embarrassment, I flushed. 'You on a diet?'

'No.' I turned away, uncomfortable being with him on my own all of a sudden. I wasn't attracted to him, I told myself furiously. I busied myself filling the kettle before turning back. 'It's because of Billy,' I muttered.

'Billy? What? Are his teeth in bits?'

'No. Hasn't Pete told you about the meeting we had with Billy's teacher?'

'Nope.'

That surprised me. The two were so close, I'd often felt the one left out. 'About her saying that Billy was disruptive in class and might need,' I swallowed on the word, 'to be assessed?'

'Naw,' Gavin's jaw dropped. 'He never said.'

I shrugged. 'Well, it was only a couple of days ago so maybe he hasn't had time. And what with his mother and all . . .' I let my voice trail off.

Gavin stared at the sweets on the table. Then he looked at me. 'So, what's the story with the sweets?'

'Well,' I said, 'maybe the sweets make him hyper. Maybe he doesn't need assessing at all. I think I'm just overfeeding him additives or something.'

'Mmm.'

'What does "mmm" mean?' I snapped. I think I'd wanted him to agree with me that yes, indeed that did sound quite plausible.

'Nothing,' Gavin began to stuff the sweets back into his jacket pocket. 'I'll buy him a toy or something the next time, ey?'

'Do you think he's disruptive?' I asked.

'Poppy, I don't think—'

'Please, Gav, be honest. Please.' I crossed towards him and stopped in front of him. 'Please. What do you think?'

'What does Pete think?' he asked instead.

'Who knows?' My voice was bitter. I shrugged, ashamed of giving out about Pete in front of his mate. 'I dunno. He won't talk about it.'

'Oh.'

'What do you think?'

'Poppy, this is between you and Pete. I like you both and it's not for me to say.'

'Yes it *is*.' I couldn't believe this. 'Come on, Gav, help me out here.' My voice broke a little. 'I can't do it on my own. I can't make a decision like this on my own. And you know Billy, you've always known him. What do you think?'

'Hey,' he stood up and caught my hand. 'Hey, don't cry. Come on, sit down.' He pulled me down on to the chair beside him. 'Don't, Poppy. Come on.'

'I – can't – help – it,' I sniffed, exaggerating just a little so that he'd feel sorry for me and give me his opinion. 'I . . . I want to do the best for Billy.'

Gavin was silent. He spent the time looking at me but I could see there was a bit of a battle going on in his head. Eventually he said, carefully, 'I don't think the teacher would have said anything if it was just a case of discipline or a sweet allergy.' He sighed. 'That's my opinion.'

I hadn't expected that. Or had I? I didn't know any more. 'So you think he's disruptive?'

Gavin shrugged. 'I dunno. He's adventurous all right. A bit of a risk taker.'

I gulped. 'My mother says it's a stupid idea.'

He gave a dry laugh. Then he said earnestly, leaning forward in his chair so that he was looking into my face, 'Look, all I know is that helping kids is never stupid. Most of the kids I work with are OK, Poppy. Underprivileged but OK. But, there are a small number who need help. They'll never get it 'cause of who they are. It pisses me off, to be honest, 'cause that lack of help will affect their whole lives.'

He caught my hand. I don't think he was even aware of it. I welcomed it though. A warm, firm hand on mine.

'If you think, even for a second, that Billy needs help, get it for him. It won't do any harm and it could change everything.' Then abruptly he let my hand go.

I nodded slowly, knowing that what he'd said made sense. 'Thanks. Thanks, Gav.'

'No probs.'

'And if Pete does mention it to you, pretend you don't know, OK?'

'Sure.' Then he smiled, 'But since Pete hasn't mentioned it by now, he won't. Pete doesn't talk about stuff unless he wants to.'

He had a point there, I guess. He hadn't talked about his mother's illness since I'd agreed that she could come and stay. He never mentioned Adrian or what was happening with the courts. Things that bothered him, he ignored. I began to wonder, for the first time ever, if he did it to protect me or protect himself.

Satan arrived just after three. My heart jumped as I heard the unmistakable sound of Pete's car pulling into the driveway. Gavin had stayed and had lunch with us. Billy was thrilled and then afterwards Gavin took Billy and a load of other kids up to the green to play soccer. They were still playing when Pete and his mother arrived. I didn't know whether to go to the door and greet them or to stay in the kitchen and pretend I hadn't heard. I decided on going to the door. Smiling, in what I hoped was a welcoming manner, I pulled the door open.

Pete was the first to get out. He shot me a comical look and rolled his eyes and the sight of it cheered me. Then he went around to the passenger door and opened it for his mother. Thelma got out and stood for a second surveying the house. I have to say, she didn't look like a woman who was sick.

'Well,' she said, 'this is a bit of a comedown, ey?'

'We like to think of it as more of a sideways move,' Pete said, grittily jovial as he pulled her bags from the boot.

'That was always your problem, Peter,' Thelma walked up the driveway, 'you could never admit what was in front of your eyes. If this is sideways, then I don't need a breast removed and aggressive therapy.'

Christ! Neither of us quite knew what to say to that. 'Welcome,' I blurted out. 'Will I show you your room?'

'Yes, if you want to, though I hardly think I'll get lost, will I?'

You can get lost if you want to, I felt like saying back. You old bitch. Instead I said, 'Well, in that case, up you go.' And I walked back into the kitchen and shut the door firmly behind me, taking a big deep breath to stop myself from killing her.

I heard Pete dragging her cases up and showing her about and some murmured conversation. He was up there for quite a bit and I had the kettle boiled and biscuits on the table and was half-way through a cuppa when they arrived back down.

Thelma sat her large bulk in a chair and Pete poured her a tea.

'I see Gav's been here,' Pete remarked. 'When did he come?'

'A couple of hours ago.'

'Oh, do you still see that ragamuffin?' Thelma screwed up her nose disdainfully. 'I thought he was leading some kind of a hippy life somewhere.'

'Yes, I still see him,' Pete said evenly.

As if on cue, Gavin and Billy came barging through the back door. Billy, as usual, slammed it and, copying my dad, I said, 'Billy, close that door properly.'

'It is closed properly!' Billy danced in front of me. 'Look, it's shut!'

'You slammed it,' I said. 'Open it again and close it.'

Billy rolled his eyes. 'Have you got sweets, Nana? I hope you have.'

Thelma turned slowly about to face him and said scathingly, 'Even if I had – which I *don't* – you wouldn't get any. Boys that ask for things get nothing.'

'Boys that don't ask get nothing either,' Gavin said pleasantly, sliding in beside her. 'Hiya, Thelma, how's tricks?'

Another scathing look was turned on Gavin. 'That's a bit insensitive, isn't it? I'm having a breast removed in the next couple of days, since you ask.'

Gavin was unperturbed. 'Well, sorry to hear that. I hope it goes well.'

She didn't seem to be able to reply to that. Instead, she spooned more sugar into her tea and stirred it vigorously.

'Maybe the worms are to blame,' Billy piped up. 'You must have loads of them now, Nana.'

Gavin chortled loudly and Pete spluttered on his coffee.

'I don't have—'

'Billy, come on,' I said quickly before the woman combusted. 'Let's go and stick some posters into envelopes for the auction.'

'WORMS!' she roared after us.

25

PETE AND I had decided on a rota for minding his mother, if minding was the right word. It was akin to minding a shark by swimming with it. Pete would be with her in the mornings as he had arranged his shifts so that he'd work from the afternoons until early the next morning. I would be there in the afternoon from two onwards. My father had insisted that he would collect Billy from school so that I could go straight from the job to the house. While I appreciated the gesture, I think I would have preferred more time with my son and less with Thelma.

The first day she was with us, however, was a Sunday. There was no escape to work for me so both Pete and I ended up having to endure her for the whole day. And Thelma was not a woman that slept on of a Sunday. Oh no. She was up at some ungodly hour on God's day of rest, pottering around our kitchen and making a fair bit of noise.

Pete and I woke at the same time. Pete rolled over, looked at the alarm clock and groaned loudly. 'It's only seven,' he hissed. 'Christ!'

'Don't get up,' I whispered. 'If we get up now, she'll think that's what we always do. We have to start as we mean to go on.'

Pete winced. 'But she's sick, and she's meant to be fasting. I can't let her make breakfast.'

He was right. 'OK,' I sat up and immediately felt faint with the sudden movement. 'Let's go down, so.'

Pete sat up too. 'Let's have a look at you,' he said.

'Huh?' I faced him. 'What?'

He touched my face, his fingers lingering on my mouth. 'There,' he grinned. 'One smile plastered into place.'

I gave a snort of laughter and caught his hand. 'No matter what she does,' I said, 'we don't fight, OK?'

'Agreed.'

It was one thing to agree, quite another to carry it out.

When we got down, Thelma was sitting at the table, a large mug of strong coffee to her right and a doorstep of toast to her left. The radio was on some sort of hymn service and she was reading yesterday's paper, which was spread over the whole table.

'Hi,' Pete said cheerily. 'Are you not supposed to be fasting, Mammy?'

'No.' She didn't even glance at him.

'Right.' Pete didn't seem to know what to say, he stood there uselessly, staring at her.

'Isn't your operation tomorrow, Thelma?' I asked. I casually took a couple of sausages and rashers from the fridge. 'I thought you had to fast for twenty-four hours.'

'Tomorrow evening,' she barked, mashed toast falling from her huge mouth. 'I'll fast tonight. Now, can we please stop discussing this?' She frowned at us both before nodding. 'Thanks.'

I gave her the two fingers behind her back but Pete didn't even raise so much as a grin. Instead he slipped in beside her. She ignored him.

I put some sausages and rashers on to our fat-reducing grill and got the frying pan out for some fried eggs. Nobody said anything until the fry was cooked, when Thelma pronounced it a 'heart attack on a plate'. Then she stood up and asked what time mass was. Pete and I looked blankly at each other.

'Well?'

'We don't go to mass here,' I said, my heart speeding up. I didn't want a row first day, but at the same time, we had to assert ourselves or she'd have us doing everything her way.

There was a long silence. Thelma glared at Pete. 'Oh, I see. So you used to go to mass when you lived at home and you go when you visit me, but it was all for show, was it?'

'Mammy, I'm thirty-five years old, I can make my own decisions.'

'Yes,' she nodded. 'And look where they've got you. No job, small house, a—'

'I'll find out when mass is,' I cut across her. 'And Pete or I will bring you.'

'Oh, don't go to any trouble on *my* account.'

I felt like telling her that we wouldn't, but I hadn't the heart. She was sick after all, and maybe the shock of it was just making her into a more horrible person.

'I'll ask Laura next door,' I said, 'but I'll have to wait a while, until she gets up.'

'I like an early mass,' Thelma said. 'When it gets too crowded there are too many children all making noise and it's hard to pray.'

'Well, maybe next week you can go to that,' I said, trying to mollify her. 'But for this week—'

'I could be dead next week!'

'Oh, don't be ridiculous, Mammy, you're not going to die.'

'And you'd know, would you, you being a hotel waiter?'

It took all my will power not to hit her over the head with the frying pan. Pete just glared at her and left the kitchen. She seemed a bit taken aback by his reaction but I saw her shake herself all over, stick her head in the air and walk out of the room like some kind of a battleship.

I ate my fry alone, which I actually welcomed.

I saw a light on at Laura's around ten so I called in to ask her when mass was. She looked surprised at the question.

'It's not for me,' I explained. 'It's for Pete's mother, she's staying with us for a bit.'

'Oh?'

'She's got,' I lowered my voice, it's something my mother always does when she mentions it, 'cancer.'

'Oh, that's terrible!' Laura looked duly sympathetic. 'Pete must be so upset.'

'Yes,' I nodded. 'I suppose he is. Though honestly, Laura, if you met the woman you'd be doing well not to strangle her.'

Laura giggled. She has a real girlie giggle, half shocked, half nervous. 'Oh, stop!'

'I mean it,' I insisted. 'She'll be with us for months. I'll probably spend the last few in jail for murder.'

Laura belted me. 'I think you need mass more than her.'

'This is my penance,' I said. 'I'll get into heaven without all that praying.'

She giggled again.

'So, what times are masses on at?'

Laura reamed off a list of times, which I jotted down.

'There is one at twelve-thirty which Tommy and I go to, I can bring her if you like, give you a break.'

I was touched once again at how thoughtful Laura was. 'Oh, I couldn't inflict her on you.'

'Aw, go on. I'm dying to see what she's like now.'

'You'll see plenty of her, don't worry.' I waved the list about. 'Thanks all the same, Laura, but I'll get Pete to bring her today.'

'Sure. But anytime you need a break or need some help with her, you know where I am, OK?'

I couldn't answer because of the lump in my throat.

26

THE NEXT MORNING there was a lot of activity. Pete, for the first time since we moved to the house, had breakfast with Billy and me, which was nice. What wasn't so nice, of course, was that Thelma was at the breakfast table too. Billy was his usual hyper self, jumping on and off his chair, knocking over his milk, going up to get dressed and coming down with nothing on. The last thing horrified Thelma. Billy danced in front of her, laughing, while Pete chased him about the kitchen and dragged him upstairs.

'That's a fine display,' Thelma said, crossing her arms over her huge chest and pursing her lips. 'Lovely.'

I said nothing. We could hear Pete attempting to dress Billy and telling him that it wasn't nice to run around with no clothes on. Billy was chanting 'Don't care, don't care,' at the top of his voice. Eventually Pete gave up and came back down. He looked at his watch and said to Thelma, 'Right, I suppose we'd better be going. I've put your case in the car so we might as well get there early and get you settled.'

Thelma stood up. 'Settled into a hospital? I'll tell you now, Peter, I'd never feel settled in a hospital.'

Pete rolled his eyes at me. 'Come on,' he said to her.

'Bye, Thelma,' I said, hoping the relief that she was leaving us temporarily didn't show in my voice. 'We'll be in to see you later, after the operation.'

She muttered something, which I'm sure was horrible, and followed Pete from the kitchen. 'Billy,' I called, 'come and say goodbye to your nana.'

'Is she leaving?' Billy called and the hope in his voice was only too evident. He stood at the top of the stairs, his school shirt unbuttoned. 'Are you going now, Nana?'

'I'll be back,' she said to him.

His face dropped and she cackled to herself. I have to say, I did smother a grin of my own.

As she was about to go, I wondered if I should embrace her and wish her luck. I mean, she was undergoing a huge operation, she was bound to feel a bit scared.

'Eh, good luck, Thelma,' I managed. My arms refused to move to hug her.

Thelma looked witheringly at me. 'I won't need luck. That's only for people who don't go to mass.'

'Right.'

She exited then and I could hear her telling Pete that he'd better drive carefully or she would probably be forced to sue him.

I had the consent form in my hand to give to Billy's teacher that morning. I really did mean to give it to her. But then, well, I chickened out, didn't I?

Being in work was a release for me that day. Sitting behind a till, watching people buy pieces of crap, was food for my soul. Add that to the fact that Maxi seemed to have taken a bit of a shine to me since she found out about the auction. There was nothing she wouldn't do for me now, provided it was auction related. Our interaction became if not friendly then slightly more positive than her calling me a posh cow. Now I was the posh cow who was organising an auction.

Mondays were always slow in the shop, I had discovered, as most of the clientele had been on the batter for the weekend and had feck all money to spend. Thursdays were the busy day as it was children's allowance day and a host of other pay out days too. Today, being Monday, it was quiet. Maxi sat at her till filing her nails and humming to the radio. I sat at my till wondering what Billy was doing now and if he was getting into any fights. I had told him that if he was good in school I would buy him something nice. I hoped it worked. I could feel the consent form folded up in my pocket. Why was I so indecisive?

'How's the auction coming along?' Maxi asked, startling me. 'Have you got any big names signed on?'

'The letters were only emailed at the weekend,' I told her, 'and I have the posters ready to send off this afternoon.'

'Posters?' Maxi asked. 'Why don't you shove one up in the shop here? There's lots of people who would be interested. I mean, what do they say – everybody knows somebody.'

'I don't think—'

'Naw, you didn't think of that, did you? Isn't it a good idea? Show me a poster, will ya?'

Reluctantly, afraid to appear too posh or snobby or whatever label she was going to attach to me, I carefully opened an envelope and pulled out a poster. 'It's for the celebrities,' I explained. 'I don't think we'll need to advertise for people to come if we get the celebrities on board.'

'Oh,' her face showed her disappointment. 'Right.'

I felt a bit bad as I returned the poster to its envelope.

She had been so full of enthusiasm. 'Thanks for the offer anyway,' I said.

'I told my friends about it,' Maxi went on, 'so we're saving five euro a week each to make a bid on someone. Do you think that would get us a person?'

I seriously doubted it. Not unless Maxi had about five hundred friends. 'Just wait and see,' I said.

There was silence for a bit. Then Maxi asked, 'Why are you working here anyway? I woulda thought that you'd be working in some posh clothes shop or something. I mean, if you know all these celebrities you must be pretty loaded.'

So, I told her. Somehow, telling people didn't seem as bad now, and so much had happened since then that it was almost as if I was talking about someone else. Though at the part where we had to sell our lovely house, my voice broke a little.

'The bastard,' Maxi exclaimed loudly, oblivious to a dark-haired, freckle-faced, stick-thin girl who had just entered the shop. 'Has he been caught yet?'

'No. Pete, my husband, reckons he's left the country.'

'Jaysus,' Maxi cracked her knuckles, 'I hope when they get him they tear him limb from limb. Imagine doing the likes of that?! Imagine.'

'Imagine talking to people you swore you'd never talk to,' the thin girl sneered, making Maxi jump about five feet into the air. She leaned her elbow on the counter and glared at Maxi, who gasped and reddened.

'Eh, hiya, Charlie, it's good to see you,' she stammered.

'I wish I could say the same,' the girl pulled away from Maxi and began a cocky strut towards me. 'And who are you?' she asked. She looked like a sick version of Maxi.

'Poppy,' I tried to say pleasantly. This young wan was

obviously Charlotte. 'And you must be Charlotte. I hear loads of nice things about you from Maxi.'

Charlotte stood in front of me with her hands on her hips. 'Oh, so she talks to you a lot, does she?'

'I don't know,' I said, feeling a little intimidated by her aggressive stance. 'I don't know how much she talked beforehand.'

Charlotte's eyes narrowed.

'Charlie,' Maxi said urgently, 'you aren't meant to be here. Isobel said she'd get the police if you set foot in the place, do you remember?'

'Isobel isn't here,' Charlotte swaggered.

Maxi pointed up to a security camera.

Charlotte stuck out her tongue and waggled her thin hips. Then gave the camera the finger. 'I only came to say hi – you haven't even rang me since last week.'

'Yeah, sorry about that,' Maxi looked guilty.

'No you're not,' Charlotte's face curled up and she sounded a little hurt. 'If you were so sorry you would have rung, and now, when I come in here, you're talking to Miss,' she looked me up and down, 'Miss Perfect Pants.'

'She's not as much fun as you,' Maxi said hastily, shooting me an apologetic look.

'Sure,' Charlotte gave every impression that she was about to throw a huge wobbler.

'Maxi, if you want to go for a coffee with Charlotte, you can. I'll mind the fort here,' I said quickly.

'We don't need your interfering,' Charlotte sneered.

'Coffee, Charlie?' Maxi asked.

'Yeah. Right.' Charlotte cast a withering look my way and on her way out she knocked over a whole display of cheap and smelly deodorants. I reckon they'd take underarm hair off too with one spray. Anyway, I had to tidy them all up.

Maxi didn't arrive back until after one-thirty. I was a bit pissed off with her to be honest. Talk about taking advantage.

'Sorry about that,' she said as she slid in behind her till.

I didn't answer. At least Billy was being picked up from school, I thought. At least I didn't have that worry on my mind.

'There was nowhere around here that would serve Charlie,' Maxi said, 'so we had to catch the bus to somewhere that she wasn't known. It was a pretty long journey.'

'What?' I hardly believed that pathetic excuse.

'Well, she's had jobs all over and mostly got kicked out of them. She starts off good and then for some reason, she just loses her jobs and she annoys people and everything. So everyone knows her. So we had to go to a place where no one knew her.'

'Right.'

Maxi coughed. 'She's my only sister so it's important to meet up.'

'Of course.'

'She can be a bit mental, to be honest. But she's OK if you get to know her, and she doesn't rob you.'

'Yeah, well, Maxi, I have to cash up now, OK?'

'And right, you know what I said the first day, about her not being a thief, well, it was true. She didn't steal the dusters but like, who'd believe that, ey?'

'Who indeed,' I said. I knew I certainly didn't.

27

PETE AND I went in to see Thelma that evening. Dad said he'd stay and put Billy to bed. To my shame, I didn't warn him that it took at least an hour to get Billy settled at night, and that's when he's tired. I'd thought it was normal, never having had kids before. But maybe it wasn't. Maybe it was another sign that Billy needed help. Of course, I couldn't ask Pete about this as he was strung out about his mother. He'd arranged a couple of hours off work to see her but they were expecting him back in at ten to make it up.

When we'd rung, the doctor had told us that the operation had gone very well and that they'd removed what they fully expected to be the whole tumour. They'd also removed some lymph glands from her armpit for examination.

Pete caught my hand as we made our way to the IC unit where Thelma had been put as a precaution after the operation. Peering through the glass, I could see her, surrounded by machines and tubes as she lay motionless on the bed. There was a nurse monitoring the three or so patients inside. She came out when she saw us.

'Hello,' she smiled, in the calm way that all nurses seem to have. 'Who have you come to see?'

'Thelma Shannon,' Pete said a little breathlessly. He indicated his mother.

'Oh yes, Thelma,' the nurse nodded. 'Well, she's doing well. She's been sedated against the pain and that's why she's a bit groggy, but her operation was a success.'

'Good. Good.' Pete swallowed hard and squeezed my hand. 'Can we see her?'

'It's one visitor only in the ICU, I'm afraid,' the nurse looked at us apologetically.

'You go,' I gave Pete a gentle push as I let his hand go. 'I'll wait here for you.'

He didn't answer me, just followed the nurse inside. I saw him stand at his mother's bed and take her hand as he began to murmur words that I couldn't hear. At this, my eyes unexpectedly filled with tears. I don't quite know what it was, I think maybe it was the fact that Pete was separated from me by glass. I could see him but I couldn't touch him or communicate with him, and lately that was the way our marriage felt like it was going. I knew he still loved me, and I knew that I still loved him, but there was something not quite right or honest in the way we were dealing with each other and I didn't know what it was. I watched him, standing beside his mother, talking to her, stroking her hand. She didn't move, but he kept standing there and trying anyway. When he came out, after about thirty minutes, he asked if I wanted to go in.

'No, it's fine.'

He nodded absently.

'Come on,' I took his hand. 'Let's go and get a burger or something.'

'But Billy—'

'Dad has him. Come on, we haven't been out in ages. And it'll do you good.'

'We can't afford it.'

'A burger?' I scoffed. 'I'm talking McDonald's, Pete.'

He shook his head. 'No offence, Poppy, but I'm not hungry, OK?' A small smile.

I bit my lip. 'Yeah. Fine. We'll go home, so.'

'Yeah.'

He hardly talked all the way home, and when he did, it was mostly one-word answers to questions I asked him about his mother. He kept his eyes glued on the road and his hands tight on the steering wheel.

We pulled up at home and Dad must have seen us arrive as he opened the door for us and asked, 'How's Thelma?'

'OK,' Pete answered. 'She's in the IC unit so she's pretty heavily sedated.' He looked about. 'Where's Bill?'

'In bed,' Dad answered as we went through to the living room. 'Oh, he's a hard man to pin down for bed – thirty minutes before he stayed there. But there was some trouble between him and the red-headed boy next door tonight and that lady next door was pretty angry with him so I think it helped him stay inside at least.'

'Trouble?' I asked.

Pete left the room and I saw him pick up the phone outside.

'Yes,' Dad nodded. 'I don't know what happened, I was replacing your light bulbs for you.'

At my startled look, he said, 'Energy-saving bulbs. Much better for the environment and cheaper for you, what with,' he paused, waved his arm about the room and didn't finish. I suppose he was going to say, what with you being so poor, or something along those lines.

'How much do I owe for the bulbs?'

'Nothing, a gift.'

I hoped Pete wouldn't notice, he'd be highly offended. As

if on cue, Pete yelled, 'What's wrong with the bloody bulb? It's dim or something.'

'It'll brighten up,' Dad called back.

'Hey, where did this come from?'

Both Dad and I ignored him. Dad was now back on the subject of Billy. 'There I was changing the bulb in your kitchen when I heard the lady next door shouting for the boys to come inside. The next thing I know is that Billy is back and looking guilty. So I asked him what the matter was and he shrugged. Anyway, he didn't go out for the rest of the night.'

'Oh.' I felt vaguely uneasy. What the hell had happened now?

'Your mother asked me to ask you if you posted the posters today.' Dad sat down on the sofa, obviously determined to stay for a while.

'I did.'

'Good,' he nodded slowly. 'At least that's something that will make her happy. She's being very grumpy lately. Oh, and another thing she told me to tell you: there's a meeting on Saturday in our house about this auction. It's at twelve.'

'OK.'

From the hall, I could hear Pete talking to someone on the phone. The conversation obviously wasn't going too well because at one stage Pete raised his voice and it sounded like he was shouting.

'He seems to be in bad form lately, doesn't he?' Dad said gesturing towards the hall.

I didn't answer.

'A bit like your mother,' Dad observed, for the second time. 'I can't do right for doing wrong.'

I wondered if I was meant to say something.

'I mean,' Dad said, 'take my retirement, for instance. I thought she'd be thrilled that the two of us could do things together, but oh no, she doesn't seem to want me near her at all.'

He sounded a little hurt and I felt sorry for him. 'Well, Dad,' I ventured, 'you were away a lot when you worked, and Mam built up her own life. You can't expect her to give it up just because you're around now.'

'I don't expect that,' Dad sounded slightly shocked. 'That's not what I mean.'

'Well, maybe you should—'

'What?' Dad said, 'Get involved in her life? You think that would be good?'

I hadn't been going to say that at all. I'd actually been going to tell Dad to get his own life. 'Well, I don't—'

'I could show an interest in her charity activities,' Dad nodded. 'I could do that. Do you think that would work?'

It actually wasn't a bad idea. 'She might like that,' I said cautiously. 'Maybe you should run it by her.'

'No,' Dad shook his head, a huge smile on his face as he stood up. 'No, she'll love it, I'm sure of it.' He picked his jacket up from the chair, a sort of jauntiness about him now that he thought his marriage difficulties were at an end. 'Well, I'll be going now, Poppy. Tell Billy he has four tanks and one more and I'll get him a surprise, OK?'

'Sure. Bye, Dad.'

'Bye now.' I walked him into the hall.

Pete slammed down the phone as I came out, a scowl on his face. Then he picked it up and dialled again.

'Bye, Pete,' Dad said.

'Bye,' Pete nodded. 'And thanks.'

'No problem.'

Dad climbed into his car and bipped his horn as he drove away.

'Hiya Michael,' I heard Pete say, and the reason for his raised voice became clear – he was ringing the brothers from hell.

Great, he'd be in an even worse mood now.

28

I T WAS COOL. I'd switched on the computer, the way Pete had shown me, and there were six emails for me.

Six.

I clicked on my inbox and the names of various agencies came up. Now how did I open them? I wasn't exactly computer literate, never having had to be before.

Eventually, after racking my brains, I dragged my little pointer thingy over the name of the first agency. Immediately the message came up. I felt very proud of myself.

Dear Poppy,

Lucy Ann and Christopher Bowen would be delighted to be involved in your auction. However, both of them are married and they say there is no question of them wanting to go on a date with anyone, but they would be willing to offer their services to facilitate actors' workshops. We hope this is acceptable.

Acceptable? Bloody sure!

Lucy Ann was a minor soap star but was, according to all show-biz reports, set to do great things. Christopher Bowen was even more minor than Lucy Ann. His only appearance to date had been in an ad for milk. But his good looks and fabulous teeth had earned him some inches in the newspapers. Neither of them would fetch an awful lot, but it was a start.

The other five agencies that had replied also offered me minor stars. It was apparent that a lot of them were doing it for the publicity they'd get. None of the major agencies had come on board yet, but that was understandable, I told myself. Obviously the bigger the celebrity the harder it would be to arrange time off. I could only keep my fingers crossed.

Slightly deflated, I switched off the computer and went downstairs. Billy was in the front room, sitting upside down on the sofa. The telly was blaring.

'Billy, come on and let's do your letters,' I said. 'Granddad told me to give you a tank if you're good at them tonight. He said you need to practise them.'

'Only Granddad can give tanks,' Billy said, looking up at me from his weird position. 'You can't.'

'I can.'

'No, you can't. I don't want to do my letters. They're boring.'

'Billy,' I made my voice really stern, though it quivered a little. 'Stand up, get your bag and let's do your letters.'

He ignored me.

'Billy!'

He started to sing over me. The more I raised my voice, the louder he sang. It used to make me laugh once upon a time, but not any more. Instead, my eyes watered and I felt a little sick. He didn't seem to have respect for anyone. Plus, his whole disobedience only underlined the fact that maybe, just maybe, he needed help, or drugs or something.

'Billy!' I shouted, determined to have him obey me.

222

'LA! LA! LA!'

I don't know what happened then. I know that I yanked him and pulled him upright. I held his arm so tight that he squirmed. 'Go up and get your bag!'

'You're hurting me!'

'I'll hurt you a lot more if you don't do it!'

'Let–me–go!'

'I will if you get your bag!'

'Let–me–go!' Then he started screaming. 'Oooooohhhhh, my arm. My arm!'

I let him go and he jumped up and ran out of the room, laughing loudly.

His laugh reverberated in my head. He was laughing at me. So I strode out into the hall and he dodged away. I grabbed him again by the arm and he still laughed. Then I slapped him. On the arm. Really hard.

And he slapped me back. Right on the face.

So I slapped him again.

And again.

He started to cry then, and beg for me to stop. Big fat tears fell from his eyes and I noticed that his arm was roaring red. I let him go and stared at my hand. It stung from the force of the slaps I'd given him. Then *I* started to cry. Huge heaving sobs that came from the very centre of me. The tears weren't only for Billy, they were for me too. What the hell was happening to my life? To me? I'd never hit him before. Even when he'd done worse things. No matter how angry I'd been, I'd retained control, the way Fanny the Fab Nanny advised.

'Billy,' I said, snot coming out of my nose. I held out my arms to him. 'I'm sorry. I really am. Please, don't cry.'

'You hit me,' he sniffed. 'You hit me, Mammy.'

'I know. I got cross.' I gulped hard. 'I'm just tired and fed up, Billy, and I got cross with you.' I sat down on the stair and put my head in my hands. Tears dripped on to my palms and I was aware that I shouldn't cry in front of my child but I truly couldn't help it. And then he came over and rubbed the top of my head with his hands.

'Don't cry, Mammy. Don't cry.'

'Sorry, Billy.'

'It's OK,' he said in his sweet little voice, the one I seldom heard nowadays. 'It's OK.'

I looked up at him.

'You have to forgive when someone says sorry, don't you, Mammy?'

'Yes,' I smiled weakly. At least one of my little lessons had penetrated his active brain.

He sat down beside me on the stairs. 'So I forgive you,' he said, and we had a little hug.

It was after ten when Laura called in. Billy had just fallen asleep after jumping about on his bed for an hour. I didn't bother to discipline him as I felt like a wet rag, completely washed out. And I hadn't the heart either, after slapping him so hard.

I was watching yet another programme on disruptive kids and some woman, dressed in a nanny uniform, was being very firm with them. The mother and father stood by helplessly as their small son told the nanny to 'Fuck off, bitch.' In fact, the mother half-giggled. But it was nerves. I did that too whenever Billy threw wobblers in public.

When the bell went, my heart skipped a beat. Who would be calling at ten at night? I went out into the hall as quietly as I could and peered through the little hole in the door.

Laura was outside, pacing to and fro on the porch and running her fingers nervously through her hair.

'Hi,' I said, opening the door to her. 'What's up?'

She smiled back, but it didn't reach her eyes. 'Can I talk to you for a second, Poppy?'

'Sure,' I pulled the door open wider to let her in. 'What's up?' It was nice, I thought, someone just calling in to me like this.

Laura cleared her throat. 'Well, I don't want this to come between us as neighbours, Poppy. I really don't. But I feel I have to say it anyway.'

Maybe it wasn't so nice her calling in. I felt hurt all of a sudden. What was it about me that people never called just for a chat? 'Say what?' I kept my voice in neutral. My heart, however, was pounding.

'I've told Tommy not to play with Billy any more.'

'What?' I couldn't take that in. 'Why?'

Laura made a hopeless gesture with her hand. 'Now, I'm not blaming Billy,' she hastened to explain, 'but whenever they get together they seem to do the most outrageous things.'

'Like?' I thought this woman was my friend. Granted, not the sort of bosom buddy that I could meet for lunch at the drop of a hat, but just someone nice. Someone different to the brittle people I'd always known.

'Well, jumping from windowsills, for instance,' Laura attempted a smile.

'I sorted that out,' I said in a dead voice. 'I apologised for that.'

'Yeah, yeah, I know you did,' Laura went on. 'But Poppy, one just seems to spark the other. Yesterday, I found the two of them walking on top of the back-garden wall with blind-folds on.'

'Blindfolds?!' The wall was about six-feet high.

'Billy was using one of Pete's ties.'

'He was?' I felt faint.

'So I think it's better if they don't mix. Tommy is easily led, you see.'

I think she was waiting for a response from me, but I couldn't give it. I didn't know what to say. 'Whose idea was the game?' I asked. I had to place my hands against the wall for support.

'Oh, I don't know,' Laura shrugged. 'I don't—'

'Whose idea do you think the game was?' The question came out like the lash of a whip. 'Well?'

Laura flinched. 'Honestly, Poppy—'

'You must have some idea.'

'I don't want this to come between—'

'Whose idea was it?' I pressed.

Laura gulped hard and said quietly, 'Tommy said it was Billy's – but then again, he would, wouldn't he?'

'And Billy?'

'He had run home.'

That sounded like Billy, all right. 'And you, Laura,' I asked quietly, 'whose fault do you think it was?'

'Aw, Poppy—'

'Please?'

She shrugged uncomfortably. 'Well, Tommy never did things like this before,' she answered. 'And you know what it's like for me, Poppy, I can't—' She stopped. 'Jesus, what's wrong? I didn't mean to upset you – honestly, I didn't.'

'I know.' I blinked rapidly, not wanting her to see how badly upset I was. 'I know, it's fine.'

'No, no it's not.' She didn't seem to know what to do.

226

'What's wrong? Look, maybe they can play together if we supervise them. How about that?'

'No. No, it's OK.' Oh God, more bloody tears. My life at the moment seemed awash with them. 'It's just,' I found it hard to say, especially to her who was a single parent and who was doing such a great job with her son, and there I was, with two of us and we weren't coping. 'It's just, well, Billy is having problems in school and his teacher has recommended that he see someone.'

'Oh.'

'He might have ADD or something.'

'Oh, Poppy.' She reached out and clasped my arm. 'Oh, that's hard.'

'Yeah. And Tommy seems to be his only friend. No one else seems to like him and he is a good kid, I know he is.'

'Oh, Poppy.' And then she did something completely unexpected. She pulled me into an embrace. I'd never hugged another woman before, never sought solace from anyone except Pete, and maybe Gavin. And for the first time, I cried over Billy and I cried over the child he might have been if it wasn't for his problems and I cried for all the horrors he was facing in school.

Laura rang her babysitter and promised her twenty euro if she would babysit Tommy for an hour. Then she sat me down at my kitchen table and bustled about my kitchen as if she'd always been there. I blurted out about Pete and my mother thinking it was a load of rubbish but how Gavin had said to get help. And how my dad said it was only a matter of proper discipline.

'He has a point,' Laura said. 'A lot of ADD children need stricter boundaries than other kids.' Then, with two steaming mugs of coffee in front of us, she said, 'And your dad is great with him, isn't he?'

'Is he?'

'Oh yeah, Billy loves him. All the parents laugh to see him charging up to him when he gets out from school. Your dad just stands there and ruffles his hair and Billy is hopping about the place, chatting away. Oh, it's such a pleasure to watch.'

'It is?'

'Yeah. He must have been a great dad to you. He's so helpful, isn't he? He spent ages looking at my TV that time I couldn't get it working and he's so nice to chat to.'

'Yeah,' I said faintly. Dad was obviously putting his best face on for the neighbours.

'So, I'd listen to him,' Laura continued, oblivious to my bemusement. 'He seems to have a way with Billy. And anyway, you should never be afraid to get help for your child.'

'That's what Gavin said.'

'Is he the artist fella with the long hair?'

'Yeah.' I smiled thinking of him.

'He's nice too. Tommy loves him. He's so friendly.' Laura put her hand on my arm. 'I wouldn't worry about getting help for Billy, Poppy. You've good friends and family.'

I suppose when she said it like that, I did have, in a way. I'd just never really thought of Dad and Gavin like that. For the first time in what felt like ages, I didn't feel so helpless.

'When Dan died,' Laura continued, draining her coffee, 'Tommy was so confused. He had nightmares and wouldn't talk to me, and like Billy, he was disruptive when he started

228

school. It took me ages to admit that I needed help, and by then Tommy had been suspended for throwing a chair at the teacher.'

'Tommy?'

Laura nodded. 'Yep. And my big regret, Poppy, is that I wish I'd done it sooner. The poor child was grieving and he couldn't grasp what death was. It made him angry and cross and he thought his dad had left him and that I'd done it somehow.'

'Oh.' Now it was my turn to put my hand on her arm. 'That's awful. You really had it hard, didn't you?'

Laura shrugged. 'I came out the other end though and Tommy is fine now. Like I said, if I'd got help when I first noticed something it would have been easier. Do what you feel, Poppy. It's all you can rely on at the end of the day.'

I nodded. She was right. And even if Billy was perfectly normal, it would be good to just be told it. 'You're right, Laura, thanks.' And I vowed, I wasn't going to wait for the school to initiate it – I was going to do it myself.

'And forget what I said about them not playing any more,' Laura stood up to leave. 'I'll keep a strict eye on them and maybe you could ask your dad to do the same?'

'Thanks.'

She smiled and pressed my arm again before leaving. I wonder what I had done to deserve her being so nice to me.

After she left, I crept upstairs and gazed down at my little boy. Love for him filled me up. Being the perfect parent, I realised, was not just about keeping calm and being the perfect disciplinarian, it was about knowing my child's faults and being able to accept them without blinding myself to the fact that maybe he wasn't perfect. In that way, I could truly help him. I could be the best I could. Which would be a first for me.

29

THE FOLLOWING MORNING, Pete went in to collect his mother from hospital. Isobel, very kindly, had given me the day off work. To my shame, I was hoping that she'd refuse. Thelma fit and well was one thing, I thought; Thelma in pain and moaning would be another.

Pete and I dropped Billy off at school, before heading over to the hospital. When we got there Thelma was waiting for us. She was dressed and had her coat over her arm. There was a doctor standing by her bed. He looked up at us as we approached and said in a jolly voice, 'Ah, Mrs Shannon, here are your son and daughter-in-law now.'

'Hi, Mammy,' Pete leaned over and gave Thelma a kiss on the cheek. 'How are you feeling today?'

'Lighter,' she snapped.

The doctor chuckled. 'A great sense of humour, Mrs Shannon. That's just what you need to get you through this.'

She glared at him and he beamed back at her. 'Tell them what you've told me,' Thelma barked.

'I was just about to,' the doctor said. 'But I'll do it in my office, if you don't mind. It's more private.'

'They found cells in my lymph glands,' Thelma said, making the doctor wince. 'It means the cancer could have spread. I'll need more treatment.' She sniffed. 'Pity they didn't operate sooner.'

Pete flinched.

I stood rooted to the spot. Jesus, I wanted to kill the woman. What a way to tell Pete. Then I thought, maybe she's in shock and it's her way of dealing with it. She didn't look shocked though, all she looked was a little paler.

Pete turned to the doctor.

'That's it in a nutshell,' the doctor said apologetically. 'She'll need to come in once a fortnight for the next four months for treatment. We've scheduled her in for Tuesday afternoons. She'll also have tablets to take at home. We'll take blood tests too just to see how she's getting on. I'm sorry,' he pulled out a chair for Pete, 'this is obviously a shock.'

'Yep,' Pete managed a weary smile.

'Well, go on, ask him,' Thelma prodded Pete. 'Ask him what my chances are.' Before Pete could react to that, Thelma said, 'Fair to good, isn't that right?'

The doctor nodded and smiled at Thelma. He obviously thought she was a hoot. 'Fair to good, that's right. Hard to kill a bad thing.'

'So, now that you've been filled in, can we go?' Thelma asked.

'Sure.' Pete hardly seemed to know what he was doing as he stood back up and pulled his keys from his pocket. He picked up his mother's case. 'Come on, so.'

I took the keys from him. 'Pete, you're in shock. We're all going to get a coffee for ourselves before we go anywhere.'

'Jesus, I'll never get out of this place,' Thelma grumbled.

Pete didn't complain, however.

We made our way to the canteen and drank a coffee in silence.

* * *

When we eventually got back to the house, Billy had come in from school. He was on a half-day as school holidays had begun. My dad was in the kitchen, fiddling about with the cooker, trying to turn it on.

'Thought I'd make us all some lunch,' he said. 'I've put some eggs in a saucepan and can't turn this thing on at all.'

He moved out of the way as I took over. I smiled to myself as I turned the childproof knobs and the ring flared red.

'Hello, Thelma,' Dad said jovially. 'How are you? I believe you were sick.'

'Well, I'm sicker now, so I was told.'

'How sick?' Billy asked, his eyes almost standing out on stalks. 'Will you maybe die and we'll find you dead in the bed?'

'Billy!' Pete snapped.

'Yes. That's a possibility,' Thelma nodded.

Billy's eyes grew wider. I think his estimation of his 'grumpy granny', as he had nicknamed her, went up a notch. 'Cool!'

'It's not cool,' Pete snapped again.

'Aw, Pete, he's only a child,' I said softly. 'Isn't it better than him being afraid?'

'Suppose,' Pete nodded despondently.

Dad looked from one to the other of us and held out his hand for Billy. 'Come on, now,' he said. 'Let's have a look at the garden and see if those flowers have come up yet. Remember we planted them yesterday?'

'Will they come up that quick?'

'You never know,' Dad tapped the side of his nose.

I watched through the window as Billy jumped ahead of Dad down the garden. Dad had to catch his hand now and again to stop him trampling on the plants but, surprisingly,

Billy didn't seem to wriggle or struggle the way he did with me when I caught him.

'I'd like a tea,' Thelma said.

'Of course, Mammy,' Pete jumped up to put the kettle on.

I let him. I think he just wanted to feel useful. What he didn't understand was that there really was nothing we could do now except wait. As Thelma sipped her tea, I noticed her pull a tablet out of her pocket and take it. In that moment, just at that tiny moment, I felt a spark of pity for her. She was obviously in pain.

I felt sorry until she said, 'Dreadful tea, Peter. I know things are bad, but can't you at least be generous with the tea bags?'

Thelma retired to bed at around three o'clock. Dad offered to take Billy out somewhere so that at least the house would be quiet and Thelma could get some rest.

'Aw, Dad, it's fine. I'll bring him somewhere. I'm sure you've got things to do.'

'I do but there's nothing pressing. No, Billy and I will go to the cinema and take in a movie. I haven't been to the cinema in ages and what was that film you wanted to see, Billy?'

'*Gruesome Ghouls*,' Billy said excitedly. 'It's got lots of blood in it. More blood than in any movie ever.'

'Great,' Dad nodded. 'Well, that's where we're going. He got five tanks and he wants the movies.'

Billy cheered and I smiled.

'I can't sleep,' Thelma called down.

'She can't sleep,' Pete hissed, coming out to join us.

'We're just on our way.' Dad caught Billy's hand and the

two left. 'Bye, Thelma,' he called. 'I'll see you tomorrow probably.'

Thelma didn't reply.

'Bye now,' Dad said to us and together he and my son left.

Pete and I had a couple of hours to ourselves. It was the first time in ages that we were alone with nothing to do. I felt that maybe I should put on some washing or tidy up, but I hadn't the heart. I wondered if I should tell Pete of my decision to get a doctor for Billy, but again, I hadn't the heart.

Pete went outside and I saw him cleaning his car. I stood by as he threw sweet papers and toys out onto the grass. I decided to go for it, to try and get him to talk about something. His mother, Adrian, whatever he wanted. His silence was scaring me a little.

'Are you OK?' I asked tentatively when I got out to him. 'You've hardly talked since Thelma came home.'

He paused briefly in his clearing out, then resumed. 'It was just a shock,' he said. 'I wasn't expecting it.'

'But you're OK?'

He ducked out of the car and looked at me. He swallowed hard and nodded. 'Yeah, as OK as I can be. She's taking it well, so that's something.'

I wondered about that, but I didn't say anything.

'Once she's getting her treatment things will get better.'

'Yeah, of course they will.'

Then he started cleaning again and I got the feeling that he didn't want to say any more.

'It's been a hard year, what with Adrian and Billy and everything,' I volunteered. 'Are you sure you're OK?'

'Uh-huh. Will you stick on the kettle for me, Poppy, and get me a cuppa while I wash the car?'

'Can we talk about this, Pete?'

'Talk about what?' He sat in the passenger seat and wiped down the dashboard. He smiled briefly. 'About you putting on the kettle? Am I offending your Women's Lib tendencies?'

I belted him and was so glad to see him smile that I let the subjects drop.

30

IT WAS A HARD couple of days. The local doctor came on Thursday and showed me how to look after Thelma's wound. There was no way Thelma wanted Pete involved. It wasn't right for a man to interfere with a woman in those regions, she told me firmly. And so, steeling myself each day to perform this task, I managed, much to my surprise, to do it. At first I nearly gagged, but after a bit it just became part of my life, like getting Billy up for school or making breakfast. Of course, the woman moaned and complained more than I'd ever heard anyone complain. But surprisingly, it didn't make me clumsy or awkward. I suppose I just knew that if I messed up I would hurt her, and much as I disliked her, I wouldn't want to do that.

It was a relief, though, when Saturday came and I had a legitimate excuse to escape the house. All week I'd been tied to it, even though my dad had offered to let me out for an hour or two. I picked up my printed-out emails with the list of celebrities that had agreed to auction themselves to take over to my mother's house. It was a little disappointing to be honest, as I still hadn't heard from anyone newsworthy. Still, the ones we had on board should raise a few thousand, but as the whole thing was my idea I really wished that we could raise a lot more. Maybe a dinner would have been a better idea after all. Still, it was early days and the auction wasn't for another couple of months so we had a little bit to go.

I was the first to arrive. Mam answered the door and I noted, with amusement, that she'd ordered in masses of flowers to fill up the hallway. The smell was lovely, if a bit overpowering.

'Come on in.' Mam ushered me into the biggest drawing room. The one with the horrible work of art and the piano. Her best china was laid out and the room reeked of polish. I wondered, for the first time, what sort of friends these were that she had to clean and show off for them.

'Hello, Poppy.' Dad appeared. 'How's it all going?'

'Oh, we've a few names, nothing earth shattering.'

'Except for your mother, of course. I'm sure she'll make a good bargain.'

Mam bristled, though I actually thought Dad had meant it as a compliment. 'I'm not going to be a bargain,' she sniffed. 'I'll fetch a good price.'

'Yes, at whatever price, you'll be a bargain,' Dad tried again.

Mam gave him a clipped smile. 'Right. Thank you, George, but Poppy and I have work to do before the others come so maybe you could go and amuse yourself elsewhere.'

'I thought I'd join in,' Dad came further into the room and I winced. There was going to be a row, I just knew it, and in all the long years of their marriage, I don't think I'd ever heard them row.

'Pardon?' Mam's voice dripped ice.

'Well, I am a businessman and I might be able to offer you some marketing ideas and such.' Dad sat opposite me on the other sofa.

'George,' Mam said, as if she was addressing an idiot. 'For the last ten years, the girls and I have organised this charity affair. We have done it successfully without any outside help, so thank you, but no.'

'You haven't heard what I've proposed yet,' Dad glanced anxiously at me. It's your fault, his eyes seemed to say, you suggested this.

'That's because you're not going to propose anything,' Mam said.

Dad took some papers out of his pocket and continued as if Mam hadn't spoken. 'I know some fellows in the media that might be able—'

To my horror, Mam crossed to him and swept his papers off the table. 'You're not listening, George. I said no!'

'This is about the residents' committee, isn't it?' he said, picking up his papers. 'You're still annoyed over that!'

'What I am annoyed with, George, is the fact that for thirty-five years of our married life, you worked every night and every day. You came home to be fed and to sleep. You left me on my own and though I begged you in the beginning to take time off, to go on holidays, you wouldn't. You always had work to do.'

'To build up a good life,' Dad said crossly. 'I don't see you complaining.'

'I got tired of complaining,' Mam took a step towards him and her face was really red. I wanted to leave but couldn't. I was rooted, with shock, to the sofa. 'I got tired of complaining so instead, I got involved in things. My things. My work. Did I ever offer to go into your work and help? Did I?'

Dad gave a nervous laugh. 'No.'

'No.' Mam folded her arms. 'So don't presume you can waltz into my things, OK?'

'But, but I'm retired now and I want to be with you.'

Mam shook her head. 'Well, George, it's a little late for that. You have to find your own life now, and when it suits both of us, we can be together.'

'Mam!' I was shocked. 'That's terrible, he only wants to help.'

'Yes,' Dad nodded. 'That's right.'

'Did you ever help me when I really needed it?'

'I don't know what you're talking about,' Dad said, flustered.

'Do you remember, Poppy, the way he was never around for your birthday parties and you'd stand by the door, waiting for your daddy to come and he never did?'

I gulped, remembering for the first time in long years how I'd cried most of my birthday nights away and yet convince myself that it would be different each year.

'Do you remember, Poppy, how he left us one year when we'd gone on holiday together? Do you remember the day of your wedding, Poppy, when he had to leave early, and the day of Billy's christening when he didn't even turn up?'

'The bottom fell out of the stock market that day,' Dad said. 'Jesus!'

'You were never there,' Mam said. 'So you don't have the right to be here now.'

'Mam!'

'I mean it, Poppy. There is nothing between us any more. We lost the art of conversation many years ago. Why do you think I live in this ridiculously big house? It's so that we don't have to see each other even when we're under the one roof!' Then she stopped and put her hand to her mouth and looked from one to the other of us. 'Oh God,' she said faintly. 'I don't know . . . I . . .'

240

Dad stared at her, his face pale. Then he tucked his pages under his arm and walked out of the room with as much dignity as he could muster.

There was silence after he left. Mam was frozen, her hand to her mouth.

I felt sick. What she had said was cruel and horrible and yet, yet she must have been hurt so deeply by Dad.

'Mam,' I ventured.

She waved me away. 'Don't, Poppy, don't.' Taking a deep breath, she instructed shakily, 'Look, ring the girls, tell them the meeting is off. Reschedule it for next week.'

'Here?'

'Well, no, not here. No, I couldn't bear it here. Maybe your house?'

And I thought of my little house and shuddered. But it was only polite if I was to reschedule that I do it in my place.

After I'd made the necessary phone calls, I thought that maybe I should find Dad. Even if it was just to tell him that I'd long ago forgiven him for not turning up on my birth-days or any other important occasions in my life. I suppose, like my mother, I'd just made the best of it. Only it hadn't hurt me as much. I wondered what I'd do if Pete had been like that and for the first time it dawned on me that maybe that's why I had married Pete – because he was mainly a nine-to-six man unless he was working on a major project like the shopping centre one. Though he'd mostly left the big ones to Adrian. When Pete had done the shopping centre, he'd worked all hours and I remember that I'd been bad tempered with him and panicky. Maybe I'd felt that I was going to turn into my mother.

I found Dad sitting on his favourite bench in the garden. It was hidden from the house by a large hedge.

'Hi,' I ventured, sitting in beside him.

He nodded.

'Are you OK?'

'She really hates me, doesn't she?' he said. It was a statement, I think.

'No, no. She's just angry.'

'It's more than that, Poppy. She can't bear to spend time with me, and I suppose I can't blame her.' He looked at me. 'I neglected you both badly, didn't I?'

I fidgeted around like Billy. 'You bought me lots of things when you were around.'

'It's not the same though, is it?'

I had paraded my new things to girls in the neighbourhood. Made friends briefly, been queen of the road, allocating rides on my new scooter, dispensing cuddles with my new doll, but when the novelty of my toy had worn off, my friends vanished until the next time.

I shrugged. 'I would have liked you around,' I admitted.

'And so would your mother,' he said glumly. 'Only it's too late now.'

'It's never too late,' I said, surprised, wondering if I was right. 'I think maybe just be around but don't push yourself on her. And get your own life.'

'I had my own life,' he said. 'Now it's gone.'

I didn't know what to say to that.

'I went into the office last week, just to say hello, but it was all rush, rush, rush. No one had any time for me. And the little time they had, it was only because they knew I could dump them all out on the street if I wanted to.'

'Oh, I'm sure that's not true.'

Both of us knew how hollow my words sounded. Dad merely looked at his hands, turning them over and over. 'David Hennel threatened to sue for unfair dismissal.'

The name rang a bell. 'Who—'

'The man that Billy walloped.' Dad smiled at the memory. 'What a great kid. Anyway, Hennel claimed unfair dismissal, the weasel. I never liked him anyway – always licking up but never meaning it. I had to pay him off, a year's wages.' He winced. 'Another battle lost.'

He was really quite dejected, I saw now. I suddenly thought of how hard it must be for him – all he'd ever had was his work. Now he had nothing.

'Forget about him,' I nudged Dad in the shoulder. 'That money will bring him no luck. Just like us with our friend, Adrian.'

Dad gave a reluctant smile. 'I suppose.' He paused. 'That must have been hard for you both,' he muttered. 'Losing everything like that.'

'Pete especially,' I said. 'His whole life blown away. He can't get a job anywhere now.'

'Maybe it's as well,' Dad said slowly. 'Otherwise you'd have to spend all day with Thelma. At least now you escape in the mornings.'

He had a point. I had a sharp image of me, living in our old house, living my old life – shopping most days, getting my facials other days, meeting Mam and her friends for lunch – suddenly being confined to four walls while minding a woman I detested.

'We could have hired in a nurse,' I quipped.

'Pete wouldn't stand for that,' Dad said. 'He'd have wanted to be there.' He smiled a little sadly, 'That's the kind of man you married, Poppy, and I'm glad of it.' In a rare display of affection, he placed his hand over mine.

It was his first ever praise of Pete. I wished Pete could have heard it.

I placed my free hand over his, my heart singing.

We sat, in silence, for a long time.

31

WITHOUT TELLING PETE – I told myself that he had enough on his mind – I talked to Laura about getting a psychologist for Billy. I wasn't sure how to go about it, and despite vowing to myself that I was going to take immediate action, I'd put it off for over a week as Billy hadn't really done anything too bad. Well, if you didn't count his plastering the kitchen in flour. I didn't want to think about the cost of his assessment, I'd cross that bridge when I came to it.

'First you have to get referred to a psychologist,' Laura said. 'Just bring Billy to the GP and have him write a letter.'

I winced thinking of GP costs. But I nodded. 'Right, I'll bring him tomorrow. I'll get my dad to sit with Thelma.'

'Your dad comes in handy, doesn't he?' Laura giggled, staring over at my dad who was pouring what looked like a whole bottle of turpentine on to the ground. 'If he's not minding Billy, he's minding your mother-in-law, or he's out doing your garden or painting your wall.'

'He's bored,' I said. 'And don't talk to me about the painting – he hasn't a clue. Look at him now. And Pete is going mad because Dad insisted on paying for the paint. Still, it keeps him occupied.'

Occupied being the right word. My dad was discovering

the joys of drenching paint all over my wall and path. Big lumps of paint were congealed on the pillar. The whole thing was a bit of a mess. He was now trying to remove all his spills from the footpath and the smell of turps was over-powering. All the kids on the road were gathered about him asking him all sorts of questions and asking if they could paint too.

'No, no,' Dad made big wide motions with his hand. 'Stay away, you'll all get paint over your clothes.'

'Yeah, you all stay away – it's my granddad,' Billy swaggered up to a tall boy who must have been about nine. 'Go on, go home!' He gave the boy a shove.

'Billy!' I called over. 'That's rude.'

'I will go home,' the big boy said. 'And you're not coming with me. Everyone else can, though. Who's coming?'

A few of his mates straggled off after him. The others were torn between their obvious fascination with what my father was doing and their even more obvious dislike of Billy. I bit my lip and Laura called Tommy back and told him he had to stay where he was.

'Now,' Dad said calmly, looking at the remaining children while pouring yet more turps on to the ground. 'If you all go home and change and get some old clothes, you can help.'

There was a second's stunned disbelief before a charge homeward began. Dad looked up and said to Billy, 'Now, the next time you're rude like that, I will let them all go home.'

'I don't care,' Billy folded his arms. 'I hate them anyway.'

'So, you don't want to help them clean up this mess?'

'Come on, Bill, and I'll get you an old T-shirt,' I called.

He came up the path, 'Well, he *is* my granddad,' he said sulkily.

246

Laura put her hand on my arm and smiled. 'Let me know how he gets on tomorrow, OK?'

It was a bit daunting talking to the doctor with Billy hanging on to my every word. The doctor seemed to realise this and he phoned his receptionist and asked her to take Billy behind her counter and give him a few stickers. When we were on our own, I explained as calmly as I could what his teacher had said. 'And he is aggressive to other children,' I admitted, my voice shaking, feeling as if I was betraying my most precious thing. 'And impulsive and hard to pin down.'

The doctor tapped his pen on his desk. 'What's his home-work like? Will he sit still and do it?'

'He gets nothing much at the moment but even to get him to colour something or concentrate on his letters is hard.'

'So he is unable to follow through on simple tasks?'

'Well, he is only six,' I gave a bit of a laugh, that even to myself sounded a bit freaked.

'OK, let's bring him back in here and just observe him. Don't tell him to sit still or behave, just let him be himself, OK?'

I winced, wondering if the doctor knew what he was letting himself in for.

Billy duly arrived back, accompanied by the receptionist who was beaming at him. It was so nice to see someone smiling at him that I felt a lump in my throat. What on earth was I doing here, I wondered suddenly? Was this the right thing? What would Pete say when he found out, as he was bound to since Billy would probably tell him.

'See the stickers I got,' Billy said, waving his roll of stickers around.

'Oh, they're lovely,' I said.

Billy threw them at me and looked about.

'Let's you and I talk,' the doctor said to me while Billy was distracted. 'Ignore him and see what he does.'

So the doctor and I proceeded to talk about treatment options, should Billy be diagnosed as ADD. I have to admit, I didn't take in a lot of it as I was too conscious of Billy's whereabouts. He lay under the chair and started kicking it with his feet, making the chair jump up and down. Then he got up and started examining the doctor's desk, oblivious to our glances.

'What's this?' he asked the doctor.

'That's a stethoscope. I use that for listening to people's hearts.'

'Really?' Billy was fascinated.

The doctor lifted it off his desk, placed the plugs in Billy's ears and put it to his chest.

Billy's eyes grew wide and round. 'Cool. Let's hear yours, Mammy.'

Without waiting for me to answer, he rammed it where he thought my heart should be.

'OK,' the doctor said softly. 'He has a lot of energy, all right. However, I'm not in a position, as you know, to diagnose him. Sometimes boys are just more energetic than girls, and every child who jumps about in school mightn't have ADD. Now, I have a list of NEPS-approved psychologists. NEPS stands for National Educational Psychological Service, and if you want the recommendations in his report to be acted on in school, you have to use a NEPS guy, OK?'

I nodded.

'So,' the doctor looked at me, pen poised, 'Billy's main

difficulty, as I hear it, is in his inability to get on with children of his own age and his impulsive behaviour. Would that be it?'

'Yes.' It didn't sound as bad when he put it like that.

'OK.' The doctor wrote me a referral note. 'Now, it's quite expensive, but there is a way of claiming it back on tax or it might be covered by your Health Insurance. You should check it out, OK?' He handed me the number of a psychologist. 'This is Jim Ryan's number. He's very good. Ring him up and book an appointment. You should get one within a couple of weeks, OK?'

'OK.'

'Now, don't forget to check out your health insurance. Most packages will not pay for medication,' he said. 'What they might do, however, is pay a contribution towards any extra counselling services you might need to get for Billy. You should find out if yours does.' He scribbled his name on the end of the note with a flourish and handed it to me. 'There you go – and good luck.'

'Thank you.' I took out my purse.

'It's forty-five euro and you can pay at reception.'

'OK. Thanks.' Forty-five euro. I winced. I'd been saving up to get my hair cut by my old hairdresser and now it looked as if that wasn't going to happen. It was going to have to be the local place again.

I waited until Pete came in that night to broach the subject of health insurance with him. I had waited up especially and had made him a small supper, to butter him up and put him in good mood I suppose. He'd been a bit morose lately and I put it down to worry over Thelma, who was due to start her treatment the following week. Though how anyone could worry about her was beyond me – even though she'd had a major operation, she looked healthier than any of us. It must be the good country air. Anyway, Pete arrived in and expressed surprise at the supper and I immediately felt guilty.

'It's actually to get you in a good mood,' I confessed, deciding to come clean.

'Am I not always in a good mood?' he asked, planting a kiss on my cheek and sitting down. 'How's Mammy?'

'Complaining as usual, so she's fine.'

We laughed a little together. It was good to see him smile. I decided that I'd wait up every night until he came in – we didn't have much time together nowadays, what with him out from the afternoons and me out in the mornings.

'So, what's the story?' He cut into a sausage.

'I'm wondering if we have health insurance?'

He paused, the sausage halfway to his mouth. 'What? Who's sick?'

'No one. Well, it's just that I brought Billy to the doctor today. You know, I decided that the sooner we get him assessed the better.'

'Oh.' He immediately resumed eating.

I tried to ignore the hopeless sort of feeling that I got when I saw him carry on like normal, regardless. I didn't want a row; I didn't want to be blamed by him; and I especially didn't want him trying to make me laugh so I'd forget about it. 'Anyway,' I continued with determination, 'he has referred Billy to a psychologist. I just want to check to see if it's covered in our health insurance.'

'A psychologist?'

'Yes.' I looked him in the face. I was not backing down. This was for Billy.

'So,' Pete said evenly, 'just because our child falls out with a few kids in school and does a few mad things, he's abnormal?'

'It's not—'

'Poppy, nothing is ever perfect. Can you not understand that?'

'What?'

'You seem to think that just because Billy doesn't do what you think he should do, that he somehow needs help. It's like you want the perfect life.'

'Yes, and there's nothing wrong with that.'

'Billy doesn't need help. He's fine. He's a boy. Boys do those things.'

'Well,' I gritted my teeth and folded my arms, 'the *doctor* referred him. Are you a doctor?'

'Don't be stupid.'

'Stupid? Me? You're the one who's stupid. Laura thinks I should bring him. And Dad. And Gavin.' I knew, by the hardening of his jaw line, that I'd said the wrong thing.

'Oh, so you've told everyone, have you? Even Gav?'

'I've told those important to us, yeah.'

'You've talked it over with them and not with me?'

'How can I talk anything over with you when you won't bloody talk about it!'

'Oh for God's sake—'

'And anyway, when I did, you just said, and I quote,' I put on Pete's country accent, '"If you tink dere's something wrong den bring him yerself" and I have!'

Pete folded his arms. 'Yeah, well, I think he's fine.'

My hand itched to shake him. It really did. But some sort of sanity prevailed and instead of getting drawn in, I repeated, 'Well, thanks for an opinion AT LAST! And I

251

hope you're right. I do, really. But in the meantime, do we have health insurance?'

He stood up, his supper not even finished. 'I'll go and look now, will I?'

'Yeah,' I said. 'Do.'

So while he looked, making a huge production out of pulling boxes and papers out of the wardrobe, I undressed and climbed into bed. I pretended to be asleep when he banged a lot of paper down next to me. Then he climbed into bed and we slept, back to back.

32

IT WAS HARD to believe – but that morning, the day after the row with Pete – I couldn't wait to get to work. My month's notice was up but I had no intention of leaving now – well, not unless I got offered a better job, which was never going to happen. And it wasn't hard to sit at a till and press buttons. There was no real responsibility in it at all. Working in the euro shop was the one area of my life left where there was no pressure. It seemed, surprisingly, to be the one area of my life that I actually had control over, and I welcomed it the way the dry earth welcomes rain.

I took the information on our health insurance with me to work, though I really couldn't understand it at all. There was a number I could ring, so I decided to call that afternoon when Pete had gone out.

'What's that?' Maxi asked, leaving her till to come and peer over my shoulder. 'Is it about your sale of the celebrities?'

'No, it's just documents about our health insurance.' I hastily tried to stuff it back into my bag.

'Oh right. Is that when you pay and then they pay for you if you get sick?'

'Uh-huh.'

Maxi leaned her huge elbows on the counter. 'Yeah, when

my fella was sick we had none of that. We had to remortgage the house to get him sorted.' She bit her lip. 'Still didn't work though.'

'Was it just the two of you?'

'Yeah. No kids.' She paused for a second and seemed to be thinking. Then continued, 'Though I would've liked kids – to remind me of him, you know.'

'Yeah.'

'He's dead five years now.' She shook her head as if she couldn't quite believe it.

'Cancer of the lungs, that's what he had. The fecking eejit wouldn't stop smoking. A heart attack would have been better. Sudden. That's the way to go.'

'It'd be a big shock though,' I said, thinking of Laura. 'At least you were prepared.'

Maxi's eyes widened and her tone was bitter as she said, 'Prepared to see the love of me life getting buried in a hole in the ground?' She shook her head again and said slowly, 'Nothing prepares you for that, Poppy.'

'No,' I said, mortified. What did I know anyway? No one close to me had ever died. 'Sorry, Maxi. That was stupid of me.'

There was a brief pause and I wondered if she was going to say any more. 'He was only thirty-four.' She turned around and hiked up her T-shirt. Her flesh wobbled. 'See that,' she pointed to her butterfly tattoo. 'I got it done when we knew he was dying. Some stupid nurse told him he was going to die and become a butterfly. When he told me, I laughed. Jesus, I said, you, a fucking butterfly? You're more like a horsefly or a cockroach. But he didn't laugh back; he liked the image, you know. So I got it done and that's him, right there.' She jabbed her tattoo. 'See?'

'Yeah,' I said softly. 'That's lovely.'

'It's him, not just 'cause it's a butterfly, but because it's always there, d'you know what I mean?'

All I could do was nod. It was such a romantic thing to say, and even more so because Maxi had said it.

She pulled away abruptly from my counter as someone came in. 'Only seems like the other day though,' she said, walking off.

The customer was a regular. The young girl who'd admired my blouse on my second day at work. She was in her early twenties, long brown hair, usually tied up in a high ponytail. She was dressed in her usual attire of a tracksuit and trainers. I always made a special point of smiling at her. She tended to buy toilet paper and deodorants, and because I smiled at her, she seemed to like being served by me. I cashed up her purchases.

'So, how are you today?'

'Good,' she handed over her money and then asked shyly, 'I, eh, bought this,' she held a bag up, 'this top in Penny's. And, well,' she faltered, 'I was wondering if, well, if you'd have a look at it.'

'Me? Why? Is there something wrong with it?'

The girl flushed and eyed Maxi nervously. 'No. No. It's just, well, I'm going for a job interview next week and, well, you always wear such nice stuff and I was wondering . . .' her voice trailed off and she went beetroot red. 'No. No. Actually, it's OK. It's OK.'

'Of course I'll look at it,' I said, ridiculously flattered. 'Of course I will. Here, show it to me.'

'Are you sure?'

'Yep.'

She opened up her bag quickly, almost as if she was afraid

255

I'd change my mind. 'It's as near to your top – the white lacy one, the one you got in House of Fraser – as I could get,' she stammered, holding it up for me to see.

It was almost the same as my lacy top – not as well made, but still, it had probably only cost a tenner or something. I studied the top and studied the girl. She was pale. I wondered if white would suit her. 'Did they have them in any other colour?' I asked.

'Yeah. Lots of colours.'

'Did they have them in,' I studied her complexion, 'a coral pink?'

'Coral pink?' she looked bewildered. 'Is that—'

'A salmon colour?'

'Uh, I dunno. They had them in a peach.'

'Yes, get one in that colour and I'd say it'd suit you a lot better. And get a brown skirt. That'd look nice.'

'OK. OK,' she said breathlessly, stuffing the top into her bag. 'Thanks. Thanks.'

'No problem.' I watched, happy and amused, as she almost danced from the shop.

'Fecking eejit,' Maxi remarked.

'How?'

'Jaysus, imagine asking for advice on a top!'

'There's nothing wrong with asking for help,' I said, suddenly realising that it was true. There was nothing wrong in it, despite what Pete thought.

It was a while later that Maxi remembered my health insurance. I'd had a busy enough morning as all the customers seemed to gravitate towards me. Maxi had stood calling out, irritably, 'there's a till free here,' every now and again. Anyway, at around twelve, after Isobel had popped her head in for ten minutes to make sure we were working. Maxi said, 'So, what's the story with the health insurance. Is someone sick or what?'

I gulped, tried to think of a lie but couldn't. My mind blanked completely. And besides, it didn't seem altogether right to lie about someone being sick. Tempting fate, my mother would have said in her ominous voice. 'Not sick exactly,' I stammered out.

'Oh.' Maxi looked expectantly at me. And when I remained silent, she asked, 'How can someone be "not sick exactly".'

Jesus. 'Well, not sick physically,' I answered, hoping to evade the subject. 'Oh, look, we're almost out of those fake antique vases. I'd better write it down to remind Isobel.'

'So, sort of mental, like?' Maxi pressed. 'As in loo-la?' She pointed at her head and made a circular motion with her finger.

'Billy is not crazy,' I snapped. 'He just needs to be assessed.'

'Is that your husband?'

It suddenly occurred to me that while I knew a lot about Maxi – her husband's name had been Jack, he'd liked Eurosport and Sumo wrestling, Charlotte was her youngest sister who she looked after like a daughter, she lived in a housing estate, she went to bingo and seemed to have loads of friends, her maiden name had been Greene – she knew absolutely nothing about me. Not even my husband's name. While she'd opened up, I'd remained very private and aloof. I suddenly wondered if that was what put people off me. That I didn't reveal myself. The only people I talked freely to were Pete and Gavin, and Gavin was Pete's friend, I hadn't even acquired him by myself. Nowadays, I chatted a little to Laura, but I still knew more about her than she knew about me, and the little she had gleaned was only because she'd caught me when I was upset about things.

'Billy is my son,' I said, blurting out the information. 'He's six and he's a little disruptive in school.'

'Aren't they all at six,' Maxi rolled her eyes. 'Sure, Charlotte was a holy terror.'

I didn't really welcome the comparison. 'His teacher thinks he might have a thing called ADD. It's where—'

'That's what Charlotte is meant to have!' Maxi said with glee, as if she'd just discovered the origin of the universe. 'At her last trial, the one where she was up for stealing packets of fags, that's what her lawyer said she suffered from. Impulsive behaviour that she couldn't help.'

'What?' My blood ran cold.

'Apparently, she's had it for ever. I dunno. All I remember is that she was always in trouble, but we all thought it was just high spirits, you know.'

'Billy isn't really bad,' I said, quoting Pete. 'I mean, it mightn't be anything at all.'

'Aw, well, let's hope not,' Maxi smiled at me. 'There's nothing worse than something being wrong with your child.'

She was right there.

When I got home, Thelma had gone to bed. She slept a lot in the afternoon, which was a relief. So, while my father was entertaining Billy in the back garden by attempting to stand still while Billy fired penalty shots at him, I rang the health insurance crowd. The woman who talked to me was lovely. She explained that indeed there were packages that gave a certain amount of money for child counselling, but that unfortunately the one we had didn't cover it. Medication wasn't covered either.

Trying not to feel total despair, I rang Jim Ryan's office.

As the phone rang at the other end of the line, I heard the thunk of Billy's ball outside connecting with something solid. The solid thing, as it turned out, was my dad. He yelled an 'ouch' and I heard Billy call out a guilty apology. Dad stumbled through the back door with Billy following close behind, and at that moment the phone at the other end was picked up.

'Hello, Jim Ryan's office.'

'Hello, my name is Poppy Shannon and I have a note from my doctor regarding my son. Apparently he has to see a psychologist. When is the earliest Jim Ryan could see him?'

I heard the woman checking through pages. She came back to me a few minutes later. 'Well, you're lucky. There's a free appointment next Wednesday morning.'

'Have you anything for the afternoon?' I asked. There was no way I was going to let Pete bring him.

'Not until . . .' I heard the flick of paper again, 'until Wednesday week at four-thirty. Would that suit?'

'That'd be fine. And, eh, how much is it?'

'Well, the first visit will just be getting to know you and your family and your son. What exactly is the problem?'

I told her.

'Right. For the assessment, which will be a full cognitive profile, it'll be three-hundred-and-fifty euro.'

I gasped.

'Is that OK?'

'Eh . . . yes. Did you say three-hundred-and-fifty euro?' I knew of course that that was what she had said, but there was some small part of me that hoped I was wrong. Maybe I was hoping for a miracle. Though, as Thelma would have said, miracles only happen when you go to mass.

'I did.'

Maybe I should leave it until Billy went back to school, I thought. But no, no, I decided, I wasn't doing that. He was having it hard enough without me being a cheapskate. And despite Pete's opposition to the whole thing, I knew that if I asked him for the money he wouldn't hesitate. 'Right. OK.' I bit my lip. But where would we get the money?

'OK. I have you penned in for Wednesday week at four-thirty. If you have to cancel for any reason, please let me know so that other people can benefit.'

'Fine. Thanks.' I put down the phone and sighed. I'd just have to manage it. Somehow. My wages were meant to go towards my car and my general upkeep. My upkeep would just have to suffer. I turned to look at my over-long hair in the hall mirror and thought that it probably already had. I was startled to see the reflection of my father standing behind me.

'What's this about three-hundred-and-fifty euro?' he asked.

'Dad, your eye! What happened?'

He shrugged and grinned a little ruefully. 'It's why I never made the football team in school,' he muttered sheepishly. 'I was really bad.'

I giggled a little. His eye was swelling up rapidly.

'I'll get some ice for it,' I said.

He followed me into the kitchen. 'You didn't answer my question, Poppy. What's the story with the money? I take it you brought him to the doctor.'

I opened the freezer and pulled out an ice-pack. From the garden, Billy was chanting 'loser' really loudly.

As Dad held it to his eye, I told him what had happened. 'So the doctor has sent us to the clinic to get him assessed.'

'And it's that expensive?'

'Yep.'

'Will you be able to afford it?'

'We're just going to have to.'

'You can ask me, you know,' Dad said, and it wasn't in the abrasive tone he'd used so often before. He smiled a little as he said, 'He's my grandchild, he deserves the best. No matter what he needs, you get it, OK?'

'We'll manage,' I said, touched. 'Honestly.'

'Well, the offer is there – I'm your dad, I'm his granddad,' he thumbed towards the garden, 'so don't you be standing on pride, OK?'

'Thanks. Thanks, Dad.' The relief of it was enormous. Not that I had any intention of taking him up on it, but it was good to know it was there. 'Thanks.' I caught his hand and squeezed it.

'Now, now.' Dad, uncomfortable with the closeness, wriggled his hand free of mine. 'I do hope that you'll at least be able to afford the court case when I sue the ass off your son for this injury.'

'Well, you might as well join the queue, so,' Thelma said from the doorway. 'From what I gather there's quite a list wanting to sue this family.'

'Thanks for that, Thelma,' I muttered.

'Thelma,' Dad smiled broadly and stood up. 'Delighted as always.' He did a mock bow.

'Yes, George. Indeed.' Thelma said dryly as she sank into one of the chairs. 'I'm sure you are.'

Dad winked at me and I smiled back.

33

Because thelma's treatment was due to begin on a Thursday afternoon, Pete had taken a day off work but, to his surprise, she had told him that she didn't want him there.

'I didn't ask you to take a day off, did I?' she said grumpily when he informed her. 'No, I'd rather Poppy brought me, thanks.'

I don't know who was more shocked, Pete or I.

'But Mammy, Poppy has to mind Billy and—'

'Why can't you mind him? He might like his father about. God knows, you should know what it's like not to have a father about the place. All he has is that old man.'

'That old man is my dad,' I piped up.

'Precisely,' she said, as if that answered whatever horrible question she was asking or whatever horrible point she was trying to make. 'Precisely,' she said again.

Pete looked hopelessly at me before leaving the room.

I glared at Thelma, who either didn't notice or didn't care, before following him out.

'Pete,' I called. 'Hang on.'

He turned to face me.

'I'll mind her,' I said. 'I promise.'

He shook his head and ran his fingers through his hair.

'It's not that, it's just . . .' he swallowed hard and said, 'Well, she is *my* mother, and you shouldn't have to mind her all the time. It's not fair on you.'

'I don't mind.' I did, actually. I was hoping for a nice few free hours with just me and Billy – and of course my dad who had virtually moved in with us too. I didn't know how things were between him and Mam because I hadn't asked. But as he was spending so much time at our house, I could make an educated guess.

'You do mind. You were hoping to enjoy your free time without her calling out for cups of bloody tea.'

I giggled. 'You know me too well, oh wise-one.'

He smiled too, before saying, 'Maybe I'll force the issue and tell her I'm bringing her and she can like it or lump it.'

'Naw, don't do that, Pete. She's sick, let her have what she wants for the moment. When she starts to get better, we'll hammer her!'

He laughed, but it was kind of a sad laugh. Then he asked, out of the blue, 'What's the story with Bill?'

I wasn't sure if he really wanted to know or if he was just asking in the hope that I'd say I'd dropped it. 'The story is,' I said slowly and firmly, 'that he's going to the place the doctor advised me to bring him.'

'Oh. Right.' He didn't say anything for a bit, and then he muttered, 'There's probably nothing wrong with him, anyway.'

'Yeah,' I said, 'I hope you're right, Pete. But if there is, we deal with it together, OK?'

'Yeah. Right. Don't lecture me.'

'I'm not lecturing you, it's just that you don't seem to be understanding this, Pete. Billy might need help. All I ask—'

'D'you know what, forget I asked, OK?' He held his

hands up in the air and walked away from me. 'Just forget I asked.'

'I think it's you who wants to forget,' I yelled after him. 'And by the way, it's three-hundred-and-fifty euro.'

He froze. Turned back to me. 'What?'

'Yeah.'

'Fuck!' He sounded a little dazed. 'How can we afford that?'

'I dunno,' I shrugged. 'My dad has offered.'

'No!' He came back towards me. 'No way.'

'Well, unless we raise the money by next Wednesday, I'm taking him up on it, OK?'

He didn't say anything. I don't think there was much he could say. There was no way we could raise that cash in such a short time.

'It'll be a loan,' I said then, feeling sorry for him. 'We'll pay him back.'

He shrugged and walked away. Maybe I should have run after him but I honestly couldn't. I was so bloody worried about Billy and it seemed I couldn't talk about it to Pete unless *he* wanted to talk about it. And it wasn't even an honest discussion. He just wanted me to say that things were fine, and if I couldn't say that, he didn't want to know.

Anyway, I let Pete walk out of the room. I heard him calling to Billy and I heard Billy call back that he didn't want to go out with Pete because Granddad was coming up and he'd promised to take him on a trip to the city.

So Pete just walked off.

He came back just before I pulled out of the driveway. Thelma was in the passenger seat moaning about her seat-belt being too tight. It wouldn't be as tight, I felt like saying, if she lost some weight.

A sharp rap on the window startled me.

'Oh, it's Peter,' Thelma rolled down her window. 'Hello.'

'Just wishing you luck, Mammy. Are you sure you don't want me to come?'

'Yes Peter, I'm sure,' she said wearily.

'OK. Fine. See yez.' With only a token glance at me, he turned and let himself into the house.

'Does he ever take no for an answer?' she said exasperated. 'I mean, did he honestly think I was going to change my mind?'

'He's worried about you.' I felt horribly hurt for him. Annoyed about the way he was treating me, but still hurt at the way his mother was treating him. 'You can hardly blame him for that.'

'Suit him better to worry about his son,' Thelma said smartly.

Her comment stunned me. Her perception stunned me.

Neither of us said anything more as I drove towards the hospital.

After we'd seen Thelma's consultant, who explained the procedures to us, Thelma was admitted on to a ward. She was to be given chemotherapy and she was going to be monitored overnight to see her reaction to it.

'Now,' the nurse said as Thelma climbed on to a bed, 'we'll just get a chair for your daughter to sit on so she can keep you company as you get your blood test and treatment.'

'Oh, she's not my daughter,' Thelma said with a wave of her hand. 'She's just my daughter-in-law.'

I bristled at the 'just' but I gave the nurse a stiff smile.

'Well, we'll get her a chair anyway,' the nurse said cheerfully. 'Daughter-in-laws sit down too.'

As she bustled away in search of a chair, Thelma said, 'You don't have to stay, you know. You can go shopping and come back later if you like. Or just come back tomorrow.'

I gawked at her. Go shopping? What sort of a person did she think I was? 'I'd hardly go shopping when you're sick in here,' I retorted, stunned. 'God!'

'Well, I don't mind.' Thelma folded her arms and shrugged.

'Well I do,' I said flabbergasted. 'And so would Pete.'

Another shrug from her, but at least she didn't tell me to go away.

I'd bought a few magazines for us to read while we sat there. I handed Thelma one with the lurid headline 'My Husband Tried To Cut My Arm Off'. The others weren't much better, I noticed. One of the others had a list of twenty places to have an orgasm before you die, while yet another had a 'My Child is a Serial Killer' article. It kind of made me glad to be the mother of just a disruptive six-year-old whose teacher thought he needed psychological help.

Thelma was reading about the arm cutting incident with glee. 'He actually told her to shove it in a mincer to see if she could fix it since he couldn't,' Thelma salivated. 'That's butchers for you. Never marry a butcher, that's what my mother always said. And wasn't she right!' She stabbed the magazine, 'Wasn't she right?'

The nurse came back with my chair and then said, 'Now, Thelma, before we begin, I just have to take a few blood samples.' She took out a needle. 'We'll do this every time so that we can see how the treatment is progressing, OK?'

'Fine.'

'Just give me your arm,' the nurse said, needle poised.

'I hope you're not going to cut it off,' Thelma cackled and I smiled.

The first joke in earnest I'd ever heard that woman tell.

About two hours later, after we'd perused most of the magazines, Thelma's medicine arrived; innocent looking bags of liquid. As I looked at them being wheeled in, I felt a little sick. Hospitals were not my thing. Thelma, on the other hand, was listening avidly as the nurse explained what each medicine was for. Then, gently, the nurse found a vein in Thelma's hand and hooked Thelma up to the bags. As the stuff trickled into Thelma's veins, she became quiet, her eyes following the progress of the liquid as it drip, dripped out.

'Are you OK?' I asked softly. 'Do you feel all right?'

'I'm fine,' she snapped. 'Just hoping this stuff works, that's all.'

In that moment, I admired her.

'Pete wouldn't have been able to bear this,' she said then. 'He's too soft. Doesn't like to confront bad things. It's much better that you're here.'

I don't think it was meant as a compliment, or if it was, it was probably a compliment for Pete.

'Yeah, I'm as hard as nails, me,' I answered. Then I picked up my magazine and said, 'But not as bad as the woman who made her children walk to school with no coats in the middle of winter as she was sick of them losing their stuff. And one of them got hypothermia.'

'No!'

'Yeah, here – look.'

She took the magazine from me and was soon busy exclaiming over it and reading it.

I started to read where to have my twenty orgasms. I'd deliberately saved it for last.

34

PETE PICKED THELMA up from the hospital the next morning, so when I got home from work she was already in bed and asleep.

'The chemo made her quite sick,' Pete said to me the minute I walked in. 'So she has to take tablets to help her feel better.'

'OK. How is she now?'

'Better, I think.'

'Good.' I plonked down on to a chair and eased my feet out of my shoes. They were high and not really designed to be stood in all day, but I liked to look good in work. And Isobel had told me that I lent the place an air of class, and that really was saying something. 'Where's Bill?'

'Your dad has taken him and Tommy off to the playground and he said he might bring them for tea somewhere.' He gave a hesitant smile. 'So you can have a relaxing afternoon.'

'Great.' I pulled off my coat.

'Oh yeah, you got these emails too,' Pete held out some printed-off mails to me. 'I was on the computer looking up stuff and thought I'd check.'

'OK. Thanks.' I got the feeling he was trying to make conversation with me, but I wasn't going to make it easy for him. I flicked through the first email. The minorest of minor celebs had agreed to take part in the auction. However, the second reply made me groan.

'Yeah,' Pete said sympathetically, 'it's a bummer, isn't it?'

Abby Amberlie had refused to be involved in the auction. According to her agent she had prior commitments that day and couldn't get out of them. Abby would have been a big draw, she had the three Bs. Brains, beauty and an enormous bust. The most famous newsreader in the country.

'I don't know what to do,' I chewed my lower lip. 'We've got nobody thrilling yet. I really thought Gav's posters would work. And my letter.'

'Aw, it'll be fine. You'll see.' He stood for a second and I sensed him looking down at me. I didn't bother to look up. 'I can get a bank overdraft,' he muttered then.

'No,' I said, still staring at the emails. 'I'm not paying interest when we don't have to.'

'Christ,' he muttered. Then, 'Well, I'll head off, so. See you later.'

'Bye.' I didn't raise my head for a kiss, pretending instead to be absorbed in the letters.

The next thing I knew he had gone.

I called over to Laura and invited her in for a coffee. I was nervous asking her in case she refused. But I think she felt she owed me one as Dad had taken Tommy off her hands.

'Your dad is great,' she said for about the tenth time as she plonked down at the kitchen table. 'He must have been brilliant when you were a kid.'

I didn't bother to enlighten her. Instead, I nodded a little and busied myself locating the coffee jar. Then I made a sandwich for myself as I hadn't had any lunch.

'So, how's the job going?' Laura asked.

'Good. I quite like it actually,' I put some plastic ham, as my dad called it, on to the bread and cut it. 'I've decided that I'm going to stay. That girl – the one who was robbing stuff – she called in and, I dunno, I think Maxi told her I was OK or something, and she hasn't bothered us since. Maxi is dead impressed, you see, because I'm organising the auction.'

'What auction?'

So I had to fill Laura in then too. I told her all about Maxi and her husband and the tattoo, and the fact that she and her friends were saving up to bid on someone. 'Only thing is,' I finished up, 'it's been a bit of a struggle to get celebrity names. I dunno, it's like they're all suspicious of what we're doing.'

Laura chewed on her biscuit for a bit. 'Well, Maxi's butterfly story is a good one. Why don't you ask her if you can use it to drum up support?'

'Oh.' I'd never have thought of that.

'What you do,' Laura put down her biscuit and leaned towards me, saying with authority, 'is, send a flyer out to them all again, this time detailing Maxi's story, and then see if the papers would run it. Personal interest stuff is always the most persuasive material.'

I gawked at Laura.

She giggled a little. 'I'm in PR, aren't I? I work from home. I've got a few contacts you might like to use. If you do get a big name I could probably get you some TV time.'

'No! Wow! That'd be great.' I stared at her. Her tiny little face and warm eager smile. I'd always thought PR people were aggressive go-getters. 'PR?' I said again, and the disbelief must have shown in my voice because she giggled.

'People are always surprised when I tell them,' she smiled. She shrugged modestly, 'I was a bit of a high flyer actually. I did the PR for a lot of new companies in their early days – that's how I met Dan, I did work for his building firm – and then when I got married and had Tommy, I dunno, I found that I didn't care as much so I gave up my job. But then, well, Dan died, and so I had to do something.' She giggled again and asked, wide-eyed, 'Well, how on earth did you think I kept the house going?'

It had never occurred to me. I just assumed people had money, I never questioned where it came from. 'I never thought about it,' I admitted. 'I suppose I just thought, well, I dunno.'

'It's handy,' Laura explained. 'I work my own hours, take on whatever business I like. It's nice – except when I have to go to meetings as getting Tommy minded can be a bit difficult sometimes.'

'Well, I'm here in the afternoons, if you're ever stuck.'

'Aw, thanks, but you've plenty of people to mind. How's Pete's mother by the way? Would she do a personal story for your auction?'

I almost choked. 'The only thing that woman does is complain,' I said.

Laura laughed and I found myself laughing too. So I told her all about yesterday.

And then she told me something.

And then I told her something else.

And before I had even time to think about it, it dawned on me that we were having a chatty, friendly conversation, just like friends.

It was just as good as I always imagined it would be.

272

35

O N SATURDAY I was panicking. Mam and her friends were due to come to my house to discuss the progress of the auction. The more I looked around, the smaller the house felt. The more I cleaned, the tinier the house grew. I'd decided to have the meeting in the television room and so I wasted most of my energies trying to make it appear bigger than it was. I even removed my favourite photos of Billy from the mantelpiece in the vain hope that the less clutter there was the bigger things would appear.

'Why is my picture in this drawer?' Billy said indignantly, yanking it out and almost ripping it in two. 'I thought you liked that!'

'Well, I do,' I explained, about to put it back in again, 'but I just need a clean room as people are coming round.'

'My picture doesn't make the room dirty,' he said back, wrinkling up his face. 'That's not nice.'

And, of course, he was right. It wasn't nice, so I reinstated the picture where it belonged. And I also reinstated everything else. This house is where we're at right now, I thought, so they'll have to either like it or lump it. The thought was quite liberating in a scary sort of way.

'There now,' I said to him when I'd finished, 'is that better?'

'Yeah, it looks like our house again.'

The 'girls' arrived over at twelve. It was like a parade of peacocks up my small driveway. Fur and feathers and floaty dresses. I reckoned some of the neighbours were gawping at them and having a good laugh.

Pete had taken Billy out, Dad hadn't come over as Mam was arriving and Thelma, much to my horror, had arisen from her bed and taken up residence in the TV room, a duvet thrown over her feet. It looked like the meeting was going to have to be held in the kitchen. The kitchen, which I hadn't cleaned as thoroughly as the TV room. A sweat broke out on my hands when the doorbell rang.

'I'll get it,' Thelma called.

'No, no, it's for me.' Christ the last thing they needed to see was Thelma, attired in her flannel nightdress and horrendous green dressing gown.

'The exercise will do me good,' Thelma said, appearing at the doorway as I raced ahead of her. Her hair was sticking up in huge spiky bits, I noticed as I scurried past. Oh God, I was a snob, I realised. But only when other snobs were present. I wouldn't notice otherwise.

'Hiiiiii,' I trilled as I opened the door. 'Welcome.'

'Hello pet,' Mam airkissed me on both cheeks before spotting Thelma. 'Thelma, hello. I've been meaning to call over but it seems that my husband has taken up residence here and I figured one Furlong was enough.' She gave a bit of a laugh. Then, her voice dripping with concern, and lowered for maximum sympathy, she asked, 'How *are* you?'

274

'Toxic,' Thelma answered. 'The drugs they give you, full of poisons.'

'Oh,' Mam recoiled slightly. Then she recovered. 'You're looking well anyway.'

Mam's friends piled in behind her, all peering over her shoulder at my tiny hallway.

'Hi,' Avril handed me a bunch of flowers. 'For your new home.'

'Oh, thank you.' I found the gesture oddly touching.

'And I've bought some lovely cakes,' Daisy produced an enormous box. 'Your mother said you probably wouldn't be able to afford these expensive ones and so . . .' she paused and flushed. 'Oh, sorry. How rude of me. I would have bought them anyway, even if you could have afforded it.'

'Thanks.'

'What's so special about those cakes?' Thelma stared at the box. 'Is it just the fact that they come in a fancy box?'

A slight gasp of horror escaped from Daisy, but she clamped it down. 'Gustav baked them himself,' she said. 'His cakes are world famous.'

'Not in my part of the world they're not,' Thelma snorted.

'Girls,' my mother clapped her hands. 'This is Thelma, she's Poppy's mother-in-law. She's staying with her for a while.'

The ladies muttered their hellos, all except Daisy who was looking very miffed.

'She'll never want any other kind of a cake once she's eaten one of these,' I whispered to Daisy as I indicated Thelma. Daisy smiled, gratified.

'So, how long are you staying?' Avril asked politely. She was looking Thelma up and down in a very obvious and disdainful manner.

'Until I die or get cured,' Thelma pulled her dressing gown tighter around her. 'I've got cancer.'

Phil and Avril gasped. Daisy however, clapped her hands gleefully and said, 'And we're raising money for cancer, how weird is that!'

'Daisy, really,' my mother chastised.

'Well, isn't it a coincidence?' Daisy gushed.

'How are you raising money?' Thelma asked, giving Avril her disdainful look back with about a five-hundred-per cent return. 'Is it by looking ridiculous in the middle of the day?'

Phil laughed. 'Oh no,' she waved her perfectly manicured hand, 'what we're doing is . . .' Her voice trailed away as the others made their way into the TV room.

I cringed slightly as I heard remarks like 'how cosy' and 'how cute'. Still, at least there would be no competitive remarks from them.

My mother came out to the kitchen to help me. 'Well, Thelma certainly looks all right. Are you sure she's not having you on? It'd be just like her. Remember the day of your wedding when she said that unless you sent a taxi she couldn't go as she'd hurt her foot? And she hadn't hurt her foot at all.'

'She is sick,' I snapped, putting sandwiches on to a plate. 'So, tell me, what's happening between you and Dad?'

'Oh, nothing. The usual.' She flapped her hand and looked about the kitchen. 'What on earth has Pete done to this room?' she asked. 'It's marvellous. And the girls are only remarking on how much use he's made of the space in the TV room.'

'Mam, don't change the subject.'

'I'm not, I answered you. Anyway, I'm sure he's happy

enough – the only things he talks about now are Billy and residents' fees.'

I placed my Denby cups and plates on to my Laura Ashley tray. I always thought the plainness of one complimented the fussiness of the other. A bit like the combination of my mother and my father.

'Pete really has surpassed himself,' Mam said, hoping, I suppose, to butter me up. 'I mean, I know he was an architect and everything but I never really *rated* him. Way too modern for my tastes. And in your old house, he had no need to show off. But I suppose the old adage is true, necessity is the father of invention.'

'Yeah. Mam, can you just put those cakes out on a plate please.'

She started to do something artistic and fussy with the cakes. 'Is Thelma going to be staying for the meeting?'

'I don't know. If I ask she probably will so if I pretend that it doesn't bother me, she might go.' I put some sandwiches on a plate.

I'd found a cookery book in one of the boxes from the old house. I vaguely remembered buying it – when our kitchen had been shiny and new and I was determined to make use of it. After a disastrous chicken Maryland, I'd given up and declared the book useless. Anyway, the cookery book had recipes for sandwiches in the back of it, really unusual combinations that worked. No cooking involved. Just fresh bread and fresh ingredients.

'We could have gone out for lunch somewhere,' Mam eyed my sandwiches with suspicion. 'You should have booked a table. I would have paid.'

I ignored her comment. It was a bit late now. She'd told me to organise it.

When we joined the others, Thelma was loudly informing Avril about how hard it had been looking after three wild boys with no husband. 'And Peter was the worst. Always climbing trees and stealing apples. I tell you, I had more grief with him than the other two put together.'

'Children can break your heart, all right,' Avril nodded solemnly.

'And how would you know?' my mother asked archly, sitting down in the seat furthest away from Avril. 'All you have are cats.'

'Which will never break my heart,' Avril said back. 'They won't go and leave me when I've nurtured them and taken care of them. They won't deny me hugs and kisses just because they've outgrown them. Oh no,' she turned back to Thelma, 'I know what children can do all right.'

'They won't come and look after you in your old age either, though, will they?' Mam said smartly. 'I can't see a cat doing your shopping for you or changing your sheets when—'

'Can we get down to business?' I said hastily. Obviously the acrimony between my mother and Avril was still going strong. 'Now, first I want to say that things are not looking too good.' That got their attention. Avril and Mam stopped glaring at each other. Daisy looked at her cake and put it back down on her plate. Thelma however, reached out and took a second cake. My next words were over the sounds of her munching and sucking cream from the centre of it. 'There doesn't seem to be much interest in what we're doing,' I said, holding the emails up.

'No!' Thelma cackled to herself. We all ignored her.

'A lot of minor celebs have agreed, but they're just looking for publicity. As for the more famous ones, they either haven't replied yet or have turned us down.'

'I knew we should have gone for a dinner,' Daisy moaned.

'Yes, well it's too late now,' Phil sat up straight and seemed about to make an announcement, before adding, 'but yes, maybe that would have been better.'

'A bit of grub, that's the only way to go,' Thelma now had her third cream cake in her hand and was speaking between mouthfuls.

'Anyway,' I continued, 'I have another idea.' I outlined Laura's idea and then I told them that she would guarantee us TV time if we managed at least one big name. That met with approval.

'The problem is *getting* the name,' I said. 'I think it's a case of contacting the celebrity directly, forget about going through an agent.' Joking, I asked, 'Anyone know Brad Pitt's address?'

'Brad who?' Avril asked.

My mother began to choke. I noted in horror that she had one of my sandwiches in her hand. The five of us turned and stared at her before Avril had the presence of mind to try walloping her on the back. The wallops were unnecessarily hard, I noted through my frozen state.

'Stop!' my mother snapped, still coughing. 'I'm fine. I'm not choking.'

'Not now, you're not,' Avril said. 'I saved your life.'

'Huh, that'll be the day. It's one thing saving my life, quite another voting for my husband instead of me.'

'What's this?' Thelma, I noted with alarm, had almost polished off the cakes. Surely that wasn't good for a sick woman.

Nobody bothered to explain. Instead, Avril muttered,

'Well, the next time you choke, don't expect me to save you.'

'I wouldn't expect anything from you,' my mother said. 'Now, what I was about to say, before I nearly had my spine shattered, was that we do know the address of a celebrity.'

'We do?' Daisy, Avril and Phil chorused.

'We do!' I couldn't believe I hadn't thought of it already. 'Yes, we do. My old house. David Dunne bought my old house.'

'He did not!' Daisy was agog. 'What an honour for you. Wow!'

'He did,' my mother said smugly. 'But it was such a lovely house.'

'Designed by my son,' Thelma said, even more smugly. 'Peter, designing for the stars. Oh, he was always a talented boy. Troublesome but talented. Now, hand us over a sandwich, Poppy. Those cakes are terrible sweet.'

'Gustav's cakes are not too sweet,' Daisy hissed in annoyance.

'David who?' said Avril.

'Do you not watch the films,' Phil asked. 'He's the lad who was in that one – *Titanic*.'

'That was Leonardo DiCaprio,' I said.

'Yeah, that was his name in the film, but in real life—'

'Leonardo DiCaprio,' I said. 'David Dunne is the Irish actor. And if we get him, we'd really have a name. Now,' I looked at them all. 'We need a personal story. I can ask Maxi – her story is a good one – but we need someone who can do a good job on Maxi's story. Who's up for it?'

They all muttered uneasily and looked down at the carpet which, I noted in alarm, was wearing thin.

'They're nice sandwiches,' Thelma said. 'Huh, when I'm on my own with you I don't get food half this good.' She reached out and took another. 'And what's wrong with my personal story? What do you need to get a stranger to talk to you for? Janey, I should have got cancer after Larry died – how I didn't with all the stress of bringing up three boys on my own is a miracle. Huh, what I have now is probably a delayed reaction.'

I gave a sort of vague smile in her direction. There was no way I was writing her story.

'I vote for Poppy,' my mother put her hand up in the air. 'Who votes for Poppy? After all, Poppy, you know this Maxi woman and you know Thelma, so you're the best person to write both.'

I desperately didn't want to do it – I had already written a letter that I thought was good and no one had responded. But every hand in the room went up. I was stuck with it.

'We can start as soon as you like,' Thelma told me graciously.

Thelma was sick that afternoon. Terribly sick. So sick that I was going to call the doctor, but she waved me away.

'It was nice food,' she said as she lay in her bed, her big face as white as the copious amount of cream she'd consumed, 'and I enjoyed it. The doctor will kill me himself if he knew, and if being sick is the price to pay for enjoying good things, then I'll pay it.'

'But—'

'Poppy, you always were the most annoying person. Read my lips. Don't–call–the–doctor. And–don't–tell–Peter– because–he's–worse–than–you.' With that, she turned her back to me and pulled the bedclothes right up to her chin.

I gently closed the door.

36

ANY THOUGHTS I might have had that maybe Maxi would be reluctant to share her story in public were dismissed by her enthusiastic 'Jaysus, I'll make yer pubes stand on end with the stuff I can give you' answer.

'And you won't mind me writing it out and posting it and everyone knowing?' I said, just to be doubly sure she understood what it all involved.

'Nope.' She handed me a coffee – the first one she'd ever made me. 'Sure, it'd be like Jack was remembered, wouldn't it? Everyone would know him and know what he went through and then they'll all feel sorry and want to be in the auction.'

'That's the idea,' I smiled.

'Well, I can tell you how it all started and how I felt and then you can take a picture of my tattoo – bring your camera in tomorrow and I'll pose.'

'Now, there's an offer I can't refuse,' I grinned.

Maxi guffawed and slapped me on the back, my coffee spilling out all over my white suit.

'He was forty when he was diagnosed. He had a cold that wouldn't shift and it was a couple of months before he did anything about it. Off he went to the doctor who sent him for an X-ray and when he got the results, time bleeding stopped.'

'Of course, with the treatment we knew we'd probably never have a chance of kids if he did survive. Oh, there's all talk of freezing sperm and stuff now, but not then as far as I could remember. Anyway, I didn't care at the time – I just wanted him to live. But he didn't respond to treatment at all. They found secondary cancer on his liver then and we knew his time was running out. He found it hard to accept he was going to die, really angry and then silent, and then one day I went into him and he smiled. I knew then that he wasn't going to fight it any more. Apparently the nurse told him the butterfly story – that he was in a chrysalis and that when he died he would transform into a butterfly. I laughed my hole off when I heard that and he got upset and then I got upset and then I got the tattoo.'

She told me the tattoo story again and I typed that up too. Then she said, 'Here, get out the camera there, I'll just roll down my trousers a little.'

Of course Thelma would not be deterred. When she heard that I'd Maxi's story typed up she snapped out, 'Where's your tape recorder? How will I know if you'll remember right if you won't tape it.'

'What?'

'My personal story. Tattoos are one thing but bringing up three boys on your own is another. Now, hurry up and get your things and we'll start.'

'Well, Thelma, Maxi has agreed—'

'And so have I.' She folded her hands together and looked expectantly at me. 'Hurry up.'

'Dropped dead on me in the middle of a field,' she began when I returned with the recorder. 'A massive heart attack they said. Well, how I didn't have one myself, I don't know. I had to bring three boys up on my own. Imagine, Billy multiplied by three. Pete took it the hardest – wouldn't go to school, wouldn't stay in the house. The child was only five so I don't think he understood. He ran wild for a few years. Then he met that awful Gavin character. Do you know how hurtful it is when your child prefers to be in someone else's house to being with you? Well, that was Pete. Spent nights in Gavin's house and when he wasn't there, he talked constantly about Gavin. Oh, sorry, I'm going off the subject. It's just I hate the way they stole him from me. Anyway, my disease. Well, I discovered a lump, just before last Christmas – but it might have been there for years – probably since Larry died. That was a shock, you know. A terrible shock. I went out into the field and there he was – dead. I stood there for just ages, and there was this terrible screaming coming from somewhere and it was me. Finding him dead was worse than finding out about the cancer. I mean, with all the stress in my life, I supposed I'd get some sort of horrible disease. And wasn't I right? Wasn't I right? And the lads were no help – Michael and Joe went away. At least Peter stayed. Well, until you took him. That was stressful too. Stress has to come out somewhere, you know.'

Four days later, I typed up Maxi's story and posted it off to David Dunne. I listened to Thelma's recording and noticed that she had hardly referred to her cancer at all. All she had focused on were her kids and what had happened in that field thirty years ago. That's what mattered to her. That's what gave her her sleepless nights. I listened and my heart went out to the three little boys who hadn't been helped to deal with their grief. My heart went out to a woman who had only known to cope as best she could but that at some level knew she had failed her family.

For the first time in the wasteland of my new life, I felt a little lucky.

37

THE PSYCHOLOGIST'S OFFICE wasn't the imposing building I had been expecting. It was a single storey building, bright and airy, and very child friendly with loads of cartoon characters and fairy stories painted on the walls. Dr Jim Ryan was young enough too – maybe in his early forties – with a boyish grin and a friendly manner, so I immediately felt at ease. Billy sat beside me, staring about. I had done my best to explain to Billy that he was going to go to a special doctor to see if he could help him make some friends in school.

Jim Ryan quietly told me not to give Billy any special warnings on how to behave. I was to let Billy do exactly as he pleased. 'It's so I can see him as he is,' he told me, 'not as his mother has warned him to be.'

So we sat there, me and Billy, across from Jim.

'Hello, Billy, I'm Jim,' he said. 'I wonder if you would colour in this picture for me?'

He passed a picture of a racing car across his desk. Billy looked curiously at it and shrugged, 'I don't like colouring, it's boring.'

'Well, try to do a little of it, would you?'

Billy gave a dramatic sigh and picked up a crayon. He lasted all of three minutes before getting up to wander about the room. He walked to the shelves and tried to jump up and see what was on them. He dragged a chair across and stood up on it and then, still unable to reach, he balanced himself on the edge of the table and managed to pull an ornament down.

We watched him in silence for ten minutes or so. Then Jim told his secretary to take him off for some stickers.

'Do all doctors give stickers?' Billy asked as he was led out the door.

'Only the nice ones,' the secretary said.

Jim Ryan turned to me, a faint smile playing about his lips. 'Now, Mrs Shannon, I've read the letter from your doctor and just looking at Billy here, he's restless. That in itself is not a diagnosis of ADD or ADHD. Basically, what ADHD means is that a child exhibits the following symptoms:' he started to list them off on his fingers. 'They can't sit still, they're easily distracted, they don't seem to listen when spoken to directly, they can be impulsive, aggressive, they lose things and they very rarely follow instructions.' He made a comical face. 'But really that describes just about every kid at some stage. What I do to diagnose ADD or ADHD is observe the child over a longer period of time and do a full cognitive profile on them. This involves a series of tests – mostly puzzles – that assess the verbal, perceptive, processing speed and working memory that Billy has.'

He made Billy sound like a computer.

'These tests, combined with some forms I'd like you to fill out, will give me a picture of just where Billy is at. I also want Billy's school to fill the forms out too.'

'But Billy's on school holidays now,' I said.

'That's fine. I'll post them to the school and they'll forward them on to his teacher and she can send them back to me.'

'OK.'

'If he is diagnosed with ADD or ADHD, it's not the end of the world. I will offer you a programme that you can follow to see if it makes any difference to his behaviour and if not, well, there always the option of medication. But we won't go down that road just yet. OK?'

'OK.'

'Now, there are a lot of things that can mimic the ADD symptoms – anxiety, depression, allergies or problems at home or school – and the tests Billy will do will rule all that out.'

'So, it mightn't be ADD at all?'

'That's what we're here to find out, ey?'

'Yes.'

'So, give me a picture, if you can, of Billy at home.'

So I told him, and in a way it was a release. It was as if I was purging myself of all my worries and doubts about Billy. I told him of even the most minor things and I didn't feel as if I was betraying my child or criticising him, I was just recounting his exploits and it was up to this man to evaluate them. 'The most worrying thing of all,' I said, finishing up, 'is that he doesn't seem to think before he does something. He does really dangerous things and he doesn't seem to be aware that he could hurt himself. That scares me.'

'He's impulsive.'

'Yes.' I was twisting my hands together – a habit I have when I'm nervous.

'Has he done this all along or has it got worse recently?'

I thought hard. His first teacher hadn't really remarked on it, except to say that he was quite lively. 'I don't know,' I admitted. 'Maybe he has been, it's just that I seem to be more aware of it now.' I gulped. 'He's my only child. I don't know about other children and what they do.'

'And no one would expect you to,' he said, his words reassuring me.

'He did have friends in his old school.'

'Old school?'

'We moved about eight months ago.'

'Right.' He wrote this down. 'And was he happy about the move?'

I shrugged. 'Well, we had to move so he had no choice really. We did bring him to see the new house a couple of times before we moved, but I don't think he quite understood what moving meant.' I smiled a little. 'It's hard to get a small boy to understand things like that, especially when he hardly sits still enough to listen anyway.'

Jim nodded.

'But he did say that he liked his smaller room,' I muttered, pathetically aware of what a crap answer this was. 'And he did make a friend on the road.'

Jim Ryan wrote this down too. 'Mrs Shannon,' he began.

'Poppy, please.'

'So, Poppy, are you agreed that this test will be carried out?' I nodded and he continued, 'I'd also like at least one parent to be there – both if possible. I find it makes it easier for parents to understand if they see for themselves what's going wrong.'

My blood ran cold. I didn't know if Pete would come, but I nodded anyway.

'I'll get my secretary to pen you in for assessment in two weeks' time, if that suits?'

'OK.'

'And in between sessions, I'd like you to observe Billy and

write down the times when he seems particularly hard to manage. That way we might get an idea of what sparks him off.'

'OK.'

'So now we'll just go and get Billy and have a chat with him, OK?' He buzzed his secretary and she came in, Billy bounding before her.

I felt like scooping Billy up and running as far away from this place as I could, but that wouldn't do either of us any favours. Instead, I listened to Billy as he chatted away, sometimes listening and sometimes not. I watched as he prowled about the room, knocking against things and pulling at things. And I listened to him laugh.

That, I thought, is my child.

38

M Y MOTHER INVITED me out for lunch the following Tuesday. 'We can shop for a few clothes and then we can go for a bite to eat,' she said. The horrible fact that I had no money for clothes wasn't going to stop me. Maybe, I thought, she'd buy me an advance Christmas present or something. Despite the fact that I was reluctant to accept money from my parents, gifts were something else. And Pete wouldn't notice, I thought. He had become so withdrawn and hard to talk to.

After Billy had visited the psychologist I'd attempted to tell Pete about it, but he'd interrupted me by asking abruptly how his mother was, and when I started to talk about her he'd said that he had to go and ring Gavin. I'd told him that he talked a lot more to Gavin now than he did to me and he said that that was just stupid. Then after his phone conversation with Gavin, he'd told me that they were going out together the following weekend.

I didn't mind – being with him was becoming hard for me. I told him that he might as well go and not come back. And he said that that was stupid. And then his mother had rung her bell from upstairs and we'd stopped arguing.

'So, Poppy,' my mother broke into my thoughts, 'where

will I meet you? I presume you've got himself to take care of Billy.' She always referred to Dad as 'himself' now.

'Yes, and he'll be minding Thelma too, so he'll be a busy man.'

'Yes, the devil finds work for idle hands,' she sniffed, and I have to say, I wasn't quite sure what she meant. 'Where will we meet? Will I meet you outside your clothes shop?'

'No!' The vehemence of my reaction surprised her. 'Eh, no,' I said again, slightly calmer. 'Let's meet in town at two-thirty. Say, outside Brown Thomas?'

'Yes,' I heard a smile in her voice. 'OK. That'd be nice.'

And so I met her and she shopped for both of us, buying me a soft grey silk dress that I had to promise to wear the night of the auction, and despite my better judgement, I bought a pair of shoes too. I love shoes, especially sparkly ones, and these were the queen of sparkly shoes. Thin high heels with beaded crossover ankle straps that snake their way up the leg. I don't know why I bought them, as I knew for sure that I didn't have the money for them, but just the very act of handing over my credit card and taking them from the cashier in the distinctive brown-and-cream shop bag was enough to give me a temporary high, to right my world – even if it was only for an hour or so.

'We should do this more often,' Mam said, sinking into a seat in the Westbury and signalling to the waiter that she wanted service. 'Two coffees and some of your scones,' she ordered.

'Yeah,' I sat down too. 'We always used to. Every Tuesday.'

'We did.' Mam rearranged her bags about her. 'And you used to buy so many things. Do you miss it?'

We paused as the waiter laid the coffees in front of us

and placed the scones in the middle of the table. When he left, I answered, 'Yeah, of course I do. This is the first new thing I've bought in ages.' I patted the shoe bag. 'Though it's more of a thrill now, I guess, because I don't do it as often.'

Mam looked at me blankly.

'Honestly,' I grinned. 'I mean it.' And I did too. The high of buying these shoes outstripped any I'd ever bought before. Maybe, though, it was because I knew I couldn't afford them. Still, sometimes, especially when I rowed with Pete, I missed our old life and the uncomplicated times we'd had. Me at home, Pete at work, Billy just being Billy before anyone started peering too closely at him. But maybe they'd been ignorant times too. I don't know.

I'd always looked good then as well. Now, parts of me had fallen into disrepair. My hair was not as sleek or groomed as it had been. My nails were chipped and broken. Worry lines had deepened under my eyes. Even the clothes I wore, hoarded from my old life, couldn't change me back into who I was. I doubted that even a good beautician could do that. I had changed, changed utterly. And I no longer had that perfectly kept air of the well-off.

'If you need any more thrills,' Mam offered, 'I can give you money.'

'No. No it's fine.'

She glanced curiously at me but said nothing. Instead, she handed me a scone. There was silence as we buttered them, then Mam gave a nervous little cough. 'OK, Poppy, I suppose I'd better tell you. It's part of the reason I asked you out today, but then you were having such a good time I didn't want to ruin it. Anyway, here it is,' she took a deep breath. 'Now, don't get upset, all right. I couldn't bear for

293

you to be upset. But here it is,' another deep breath, 'I'm leaving your father.'

My mouthful of scone got wedged in my throat. My eyes watered as I tried not to show I was choking. I took a huge gulp of very hot coffee which burnt my tongue and throat but mercifully sent the scone on its way. 'What?' I gasped, in shock and in pain. 'What did you say?'

'Poppy, please, don't react badly. It's for the best. What is the use of us being together when we've nothing to say to each other?'

'You haven't even tried!' I spluttered, my voice rising. 'You just haven't tried talking to him. He's nice. He's a nice man.'

'Well, you would think that, he's your father.'

'And he's your husband!'

'Poppy, please, not so loud.' Mam began to stir her coffee really hard. It swirled around and around until it came out the top and splashed on to the saucer. 'He and I have nothing in common. It's too late now. He wants me to fit into his retired lifestyle and I can't.'

'He was prepared to fit into yours.'

'Take it over more like. No, Poppy, it's been decided,' she looked at me again. 'We're selling the house and I'm getting a little apartment for myself and he's getting a little apartment for himself and he'll pay me an allowance. It's all very amicable.'

'Great!' I stood up. My parents. Splitting up. They were old, for God's sake. Old people didn't split up. 'I'm so happy for you.'

'Oh, now, Poppy—'

'Enjoy your apartment. Enjoy your single life.'

'Poppy!'

'And you can take this dress back!' I picked up the bag with the grey dress in it. 'I don't like to be bribed!'

Everyone was looking at us. Some people were a bit alarmed but the younger ones were relishing the bit of afternoon drama.

'You're not a politician then?' some young fella called out and there were a few sniggers.

I left my mother sitting in the middle of the room while I half walked, half ran out the door.

Once outside, I didn't know where to go. So I just walked. Walked and walked and walked. Over bridges and rivers, past shops and factories and houses. Walked until my feet started to ache and my head started to hammer. Walked until my thoughts stopped swirling like hurricanes in my head. Walked until the light went out of the day and I was standing on a street, in the middle of I didn't know where. Then my mobile phone started to ring. I listened to its stupid ringtone – 'Happy Talk' – and waited until it stopped. I didn't want to talk to anyone. When it finished, I fished it out from my bag. Four missed calls. Four messages. Two messages from my mother, two from my dad:

'Poppy, this is Dad. Where are you? Your mother is going crazy with worry. Call the house. Please.'

I felt a little guilty at this last frantic message, so I rang him.

Dad picked up and before I could say who I was, he asked, 'Poppy, is that you?'

'Yeah,' I gulped hard. 'She told me, Dad.'

'Yes, I know. You've had a shock. Where are you? I'll send a taxi to pick you up.'

'I don't know where I am.' That was true in many ways,

295

I reflected sadly. I didn't even know who I was any more, or where the hell I was going.

'Describe where you are.' Dad sounded like his old self – in control, ready to sort out the crisis.

I looked about. 'A street. There's a dry cleaners called Cut and Dried, there's a vegetable shop and some houses.'

'I'll look up the dry cleaners in the phonebook, hang on now.'

'Can I have a cup of tea?' I heard Thelma calling in the background.

'One second,' Dad called back. I heard him rifling through pages before announcing that he'd found out where I was. 'You stay put and I'll have a taxi out to you very soon. You were making your way back here, you're on the west road,' he said proudly, as if I'd done it on purpose.

'Dad, I need to pick up my car from town.'

'No you don't. You'll get a taxi to work tomorrow, then go off into town and pick up your car afterwards. You're far too upset to drive now.'

'But the car parking fee!'

'I'll give you the money for it. It's our fault you're in such a state. Now stay put.'

I got home at nine-thirty. Dad had the door open before I'd even put the key in the lock. 'You gave us a fright,' he said simply, as he stood looking at me. And that's when it hit me. My parents. The ones who are there for me, fighting my corner, and now they'll be apart. I'll be the glue holding them together, telling one of them something and then telling the other. It didn't seem fair. It wasn't right.

'Come in, come on,' Dad touched my arm and I realised

that I was still standing on the step, my new shoe bag clutched in my hand. 'I'll make you a coffee.'

'More than he's made me all afternoon,' Thelma said from the top of the stairs.

'Get away,' Dad flapped his hand at her and chuckled. 'Sure, a camel wouldn't drink the amount of stuff I've made you this afternoon.'

'Undrinkable, it was,' Thelma snorted. 'Poppy makes a fine cup. I missed you today – don't leave that old man in charge any more.' With that she stomped back into her room.

Dad smiled at me. 'A right auld bitch,' he said loudly.

I gave a shaky smile in return. 'Like Mam,' I muttered.

'Oh now,' Dad patted me on the back as he led me into my own kitchen. 'At least she's honest. I wouldn't have left her but she's right, we don't have a life together any more, and I've only myself to blame.'

'No,' I said. 'She won't try.'

'I didn't try either,' Dad said.

'That's not true.' I sat down and watched him fill the kettle – only enough in it for a couple of cups, my dad wasn't the sort to boil a full kettle of water for one cup of coffee.

'It is,' Dad sat down beside me. He gazed at me and for the first time I noticed his eyes. I'd always been slightly scared of my dad's gaze – dark brown eyes that seemed bottomless – but now, they were turned on me and they seemed the softest eyes I could ever imagine. 'I worked all my life, Poppy, because that's what I supposed men did. I stopped talking to your mother once I'd married her. I never asked her how she felt or things like that. I never asked you.'

'Yeah, but—'

He held up his hand. 'It was easy and safe. And to be

honest, I've never been an emotional man – which is why I'm good in business and bad in relationships.'

'You can learn! She hasn't given you a chance.'

He shrugged. 'She doesn't want to, Poppy. That's the bottom line and there is no use fighting it.'

I scrambled for something to say, some word that would make him chase after her and win her back. 'But you have to fight it! She's your wife. And you can learn to be what she wants.'

He smiled. 'No, I can't. I can only be me and she doesn't want me, and it hurts. It does. But at least I have you,' he grasped my hand, 'and Billy. And he's teaching me all sorts of things, things like how brilliant he is. You know I never had much time for him before, but at least it's not too late with him, and that makes me glad.'

'Good,' I sighed.

'And at least I'm getting to know you now too,' he said. 'That's better than good.'

I managed a shaky smile.

'So, in a way, the fact that you lost all your money has worked out well for me,' he grinned.

It made me laugh.

298

39

I WAS STILL up when Pete came home from work. He usually got in at around one in the morning, and even if I was awake I'd pretend to be asleep. We were dancing elaborately around each other now – there was a huge rift between us and yet we were still retaining eye contact and trying to ignore it.

'Hey,' Pete arrived in, dressed in his ridiculous uniform. He threw his coat across the kitchen chair and went to fill the kettle. 'How come you're still up?'

I remained at the table, my chin cupped in my hands. 'They've separated,' was all I could manage.

'Who?' Pete was oblivious. He took some bread out of the press and began a search for the butter.

'My mother and father.' There was a silence, and in the silence I turned to look at him. 'She told me, today, when we went shopping.'

'Separated?' Pete gawped. 'Seriously?'

'Yeah.' My voice wobbled. 'And Dad is being so good about it, but I know he's devastated. And he was trying to do what she wanted and she just, she just . . .' For the first time since I'd been told, a tear slipped out from the corner of my eye. I hastily brushed it away.

For some reason, I didn't want to cry with Pete there. He must have seen it though, because he dropped his knife on to the counter with a clatter and crossed over to me, wrapped his arm about my shoulders and hugged me hard, whispering 'hush' in my ear. I liked him doing that. It was the first time in a long time that we'd had any sort of connection. I started to blubber a little and then I sniffed and then with a sudden release of emotion it all came out – what she'd said, what he'd said, what I thought. All the time he held me and stroked my hair. And then something shifted in my head, I don't know what. The blinding light of clarity intruded into the lovely safe warmth of his arms. Suddenly I knew why we were floundering: slowly but surely our roles were reversing. Pete was retreating from the marriage because he wasn't in control any more. It scared him that I was becoming stronger. I had to do the majority of caring for his mother – tending to her every afternoon and evening and bringing her to the hospital. I had to get a job, crap and all as it was, to help pay our way. And I had to help Billy because Pete was refusing to see that anything was wrong in the perfect life he had conjured for himself. Weaknesses in our lives were being exposed and I was the one trying to plug the gaps. And now, because I was upset, he was wading in and being his old self again.

Maybe I should have let him. Maybe I should have ignored my building irritation, but I didn't. Softly, I asked, 'How come you can't put your arms around me when I get worried about Billy?'

'What?'

'Or why don't you let me put my arms about you when you worry about your mother?'

'What?' He pulled away slightly.

'You're only doing this because you feel good that I'm upset.'

His eyes widened in shock. I had hurt him. 'What?'

'You just want to be in control, don't you, Pete? Comforting me is what you're used to, isn't it?' My voice rose. 'Well, newsflash, this is not the only thing upsetting me at the moment, but you don't want to acknowledge the rest, do you?'

He continued to stare at me. He opened his mouth to speak but nothing came out. His arms dangled uselessly by his sides.

'I'm going to bed.' I pushed past him.

He still said nothing.

That moment, I reckon, was the lowest point in our marriage.

My mother rang me the next day but I couldn't bring myself to talk to her. I told her, in a clipped voice that wasn't mine, that I would discuss the plans for the auction but that I didn't want to chat. Oh, she tried to explain that what she was doing was for the best, and I said back, 'How can discarding Dad like, like an old shoe you don't want any more be for the best?'

'I'm not discarding him.'

'Yes you are!'

'Well,' she said, and I think she sounded as if she would cry, 'he discarded me for thirty-five years, think how hurtful that was. Wedding anniversaries, birthdays, all forgotten, and only flowers sent by his secretary to mark the day. How would you feel?'

'So, you're out for revenge, is that it?'

'No!' She tried to explain, her words tripping over themselves, 'Poppy, we have *nothing* in common, it all died along the way. I can't live the rest of my life with him. We've grown too far apart.'

'Yes, well, enjoy the rest of your life, so!'

'I brought you up, Poppy. I was there for you when he let you down. How can you do this to me now? At least try and understand!'

'You're letting me down now, Mam.' And I hung up the phone.

I really, really didn't want to talk to her.

Pete had been very cool with me since our row. It was for this reason that I was petrified of asking him to accompany me for Billy's assessment. Bad as we were, I didn't want to drive a permanent wedge between us.

I waited a few days and then on the Sunday evening before Billy's assessment, I asked Pete if he was working on the coming Wednesday afternoon. It was a stupid question, as I knew he was.

'Yeah.'

'Oh. Right.' I studied my nails, hoping he'd ask why I'd asked him. My heart was pounding.

'Why?' he asked.

'It's just that Billy is having his assessment and the doctor thinks it would be good if we were both there.' I tried to sound casual about it.

'Oh,' Pete nodded. 'Right.'

'So you'll come?' I hardly dared believe it.

'He's my boy.' Pete said.

I suppose it was a 'yes'.

*　　*　　*

That week, the last week in July, the 'weekus horriblus', was when I noticed that the chemo was beginning to take its toll on Thelma. She seemed a lot more fragile, a lot less caustic, and her hair had started to fall out. She never referred to it though. Instead, she began to complain that things had started to taste funny, so I joked that my food always tasted funny, and she did a strange thing. She reached out and took my arm. 'Never belittle yourself,' she said earnestly. 'Never do that.'

'It was a joke,' I said startled.

'It wasn't a joke,' she snapped, taking her hand away abruptly. 'You *are* a terrible cook, but don't admit it.'

Jesus, I thought.

'Poor Peter wouldn't be so thin if you cooked properly,' she went on, wiping her hand along the bed as if it was contaminated from touching me. 'Still, at least he gets a decent feed in the hotel. Maybe it's as well he works there. He'd probably be dead by now otherwise.'

'Thank you, Thelma,' I said crossly. 'Thanks for those confidence-boosting words.' I slammed the door on her as she cackled to herself.

And that, pretty much, was the horrible taste of July.

40

PETE DRESSED UP for Billy's assessment while I wore my jeans and runners. I literally hadn't the energy to bother dressing up, and anyway, what difference would it make to the outcome?

I told Billy that we were going on an outing, that Jim Ryan was going to give him tests and that if Billy did his very best, we'd all go and get a McDonald's.

'I will do my very very best,' Billy promised earnestly as he ripped off his seatbelt and bolted from the car the minute I had the car door open. 'Come on, hurry up,' he shouted, dancing from foot to foot outside Jim's offices.

As Pete joined me on the footpath, I wished he would take my hand, do something, to take the nervous feeling from my belly, but I think he was unsure of what to do himself. Ever since I told him that he was only happy when he was in control, he had withdrawn little by little. I don't know if he was even aware of it, but I missed the hand holding and soft kisses.

'Come on,' I tossed over my shoulder to him, 'let's go.'

He followed me up the steps and into the clinic.

Jim was waiting for us. He had a small desk set up in his room and Billy immediately bounded over and began examining the things on it. Jim shook both our hands, telling us he was delighted we could make it. Then he asked his secretary to bring us in a coffee.

While Pete and I sipped our drinks, holding on to our mugs as if they were the most comforting things in our lives, Jim explained what he was about to do. He made it simple so that Billy could understand too. He said that he was going to give Billy a series of tests since ADD children tend to have a hard time with maths as the rules for solving problems kept changing, whereas they could be great at other things once they were stimulated and motivated. 'ADD children,' he said, looking over at Pete as if he somehow knew Pete was having a huge problem accepting this, 'have a lot to offer. It's just a case of management.'

Pete nodded silently and his gaze dropped back to his cup.

I found the whole process fascinating, despite my jangling nerves. Billy was given tasks suited to his age. He had to code symbols to letters and simple things like that. Jim was great with him and even when Billy veered wildly off course, he had a wonderful way of steering him back again. It was a long few hours and with Billy jumping about every time he lost interest, two hours turning into three.

'That's it,' Jim stood up and tousled Billy's hair. 'You're a great chap. I'll see you again when I collate the results.' He turned to us. 'Thanks for coming. I'll get my secretary to ring you with an appointment as soon as possible. Again, it would be great if you could both come.'

'Sure,' I said, as brightly as I could. 'We'll be there.'

Pete, however, didn't answer.

We left the office and once out on the street, Billy said, 'Wasn't I good? Did I do good?'

Pete crouched down to his level. He held out his arms

and Billy hugged him. 'You're the best boy,' he said with feeling. 'The best.' Then he hoisted Billy on to his shoulders and with Billy screeching and laughing he jogged down the street with him.

The last time I'd seen him do that, we'd been happy.

41

THE 4TH AUGUST was a bright, sunny day with lots of blue sky. It was the first decent day of that summer and I was due to spend it sitting in the hospital beside Thelma as she got her treatment.

Just as I was about to lock the house up, the phone rang. I considered leaving it, but I can never resist a phone call. I knew I'd spend the whole of the time in the hospital wondering who had rung, so I picked up.

'Hello, I'm looking to speak to Poppy Shannon?' a male voice said.

I hoped it wasn't anyone selling things. Honestly, someone had rung one week and offered me an alternative phone line. I'd told them that I didn't have a phone. 'No phone?' they said puzzled, 'But, but, I'm talking to you on a phone.' 'I've no phone,' I insisted, grinning. They'd hung up, convinced, I'm sure, that I was mad. I probably was, I thought afterwards, if that was my only source of amusement.

'Poppy here,' I said in as disagreeable a voice as I could, so I might put them off.

'Hiya Poppy, this is David Dunne – you know, I'm—'

'No way!' I gasped out. There was a startled pause. I silently kicked myself. 'David Dunne . . . the . . . the actor?' I stammered.

'Poppy, I'm going to be late,' Thelma shouted out of the car.

I closed the front door on her. 'That David Dunne?' I asked.

'Yeah. I got your letter.' He paused for a second. 'My mother died of cancer, just last year.'

'Oh. Oh dear. I am sorry.' I didn't know what else to say. Part of me screamed *are you going to agree to do the auction? Are you? Are you?*

'I'd like to do the auction, if that's OK. I'm sorry for taking so long to reply, I was out of the country for the last couple of months.'

'If that's OK?' I couldn't help it. I giggled. Then I giggled again.

Thelma began to ring the doorbell over and over again and knock sharply on the door. She was yelling too, only I blocked her out.

'It's *so* OK,' I answered.

'Sorry?' he sounded confused.

'David,' I said, and I didn't know if I was going to laugh or cry or scream or what, 'it is *so* OK for you to do this auction. It is the *best* thing for you to have agreed. Thank you so much.'

'Yeah, well, once some gorgeous babe gets me, I'll be wrapped.'

I giggled again. 'We'll try to organise that for you. Thanks.'

'Right, well, you can email all the details to my agent. I've told her that I'm doing it.' With that he gave me his agent's home email. Her *home* email. And then he hung up.

I stood for a second just staring at the phone before giving a huge screech of delight, which momentarily stopped

Thelma in her tracks. Then I flung open the front door and grabbed my mother-in-law about the waist and shouted, 'David Dunne is doing the auction! David Dunne is doing the auction!' I did attempt a dance with her, but she was having none of it. She pushed me off.

'And I am getting chemotherapy. Have a bit of respect,' she muttered, though I do think she smiled. But even if she hadn't, I would still have enjoyed that moment.

I had done this thing right. I had got David Dunne. I had done this right and nobody, least of all my cranky mother-in-law was going to ruin the moment. Only she did. But it wasn't her fault.

Apparently, from all the blood tests and treatment, her veins had collapsed. It was hard for the nurse to find a vein to administer her her medicine. She kept trying and trying and in the end, unable to stomach any more, I snapped, 'Look, you're hurting her. Can't you see it?'

The nurse flushed. 'I know, I'm sorry. Look, maybe I'll go and get a hot-water bottle to see if we can make those veins pop up, all right?'

'You should have done that first,' I grumped. I turned to Thelma, who had remained admirably silent throughout the exchange. 'Are you all right?'

'Fine.' She was lying because there were tears in her eyes. She turned away from me and started to examine her hands. 'Jesus, they're in a terrible state, aren't they?'

And they were. Thelma's big rough hands were totally bruised and sore. I touched her shoulder and said gently, 'Two more sessions, Thelma, and then you'll be finished. It'll be over then.'

She nodded but said nothing.

The nurse came back with a hot-water bottle and placed

it on top of Thelma's hands. Then she wrapped a blanket around her and told her to wait a few minutes.

We sat there in silence, both of us praying, I think, for Thelma's veins to pop up. I searched for something to talk about but couldn't think. Being in the hospital with Thelma always made me feel slightly nauseous. I held out my bag of boiled sweets to her. Apparently they're good to suck when you're having chemo.

Thelma shook her head and gave me a wry smile. 'When I go, I want to go with all my teeth intact. Do you know, I don't have a filling or anything. Peter takes after me for that – his father's teeth were terrible.'

'Were they?' I was glad she was talking.

'Oh yes, a terrible man for the sweets. A terrible man for food. He ate all about him. He'd eat the pus out of acne spots, so he would.'

My stomach heaved.

'I reckon he died from eating too much. A big man, he was. Big Lar, they used to call him. It took eight men to carry his coffin out of the church.'

'Wow.'

Thelma stopped abruptly as she was remembering. There was a rare smile hovering about her mouth. She looked human all of a sudden.

'What was he like?' I asked softly. It was the one area of Pete's life that he never talked about. 'Pete never says.'

'Sure, Peter was only five when he died, he'd hardly remember. Though he loved his daddy, so he did. Lar would put Peter up on his shoulders when he was rounding up the sheep or the cows and they'd walk across the fields together. I always thank God Peter wasn't with him the day he died.'

'Was he like Pete? Did he look like Pete?'

'No,' Thelma shook her head impatiently, 'Peter is like me. Michael and Joe are more like Lar.' I must have looked doubtful because, she said again, 'Peter and me, we share the same eyes and the same temperament.'

I suppressed a smile. 'Sunny and good natured?' I asked.

Thelma threw me a look of pure distain. 'Huh, if he's so sunny and good natured, why are you constantly picking fights with him?'

'I do not!'

'Well, that's not what I hear. Bicker, bicker, bicker, the two of you. Huh, even the night he went out with his friend, that eejit Gavin, you got on to him.'

'He came home drunk. He had spent money we don't have.'

'Not like you, ey, with your fancy shoes. I saw them.'

I glowered at my bag of sweets. How dare she, it was none of her business. 'Well, you don't miss much, do you?'

'Nope.' She paused. 'Just my breast now and again.'

I looked up and she was smiling. And I smiled too.

'Go easy on him,' she said softly. 'He's not as strong as you.'

Before I could reply, the nurse came back and declared herself well pleased with Thelma's veins. And as she attempted to inject her again, I saw Thelma wince. Now there, I thought, was one strong woman.

42

'JAYSUS, WHAT A gaff!' Maxi exclaimed over her morning cup of coffee. 'A snip at its valued price of ten million,' she read out, guffawing loudly. 'Ten million. And would you look at it!'

I peered over her shoulder and saw, to my horror, my parents' house as the featured property on the property pages of the morning newspaper. They'd decided to auction it. My father had already moved out and bought himself a penthouse apartment while my mother was in situ until the place sold. I still wasn't talking to her, except to inform her that David Dunne had agreed to the auction.

'Some people, ey?' Maxi said, gawping at the photos.

Various shots of the outside of the house were shown, including my father's attempts at gardening, which marred the print a little. The inside pictures, however, more than made up for it. The wide sweeping staircase that dominated the entrance hall, before splitting in two when it reached the landing. The gleaming marble foyer. The gorgeous shaker kitchen with granite counter tops and island.

'What a gaff,' Maxi whistled.

'Yeah,' I agreed.

Maxi read on haltingly. 'Home of the entrepreneur George Furlong and his wife for the last twenty years, it is a shrine to class and taste.' Maxi raised her eyebrows, 'Jaysus, if we had their money, we'd have class and taste too, ey. What would you do if you had ten million, Poppy?' Before I could answer, she said, 'I know what I'd do. I'd buy a villa in Benidorm in Spain. Then I'd get plastic surgery to have bigger boobs and then I'd head off to Spain and lie, topless, in the sun all day.'

'Sounds great,' I lied brightly.

'But there is no way,' Maxi jabbed the paper, hard, 'no way I'd ever buy a poxy house in Dublin. Jaysus, there's no sun, no decent men and who wants a big garden anyway? I mean, look at the mess this crew have made of theirs.'

My dad would be highly insulted, I thought, amused.

'Auction on Thursday next,' Maxi finished reading. 'Aw well, it won't be as exciting as auctioning David Dunne, huh? I can't believe you got him. And with my letter and everything.'

She had told everyone about her letter to David Dunne. All the customers in the euro shop were full of it. Isobel had even ordered in David Dunne posters in honour of Maxi and they were to be sold at a euro each.

'I got the job,' I heard someone say later that morning. I was busy arranging some Halloween brooms on a shelf. It was still only early August, but Isobel thought that it would be good to beat the Halloween rush. And besides, Isobel had added, you never know who might want a broom before then.

Indeed.

'Sorry,' someone tipped me on the back. 'I just came in to say that I got the job that time you helped me out. That's why I haven't been in. I've been working, and now that I've got a day off work I thought I'd come in and tell you.'

It was the young girl who'd asked my advice on what to wear.

'Oh, that's great.' I was delighted for her and chuffed for me. 'Well done.'

'Yeah, I'm a receptionist in a builders' supply yard.'

'Great! Do you like it?'

'Yes. I like the money.'

'Don't we all,' I grinned.

'And I wouldn't have got it, only I had nice stuff on. They even asked me where I'd got it. Imagine.'

'Imagine.' I didn't know what else to say. The girl was shifting from foot to foot and swinging a bag to and fro. I finished putting the final broom beside a big pretend pumpkin before saying again, 'Well, well done.'

'This Saturday,' the girl followed me up the shop, 'I'm going on a date with one of the builders who comes in. He specialises in building walls. He's very nice.'

'Good.'

'Are you actually going to buy something?' Maxi asked crossly.

'And, well, I don't know what to wear,' the girl continued, ignoring Maxi. 'We're going for a meal. It sounds posh.' She opened up her bag. 'Would this go nice d'you think?'

She held up for my inspection a pair of very tight-looking black trousers and a vest-top. They were horrendous.

'Eh, maybe you should just wear what you're comfortable in,' I muttered, not wanting to hurt her feelings and wondering too if she was going to come in and pester me to dress her for every important occasion of her life.

'So, I should just wear my tracksuit, then?'

'No!' God, had she no clue? 'Eh,' I pretended to study the jeans. 'They look very tight.'

'They are,' she nodded enthusiastically. 'They show off

everything. And the top just comes to here.' She indicated her navel. 'What do you think?'

'Sometimes less is more,' I said.

'So I should get a smaller top?'

'No, you should aim for a nice loose pair of trousers – not a tracksuit,' I said hastily, 'but a stylish pair, that maybe flair out a little to compliment your hips.' I looked at her. 'You've a nice figure and a good bust. Go for a v-neck top, show a little cleavage, but make it a top that flairs out slightly to cover any tummy.'

She winced. 'Oh, that's a lot to think of. Can I write it down?'

I got a piece of paper and drew a diagram of what she should wear based on her body type. I also wrote down a list of colours that would suit her. 'OK?'

'Cool. Yeah, OK.' She held the paper to her as if it were a diamond. 'I'll let you know how it goes.'

As she danced out the shop I found Maxi glowering at me. 'What's wrong with tight things?' she snapped. 'I wear tight things.'

'Yes, but sometimes it's better not to.' I smiled in what I hoped was a nice way.

'Do you think my tight things make me look crap?'

'Oh no, not at all.'

'You fucking do!'

'No.' God, she was cross.

'You do!'

'No, not crap,' I said weakly. 'Just, you know . . .'

'I don't know,' she said through gritted teeth.

'Tight things are fine if you're thin,' I said. 'Otherwise they can make certain people look . . . well . . .' I gulped. 'Just make them look a bit fat.'

'Fat.' Maxi stared down at her huge frame. 'I'm not fat. Just big boned.'

'Yeah, but tight things can make big-boned people look fat too,' I said.

A big frown-line appeared between her eyebrows. 'You think I look fat!' It was a statement.

I wondered how to extract myself from this conversation. 'No,' I lied, my poor brain working frantically. I did not want to fight with this woman, she could make my life hell. She could get Charlotte to do something horrible to me. She could call in sick again and leave me on my own. 'No,' I said again. 'I just think that . . . that maybe, with some different things, you could look,' I floundered for the right words. 'Well, you could look even thinner than you do now.'

'I'd fade away,' she snapped with the confidence of one who is blinded by denial.

'Yes, but you'd look nice,' I said back.

She rolled her eyes, walked across to our special-promo hall mirrors and studied herself. 'Nic*er*,' she clarified.

'Absolutely,' I nodded.

She twisted about, her tattoo appearing and disappearing among her acres of flesh like a real fluttering butterfly. Then she walked back to her till and pretended to study it.

I sighed, relieved, and turned back to my till.

'What should I wear?' she barked out, making me jump. 'Go on, tell me if you're such a fashion guru.' She made it sound the most despicable thing to be.

'I'm not a fashion guru,' I said. 'I—'

'Short skirts? Pedal pushers? What?' She had me fixed in her gaze and I squirmed.

'None of the above,' I chortled nervously. Then, when

she didn't smile back, I said, 'Well, the idea of clothes is to make the most of your assets and minimise your flaws.'

'Flaws? What flaws have I got?'

Christ.

'I've a fairly good bust.' She shoved her chest out. 'I'd like it bigger but it's acceptably big, don't you think?'

Exceptionally big would have been my choice of words. 'V-neck,' I said. 'That shows cleavage. Go for a nice loose v-neck top.'

'Loose? Why?' Her questions were being fired like a hail of bullets at me. One of them was going to do me serious damage if I didn't watch myself.

'To show off your figure.' To cover her tummy, more like.

'A loose top will show off my figure?' she spoke doubtfully.

'Uh-huh,' I walked towards her. 'See, get something that catches you about here,' I indicated under her bust, 'because they're your best feature, and then flares out and comes down to about waist level – that's your thinnest part, see. That way, the eye is drawn to the waist and not the hips.'

'What's the matter with my hips?'

'There's nothing wrong with your hips, just your waist just looks better.'

'So, I wear a top like that and what do I wear below?'

'Nothing gathered,' I said, 'that'll only draw attention to the tummy area. Maybe a pair of wide-legged trousers, the same width all the way down.'

'Do I not want people to look at my tummy?'

I ignored the question. 'The same all the way down and get them to come to the floor. That way, they add length to your leg and make you look taller.'

'My tummy?'

'Will I write it down for you? You can go shopping and ask someone. Just try the stuff on and see.'

Maxi shrugged. 'If you want to, I don't care.'

So I did. 'In repayment for the tattoo story,' I said, pushing it towards her.

She shrugged, but I noticed her glancing at it on and off through the day. And then, just as I was cashing up, I saw her pick the slip of paper up and tuck it down her bra.

There was an envelope, addressed to Mr and Mrs Pete Shannon, on the table when I got in. It had been addressed to our old house and then been readdressed by the post office. I opened it up and saw that it was a card bearing a bunch of flowers with the word 'Sorry' underneath. Hand shaking, I opened it. It was from Jane, Adrian's wife.

Pete and Poppy,

I've so often wanted to write to you both since Adrian left but I didn't know how. Or what I could say. Or what I should say. I couldn't think straight either, it was such a shock. He took all our savings and I lost the house as I couldn't pay the mortgage. My new address is on the back of the envelope. I don't know why he did what he did. I feel I should have noticed something different about him but I didn't. The police reckon he has been taking money since last year, but I can't say that I noticed him being different. He was happier and even more hyper than normal, but I just put it down to things going well for him and Pete.

*I know you both counted him as a friend –
I counted him as my very best friend and
husband and I'm as shocked as you both
are. I'm just pulling my life back together
again and want to write to you both to thank
you for your friendship down the years and
to say it did mean a lot to us.*

*Pete, I'm sorry for refusing to speak to
you the day you phoned to see if I was OK,
but I felt so guilty and bad and horrible.
Poppy, what can I say? I do hope you're
both happy in your new home and that Billy is
keeping well. Please accept my apology on
Adrian's behalf as I can't imagine he is
happy wherever he is. I would have given my
life on his honesty.*

With all good wishes for your future,
Jane Kilbane

I traced my finger over her signature and felt so sorry for
her. At least I still had Pete. At least he was honest. Poor
Jane had no one. And I felt all warm and fuzzy that Pete
had been nice enough to ring her to see if she was OK.
That was Pete all over. Yeah, the cross part of me said, he
can do it when someone else is hurting. He's not so good
when he's hurting.

I pushed the thought from my head and resolved to write
back to Jane, giving her our new address and telling her
that we didn't blame her or feel angry at her. The fact that
we would disembowel Adrian should we ever meet him, I'd
leave out!

43

M Y HOUSE SEEMED to be in a permanent mess. When we'd lived in our old home, I'd enjoyed cleaning its wooden floors, polishing our oak furniture, shining up our mirrors and dusting the ornaments. I knew I could do those things, and I knew that I could do them well. Our house had even featured in a Sunday newspaper once – Pete and I smiling happily from our light-drenched kitchen. Now, even though the house was smaller and therefore should have been easier to keep, it wasn't. People seemed to come and go every moment of the day. There was never a time when I was alone in it.

Dad arrived over most mornings and plonked down at the kitchen table after first making himself a cuppa. I don't know if he and Pete talked, but I do know that Dad entertained Billy either by rolling around on the floor with him or by taking him off for an afternoon. Dad looked after Billy and that was it; cups and plates and crumbs stayed exactly where they were. Pete looked after his mother and Billy, and if I was lucky he thought to put a wash on.

Thelma was useless. Even if she had been well she would have been useless. Her own house was a cavern of darkness and mess. The relative neatness of my house only challenged her. She walked through the rooms dropping bits and pieces of her clothing as she went. She dragged duvets down so she could lie on the sofa and watch Rikki Lake and Oprah. Empty mugs littered the carpeted floor of the TV room. Her half-eaten lunches were left on seats. And arriving in from work in the afternoon, there was no way I could face a big tidy-up, so all I did was dump things into the dishwasher and turn it on. I ironed on demand and cooked as best I could for Thelma, Billy and me. Most of the time we had shop-bought pasta and shop-bought sauces. Thelma always examined hers as if she was about to ingest some form of toxic waste. Which, being honest, my cooking could probably rival.

It was a rare afternoon when there was peace in the place, so it was a great surprise when I came home and found a note from my dad saying that he had taken Billy to the cinema. Back when we're back, he'd written.

Pete was on his way out as I came in. 'My mother is asleep,' he said. 'She says she wasn't feeling great last night so don't do her a dinner.'

'Is she OK now?' I asked.

'I dunno, she's asleep.'

'Have you checked on her?'

'Yes.' He glared at me as he pulled on his coat. 'She's asleep.'

'OK.' I turned away from him and pretended to busy myself looking for a cup. As usual there were no clean ones. 'It would be nice if someone would bother having clean cups ready for me when I come home,' I griped, fishing one from the dishwasher and rinsing it under the tap. 'Or even had a lunch ready for me.'

'You never asked,' Pete muttered. 'I'll do you something tomorrow.'

'Great,' I said in a voice that implied that it was about time.

He didn't respond. Instead, he kissed me briefly on the cheek and left.

I have to say, it was a nice afternoon. My mother rang once but when I saw her number on caller ID I didn't bother to answer it. She left a message with her new home phone number and address. 'It's a lovely apartment in Ballsbridge,' she said, 'please come and visit when you have the chance. And bring Billy, I do miss him. And tell Thelma I was asking for her. Avril was also wondering if Pete would ring her. Tell him to be careful of her – she's notorious for younger men.' She then gave me Avril's number and urged me again to bring Billy to see her.

I felt a little sorry when I heard her mention Billy. She had always been his greatest fan. Even when he'd pulled her curtain rail down and wrestled with it she had only said that she was getting rid of those curtains anyway. My hand hovered over the phone but then I began to think ahead and I wondered what I would say to her. She had destroyed our family with her decision. She had shattered my illusion of her and Dad happily heading off into the retirement sunset, content to be together. I resented her for that, I realised, and so I pulled my hand back and I shoved it into the pocket of my jeans. Instead, I wondered why Avril wanted Pete.

Laura arrived later on. She came around the back of the house and frantically knocked on the door. I was trying to clean the kitchen floor which hadn't been done in ages.

'Come in,' I called. 'It's open.'

Laura arrived in, her boots marking the floor, and all I

could do was grin. This house was never destined to be clean, I thought.

'Ooooh, am I after making a mess?' Laura teetered around on tiptoes as if that would lessen the impact of her dirty shoes. 'Sorry. Sorry. Sorry,' and before I could say that it was OK, she said, 'But it's just that I have some news for you.'

'Yeah?'

Her face was flushed and she was grinning hugely. 'Yeah! Yeah!' she nodded. 'I've only gone and got you TV time.'

'For the auction?' My mop fell to the floor, upturning the bucket, which splashed on to the tiles. 'Shit!'

'The producers of *Anne in the Afternoon* rang and they want you all to go on and talk about the auction.'

Anne in the Afternoon was the most watched afternoon show in the country. 'No!'

'Yes!' She grabbed me by the shoulders and did a little dance. 'The David Dunne element swung it. In fact, I'd say that you'll have a lot more publicity before it's over.'

'Laura, that's great!' I hugged her. 'Fab! Thanks so much!'

'It wasn't me, you'd have got on anyway. But yes, it is fab!'

We laughed and squealed like two schoolgirls, then we splashed about in the water.

Thelma rang the bell we'd given her from upstairs.

'Sit down, Laura, I'll make us a cuppa and I'll even open up my secret stash of chocolate biscuits. Just wait until I go up to Satan.'

Laura giggled and began to fill the kettle.

Thelma's bell continued to ring as I made my way up the stairs. I knew by the insistence of her ringing that she was angry. In the beginning, this angry ringing would have me quaking or on the defensive, now I took it in my stride.

'Yes?' I stood in the doorway.

Thelma hauled herself up in bed. 'I wasn't well this morning, you know. Did Peter tell you?' She didn't look well now either. She was quite flushed.

'He did. How are you now?' I crossed towards her and knelt down by the side of her bed.

'Well,' she licked her lips. 'I would have been a lot better if I hadn't been woken up by people screaming. It gave me a shock, so it did.'

'Sorry,' I said meekly. 'It's just—'

'Can you keep it down? I have cancer you know.' Then, in case I didn't know, she spelt it out for me. 'C-A-N-C-E-R.'

'And I have news,' I said. 'N-E-W-S.' I waited for her to ask what it was. Thelma couldn't resist news. 'Go on,' I gave her a gentle shove. 'Ask what it is?'

'No point,' she sniffed. 'You're going to tell me anyway.'

And so I told her.

She pulled her covers up to her chin. 'So you'll be even more cocky than you are now,' she said, rolling over away from me. 'Wonderful.'

'Isn't it?' I said brightly. It really was getting harder to be intimidated by her, especially as she did look quite frail. 'So, would you like something to drink? I've got nice fresh fruit juice.'

'You can save that for your hyperactive son, I'll have tea, as usual.'

'Yes,' I said over my shoulder as I walked away, 'I do tend to save the tea for my underactive mother-in-law.'

'That's 'cause I have cancer,' she shouted after me. 'C-A-N-C-E-R.'

324

Laura looked at me askance when I came back down.

'Don't mind her,' I grinned. 'That's the way she likes to carry on. It keeps her going, I reckon. The woman is completely dysfunctional.'

'You're great to put up with her,' Laura mused.

'There's no putting up with her,' I said, as I rummaged for my nice biscuits. 'She says what she wants and I say what I want back and we get on fine. I prefer her that way.'

Laura giggled a little, and I suppose I probably did sound odd. A year ago I'd never have said anything like that. A year ago I'd have withered up and died rather than give as good as I got to Thelma. But now I found myself admiring her. And I meant it, I think our sparring kept her going.

I poured Laura a coffee and carried Thelma's tea up. In the spirit of generosity, I'd given her two nice biscuits as well. She eyed them suspiciously.

'Did you get a pay rise?' she asked.

'Ha. Ha.'

I noticed a flicker of a smile as she took it from me.

When I got back down again, Gavin had arrived. He was sitting across the table from Laura and they were making awkward conversation. Laura was haltingly explaining to him the good news and he was mumbling out a reply of some sort.

'Did you hear it?' I asked.

'Yeah. Cool.' He grinned up at me. Then he indicated the biscuits. 'Am I allowed?'

'Just one,' I told him sternly. 'Well, not unless you have guaranteed *The Late Late Show* for me?'

'Just one then,' he said, taking one from the packet. 'So,' he turned to Laura again, 'you're in PR?'

'Uh-huh.' She flushed. 'And don't say you're surprised.'

'OK. That stops that thread of conversation then.'

Laura giggled.

Gavin smiled.

I looked from one to the other and wondered what subject to chat about that would include us all and put us at ease with each other. 'We're expecting Billy's assessment results soon,' I said, and that put us back on track.

Gavin stayed after Laura left. I made him some chips and eggs (my speciality) and we talked about trivial stuff. Then, out of the blue, he asked, 'Poppy, what's the story between you and Pete?'

'What?'

'You.' Gavin nodded. 'And Pete.'

'Nothing.' I concentrated on my runny fried egg. I like them runny, especially when they go sort of cold and hard and you can scrape them off the plate with some toast. 'And anyway, what's it got to do with you?'

Gavin was unperturbed. 'Well, I guess, it's that he's a mate and you're a mate and I don't like getting caught in the middle.'

'You're not caught in the middle.' I looked up to find Gavin staring oddly at me.

He shrugged. Then he jabbed at his fried egg and it began to run all over his plate. 'Just, you know, he seems a bit odd these days.'

'Odd?'

'Yeah, quiet and stuff.'

'Well, his mother is sick, so I suppose that worries him.'

Gavin shook his head. 'It's more than that. You and Pete, right, you're both so sound. And, like, I'd hate it if anything ruined that for yez.'

He sounded like a kid looking for reassurance from his parent. Big eyes looked up at me as he twirled his fork absently in his hand. Only he wasn't a kid. He was Pete's friend. And mine, I suppose. So I said, 'Has Pete said anything?'

Gavin shook his head. 'That's the problem. Even when we went out last week he wasn't great.'

'Well, when he came back he certainly wasn't!'

Gavin smiled ruefully. 'Sorry 'bout that.'

There was silence for a bit. Upstairs, I heard Thelma shifting around in her bed. She turned on her radio and the sounds of music drifted down to us.

'He won't discuss Billy with me,' I blurted out suddenly. 'Or his mother. Or Adrian. Or anything else that makes him uncomfortable. I used to think that it was to protect me, but it's not. I told him that he was only happy when he was in control.' I glared at Gavin. 'So there. Now you know.'

'Right.' Now that he had an answer of sorts, Gavin didn't seem to know what to do. 'OK. Right.'

'So you can tell your precious friend that unless he starts opening up his eyes to the situation, things will not improve.' I stood up from the table and dumped the rest of my dinner in the bin.

'Maybe that would be better coming from you,' Gavin cracked a grin.

I didn't answer. Instead, I turned from him and wrenched open the dishwasher. I shoved my plate on to the bottom shelf and slammed it shut.

'He's mad about you, you know,' Gavin said. 'Always was. The first time he met you, he kept talking about you. Bored me stupid, to be honest. You know Pete, when he gets

327

excited about something you can't shut him up and he becomes really boring. Well, he was like that about you.'

I couldn't look at him. I stared out the window, into the back garden.

'When I met you, I knew what he meant. You were pure class, Poppy. We'd never seen anything like you. Pete was scared in case he'd mess up and you'd see him for what he was – a country red-neck. Jesus, he even decided there and then to set up business with Adrian to impress your folks.'

'What?'

'Yep. That's what he decided to do. Adrian had been on and on at him for ages and he kept muttering that he wasn't sure and then, he did it.'

'But . . . but he liked it. He did it because he liked it,' I said.

'Aw yeah,' Gavin said. 'Yeah. But what I'm trying to say is that he is mad about you. He'd do anything for you.'

Anything, I felt like saying, except what was important to me. 'We'll be fine,' I found myself saying instead. 'Don't worry about it.'

'Good.' Gavin came across to me with his half-eaten dinner. He deposited it on the draining board. 'Good.' He gently pulled at my hair.

'Ow!' I grabbed his hand and he unexpectedly caught mine in his. And we stood there, hand in hand, body to body. His eyes were a deep, beautiful grey and his fingers were long and lean. He gently pressed my hand with his, rubbed it between his long fingers and I felt an unexpected rush of desire for him. His face bent towards mine and I lifted mine to his when suddenly my mind started to scream. I jerked away abruptly. Gavin stumbled back too.

328

'Jesus!' he said. 'You're Pete's wife.' Then he shrugged, flushing. 'I'm just his mate, I'll always be second best.'

'Sorry,' I stammered out. 'I'd never – oh my God!'

'Yeah, me neither.' Gavin took another step back. 'I, eh, I,' he indicated the back door. 'I'd better go, OK?'

'Yeah, yeah. See you.' I could barely look at him as he left.

Once gone, I had to sit down. My legs were weak. I was shocked at what had almost happened and yet, in a funny way I understood. And Gavin understood too. He was the closest thing to Pete I had. If I couldn't reach Pete, then Gavin was right, he was the second best. But I would reach my husband, I vowed there and then. I would reach him and I would make him live this new life we'd forged.

Pete rang Avril the following morning. I hung about until it was time to go to work. He did a lot of uh-huhing and nodding. Once or twice he grinned slightly and as I was about to leave the house, he gave me a thumbs up. This little positive sign made my heart lift.

He rang me on my mobile when I got into work. Apparently Avril wanted him to redesign the inside of her house so that it was brighter. 'And she's prepared to pay for it,' he said cheerily down the phone to me. 'We can at least pay your dad back the money he gave us for Billy now and have loads of change.' He stressed the 'loads'. I was thrilled for him but slightly annoyed at the way he had focused first on paying my father back.

'Dad's not exactly waiting on the three hundred odd euro he gave us,' I snapped. 'He hasn't even mentioned it since.'

'Yeah, well now he won't have to wait, will he?' Pete snapped back.

We both stumbled out a 'goodbye' and my vow for us to live our new life seemed to wither slightly.

44

J IM LOOKED QUESTIONINGLY at me as I sat down. 'Only you today?' he asked as he shuffled what I suppose was Billy's file between his hands.

'Pete had to work,' I muttered flushing. We'd rowed about it actually. Pete was meant to come with me to get Billy's final results but instead he'd used his afternoon off to go to Avril's and look at her house. I'd accused him of not wanting to come and he'd said that of course he didn't want to go, that the whole thing was nonsense, but that he would have gone because it was for Billy.

'So go,' I'd spat.

He'd shaken his head and glared at me. 'And when am I supposed to go to Avril's?' he grouched. 'Mornings are out as I've my mother to mind. I work all afternoon and when I get back it's too late. What do you want me to do?'

'Dad will mind your mother.'

'She's my mother.'

'Billy is your son.'

He looked hopelessly at me. 'We need the money, Poppy. If Billy,' he gulped on the words, 'needs tablets or whatever, we'll need the money.'

I couldn't dispute that so I let him go. It was his first acknowledgement of Billy needing help.

'Well, you can explain this to your husband anyway,' Jim said, interrupting my thoughts. 'It was more important that he be here for the testing – at least that way he saw where Billy's difficulties lie.'

I nodded. We hadn't even discussed it since. Pete seemed to be on autopilot or something.

'Right,' Jim looked at me across his desk. 'I've had a look at the tests and the reports from Billy's teacher and your-selves and the bottom line is that yes, Billy is indeed affected by ADHD.'

I'd been expecting it, yet not expecting it, if that makes sense. I think that during the time there was no diagnosis, I still had a little banner of hope fluttering away in my heart. I swallowed hard and managed a nod of sorts.

'Are you OK?' Jim asked.

'I'm fine!' Billy, from his position on the windowsill yelled over.

It made us both smile.

'Just a little shocked,' I admitted. 'I dunno, I thought . . .' I let the words trail away. What had I thought? I didn't know. A bit like Pete, I hadn't actually voiced any opinions.

'You thought there might be a mistake?'

I shrugged.

'That's normal,' Jim said. 'Any diagnosis is a shock.' He smiled sympathetically and turned to Billy's file. 'He's a bright kid though,' he continued. 'But like most ADHD sufferers, he has problems with processing speed and his working memory. You saw for yourself that he has difficulty converting words into concepts, but his visual thinking is good. He's disorganised and has a very short attention span, but then when he's interested in something his focus is very intense.'

He kept talking and talking and words occasionally jumped out at me but I couldn't concentrate at all. All I kept wondering was whether it was my fault. What had I done? How could I make it better? Was it too late?

'Now,' Jim said, after what seemed like ages, 'it's important to realise that this is not your fault, though sometimes changing parenting styles can help. As can diet and other small changes you can make.'

'It's not my fault?' I repeated softly.

'No,' Jim smiled a little. 'It's no one's fault. It can be hereditary all right. And to be honest, moving house has been a little disruptive for him. He worries about being poor.'

I grimaced. 'He's right to worry,' I half joked, feeling a little better. And after all this our finances would be decimated.

'Now,' Jim took some papers from another folder on his desk. 'Here are some things I recommend that you do.'

I wanted to ask if Billy would have to go on drugs, but I hadn't the nerve.

'Firstly,' Jim said, 'the approach to handling ADHD children is complex as all children are different. However, it has been found that these approaches can help and if there is a significant improvement after three months, the need for medication will be minimal. If I do find that Billy needs to be medicated, I'll refer you on to a psychiatrist. But first, I'd like you to try these.' He came around his desk and placed a page in front of me. Both of us ignored Billy as he began to pull at the curtain rail. 'The first thing that has to be altered is your parenting styles. Kids like Billy can be very stubborn; there is no point in getting into a head-to-head argument with them, as you probably know.'

I thought of our disastrous breakfast in Pete's hotel and winced.

'What you should do is try to diffuse the situation, distract the child with something else. Easier said than done, I know.' He gave a wry smile.

That's what I do already, I wanted to shout with joy. Pete was the one who wouldn't give in. At least I was doing something right. It wasn't mollycoddling, it was 'diffusing the situation'.

'Don't show any reaction. Don't get angry or sad or anything. Be a parent, OK?'

I nodded.

'Billy is quite hyperactive and impulsive. The best way of handling that is positive—'

'Positive reinforcement,' I said wonderingly. Jesus, my dad should be getting a medal for his work with Billy.

'Exactly. Reward the good behaviour and ignore the bad. Reward effort not achievement. Focus on one behaviour at a time. For instance, Billy tends to shout a lot. Divide the day into half-hours. If he doesn't shout for a half-hour, give him a star. If he gets two stars, give him a treat. Things like that.' He indicated the page. 'It's all there for you.'

He went into other things after that. Things like Billy's diet and strategies for getting Billy to sleep at night and how to handle homework. It all seemed so logical and sensible and yet I knew it would be hard.

'So,' Jim placed the final page down in front of me. 'I want you to monitor Billy for the next three months, putting these strategies into place, and we'll see you back here again, all right?'

'And if it doesn't work?' I asked.

He smiled, 'We'll worry about that when the time comes.

He may need medication, but if he does, it's not the end of the world, you know.'

But it would be, I reckoned. I didn't want my child to be on drugs. I really didn't. But neither did I want him friendless and unhappy. I picked up the pages and nodded to Jim. 'I'll make it work,' I promised. 'I really will.'

'All you can do is your best,' Jim said. 'And no matter what happens, he'll still be Billy.'

The words were a comfort of sorts, but at the same time, I wondered if they were true. Would Billy still be Billy if he didn't swing fearlessly from the swing in the garden, or shout louder than any kid on the street? Would he stop risking life and limb to dive to save a football? Would he cease chatting to me about rubbish for hours on end? And yes, would he never ever again hit perfect strangers with swords because they'd insulted his granddad? My gaze strayed towards Billy. He saw me looking and jumped down from the windowsill, making the floor shake.

'Can we go now?' he said. 'I'm bored.'

'I'll get my secretary to pen you in for an appointment in three months' time. Is that OK?'

I nodded. I wondered if it would be expensive. Money. Everything these days boiled down to money. We had no bloody money. Maybe Pete was right to go to Avril's, I conceded.

'Thanks,' I said.

'Take care,' he smiled. He tousled Billy's hair as Billy went past him. 'Be good, buster,' he grinned.

Dad was waiting anxiously for us when we got in. 'Your mother rang to see how he is,' he said, the minute I entered. 'And herself,' he indicated upstairs, 'is moaning that the coffee tastes awful. Blaming me, she is. I told her I can't help it if you buy instant. I know it's not as good, I said to her, but you should be lucky you're getting coffee at all.'

I threw my coat across a chair and told Billy to go and play in the back garden. Dad fell silent, and once Billy had slammed the back door, I told him what the doctor had said.

Dad nodded. 'Makes sense,' he murmured, studying the pages quickly and yet managing to take them in. 'Lots of this could be applied in the work force too.'

'Mmmm.' I didn't care about the work force. 'I've to bring him back in three months' time to be assessed again.'

'Right.' He was still studying the pages. 'That's good. Is it part of the initial fee?'

'I dunno.'

'What do you mean you don't know?' Dad was appalled. 'What if it's not and you have to fork out more money? How will you afford it?'

'We can claim it on tax, I think?'

'You can't claim what you can't pay,' Dad spluttered. 'What'll you do then?'

'Cross that bridge when we come to it,' I answered, copying Jim's answer.

'You'll take it from me, that's what you'll do,' Dad said, sitting down opposite me and placing the pages on the table beside him. 'I told you already, I have the money. I could pay for him to have a brain transplant if it'd work. You get all he needs and I'll pay.'

'Dad, I can't—'

'I don't care.' Dad was suddenly the father of my child-hood. 'I don't care if it offends you or your husband. It'd offend me if I wasn't allowed to help my grandson.'

'It's not—'

'Yes it is.' Dad stood up. 'I'll tell you something, shall I, Poppy? I'd be offended because it's OK for me to mind your child during the day, which is a far more responsible job than shelling out a few quid for him. So, if I can't spend money on him, then I shan't mind him.'

'That's . . . that's blackmail!' I spluttered.

'No, it's not,' Dad said calmly. 'It makes perfect sense, and you can say it to that husband of yours if he objects.'

That husband of mine would object, I was sure of it. 'He'll go mad.'

'He won't,' Dad said. 'Because putting your pride before your child is not the way to parent.' He looked strangely at me. 'I did it for years, being the big man earning lots of money but neglecting you and your mother.' He licked his lips and shifted uncomfortably. 'Don't say I did it for nothing.'

He looked so vulnerable and lost that I just had to nod. And it was a huge relief to know that money was there if we needed it. 'OK. OK, Dad.'

'Good girl,' he smiled widely. 'I just knew that little speech at the end would clinch it!'

Despite his jocular tone, I knew he'd meant it.

Dad refused to ring my mother to tell her and so I was forced to. Of course, she went hysterical. 'You shouldn't have brought him. Those doctors just want to feel useful and that's why they go on like that. Parenting, pah. And what if he needs drugs, what'll you do then?'

'Get the drugs and give them to Billy,' I replied through gritted teeth. 'And Dad,' I stressed the 'dad,' 'has offered to pay for it all.'

'Oh, he would,' she sniffed. 'He's just trying to buy you over, that's all.'

'He's trying to help,' I snapped.

'Billy is a great little boy and I just can't understand it at all. I never noticed anything wrong with him.'

How could she be so blind? Even I'd had my worries about Billy, though I hadn't fully acknowledged them. How could she not have seen . . . but she'd never *seen*, had she? Her blindness was a result of a lifetime in denial. All through her marriage, she'd blithely ignored the fact that she and Dad were growing apart. She'd only confronted it when the reality became too much for her. But I'd been blind too. I'd been blind as to how bad Billy had actually been. Maybe I'd been afraid or ignorant or stupid. But I knew that in trying to get *her* to understand, *I* suddenly understood.

'Mam,' I half laughed, 'one day he walked the dividing wall between my garden and Laura's totally blindfolded.'

'That's boys for you.'

'He stood on the windowsill of his open bedroom window and jumped down on to his bedroom floor. He flooded our old house before we left. He broke your curtain rail.' Little incidences of his childhood suddenly swamped my memory. 'He didn't do jigsaws, he couldn't sit and colour, he interrupted people constantly, he's broken most of his toys and he never sits still.'

'And it never bothered you before,' Mam said.

'It did,' I said. 'It did bother me. I used to wonder why he wouldn't learn poems like other kids, but I just said, hey, he's not interested in rhymes. And then it was hey, he's not interested in jigsaws, and then it was, hey, he doesn't like the kids in his class. I can't keep making excuses for him, Mam.'

'Well, I don't know, he sounds like you when you were small.'

At first I thought she was being mean about it, but then I realised that it was true. I could never learn anything in school, I couldn't sit still long enough. I'd barely scraped my leaving cert. I'd made no friends at school, no friends anywhere. So, in desperation, I'd ask Mam to buy me the latest toy so that I could impress them with all my stuff. And they had been impressed until I'd tried to take over their games and they'd dump me again. And I'd got Mam to buy me bigger and bigger things, and when that had failed, I'd stopped trying. And Billy was doing the same, I thought. Telling all the lads in school how he was getting this wrestler and that wrestler in the vain hope of making them his friends. Tears pricked my eyes.

'Poppy,' Mam said, 'are you still there?'

'I . . . I have to go now, Mam,' I said and I hung up.

I cried for ages. No one was about. Dad had taken Billy off and Thelma was asleep. She slept a lot these days. I cried for the young me, the kid that had tried too hard. The person that had gone and got a husband who had set up a business just to impress her because at some level, he must have known how I craved possessions. How I needed them in order to feel valued. How without them, I was just me. And the 'just me' hadn't been good enough ever before.

But it was the same me who was surviving now, I thought. The same me who had made a friend. The same me who had written a letter to David Dunne and got him to agree to auction himself off. The me who was the real me.

45

I WAITED FOR Pete to come home from Avril's. I didn't want to phone him. It wasn't the way to break news to anyone. I washed my face clean of its tears and sat, totally at ease, at the kitchen table when he arrived in. He looked tired, I thought. But there was a bit of a grin about his mouth. Designing stuff made him happy like that.

'You OK?' I asked.

'Tired,' he managed a weak smile. And I thought of Gavin and what had almost happened and I thanked God that it hadn't. Pete's smile was the reason I was still with him after this length of time. A sort of quirky, lop-sided grin which showed a chipped front tooth in a row of even ones. The chipped tooth was him – not too perfect but totally endearing. Every time he smiled I was reminded of the first time we met, of our first date at the pictures, of the first time we made love two weeks after we'd met, of the day when Billy was born and Pete had held him and looked at him and then looked at me. He'd smiled then. He'd smiled and put his arm about me and said, 'We're a family now, ey?'

'I've made a sambo for you,' I indicated the fridge. 'Thought you might want it.'

'Great. Thanks.'

I admired his bum as he bent into the fridge to get the sandwich. God, he could wear a pair of jeans. I waited for him to ask about Billy, but he didn't. And he probably wouldn't either, I realised suddenly, with a bit of a heart wrench. So, I said, 'Do you want to know Billy's results?' For the first time, my voice cracked. I didn't wait for him to answer. 'He has Attention Deficit Disorder with Hyperactivity.'

Pete paused, sandwich in hand. 'He hasn't,' he said.

'Yes, he has,' I replied firmly. 'It's been confirmed.'

Pete shook his head and gave a shaky laugh. 'I don't care. I don't believe it.'

'Well, Pete, whether you believe it or not, it's a fact.' I stood up and walked towards him. I kept my voice deliberately low. I didn't want to shout at him. 'And you saw for yourself the difficulties he had in those tests.' I picked up the sheets on parenting and diet and held them out to him. 'And here's what we have to do about it.'

Pete brushed past me and sat at the table. Very deliberately he took a bite out of the sandwich and waited until he'd swallowed to respond. 'Right. Good. Go on, tell me. You know everything.'

I glared at him. I stood opposite him and laid both my hands on the table. 'All right, I'll tell you, will I?'

He shrugged.

'We're going to change the way we deal with Billy. You are not going to get into fighting matches with him. Instead, you have to distract him. It's all there, in those sheets. Read them.'

'So it's my fault, is it?'

'No, no it's not. Just read the stuff there, OK?'

'Yeah, I will.' He sounded as if he would. He took another

bite from his sandwich. 'But I'm just in, I'm tired and I don't need this just now.'

'Well, when?' I said. 'When would be convenient, seeing as we hardly see each other these days. Or talk for that matter!'

'I'll read them and we'll talk then, right?'

'Oh, well I won't hold my breath, so. It'd be like the way you talk about your mother being ill or Adrian stabbing you in the back? All that sort of talk?'

He flinched.

'One thing we will not be talking about, however,' I continued, my voice rising despite my best efforts, 'is the fact that my dad has offered to pay for anything we need to help Billy. I have accepted it and that's final.'

'Your dad is paying for nothing!' He glared at me and would have sounded angry if he hadn't a load of mashed-up sandwich in his mouth.

'Did your mother never tell you not to speak with your mouth full?'

That really annoyed him. 'Your dad is paying for nothing,' he shouted. 'Nothing! Do you hear me?' He stood up.

'Oh,' I squared up to him, 'so what are you going to do? Are you going to get all our money back from Adrian?'

'No.'

'Well then?'

'Billy is fine.'

'He's not bloody fine!' I slammed my hand on the table, making the sandwich jump. 'You are an architect, Pete, not a doctor. Billy needs help. I'm going to get it for him and if you think that your pride will stand in the way of me getting help for my son, then you're so wrong!'

'Fine. You do what you want, Poppy. It's what you're good at!'

'What?'

'Well, I guess it's hard to listen to other people's opinions when you've been spoilt rotten all your life.'

'What!'

'There wasn't a thing you didn't have, was there? There wasn't a thing you couldn't get. Your mother and father treated you like porcelain and so did I. Nothing in your world was ever bad, was it? And now, now that Billy's not conforming to what you think is acceptable, you want him treated.'

'Fuck off!'

'Oh, Mammy and Daddy would love to hear that, wouldn't they?'

'Nothing in my world was ever bad, Pete.' I wanted to slap him. I wanted to shake him as I moved nearer him. 'Nothing in my world was ever bad,' I repeated, 'but nothing in your world was ever good, was it?'

'What?'

'You hated your life, didn't you? Let's face it, your dad, whom you loved, died, and your mother had to buckle down and bring up the three of you. And she hated that, didn't she? And you hated that she was always complaining, and you hated that your brothers left you with her. And you hated the fact that your house was dirty and that your mother was grumpy, so you found Gav and his family and they became your home for a while. And then you met me. And I became the woman you married. Spoilt little rich girl who only needed holidays and clothes to be happy. You could do that. And then, along came Billy and you had the family you always wanted.'

He didn't move, he just kept staring at me.

'And now, it's less than the perfect dream, isn't it? You

343

can't give me the clothes and the holidays any more, can you? You can't control your mother's illness and you sure as hell can't make Billy better by pretending it's not happening.' As soon as I'd vomited it all out, I wished I could take it back. I was horrified by what I'd said and yet, weirdly relieved.

He startled me by grabbing his jacket from the chair. 'I'm not pretending.'

'Wha— where are you going?'

'Out.'

'But, but you've only just come in.'

'Yeah. Yeah, I know.'

'Pete, please—'

'Just let me go, hey?'

And I did.

My mobile phone bleeped at around one in the morning. I'd lain awake all night and the sound of it scared me stupid. It was a text:

At Gav's. Pete. And about ten minutes later:
Pete wid me. Don't worry. Gav.

I felt sick.
And worried.
And sick again.

46

I BROUGHT A cuppa up to Thelma the next morning. She hoisted herself up in bed and looked balefully at me. 'Where's Peter? He normally does this.'

I couldn't look her in the face. 'He's not here this morning. Now, do you want this or not?'

'Yes, I do want it, thank you,' she snapped, taking it off me. 'There's no need to be so cheeky.' Sipping it, she winced slightly before saying, 'I don't know, it must have been some row yez had.'

'You're right, you don't know,' I walked to her curtains, drew them apart and the light streamed in.

'Well, I know I heard raised voices yesterday evening so unless you were playing bingo, it must have been a row.'

'Playing bingo?' I snorted. 'God, Thelma, where do you get them from?'

She smirked. 'I make them up. Good, aren't they?'

'If anyone actually still played bingo, it would be good,' I smirked back.

'So, was it about the young fella?'

'Thelma, it really isn't your business what it was about.'

'So you did have a row?'

'Haven't you got cancer or something to be worrying about?'

Her laugher surprised me. A huge bellow of laughter that filled the room. 'Jesus, but you're good,' she chortled, clapping her hands together.

'What's wrong?' Billy hurtled into the room and stopped, stunned at the sight of Thelma laughing. 'Is she dying, Mammy?' He was torn between fear and curiosity.

'Your mother,' Thelma pointed a finger at me, 'is the only one who doesn't creep about me with kid gloves. Jesus, everyone else puts on mournful faces and doesn't talk about the fun they had in case I feel left out. And your mother, well, she's just a complete bitch to me.'

'My mammy is not a bitch!'

'I'm not a bitch!'

Billy and I spoke together.

Thelma smiled merrily. 'Josie, my friend from down home, called in last week. Well, you'd swear I'd a week left to live the way she went on. I told her to go home in the end. Can't stand that sort of thing.'

'Billy, will you go and get dressed please?'

'Nope.' He danced away from me.

'Please?'

'No. No. No.'

'Get dressed for your mother, now!'

Billy jumped.

'Thelma, really—' I began as Billy slunk out of the room.

'Your father talks like that to him during the day. He says a firm voice works well. A reward system is good too.' Thelma smiled smugly. 'So, now, Poppy, what was it about last night? Was it about Billy?'

'I have to get ready for work.' I made to leave.

'Poppy,' she said urgently, 'just let me say one thing.'

'One thing? You promise?'

346

'If Billy needs help, you get it for him.'

I was so stunned, all I could do was stare at her.

'Maybe when Lar died I should have got help for the boys – Peter especially – but it wasn't done then. Poor Peter, I suppose he was grieving just like me only my way of coping was to get on with it.'

Just like she was doing now, I thought.

'And I ignored the boys' sadness because, well, I would have had to face my own sadness, and I couldn't have coped with that.'

'Aw, Thelma . . .'

'Now, now. Don't go feeling sorry for me, it doesn't suit you. All I'm saying is, if you think Billy needs help, get it for him. That's all I'm saying. Me and Peter, we're alike, I told you that.'

We looked at each other for a long time. Eventually, I mumbled, 'Thanks, Thelma.'

'For what? And send Peter up when he gets in, I want a word with him.'

Pete came in just as I was leaving for work. He gave me a hesitant smile.

'Thanks for coming home last night,' I said coldly.

His expression darkened. 'How's my mother?'

'Upstairs. She wants a word.'

'Hiya, Daddy,' Billy, half dressed, appeared on the landing. 'Where were you this morning?'

'Just out,' Pete grinned at him. 'Now go get dressed, OK?'

'See what I can do, Daddy,' Billy hopped on to the banister and proceeded to slide all the way down.

'Billy!' I shouted.

He fell off.

'Good one, Poppy,' Pete said as he went to pick him up. 'Great parenting there. He wouldn't have fallen if you hadn't shouted.'

'He wouldn't be doing it in the first place if you'd acknowledge there's a problem.' And with that I slammed the door.

The shop was busy that morning, which was good as it kept my mind off what was now my crumbling marriage. I kept telling myself that it couldn't be happening to Pete and me, but it was. He was being deliberately difficult and hurtful and stubborn. But maybe he thought the same of me. I suppose he did. And then, just as I'd start to despair, an image would pop up. Pete and me building a snowman, Pete and me having an ice-cream fight, Pete and me laughing over *My Cousin Vinny*. We loved that film. It was Pete's all time favourite while it was my second. I loved *Dumb and Dumber* the best. And we both loved holidays and candyfloss.

And each other?

I didn't know. But if not, how could I mend it? How could *we* mend it?

'I got them poxy trousers,' Maxi said at around one. I was just finishing up and was anxious to go home. To be honest, I was a bit apprehensive about what Pete and my father would say to each other. They may not have been each other's biggest fans, but all-out war had never been declared before.

'What poxy trousers?' I started to count my cash and write it up.

'Them big wide ones you told me to buy.'

'Good,' I said absently. 'And are they nice on you?'

'Well, I don't bleeding know,' Maxi stuck her face in under mine to get my attention. 'I wasn't going trying them on in the shop in case they looked poxy, was I? No, they'd be all looking at me then. So I brought them here for you to have a look at.'

'Aw, Maxi, I'm in a bit of a—'

'And I got the top. Would you like to see that too?'

'Maybe tomor—'

'OK, you mind my till and I'll slip into the coffee room and get changed, right?'

'You'd better be quick,' I snapped, writing in my fifties total and adding it up.

I'd actually balanced, which was good. I filled out my form, rolled all the cash up and shoved it into the safe. Then I went to Maxi's till and waited for her.

Twenty minutes later and she still hadn't appeared.

'Maxi,' I called, 'come on – I have to go.'

'You'll have to come in here,' she yelled back. 'Jaysus, I can't go into the shop, someone might come in.'

'The idea of wearing clothes is that you wear them in public,' I called. 'Now come out or Isobel will see on video that there's no one in the shop.'

'I don't give a fuck what Isobel sees or not,' Maxi snarled.

'Well, I do and I don't want to lose this job, so you either come out or I'm going.'

Nothing.

'Maxi!'

She wrenched the coffee-room door open and stood, glowering, in the doorway. Her head hung down and her shoulders slumped. 'Well?' she barked.

'Stand up straight, I can't see it properly.' She was nervous, I thought amused. Nervous of looking different.

Slowly, she straightened herself up.

The change was nothing short of miraculous. Yes, she

still looked big. Yes, her face could have done with a smile and a touch of make-up, but God, she looked classy. I smiled delightedly at her. 'Brilliant!'

Her face was unsure. 'Are you laughing at me? I wasn't going to show you 'cause you were in such bad form, but then I thought, well, it might give you a laugh and—'

'Maxi, I'm not laughing at you. I swear.' I shook my head. 'You look,' I paused, 'just great. One million times better.'

'Fuck off!'

'You should wear that for the rest of the day. Amaze the customers. Amaze Isobel.'

'Aw,' she flushed, 'I dunno. I kind of like my jeans and—'

'Well, whatever. But,' I gave her a thumbs up, 'look-king good!'

'Don't fucking fraternise me,' Maxi snapped.

'Wouldn't dream of it,' I laughed.

47

'NANA HAD A fight with Daddy,' Billy announced to everyone on the road as I pulled up in my car that afternoon. 'And then Granddad came and he had a fight with Daddy too. And now Daddy's gone to work and Granddad and Nana are drinking tea in the kitchen.'

'Wow, it's all happening in your house, ey, Poppy!' one of the neighbours called over, laughing.

'I'm selling tickets,' I called back and she laughed again.

I trudged into the house and found Dad and Thelma at the table having a cuppa. As usual, every cup in the place was lying about the kitchen.

Dad stood up, 'I'll just rinse you one,' he said. Then added, 'There's a bite to eat in the fridge. I went out and bought a big cake today.'

I wondered what the occasion was. Dad never usually bought cakes, and my favourite one at that – an enormous cream and chocolate affair. I took a huge slice of it over to the table. Both of them looked guiltily at me.

'Yes?' I queried.

'Pete is a bit annoyed with me,' Dad murmured. 'Eat that up now, there's a good girl.'

'He's annoyed with me too,' I said.

'And he's annoyed with me,' Thelma said. 'In fact, I think it's my fault that he's annoyed with your father.'

'Oh no, I annoyed him all by myself now, Thelma. Don't worry yourself on that score.'

'What happened?' I looked from one to the other of them. 'Did he have a go at you for paying for Billy?'

Dad made a face. 'Well, in a manner of speaking. You see Thelma, not that it was her fault, well, she told him that he had to cop on and stop running from reality. Isn't that what you said, Thelma?'

They were being very nice to each other. I began to feel a sort of dread growing somewhere in my stomach.

'Yes,' Thelma nodded. 'I told him to cop on and get Billy sorted out and not to be taking it out on you.'

'Oh. Thanks.'

'I said to him, "I know that Poppy's a bit stuck up but that's just the way she was reared," but that you're a good mother for all that.'

'Right.' Was that a compliment? I wasn't sure.

'And he shouted at her,' my dad said indignantly. 'Shouted at a sick woman, didn't he, Thelma?'

'He did,' Thelma nodded vigorously. 'He told me to mind my own business and that just because I was living here, it gave me no right to interfere. Asked me what the hell I knew about motherhood. That hurt, it did.'

'And then I arrived in,' Dad chimed in.

They were like a double act.

'And?' It was coming. I could feel it hurtling towards me and what made it so scary was that I didn't know what 'it' was.

'And I told him to have a bit of respect for his mother and not to be shouting at her. And then he turned on me and said that me and Thelma were the same – interfering old busybodies. And he said that I was only interested in his life because I'd none of my own!'

Jesus. 'He didn't!'

'He did,' Dad nodded. 'Wasn't that shocking, now?'

In all of my life, I don't think anyone would have dared to speak to my father like that.

'Shocking,' Thelma murmured. 'But he is a good lad. He's kind, and I suppose we shouldn't have said anything to him.'

'So what happened?'

'He went to work,' Dad said, 'and, well, he just told us that he was staying in Gavin's.'

'*What?*'

'For a while,' Dad added.

'He told you that?' I gawped at them. 'You mean, he walked out on me and he told you to tell me *that?*'

Both of them nodded.

Dad went to say something, only I had jumped up and grabbed my coat. 'The nerve of him,' I spluttered. 'How dare he. How dare he do that!'

'Now, now, Poppy, come back,' Dad called, but his words were lost to me.

I jumped back into my car with Billy calling after me, but I ignored him as I reversed out of the driveway. I barely thought about what I was going to say to him. God, I was furious. FUR-I-OUS. How dare he do that to me? How dare he!

I drove like a maniac towards his hotel. I was on autopilot, I can't even remember the journey. Signs and traffic lights flashed by in an incomprehensible blur. One minute I was driving along the motorway and the next I was pulling up outside the front entrance to the hotel, gravel spraying out behind me. It was like something from a police movie. I jumped out of the car, slamming the door forcibly behind me. Some people, who were about to leave the hotel looked at me in shock and jumped out of my way as I came hurtling towards them. There was a little man at the door and he attempted to stop me as I barged through.

'Excuse me, Miss,' he said, 'You can't park there.'

I looked from him to my car and back again. 'Well, I did, so obviously I can.'

'No, no, Miss, what I meant was . . .' he followed me towards the reception desk, chattering away like an anxious budgie as I strode ahead.

The old man was there – Les or Lenny or whatever his name was – and he recognised me and his face broke into a big warm smile, which totally disarmed me and brought my purposeful walk to a halt.

'Hello, hello, Poppy,' he beamed, his hand held out in welcome. 'And how are you? Come to meet your husband for his break have you?'

More like break his arms and legs, the way I felt. 'Mmm, where is he?' I tried to sound friendly.

'Excuse me, excuse me,' the little man tapped me on the back. 'You can't park in front of the hotel. You just can't park there.' He turned to Lenny – that was his name, it was on his nametag – 'She's parked right at the front door, Lenny. You can't park there, sure you can't.'

'I'll only be a second,' I said.

'Oh, no, now, Poppy,' Lenny shook his head very regretfully and said in a slow, measured, rueful way, 'I'm afraid you're not allowed to park there. Insurance purposes. Fire hazard. All that malarkey.'

'But—'

'You'll have to move it into the car park. You passed it on your way in. In fact it's just beside where you parked.'

'But—'

'It'd only take a minute.' His look brokered no argument.

Feeling ridiculous, I tramped back out to the entrance, followed by the little man.

'I did try to warn you,' he chirruped victoriously. 'But you wouldn't listen. You have to park where all the other cars are parked, you can't just go parking where you want to park, that's the rules in this hotel and if you . . .'

I got back into my car, which I hadn't locked, and left him still chattering. I felt like reversing over him, but of course you can't go doing stuff like that. Instead, I revved the car hard so that he jumped out of my way and I zoomed off into a parking space that in normal circumstances I would have found way too tight for me even to attempt. As I got out, my door clattered against the door of the car beside me.

Shit! Shit!

There didn't seem to be any damage done. Chastened, I slid cautiously out of my car, careful not to make contact with the car beside me again. Then, trying to regain some of my ferocity, I strode back to the hotel.

'Satisfied?' I snarled at the little man.

'Oh yes,' he returned smugly, not at all intimidated.

Lenny smiled at me again as I approached him. I had to smile back. He said, 'I've paged Pete and he'll be down in a minute. I hope there's nothing wrong.'

I didn't answer. Instead, I began to pace up and down the reception while I waited for Pete to appear. He arrived ten minutes later.

'Hiya, Poppy,' he looked anxious, as well he might. 'What's wrong? Is there something wrong?'

'How could you?' I whirled on him. 'How on earth could you?'

'What?'

I gave a big howl of laughter. Turning to Lenny who was looking uncomfortable I said, 'Do you know what this guy has done? Do you?'

'Eh, God, now,' Lenny made a production of shuffling some papers, 'that seems to be a matter for between yourselves, now.'

'Oh no,' I shook my head. 'OH NO!' I shouted making everyone within five miles jump, 'Oh no, it's between my mother-in-law, my father and his,' I jabbed a finger at Pete who was looking confused, 'his best friend! Nothing to do with me at all.'

'Poppy, what are you on about?'

'Ha!' I gave another hoot of laughter and walked in a big circle. People, I noted, were hurrying away from the two of us. 'I'm on about you. Walking out on our marriage! Going to live with your friend!'

Now people stopped walking and looked at us. And looked at Pete and nudged one another.

'Oh, now, oh now,' Lenny clucked, still shuffling his papers. 'Maybe it would be better to discuss this somewhere else.'

'No, it wouldn't,' I said, still glaring at Pete, who was beginning to grin slightly.

'Sure, he discussed his arrangement with his mother and my father. Never thought to tell me. Huh, does Gav know you're coming to live with him?'

'Are you gay?' the little man at the door was back, his face agog.

356

'Poppy, can you calm down?' Pete asked. He attempted to touch me.

'I can't! How can you do this? How can you?' I fended his hands away, 'Don't you touch me!'

'I'm not leaving you,' he shouted then. 'Jesus, you eejit, what made you think I was leaving?'

His words wrong-footed me and then I understood. He was only saying it so that I wouldn't make a scene. 'You are leaving,' I snapped back. 'You told my dad and your mother that you were staying in Gav's for a while.' I folded my arms and made a snotty face. 'Now if that's not leaving, I don't know what is!'

'That sounds like leaving to me,' the little man said.

'You mind your own business,' I snapped at him. I turned back to Pete. 'Now, didn't you say that? Didn't you?'

'Yeah,' he was looking curiously at me. 'Yeah.'

'See! See!' I pointed to him. 'See!'

'But I didn't mean it. Not really.'

'Oh *please*!'

'Poppy, can we do this somewhere else?'

A little crowd had gathered around by now. Some big fat man was saying loudly to his wife, 'I'd like to see him get outa this.'

I turned to the fat man. 'I'd like to see him get out of it too.' I sat down on a sofa, feeling superior and in control. 'Go on,' I said. 'Go on.'

Pete, who usually thrived on being the centre of attention, was mortified. He gave me a look that said, please, let's go somewhere else, but I continued to gaze at him with my arms folded.

'Right,' he said, jamming his hands into the pockets of his uniform. 'Here it—'

'You shouldn't put your hands into your pockets,' the little doorman said. 'It ruins the line of the trousers.'

Some people shushed him.

'Well, it's true,' he sniffed.

Pete was biting his lip and shaking his head at me in total amazement. 'I didn't mean it,' he said. 'Your dad was giving me grief and so was my mother – God, that woman, I swear – anyway, they were both so bloody superior, doling out advice on Billy and you. Like, what do they know?'

I shrugged.

'I mean, the two of them would win worst parent awards.'

'They were trying to help.'

'Would you take advice from them?'

'We're not talking about them, we're talking about us.'

'Yeah, that's right,' someone said. 'He's only trying to get off the subject.'

Pete glared at the speaker then turned back to me. 'I said that I was leaving to, you know . . .' he bowed his head and shrugged and a faint smile pulled on the corners of his mouth, 'Well, I said it to give them a fright – to make them think that their interfering had driven me away.'

Everyone, including me, was stunned.

'*What?*' I eventually spluttered out.

He had the grace to look a little ashamed. 'Well,' he said, 'I betcha they were all guilty when you came home.'

They had been. That explained the cream cake and the reason they were actually getting on and being nice to each other.

'Well?' Pete asked. 'Weren't they?'

'They were,' I muttered, some of my anger ebbing away. But then it came right back. 'But Jesus, what did you think I'd do when I heard? Did you not care about me?'

'Yeah,' some woman said. 'What a thing to do!'

Pete looked at me hopelessly. 'I thought you knew me,' he said dejectedly, 'I thought you'd know that I could never leave you.'

And that small statement took the wind right out of me. It left me feeling stupid and foolish and, worst of all, it left me wondering exactly what Pete and I did have left.

The fat man was saying in admiration how well Pete had extricated himself from the situation.

On shaky legs, I stood up from the sofa. Pete's eyes followed me. 'Sorry,' I said.

'You came after me,' he said, smiling a little. 'I like that.'

'I didn't come to win you back,' I said, not sure if I should be cross or sad or flirty. 'I came to kill you.'

'Shows you care enough,' he muttered. He turned to the crowd. 'Shows over now, you can all go back to your rooms.'

They began to disperse in ones and twos. Some people stayed around though, under the pretext of examining the dinner menu. Pete and I stood looking at each other.

'I got a fright,' I sniffed. 'And—'

He crossed to me and wrapped his arms around me. 'Sorry. I just never thought that you would believe—'

'I never normally would have, but these days . . .' I let the sentence hang in the air.

'Come on,' he pulled me towards the door. 'Let's take a bit of a walk, OK? Lenny, I'll be back on in about an hour.'

'No problem.' Lenny gave me a thumbs-up. 'Wish I had a pretty wife who shouted at me like that.'

I gave him a watery smile.

Pete walked me outside and we went around the back of the hotel and into the gardens. It was a damp day and there weren't many people about. He led me to a bench under an awning and we both sat down, side by side, our legs touching.

'I didn't think you'd take me so seriously,' he said again.

I didn't reply.

'Have you lost every bit of confidence in me?' he asked quietly. 'Don't you think I'd stay with you?'

'I've lost confidence in us,' I said, just as quietly. 'We can't seem to talk any more.'

He didn't say anything, and the drip, drip of the damp leaves about us was the only sound. 'Poppy,' he said haltingly, 'when the company folded, it half killed me, you know.'

'Me too.'

'But it killed me *because* of you,' he said. 'I never cared much about money, but I knew you loved our life and our house and that you'd be devastated, and it killed me to see you pack up and cry over all our stuff when we moved.'

'I survived,' I said softly.

'No, you didn't.' Pete shook his head. 'The Poppy who bought clothes and booked holidays and did all the stuff she loved didn't survive. And all I could do was kill you some more going on about money all the time. But I had to.'

'I know.'

'I got on with it because I had to. I mean, I hate this job.'

'Do you?'

''Course, yeah. I'd love to be out doing big projects and stuff, but I can't. And so I grit my teeth and I said, right, I'm gonna get on with this, make it as good as I can, be happy, and, like, I'm so busy getting on with it that I can't leave room for any extra problems.'

'Like Billy. Like your mother.'

He sighed and nodded slightly.

I started to smile a little. I don't think he noticed.

'And on top of that, while I'm fucking up, your parents wade in and start buying you things and making you into what you were before, and I'm thinking, that's my job. That's what I should be doing. You were right, too, about what you said the other night. You and Billy, you are my perfect family. I always wanted that, and some faceless person telling me that my son needs help, well, I could kill him.'

'He's a doctor, Pete.'

'Yeah, I know that. But looking after Billy, looking after you, that's my job. Everyone else is doing what I should be doing – even me own mother won't let me bring her to chemo. And yeah, I hate that I'm losing control.' He winced a little. 'You know me well, Poppy Furlong.'

'To know ya is to love ya,' I said back.

He took my hand in his and examined it, turning it over and over. 'I went out the other night to get some headspace, just to sort my mind out. I ended up in Gav's and he gave me a right ear bashing. Jaysus, if you heard him you'd know there is no way I could ever go back there, anyway.'

'What did he say?' The feel of his hand touching mine was sending goosebumps down my spine. His touch on me, slight as it was, was akin to the sun on frozen soil. It was melting me, right down to my very core.

'He said, right, that I was a fool, that I had the best girl on the planet and that I'd be a thick to risk losing you. And I told him I wasn't losing you and he just gave me such a look and said, "Aren't you?" And it made me think. And this morning I was all set to apologise and reform and talk if I could, until Billy slid down the stairs.'

I smiled a little.

'I think Gav loves you a bit,' Pete said jokingly. 'I reckon that's why he's never found anyone else.'

'Get lost,' I gave Pete a shove trying to laugh to show how silly I thought the whole idea.

'But I love you more,' Pete planted a kiss on my palm, his eyes staring up into mine. 'And I'm sorry. But Poppy, all I ever wanted was to give you all you wanted.'

I smiled. Said quietly, 'All I ever wanted was you.' Then I remembered something Gavin had told me. 'Did you only set up in business to impress me?'

Pete froze. 'What?'

'Gav told me. He said you only set up in business to impress me.'

'Well, it was more to impress your dad, actually,' Pete admitted ruefully. 'Imagine, marrying a multimillionaire's daughter and just being an office boy, ey?'

'Yeah, it would have scandalised him,' I giggled. 'Still, he mightn't have noticed – he was never around.' Then I asked, 'What did you want to do before that?'

Pete shrugged. 'Much the same, only I didn't want the responsibility of my own business. That's why I left so much of it up to Adrian.'

'Aw, well . . .'

Pete laughed a little. 'Aw, well,' he echoed, 'he only stole a few hundred thousand or so.'

'Yeah,' I nodded, 'that's all.'

'Yeah, all we bloody had.'

'No,' I said. 'That wasn't all we had, Pete, and you know it – and I know it too.'

Pete put his hand to my face and caressed my cheek. Then he kissed me for a long time.

Nothing could steal what we had – not even life.

48

BILLY HAD A new teacher for first class. It was weird him being in first class – it made him sound more mature or something, and yet he was only about to turn seven. Things were improving slowly with him, I thought. He didn't shout as much, though he was still prone to extreme behaviour.

I had taken the morning off work, allegedly sick. Maxi had told me to do it. 'I'll cover your shift,' she assured me. Then, when I was in the middle of thanking her, said, 'You can repay me after you come back.' I didn't ask. Pete came with me and Billy as Dad had offered to look after Thelma. Dad was going to miss minding Billy for me in the mornings, though I'd told him that he could still pick Billy up from school for me. That cheered him up.

'I'm going to spend the day researching ADHD on the internet and ringing up therapists to see what might work with him,' he announced. 'And if it takes me a month, that's what I'll do.'

'At the rate you do things, that is how long it'll take you,' Thelma griped, coming to stand in the kitchen door. 'Jesus, I asked over twenty minutes ago for a cup of tea and has one arrived? No chance!'

'I'll bring one up, Mammy,' Pete said.

'No, let the old man do it, he promised he would.'

'I may be old, but I'm healthy,' Dad joked, making a face at her.

She shook her head and stomped back up the stairs.

'One-nil to Dad,' I giggled.

'Oh, she'll get me back yet,' Dad said, pouring some boiling water into a cup. 'She's a great woman your mother, Pete.'

'Huh?' Pete's face was a picture of disbelief.

'Well, it can't be easy for her being in so much pain, and she's bound to be frightened, but she keeps it hidden well, doesn't she?'

I think it was the first time Pete had looked on it like that.

'And she's great fun – always moaning, but I love the craic with her, so I do.'

'Billy, are you ready?' I shouted suddenly, glancing at my watch. 'Come on, it's nearly time to go.'

'Is Nana down there?' Billy shouted back.

'Why does everyone shout in this house?' Thelma shouted down herself. 'No, Billy, I'm not downstairs. I'm in my room.'

From upstairs there came the sound of a door opening and then the sound of Thelma exclaiming, 'Oh, good boy, you've got dressed all by yourself. I'm so glad you don't go about naked any more.'

'That's a big massive nuclear bomb to me now,' Billy yelled over the banisters. 'Mammy, that's five bombs. I can have a treat on the way home from school!'

'Yep,' I said back.

'And if you stop shouting for thirty minutes, I'll give you a big sloppy kiss,' Pete shouted, which made Billy giggle.

'You're shouting now too, Daddy!'

Pete grinned at me.

Billy bounced down the stairs, his tie askew and his shoes on the wrong feet, but he was DRESSED, and he'd done it himself. I had discussed with Pete the best things to start on with Billy, and despite his initial reservations he had done his best to be enthusiastic, and the getting dressed in the morning had been his idea so I'd agreed. Dad, Pete and I gave him a little cheer as he entered. 'Well done you!' I clapped. 'Look, Pete, he's dressed himself.'

'Good man,' Pete clapped him on the back and lifted him up in the air. 'Will we bring you, so?'

'Yeah!' Billy cheered. 'I can't wait to go!'

I hoped his schoolmates felt the same about having him back.

His new teacher was a middle-aged motherly looking woman and she escorted us into the classroom before the boys came in. Pete stood nervously beside me, fidgeting and saying very little. I know he was still uncomfortable with the situation, but he was trying. I'd catch him studying Billy sometimes. And there would be such a look of sorrow on his face that I'd want to cuddle him, but like his mother, he'd mask it well and come out with a wisecrack.

I explained to the teacher about the measures we were taking at home. She said that she'd got the psychologist's report and that they'd have a meeting about Billy as soon as they could and that we should come. 'We'll put learning strategies into place for him,' she said. 'And we'll do up a progress report as well.'

'Thanks,' Pete blurted out.

I smiled at him and he caught my hand.

'Now, don't worry your heads about it,' the teacher went

on. 'I've had a few ADHD children over the years and some of them, well, it wasn't recognised at the time and they ended up in a terrible way. Couldn't read or anything.'

I wanted to hug her for those words – they were exactly what Pete needed to hear.

When we left, Billy's class were going in. He was chatting animatedly to a boy walking beside him. The boy seemed to be listening. And then the boy laughed and told Billy he was funny.

And I knew then, that he was still Billy. Still my little boy.

When we got into the car, Pete sat for a bit.

'What's up?'

'Sorry,' he blurted out. He turned to me and wrapped his arms about me and planted a soft kiss on the top of my head. 'You were right about Billy. Jesus, he actually got dressed today.'

'He did, didn't he?'

We smiled at each other. That nice, quiet smile, just between us.

'And you were right to do what you did,' Pete said softly. 'I was an asshole. I promise, Poppy, I'll never let you down, not ever again.'

'Good,' I gave him a bit of an arm poke. 'So you're gonna get the weather-glaze windows I want?'

He laughed. 'Oh, I love it when women take advantage of me.'

'I haven't even started!'

'The hospital rang,' Dad said when we got home. He glanced at Pete. 'They'd like to see Thelma tomorrow instead of next Tuesday.'

'Oh.' I took off my hat and scarf and walked into the

kitchen, Pete and Dad following. 'That's strange, they must have a free slot available or something.'

'They said for her to be accompanied by someone.'

'Yeah, that's no problem. Sure, I always go in with her. Tea anyone?'

Their lack of response made me turn around. Pete was looking oddly at my dad.

'You think it's serious, don't you?' he said.

'No, Pete, he doesn't,' I answered. 'It's just—'

'It did sound pretty urgent,' Dad interrupted apologetically. 'I mean, I took it to mean that it was urgent.'

The three of us looked at each other.

'Well, we don't know for sure,' I ventured.

'I haven't told Thelma,' Dad looked at Pete, ignoring me. 'I didn't think it was my place.'

'For once,' Pete half joked, then the smile slid from his face. 'So, what do we do?'

To my horror, they both looked at me. I gaped at them. 'Well, I don't know. I mean, we don't even know if it's serious.' My appetite for tea had gone. Their faces were still trained on mine. 'Well, I suppose we have to tell her. I mean, we have to bring her to the hospital tomorrow so we have to tell her.'

They nodded.

'When?' Dad asked.

'Now, I suppose.'

'Who?' Dad asked.

'How did Billy get on this morning, Poppy?' For such a big woman, Thelma had the footfall of a cat. She had dragged her quilt down and was obviously going to spend the day in front of the telly watching the soaps.

'Oh, fine. He got on fine.' My mouth went dry.

'Good,' Thelma nodded. 'Let's hope he stays that way. The house was so peaceful without him – I had a great sleep, didn't I, Georgie?'

'You did,' Dad nodded vigorously.

'I wouldn't get a sleep the likes of that if he were here.' Thelma sat down in a chair. 'Now, who's making tea?'

'The hospital rang, Thelma,' I blurted out before I realised what I was doing. 'They need you tomorrow.'

'Morning.' Dad said. 'Tomorrow morning.'

'Right,' Thelma didn't seem too bothered. 'Just as well I got my sleep in this morning, so. Huh, they'll want to be pricking me with needles and everything again tomorrow probably.'

'Brave people to go near you at all,' Dad remarked and dodged a wallop from her. If she'd got him, he would have been bruised for a week.

'How did you marry into such a family?' Thelma barked at Pete. 'Honestly, but sure you were always an odd child. Do you know,' Thelma turned to me, 'he used to be afraid of the bath for years. Kept thinking things were going to come up the plughole.'

'Mammy!' Pete glared at her. 'Jesus!'

'He made his daddy sit in the bath before him to frighten the plughole people away – do you remember that, Pete?'

'Nope.'

'Aw, was you the scaredy cat,' I made a big baby voice.

'The plughole people,' Dad said. 'Well, that's a new one – gives you a whole new dimension, Pete.'

'And his daddy would have to shout down at the plughole for them to go away.'

Dad and I laughed while Pete stood silent, his hands in his pockets. He was smiling a little though.

'And,' Thelma was relishing being the centre of attention, 'another thing Pete did was to convince himself he could talk to the animals. His daddy would shove him on his shoulders in the evening and they'd walk across the farm, wouldn't yez?' She was gazing hard at Pete and he nodded. There was a weird look on his face. 'And his daddy used to tell me that Peter would make all these noises, like as if he was talking to the sheep and the cows, and his daddy would pretend that he could hear the sheep answering back.'

The three of us were silent now, the mood had changed a little, shifted slightly.

'You never did that after he died, Peter, sure you didn't.'

It was an eternity before Pete spoke. 'The fun was gone, Mammy.'

'I did try once – to make it happen – but you said the animals were too sad to talk.'

'So were we all,' Pete muttered.

'So were we all,' she said back. Then she held out her hand. 'I look at you and Poppy and little Billy and I think how good it is that you can all talk.'

Pete took her hand in his. His eyes were suspiciously shiny. 'You did your best, Mammy.'

'Yes, Peter,' she said, clenching his hand so her knuckles went white. 'Yes I did.'

Dad and I left then, and in the sitting room I turned to Dad and he held out his arms. I knew, Dad knew and Pete knew what the doctor had in store for us tomorrow. And from what Thelma was saying, I think she knew too.

49

'YOU OWE ME big time now,' Maxi said down the phone. 'The place was hopping yesterday and that interview girl brought in two more of her friends for fashion advice. You should charge, Poppy, I'm telling ya, you'd make a fortune. Anyway, I ran them.'

'So, you'll cover my shift today?'

'I will.'

'Thanks, Maxi, you're a little gem!'

She grumbled out something but I put the phone down on her. Dad had taken Billy off to school and was then going to head into town to visit a few therapists for Billy. Apparently, he'd discovered something about cognitive therapy being good for ADHD. I grinned as I pictured him firing out questions – they'd probably need therapy themselves by the end of his tirade.

'Now,' Thelma came downstairs, wrapped in a voluminous cape-like get up, 'are we ready?'

'Yes. I'll just get Pete.'

Thelma made a face. 'Is he coming? Well, you'd better tell him not to make a show of himself.'

'He's like you, remember?' I said, opening the front door, 'so he's bound to make a show of himself.'

'Bitch!' Thelma shook her head wonderingly.

*　　*　　*

We checked in at the reception desk, Thelma leading the way. We were told to go on up to the consultant's office and the three of us crowded into the lift in silence. A sharp 'ping' told us when we'd arrived at the third floor and out we got.

Thelma's doctor was quite a bit down the corridor and his secretary asked us to take a seat outside. 'He'll be with you in a minute,' she smiled, then turned back to her typing and filing.

There was an air of calm about the place. And it was silent too, being so far up in the building. None of us looked at each other. Pete's leg jiggled nervously up and down, the clock on the wall ticked away the time and shoes squeaked in a corridor somewhere around the corner.

And then the phone buzzed, the secretary picked it up and said, 'You can go in now. He's ready for you.'

Pete and I jumped to our feet. Thelma, however, stayed sitting on her chair.

'Mammy?' Pete said, turning to her.

'Just a minute now, just a minute,' she said, as she got unsteadily to her feet.

'Are you OK?' I asked.

'Fine,' she brushed away my hand and strode determinedly to the door.

Dr Costolloe sat behind a big walnut desk. It gleamed richly in the light coming through the window. 'Aw, Thelma, how's my favourite patient?' he smiled.

'Well, that's what you're bound to tell me, isn't it?' Thelma folded her skirt under her before sitting down. 'Now, this is my son and daughter-in-law, Peter and Poppy.'

'Yes, yes, we met a while back,' Dr Costolloe's eyes appraised the two of us. 'And I'm glad you brought people with you today, Thelma, because,' he paused and it seemed to go on for ever, though it could only have been a second or so, 'because I have some bad news for you, I'm afraid.'

I reached for Thelma's hand and she clasped mine. Her other hand was in Pete's.

'Not as afraid as I'll be, I reckon,' Thelma said.

The doctor smiled a little before saying, 'You know when you got your operation and we removed the breast?'

Thelma nodded.

'And we found cells in your lymph glands?'

She nodded again.

'Well, what that told us was that the cancer may have spread so we gave you chemo to try to get rid of any other cells.'

'Yes, yes, I know all this,' Thelma shook her head. 'What are you trying to tell me?'

Dr Costolloe clasped his two hands in front of him and his gaze took in the three of us. We must have looked a right sight: me, straining forward in my best designer jeans and a cheap top, my hair a complete mess from not being cut in ages; Pete in his suit, his hair butchered from the local hairdresser but still looking awful sexy; and Thelma in her horrendous cape with her mismatching brown skirt and black top. Her hair had never been cut and now it hung sparsely, in tiny wisps on her scalp.

'Your bloods weren't great the last few times, Thelma, and unfortunately, in the scan we did the last time you were in, we found cancer cells in your liver, heart and kidneys.'

I was expecting bad news, I'd prepared myself for it, but I wasn't expecting to feel physically sick when it was delivered. There was more horrible silence as we all tried to digest what he had told us. I broke it. 'Are you sure?' I asked. 'Like, could it be something else?'

'We're sure,' Dr Costolloe said. 'I'm very sorry.'

We sat there, the three of us, stunned, each in our own world of shock.

Pete spoke then, in a shaky voice that wasn't his, 'So, what happens now?'

'The chemo isn't working,' Dr Costolloe said gently. 'It is highly unlikely that anything else will either.'

'No!' Pete stood up. 'No, you have to be able to do something!'

'Peter,' Thelma grasped his hand. 'Stop. Come on now.' She pulled him down. 'I knew he'd make a show of himself,' she said lightly.

Dr Costolloe smiled again but didn't say anything. I think he was waiting for us to ask questions or maybe just one question. I knew I couldn't ask it. In the end, Thelma did with admirable composure.

'How long have I got?'

The doctor fixed his gaze on her. 'Anything from a month to six months. It could even be longer.'

'Well, there's a big difference between a month and longer than six months, isn't there?'

'Cancer doesn't spread as quickly the older you get so it's hard to say.'

'So can you not get rid of it?' Pete asked. 'Jesus, you must be able to do something!'

'He's not Jesus,' Thelma said. 'I mean, if he was, don't you'd think I'd be cured now?'

The doctor laughed and so did I. I realised how much I was going to miss her. How much I was hurting for her. I put my arm around her and she put her arm about me. Pete put his arms about the both of us.

* * *

373

My own mother was there when I got home. She was sitting in the kitchen with Dad and they fell silent when I came in. Pete was in the hall, escorting Thelma upstairs to her bed as she'd said that she was tired.

'Hello Poppy,' my mother said nervously. She looked tired too, I noticed.

'Hi,' I said back, not having the energy for a fight. I didn't even have the energy to ask her what she was doing there. I didn't have the energy to order her out.

'How is she?' Dad asked me.

I shrugged, afraid I'd cry if I had to answer.

'Oh, Poppy,' my mother stood up. 'Come here, don't cry, come here.'

And without thinking, I fell into her arms and she hugged me hard and I cried. This was the person, I realised, that all through my childhood, whenever I was hurting, had comforted me. She wiped my tears when I'd fallen off my first bike, when I'd caught my hair in a bush and it had to be cut off, when the kids at school wouldn't play with me. She'd minded me and loved me and told me stories at night-time.

She was my mother.

Dad had accepted her decision so I had to too. And she'd been a better mother than Thelma had been and Pete loved her all the same.

'She's dying,' I sobbed.

'Oh, Poppy, don't cry. Come on.' And just like all the other times in my life, she hugged me and cuddled me while Dad, uncomfortable with the emotion, went off to do some more awful DIY handiwork for us.

Later that night, after Billy and Thelma had fallen asleep, I sat beside Pete on the sofa. He put his arm about me and absent-mindedly kissed my head.

'You OK?' I asked.

'Yeah,' he kissed me again. 'Will you be . . . it'll be tough, you know . . . we'll have to decide what we're going to do.'

'Going to do?' I pulled away and stared incredulously at him. 'Pete, she's staying here.'

He swallowed and smiled sort of sadly. 'Do you mean it, you don't mind?'

'No, no I don't mind. Pete, your mother is great. She's great. I don't know why I hated her. Well, I do, she was a bitch.' Pete laughed quietly as I continued, 'But she's great – I wish everyone could meet her. You should be so proud that she's your mother.'

'That has to be the greatest turnabout of the century,' Pete slagged, but he wasn't smiling.

'No, you telling my mother and father that they were welcome any time has to be up there with that!'

'Yeah, but I didn't mean it!'

'Oooh!' I hit him. And he caught my hand and he pinned me down on to the sofa and one glorious thing led to another.

50

THERE WAS A queue outside the euro shop when I got in to work the following morning. I went around the back and Isobel and Maxi were in deep discussion with one another. It all sounded very serious.

'Ah, here she is,' Isobel beamed at me, which was a bit suspicious since I'd been out of work for two days. 'Better, Poppy?'

'Eh, yeah, thanks.'

'Maxi and I were just having a chat about you,' Isobel went on in a silky smooth voice.

I shot a sharp glance at Maxi, who merely stared mutinously at me. 'It wouldn't have happened if you had've come in yesterday,' Maxi snapped.

'Isobel, I can explain—'

'No, no need to, Maxi has explained everything.'

'Yes, but, you must see how I had to—'

'Doing things for free means you're never valued,' Isobel said sweetly. 'Sometimes, you just have to charge.'

'What?' Was she suggesting I pay Maxi for doing my shifts? She'd never bloody paid me any time.

'Now,' Isobel patted a seat, indicating for me to sit down, 'what I suggest is this: You charge ten euros and because you're working from my premises, I'm going to take four of that.'

I had no idea what she was on about.

'Well,' Maxi snarled, 'she has to see my friends for free. She can't charge them anything because they came in looking for her yesterday and she wasn't there. You can't charge them because them new charges hadn't been thought of then.'

'Yes, Maxi,' Isobel said, 'I do have *some* business ethics.'

'And Charlotte wants to see her too. You have to let Charlotte into the shop.'

'Maxi, please, go to your till.'

'I'm just saying—'

'Maxi!'

Both of us jumped at the order and then Maxi slouched out. She was wearing, I noticed suddenly, a nice top. One that covered her. Unfortunately, she wore jeans with it, but sometimes miracles happen in small degrees.

'Now, what do you say?' Isobel asked. She thumbed to the door. 'Word has spread, you know.'

'On what?'

'On the business you were running from this premises. But I'm prepared to overlook it on condition that I can profit from it in the future.'

'Business?'

'Advising our customers on their wardrobes?'

'That wasn't a business, I was making no money.'

'Lots of businesses make no money – consider yourself lucky it wasn't a loss!'

'I meant—'

'So, what's your answer?'

This was very surreal. That morning, I'd sent Billy off to school with his granddad because Thelma had insisted on having a shower. Why she couldn't have had one that evening when I was home, I don't know. So I had to wait while she washed herself and then I had to help dress her, and then she wanted me to make her toast. Done on one side only.

And now I was being asked to help piles of people I didn't know dress themselves, albeit in a different way. I was going to be toast.

'OK,' I agreed, trying to match my smile with Isobel's. 'I'll give it a go.'

'You can use this office until we sort something else out,' Isobel said happily.

Maxi's friends were like her: rough and ready. Unfortunately, some of them weren't ready for my advice. Until I said the magic words, 'Think of Maxi,' and they all agreed that yes, indeed, Maxi looked good now. But then again, they said, wasn't anything an improvement? Still, I sent them all off with their little pieces of paper.

And then the paying people started to arrive. The money rolled in. Ten euro, it seemed, was cheap.

When Charlotte came in, Isobel stood behind her, arms crossed.

'Hi Charlotte,' I smiled, 'how are you?'

'All righ',' she said as she sat astride a chair. 'You don't look as stuck up as the last time I saw ya.'

'I'm wearing flatter heels,' I said.

She laughed and Isobel smiled.

'So, Charlotte, what can I do for you?'

Charlotte stared at Isobel. 'A bit of privacy please,' she snapped.

'We'll be fine,' I told Isobel. I wondered whether if Charlotte had got therapy she would be different now. Would that aggression be gone?

'Watch her,' Isobel nodded. 'She's a sly one.'

Charlotte made a face. 'Not half as sly as her, auld cow,' she hissed.

When the door closed behind Isobel, Charlotte looked me up and down. 'Your hair could do with a cut,' she remarked.

'I know. So, what could you do with?'

'I'm going for a job, next week. Maxi said I should talk to you about what gear to get.'

'OK, what kind of a job?'

'Well, it's a charity shop. I'm sorting out their clothes and working on the till and stuff.'

'Oh, good for you!'

'Well I haven't got it yet. I want to look respectable.'

'Well, stand up and I'll have a look at you.'

She stood up, all five foot nothing of her, thin as a lollipop stick with long hair that did nothing for her elfin face.

'You're thin,' I remarked, 'nearly too thin. You need something to make you look more womanly. And your hair could do with being cut. Short would be nice.'

'Pot calling the kettle black,' she snorted. 'It took me years to grow this,' she swished her hair about her face. 'No bleeding way am I going to cut it.'

'I'm only telling you what I think – that's what you're paying me for.'

'I'm not paying. I'm Maxi's sister and she said that—'

'OK, fine. Do what you like. All I'm saying is that you'd look nicer with short hair.'

She made a face and didn't reply.

I drew pictures of a couple of things that might suit her – nicely tailored trousers, over-the-knee skirts, different types of tops that would make her look as if she had a bust. 'OK?'

'Yeah.' She stood up. 'Thanks.' Then, eyeing me, she said, 'I'm going out right now to get some of this stuff.'

'Good for you.'

'Only hope I don't get caught.'

And before I could react, she was gone.

Isobel was thrilled with the takings at the end of the morning. 'A right little goldmine,' she chortled as she added it up. Then she gave me my cut and it was great to earn some unexpected money. I hadn't really thought of it as work. I'd enjoyed my day, meeting people and having a chat with them, and best of all getting to talk about clothes and hair.

'Tax free, just for the first day,' Isobel said as she deposited her share in the safe. 'You'll have to come and work a full day now and again and earn lots more.'

I didn't answer. There was no way I was going to do full days. Not if I couldn't see Billy and not if Thelma had to be looked after. 'Thanks Isobel,' I said instead, shoving the cash into my purse. On the way out I passed Maxi. She was bad temperedly serving a customer. 'Bye, Maxi.'

'Yeah, bye. By the way, I've told Isobel she needs someone in the shop again. I can't cope with all this work.'

I grinned as I remembered her hostility to my arrival and her insistence that she could do it on her own. 'I'm sure she'll sort something out.'

'I'm not wearing me trousers today, they're dirty,' she said as I went to leave. She sounded almost shy, 'That's why I have me jeans on.'

'Oh, good. Those trousers suit you better.'

'Yeah, I know.'

We smiled at each other then.

* * *

380

Gavin was there when I arrived back. Pete was at the table eating lunch with him.

'Hi Poppy, there's a sambo in the fridge.'

'Great.' I couldn't look at Gavin, though I was aware that he was looking at me. 'Hi Gav.'

'Hiya.' He sounded so normal and cheerful that it was a relief. He hadn't been about the place in weeks, though Pete had met him a couple of times for a drink.

'Well,' Pete stood up, 'I have to go. I'll just head up and see how my mother is first.' He kissed me lightly before heading upstairs.

'Where's Billy?' I called after him, not wanting to be left alone with Gavin. 'He's usually home by now.'

'Your mother and father took him to the park.'

'Oh. Right.' I wondered what to say to Gavin. I smiled a little too brightly at him and neither of us said anything for a bit.

'It's good to see you,' he said eventually.

'Good to see you too,' I answered, meaning it. 'Have you been here long?'

'A couple of hours.' His eyes met mine. 'I was just telling Pete that I've got a permanent job in the US doing art workshops.'

'Bye!' Pete popped his head back in the door. He looked at Gavin. 'Have you told her yet?'

'Just doing it,' Gavin said back.

'Right, Bye.' Pete exited and we heard him slam the front door.

Upstairs, there came the rumble of Thelma grumbling to herself. I kept my gaze on Gavin. 'The US?' I said, taken aback. 'You've got a job in the States?'

He nodded. 'Uh-huh.'

'America?'

'Yep.' He was fiddling with a piece of tomato on his plate, squishing it between his fingers.

'And you're going to take it?'

'I think it's about time I took something.' He smiled a little. 'Can't keep drifting the way I am.'

'You don't drift.'

He quirked his eyebrows as if to say, yeah right! 'I do,' he answered softly. 'I've been hanging on to you and Pete like crazy since for ever. I've no money, I don't have a place of my own, I don't have any family of my own – it's about time I found something to ground me.'

'I never knew you felt like that,' I whispered, slightly horrified.

'I never knew myself until, well, until I almost messed up you and Pete.'

'You almost did nothing,' I said. 'It would never have happened.'

'Exactly,' Gavin nodded and said wryly, 'It's a lonely old life being the best friend.'

I didn't quite know what to make of that.

'I need more, you know. And I guess I need to commit to something to make a commitment to other things. Maybe if I'm actually earning money and doing a real job of sorts other things will come.'

I didn't want him to go. Gavin was part of our lives. Biting my lip, I asked, 'So when do you leave?'

'Couple of months.'

'We'll miss you. Billy will miss you.'

'I'll miss you all too, but hey, I'll be back.'

'D'you promise?'

'Cross my heart.'

'You don't have a heart!'

He laughed a little. Then said, 'I'd better go now. Thanks for lunch.' He stood and I stood.

'Hug?' I said.

He hesitated slightly before coming to wrap his arms about me.

'Take care, OK?'

'And you.'

He planted a soft kiss on my forehead, then held me at arm's length. 'See ya.'

I watched him walk out of the door and I hoped that wherever he was going he'd find his perfect life.

51

*A*nne in the Afternoon was a live show, which made the TV appearance more nerve-racking than it might have been. Laura tried to calm me down as she drove me to the studio – she had sort of appointed herself our unofficial PR woman for the auction.

My mother had, very kindly, I thought, given me back the grey silk dress we'd bought that disastrous day in town, and Pete had admired it without wondering why my mother had bought it for me, which was a huge thing for him. And even when Dad announced that he had found 'the perfect therapy' for Billy, Pete had asked how much it was and declared that we could probably afford to pay half. Dad had said that that would be fine and Pete had asked that a tab be taken so that if at any point we could repay him we would. That had seemed to make everyone happy.

'Now,' Laura was telling me when we arrived, 'because you're the one who got David Dunne on board, she'll probably ask you most of the questions. Just be relaxed and answer as best you can.'

'Easy for you to say,' I muttered, sweat breaking out on my palms. 'I've never done this before.'

'Well, if you're just yourself, you'll be fine.'

'Ha!'

'You will,' Laura squeezed my arm, 'you're very interesting to talk to, you know.'

Her words stunned me into silence.

'Holy God, look at them,' Laura gawked at my mother and her friends who were dressed in all their finery for their television debut. Each of them, as usual, had tried to outdo the others in the fashion and diamond stakes. Their hairstyles were elaborate and their make-up was, well, quite elaborate to say the least. They floated towards Laura and me in wads of loose-flowing material.

'Hi,' my mother waved genteelly. 'All set?'

'I told you not to wear make-up,' Laura said crossly.

It was the first time I'd heard her sound like that and it startled me.

'Yes, well,' Daisy giggled nervously in the face of Laura's hostility, 'a woman's make-up is a *personal* thing. Surely they won't mind?'

'I am the expert here,' Laura's tone was icy. 'I may not know much about anything else, but going on TV, I know the procedure.'

'Sorry,' Daisy meekly bowed her coiffured head, full of plaits, that twisted about one another and reminded me of sleeping snakes.

'I'll have to go and chat with the make-up people, see what we can do.' With a confidence I hadn't seen in her, Laura strode before us into the building. We trotted behind on our high shoes. 'We're here for *Anne in the Afternoon*,' she announced to the receptionist, who paged a researcher from the show to come and get us.

The researcher was a young girl who couldn't have been more than twenty. She showed us into a corridor, informed

385

us that we would be going on in about forty minutes' time and asked did we want coffee.

'No,' Laura answered for us. 'The stuff they serve here makes you jittery,' she announced. 'Now sit down there and I'll go and have a chat with make-up.'

We all sat down. Mam and her friends were a little miffed at Laura's treatment of them.

'She's a very bossy girl,' Daisy said quietly. 'Is she married?'

'Her husband died, tragically,' I informed them. 'She's trying to bring up her little boy on her own.'

They all made sympathetic noises and put on suitably shocked expressions. They'd be eating out of her hand now.

'Here,' Laura arrived back with a girl in tow. 'Look.' She pointed to the four ladies.

The girl made a face and nodded slightly. 'Well, their make-up's quite dark, so they should get away with it.' She beckoned me in. 'Come on, I'll do you, so.'

'Dark?' I heard my mother say in disgust. 'This is my natural colouring.'

I followed the girl down the corridor into a tiny make-up room where I had to sit on a chair while she studied my face and got out various types of make-up.

'Love the dress,' she remarked as she began cleansing my face. 'Really suits you.'

'Thanks.'

She chatted away about silly little things, in between telling me to close my eyes and look up and purse my lips and all the things you do when you're putting on make-up at home. 'So, anyone watching you today?' she asked.

I laughed a little. 'Well, my husband works in a hotel, so he's got it on in work, and my son Billy,' I grinned, 'he told his teacher and they've ordered a TV into his classroom specially. And I suppose a few of the neighbours might watch too. And my boss is watching it – she's got a telly in the shop for her and the woman I work with.'

'You're a popular woman, huh?'

'Aw, I dunno.' I'd never been described as that before and it was nice to think that this stranger thought so, even if it wasn't exactly true.

She made a great job of my make-up, though it was a bit dark.

'It's so you look natural under the bright lights,' she told me. 'Not too pale.'

'OK.' I stood up and smoothed down my grey dress. This had to be the scariest thing I'd ever done.

'And now we've five wonderful women here.' Anne stared like the pro she was into the camera as we sat nervously on the sofa, my mother practising various smiles ready for when the camera panned her. 'They've organised a unique charity event to raise money for The Irish Cancer Society.' She turned to us and smiled, 'You're very welcome, ladies.'

We all murmured thankful noises and smiled like loons. Daisy however, clasped my hand hard and I noticed that she seemed completely frozen, gaping with wide staring eyes as the camera swooped across us.

'Now, whose idea was it?' Anne said.

'My daughter, Poppy's.' My mother had her extra-posh voice on, the one she used when she was talking to people richer than herself. However, as the years went by, she'd had very little cause to use it. She waved her hand in my direction. 'Poppy thought it would be far more interesting than a dinner and we all had to agree with her.'

The ladies nodded. Made approving noises. All except Daisy who remained rigid.

'So, Poppy, tell me how you went about it.' Anne looked encouragingly at me.

Daisy was hurting my hand and it was hard to speak normally. 'Well, Anne,' I began, 'initially we had posters done up.' I was relieved that at least I had a voice. I went through the whole story and eventually came to the part about Maxi volunteering her story.

'Tell me Maxi's story,' Anne said. 'It's lovely.'

And I did.

'And how did you meet Maxi?' Anne asked.

'I work with her in a shop.'

'What shop?'

My mouth went dry. Oh shit. I hadn't foreseen this. And I couldn't lie as Maxi was watching. And Isobel would kill me if I didn't give her the publicity. Not that I cared about that, not really.

'A clothes shop,' my mother chimed in. 'They sell really unusual labels in it, don't they Poppy?'

'Eh, no,' I sat up straight. I wondered if I'd have the courage to tell her, to throw off this last bit of pretence I'd been living with. And then, I chickened out. Sort of. 'I left that shop, Mam. I work in a . . .' I faltered, 'a euro shop now.'

'Oh, right.' Mam looked faintly surprised but I don't think she had a clue what a euro shop was, which was good.

'Maxi is on the till with me.'

'A euro shop?' Anne looked at me in surprise. 'And how did you end up there?'

Oh shit!

'A horrible little man ran off with all her husband's money

388

and wrecked the company he ran,' Avril said. 'And her husband is being investigated about it and it's such a shame as he's hugely talented. He made my dark house lovely and bright. If you want your house to looks its best, you should employ him. He's wonderful. Pete Shannon, that's his name. But anyway, to keep things going, Poppy had to work and we all felt so sorry for her.'

They all looked at me, even Daisy. I wondered if the viewers could see my dignity as it peeled off me.

'That's awful!' Anne exclaimed. 'And yet you still had the good nature to go and organise this auction. Well done!' She gave a little clap. Some of the cameramen joined in. 'I must admit,' Anne said, 'that when you all came in I thought to myself, what do these women know about suffering?'

'Poppy is looking after her mother-in-law too,' Daisy said, squeezing my hand so hard that it hurt. 'And she has cancer.'

Anne's eyes widened. 'You have cancer?' she asked me.

'No, my mother-in-law has,' I gave Daisy a dig to shut her up.

'Terminal cancer,' Daisy added.

'And just because we've money doesn't mean we haven't suffered,' said Avril. 'I mean, my first marriage was a disaster. The man was an alcoholic. I lasted two years before I had to leave him. I made my money myself through investments. I started off as a shop girl too.'

We all gawped at Avril.

'Now I just have cats,' Avril said. 'They're better.'

'I was anorexic,' Daisy volunteered. 'But I got over it.'

That much was obvious with her passion for Gustav's cakes, I grinned to myself.

'And you,' Anne turned to Phil with amusement. 'Have you any stories for us?'

'Not at all,' Phil smiled regally. 'My life has always been fine.'

'So there you have it,' Anne turned back to the camera, 'five wonderful women who have managed to put their own problems behind them and organise this auction for people who need help. And now over to Patrick, who's going to cook something lovely for us, ey?'

The camera went to the chef and Anne shook our hands. 'Great stuff. Thanks ladies, well done.'

Isobel rang my mobile the minute I got out of the studio. 'Well,' she said crossly, 'thanks for saying where the shop was. Huh, it might have been anywhere.'

'Sorry, didn't think.'

'Mmm,' she seemed slightly mollified. 'Well, just to let you know that there are at least fifteen women booked in for a fashion consultation tomorrow and I've upped your fee to twenty euro.'

'Twenty?' God, it sounded a lot for someone just to talk to me.

'What?' Isobel demanded. 'Do you think I should have charged more?'

'Poppy, come on!' My mother waved over at me. 'We're going for lunch, are you coming?'

'Just a sec,' I waved back at her. 'Isobel,' I stuttered, 'are you saying that people are going to pay twenty euro just to talk to me?'

'Well, I hope you'll do more than talk,' Isobel sniffed.

'Poppy!' my mother called again.

'Well?' Isobel demanded, 'what do you think? Is twenty too cheap?'

'Can I ring you later?' I asked. 'I'm a bit tied up now.'

'Fine,' she sounded miffed. 'Later.'

I hung up. I stood there, dazed, until Laura almost ran me over in her car.

When Laura and I eventually made it home the neighbours came out to greet us. Many of them I'd never spoken to before but they all came up and congratulated me and told me they'd never known about all our money being stolen and how good I was not to have moaned on and on about it. I didn't say that it was because I had no friends to moan to. And they told me that if they could help out with Thelma in any way, I only had to ask. 'Yez wouldn't say that if yez met her,' I joked, and they laughed. Then we all went into Laura's for coffee.

Later that evening, after Billy had gone to bed – he was sleeping so much better now that we had developed a bedtime routine for him of bath, story and bed, though Dad was better at it than me and Pete – Dad sat in beside me on the sofa and handed me a glass of wine.

'You and your mother were great today,' he said. 'Your mother was right, I shouldn't have been involved.'

I didn't reply. I hated talking about them being split up.

'This is your achievement,' he went on. 'And I had no right to try and gatecrash it.'

'Talking about achievements,' I changed the subject. 'There's something I want to ask you.'

52

ISOBEL MET ME at the shop the next morning. 'Well,' she demanded, 'are you ready to work?'

I nodded back. 'Yes, I am.' I fingered my little speech which was all written down and nestling right at the bottom of my pocket. 'Let's talk first though.'

The two of us walked right by Maxi as she was setting up her till.

'Huh,' she called after us, 'flavour of the month, aren't ya?' Then, 'Still, most people hate puke flavour.'

Once in the office, I delivered the lines I'd been practising. Isobel was gobsmacked.

'You're leaving?' she gasped. 'But why? I thought you liked it here?'

I didn't answer her. Instead I said, 'I'm giving a month's notice, like it says in my contract, and then I'm going. I'm sure you'll have no problem replacing me.'

'Have you another job?' she asked suspiciously. 'Are they paying you more? Are you going to work for the two euro shop in the centre of the village?'

'No,' I shook my head and swallowed hard. 'No.' I almost didn't tell her, but then I decided that I might as well. 'I'm going to work for myself.'

'For yourself?' she looked incredulously at me. 'Doing?'

I shrugged.

Then the penny dropped and so did her face. 'You're going to set up as a fashion adviser?'

'Yep.'

Isobel glared at me. 'It was my idea,' she snapped. 'It was my idea to charge people. You're trying to profit from my idea.'

That's what I'd said to Dad when I'd told him about the situation. I had initially considered taking Isobel on board because she had made me think that maybe I could actually be good at something in my life. Dad had asked me if I liked her. I'd shrugged. Then he'd asked how much profit she was currently taking from me and when I'd told him that it was four euro out of every ten he almost had a heart attack. 'Forty per cent!' he'd spluttered. 'You don't need her!'

'It's my skill, Isobel,' I said back the way Dad had told me. 'You were, in fact, trying to profit from my skill. And forty per cent was too greedy so I decided that I could make more on my own.'

She opened and closed her mouth then snapped out, 'Huh, you'll need premises.'

'I have a backer.'

'You know nothing about business.'

'My backer does.'

Isobel stood up. 'Well, for the next month you work for me and forty per cent is what I'm taking.'

Dad had told me not to do any more work for her, to just work on the till, but I had never been my dad's daughter when it came to decisions, and despite everything, she had given me a job when I was hopeless. 'Twenty-five per cent,' I said, surprising myself. 'And that's it.'

To my surprise, she smiled a tiny bit. 'Right. Fine.'

'I just want to go out and talk to Maxi first.'

'Well your first appointment is in five minutes,' she warned.

Maxi glowered at me. 'I'll be on my own again,' she grumbled as I crossed towards her. 'This isn't fair, you know.'

'Just to let you know,' I said, 'there is a job going in a new company called Perfect Fit. They're specifically looking for someone called Maxi to take bookings. Interested?'

'Huh?' Her face was comical. 'Are you trying to get rid of me outa here.'

'Yep.' I grinned. 'How would you like to work for me?'

'Huh?'

'I'll explain it all when Isobel goes.'

She snorted and turned back to her till.

When I got in, Dad asked me how it had gone and I told him.

'I told you not to work for her any more on your business,' he grumped.

'Yeah, well . . .'

He rolled his eyes, then said, 'You'd want to start advertising for staff – a receptionist and what not.'

'I've got the receptionist,' I smiled.

'Someone with a bit of class, that's the impression we want to give.'

'Someone who's honest and a good worker and who can look classy when needed,' I said back.

He snorted and handed me the paper. 'We'll start looking at premises at the weekend, right?'

'Right.'

'Oh, this is going to be exciting,' he rubbed his hands together. 'I've missed the thrill of new business. Oh yeah, by the way, the researcher from *Anne in the Afternoon* rang.'

'Yeah?'

'Apparently they've been flooded with calls from viewers looking for Pete to design their homes. Avril's little speech yesterday was the best advertisement he could have got.'

'No way!'

Dad nodded. 'So, I think he's found himself a new business too.'

'Have you told him?'

Dad walked over and picked up the telephone. 'I thought you'd like to do that.'

53

OVER A HUNDRED people had rung Pete, apparently. He took a week's holiday from work and spent most of the time returning calls and listening to what people wanted him to do. He tried to do it when Billy wasn't around as Billy had a habit of doing the most extraordinary things when either of us were on the phone.

Then, on the Friday night, when Billy was tucked up in bed with promises of a day out on Saturday if he stayed there, and Thelma was sleeping, the front doorbell rang. Pete lifted himself from the sofa where we'd both been watching a DVD. 'I'll get it,' he said. I froze the picture on the screen and wondered who it could be. Most people I knew knocked at the back door or just walked in if the back door was open. It had to be someone selling something.

I heard Pete open the door and the murmur of a voice and then silence.

'Who is it?' I called out.

Nothing.

Feeling uneasy, I poked my head out the sitting-room door and I too was stunned into silence.

'Hi, Poppy.'

Standing there was the man I'd wanted to kill for so long.

Visions of me screaming into his face and doing unlawful things with a sharp object had comforted me on many a night, but now all I could do was stare.

'Can I come in?'

Pete held the door open a little wider.

'No!' My voice surprised even me. 'Get out! Go on, go!'

'Please?' Adrian said. 'I just want to explain.'

'Explain what?' I advanced towards him. 'Explain why you landed Pete in shit? Why he's being investigated by the police and the RRA or whatever it's called.'

'RIAI,' Pete corrected softly.

'Yeah, all that,' Adrian said.

Pete looked at me and I looked away. 'Come on in,' I heard him say. He didn't sound angry or flustered or anything. 'What you did upset Poppy, a lot.'

'Upset?' I snorted. 'It did more than upset me. And you, God, you were ruined.' Jesus, I wondered, was this guy I married a complete pushover?

Pete didn't answer. I heard the door click closed behind Adrian and then the three of us stood in silence in the narrow hallway.

'I got your address from Jane,' Adrian broke the quiet.

'I don't give a fuck where you got it from,' I said crossly. 'Why are you here?'

Adrian flinched. 'I'm here to say sorry,' he said slowly. He was so skinny, skinnier than he ever was, and his hair needed a wash and his eyes were deep hollows. 'What I did was awful and I'm going to turn myself in. I'm going to tell them you knew nothing, Pete, and that it was all my fault. Jane,' he bit his lip and his eyes suddenly welled up, 'well, she's told me she'll give me another chance if I do that. But I was going to do it anyway.'

I looked at Pete. He didn't seem relieved or happy. Instead, he seemed slightly devastated. 'Why?' he asked then. 'Jesus, A, we had it all.'

Adrian bowed his head. He rubbed his long hands up and down the leg of his trousers in a nervous jittery way. 'It just got too much.'

'What?'

His eyes met Pete's. 'I liked a flutter, you know the way I did. Just a bet now and again. But it got out of control. I dunno how. I'd win one week and lose the next and bet bigger to win it back and lose it and bet bigger again and soon, Jesus, I owed so much that the planning permission seemed the only way to get it all back.'

'You gambled it all?'

He nodded.

'Why didn't you tell me? Tell Jane?' Pete pressed.

'I thought I'd get it back,' he said. 'I really did. Christ.' He swallowed hard and rubbed his hands down over his face, dragging at his skin. 'The house was gone, the company insurance wasn't being paid, the accounts were in shit. It was like this nightmare that I couldn't stop. So I ran.'

Neither of us said anything.

'Where to?' Pete asked after a bit.

'Just around. It's easy to disappear – easier than you'd think. But I couldn't live with myself. I missed Jane and felt so bad about you. I hated myself. It got easier to think of coming home than staying away.'

He looked so broken, so defeated that all my hostility disappeared. However bad Pete and I had had it, he and Jane were a hundred times worse. 'Come inside,' I found myself saying.

He didn't seem to hear me. 'I'll tell them you're

innocent,' he said fervently to Pete. 'You're my best mate, Pete, I'm so bloody sorry.'

I watched as Pete held out his hand and Adrian took it. I watched as Pete told him that he'd be there for him – whatever Adrian needed, Pete would help. I watched Adrian try not to cry, but he cried anyway. And in that moment I knew why Pete hadn't been angry. What was the point when we were happier than we'd probably ever been? We were closer, we had learnt how to deal with Billy, I finally had a dad who believed in me enough to invest in my new business, I had new friends, Pete had found his mother before it was too late and both of us were setting up our own businesses and money would surely follow. We weren't out of the woods yet, but we could see the shining path beyond. What was there to be angry about?

54

IN THE WEEKS before the auction, Thelma weakened rapidly. She had been on an even keel for a while, and then all of a sudden she became unable to do even the smallest thing without feeling pain. I left my dad looking for suitable premises for my business and spent my time nursing Thelma.

Pete left his job in the hotel and began building up his new business venture, and though he could have walked into an architectural job if he'd wanted – as his name had now been cleared by Adrian's reappearance – he decided not to. But for those couple of terrible weeks, he too abandoned his work and focused solely on Thelma. Money was tight but we had good friends and family. Dad, with Pete's consent, paid for all of Billy's therapy and Mam surprised us with bags of groceries. Her friends too rallied around and Daisy brought cakes and sat in the kitchen and ate them. Avril brought a mass card and some flowers and Phil brought herself. And then proceeded to clean up my house. 'It's why I never got a monstrosity of a home like the other girls,' she whispered to me. 'Too much cleaning. Your house now, is just the right size for me.' It was the first time in ages that the place sparkled.

Neighbours too popped in to ask how Thelma was and their concern touched me. Pete's brothers came from England

and hung about the house like spectres, floating in and out of Thelma's room unable to say much to her. They didn't talk to Pete much either, but we did try to make them as welcome as we could. Gavin and Dad took turns looking after Billy and bringing him out. I think it was Gavin's way of saying goodbye to him.

Then one evening, when everyone had left and the house was silent, I sat at the end of Thelma's bed. She was awake and alert.

'Poppy,' she said, and her voice was just a whisper of what it had been.

'Yeah?' I walked up to her. 'How are you feeling?'

She laughed a little at that. 'What a stupid question,' she commented.

I smiled too then.

'I feel like I'm dying,' she said. And added, 'I'm scared, Poppy.'

She'd never admitted that before. She must really have been frightened, so I took her hand in mine. 'I'd be scared too,' I said, 'especially if I was in heaven and you were coming to join me.'

'You bitch.'

'Yeah. Old habits die hard.'

There was a pause. 'I didn't like you when I met you first,' she said. 'I thought you were a right stuck-up bitch.'

'I know, so you've told me before. And I didn't like you either.' I picked up a wet facecloth and wiped her face down. She was hot.

'Will you stop doing that, I hate it.'

'Sorry.' I put the cloth back and dried her face as gently as I could.

'I thought, you see,' she went on, 'that you were leading

Peter away from what he wanted to do, changing him. Taking him away from his true path.'

'I'd never change Pete.'

'Yes, I know. I know that now. You are his true path.' Her hand squeezed mine and then . . . nothing.

'Thelma?' I said. Then, trying not to panic or cry or whatever I should have done, I said again, 'Thelma?'

But she was gone. Just like that.

I stood, stunned, holding her hand, half expecting her to say more, but she didn't. Her eyes were half closed, her breath sinking out of her body and Thelma was gone.

55

'THIS AUCTION IS in memory of Thelma Shannon, who passed away from cancer a fortnight ago,' my mother spoke into the microphone.

People clapped and I squeezed Pete's hand in mine. It was going to take us both a long time to get over it. I missed Thelma more than I could ever have thought possible. Sometimes, when I was in the kitchen, I'd even imagine that I could hear the bell or her big cross voice in the room above. I missed our sparring and I missed constantly running up and down the stairs with cups of tea for her. It was hard to fathom that such an enormous presence was gone. We really had expected her to last longer and she hadn't even lasted six weeks. Maxi had been right, I knew now. No matter how bad or sick someone is, you're never prepared to bury them. The only positive thing was that Pete wasn't running away from it the way he had when his father died. He was talking about her and he was letting me in. And best of all, my mother had said to him, 'You can consider George and me your parents, you know.' It was the one thing he'd laughed at since his mother had died.

'Well,' my mother got down to business. 'We've a very successful businesswoman here – Avril Doyle.'

Avril took to the podium to much applause. She gave a

big fake smile and stood very straight so her tummy looked flat.

'Now,' my mother said, 'Avril is willing to be auctioned off and she will do *anything*.'

'Not anything,' Avril said, sounding slightly panicked. 'I'm just auctioning my company.'

'You've a company have ya, love?' some wise guy shouted out. 'I wouldn't mind one of them!'

Avril flushed and tossed her hair back.

'Right, we're starting at fifty euro,' my mother said. 'Who'll give me fifty?'

The wise guy raised his hand. Someone else bid sixty, and eventually, much to her horror, she was sold to a dirty-looking chap for four hundred euro.

'And now,' Mam sounded faintly embarrassed, 'I'm auctioning myself. A single woman about town. I'm great company, very funny and I'll treat the lucky buyer to lunch. So, who'll give me fifty?'

It must have been the desperation in her voice to beat Avril, but they were slow to start. The bidding stalled at one hundred euro

'Any more?' my mother called out gaily, trying to cover her discomfort. The place was silent. 'Even two hundred?'

'Thirty thousand,' my dad called causing a gasp to go up around the hall. 'I'll give thirty thousand to go to lunch with that woman!'

People clapped and laughed. My mother looked every bit as if she wouldn't have expected to go for any less.

Dad winked at me. 'She's still a bargain at that price,' he said.

'You can't bid on your wife,' Avril came over, looking very annoyed. 'That's not allowed.'

404

'That's something else that cats can't do,' my mother called down from the podium. 'Make a bid at an auction – isn't that right, Avril?'

She glared at us and stalked off.

Dad laughed.

Mam was sold to my father for a lunch date.

Maxi and her friends put a bid on a weatherman. They'd saved up a thousand euro between them and they all arrived at the auction in their new stylish clothes, making a complete show of themselves by jumping up on to the podium and dragging the poor guy down when they'd won. I'd say he was going to be savaged alive.

The evening ended with David Dunne. In the flesh, he was even more handsome than on screen. Daisy wasn't impressed though. 'You impostor,' she called out, waving a wine glass wildly, 'you were never in *Titanic*!' Some people laughed but David was unperturbed. He stood up there, a total sex god in his faded jeans and white T-shirt.

'And now,' Mam almost fainted at the sight of him, 'we have,' she giggled slightly, 'as you can see, the *very* gorgeous David Dunne here. Who'll start me off at a thousand?'

Maxi raised her hand. 'Can we give back the weatherman?'

Some people laughed but my mother wasn't impressed. 'No, you can't. He's yours now. OK, a thousand?'

Someone raised their hand. The bidding went up and up. When it got to a hundred thousand, Mam looked expectantly about. 'Going once . . .'

Pete looked at me.

I looked at him.

'Going twice . . .'

Slowly I nodded. Both our businesses were going well.

We were confident of making a lot of money over the next few months.

'Two hundred thousand,' Pete called out.

There was a gasp.

Mam gawped at him.

'Two hundred thousand,' I confirmed.

'Any advance on that?' Mam asked faintly.

Murmurs of 'no' were heard.

'Sold, for two hundred thousand,' Mam brought her gavel down.

And so Thelma bought David Dunne.

She had left the house and farm to Pete and his brothers. Pete's brothers had given it to Pete. They didn't need the money, they said, and Pete deserved it for putting up with their mother for the last few years. Pete and I decided that we wouldn't need the money either. So David Dunne was what we spent the money on.

Thelma would have loved that.

Epilogue

I HEAR PETE calling to me as I sit in the garden, sunning myself on our new patio. The garden is in full bloom thanks to my dad's new-found interest in how to fill a small garden.

'Poppy!' Pete doesn't wait for me to join him. He comes out holding the newspaper and hands it to me. 'Read. Go on.'

I take it from him and the first thing I see is the headline 'Kildare Girl Charged with Charity Shop Robbery'. A very pretty, short-haired Charlotte stares brazenly out at me from the paper.

> A Kildare woman, Charlotte Greene, who has a string
> of convictions for theft, pleaded guilty in court today
> on charges of theft from a charity shop. The owner
> said that Ms Greene had always been a good worker
> and that she was surprised that this had happened.
> 'We had no idea of her previous record,' she said.
> 'She was a neat, respectable-looking girl.'

I groan as I realise that I'm probably responsible for getting her that job.

'Not that,' Pete says, turning the paper over. 'This.'

Pictures of David Dunne launching both my business and Pete's business dominate the page. There's a whole story attached of how we'd bought him at auction and of our husband-and-wife status.

'Great publicity, ey?' Pete sits in beside me and kisses my head.

'Yeah. Great.' I wrap my arm about him. 'The best.'

We sit in silence for a bit, stealing glances at the paper and at each other.

'Oh yeah,' I suddenly remember, 'Mam and Dad are coming over tomorrow – apparently they've an announcement to make.'

'I know what it is,' Pete grins, 'your mother is pregnant!'

'Feck off!' I belt him and he laughs. 'Mind you, they're spending a lot of time together these days. Mam even confessed to being fascinated by Dad's tour of the Natural History Museum.'

'Well, she must be mad after him, so,' Pete declares, 'I mean, come on . . .'

We both laugh. If there was a scale to measure boringness, Dad and his museums would be right up there at the top.

Pete gets up to get us both a glass of wine and as I watch him leave, I listen to the noise coming from next door. Billy and Tommy are sword fighting. Billy's voice dominates as usual. I think he's just a shouter. I don't think we'll ever get that out of him. But he's come a long way from the reckless kid he was.

We've all come a long way.

And hopefully, we've an even longer way to go.